THE BEST
HORROR OF THE YEAR

VOLUME SIX

Also Edited by Ellen Datlow

THE BEST
HORROR OF THE YEAR

VOLUME SIX

EDITED BY ELLEN DATLOW

NIGHT SHADE BOOKS
NEW YORK

Night Shade books may be purchased in bulk at special discounts for sales promotion, corporate gifts, fund-raising, or educational purposes. Special editions can also be created to specifications. For details, contact the Special Sales Department, Night Shade Books, 307 West 36th Street, 11th Floor, New York, NY 10018 or info@skyhorsepublishing.com.

Night Shade Books™ is a trademark of Skyhorse Publishing, Inc. ®, a Delaware corporation.

Visit our website at www.nightshadebooks.com.

10 9 8 7 6 5 4 3 2 1

Library of Congress Cataloging-in-Publication Data
The Best Horror of the Year, Volume Six / edited by Ellen Datlow.
    pages cm
 ISBN 978-1-59780-503-2 (paperback)
 1. Horror tales. I. Datlow, Ellen, editor of compilation.
 PN6120.95.H727B47 2014
 808.83'8738--dc23
                    2014009354
 ISBN: 978-1-59780-503-2

Interior layout and design by Amy Popovich
Cover illustration by Pierre Droal

Printed in the United States of America

ACKNOWLEDGMENTS

I'd like to thank Kris Dikeman for being my first reader. I'd like to thank Charles Tan for introducing me to so many exciting books and writers from the Philippines, as well as Steve Berman and Dave Truesdale for recommendations.

I'd like to acknowledge *Locus*, *British Fantasy Society Journal* for their invaluable information and descriptions of material I was unable to obtain. Thanks to the editors who made sure I saw your magazines during the year, the webzine editors who provided printouts and efiles, and the book publishers who provided review copies in a timely manner. Also, the writers who sent me printouts of your stories when I was unable to acquire the magazine or book in which they appeared.

Thanks to Merrilee Heifetz and Sarah Nagel at Writers House.

And thank you to my in-house editor Jason Katzman, for his patience.

TABLE OF CONTENTS

SUMMATION 2013

First, here are some numbers: There are twenty-three stories and one poem included this year. They were chosen from magazines, webzines, anthologies, single author collections, chapbooks, and a newspaper. Five of the stories were originally published by *Black Static*. Twelve of the stories are by writers living in England, Ireland, and Wales—the first time that's ever happened. In addition, there are two stories written by writers living in Canada and eight by writers living in the United States.

Three pieces are more than 10,000 words, the longest is 15,800 words. The shortest is 1,100 words.

The authors of the one poem and ten of the stories have never appeared in previous volumes of my year's bests. Eighteen stories are by men. Five stories and the poem are by women.

There are always a few novellas that I wish I could have taken but were just too long. Here are the ones from 2013: Nina Allan's "Vivian Guppy and the Brighton Belle" from *Rustblind and Silverbright*; Norman Partridge's "The Mummy's Heart" from *Halloween*; "Black Helicopters" by Caitlín R. Kiernan, published as a hardcover chapbook included with the limited edition of Kiernan's collection *The Ape's Wife*; "Mother of Stone" by John Langan from his collection *The Wide, Carnivorous Sky*; and Laird Barron's "Termination Dust" from *Tales of Jack the Ripper*.

AWARDS

The Horror Writers Association chose a historic hotel in the haunted city of New Orleans to announce the winners of the 2012 Bram Stoker Awards® June 15, 2013. The presentations were made at a banquet held as the highlight of the Bram Stoker Awards Weekend, which, in 2012, incorporated the World Horror Convention. The winners:

Superior Achievement in a Novel: *The Drowning Girl* by Caitlín R. Kiernan (Roc); Superior Achievement in a First Novel: *Life Rage* by L. L. Soares (Nightscape Press); Superior Achievement in a Young Adult Novel: *Flesh & Bone* by Jonathan Maberry (Simon & Schuster); Superior Achievement in a Graphic Novel: *Witch Hunts: A Graphic History of the Burning Times* by Rocky Wood and Lisa Morton (McFarland and Co., Inc.); Superior Achievement in Long Fiction: *The Blue Heron* by Gene O'Neill (Dark Regions Press); Superior Achievement in Short Fiction: "Magdala Amygdala" by Lucy Snyder (*Dark Faith: Invocations*, Apex Book Company); Superior Achievement in a Screenplay: *The Cabin in the Woods* by Joss Whedon and Drew Goddard (Mutant Enemy Productions, Lionsgate); Superior Achievement in an Anthology: *Shadow Show* edited by Mort Castle and Sam Weller (HarperCollins); Superior Achievement in a Fiction Collection: (tie) *New Moon on the Water* by Mort Castle (Dark Regions Press) *Black Dahlia and White Rose: Stories* by Joyce Carol Oates (Ecco Press); Superior Achievement in Non Fiction: *Trick or Treat: A History of Halloween* by Lisa Morton (Reaktion Books); Superior Achievement in a Poetry Collection: *Vampires, Zombies & Wanton Souls* by Marge Simon (Elektrik Milk Bath Press).

The Shirley Jackson Award, recognizing the legacy of Jackson's writing, and with permission of her estate, was established for outstanding achievement in the literature of psychological suspense, horror, and the dark fantastic. The awards were announced at Readercon 23, July 14, 2013, held in Burlington, Massachusetts. Jurors were Laird Barron, Ellen Datlow, Chesya Burke, Jack Haringa, and Graham Sleight.

The winners for the best work in 2012: Novel: *Edge*, Koji Suzuki (Vertical, Inc.) Novella: *Sky*, Kaaron Warren (*Through Splintered Walls*, Twelfth Planet Press); Novelette: "Reeling for the Empire," Karen Russell (Tin House, Winter 2012); Short Story: "A Natural History of Autumn,"

Jeffrey Ford (*Magazine of Fantasy and Science Fiction*, July/August 2012); Single-Author Collection: *Crackpot Palace*, Jeffrey Ford (William Morrow); Edited Anthology: *Exotic Gothic 4: Postscripts #28/29*, edited by Danel Olson (PS Publishing).

The World Fantasy Awards were presented November 3, 2013, at a banquet held during the World Fantasy Convention in Brighton, England. The Lifetime Achievement recipients, Susan Cooper and Tanith Lee, were previously announced. Brian Aldiss and William F. Nolan were given special awards.

Winners for the best work in 2012: Novel: *Alif the Unseen* by G. Willow Wilson (Grove; Corvus); Novella: *Let Maps to Others*, K. J. Parker (Subterranean Summer '12); Short Story: "The Telling," Gregory Norman Bossert (*Beneath Ceaseless Skies* 11/29/12); Anthology: *Postscripts #28/#29: Exotic Gothic 4*, Danel Olson, ed. (PS Publishing); Collection: *Where Furnaces Burn*, Joel Lane (PS Publishing); Artist: Vincent Chong; Special Award: Professional: Lucia Graves for the translation of *The Prisoner of Heaven* (Weidenfeld & Nicholson; Harper) by Carlos Ruiz Zafon; Special Award: Non-Professional: S. T. Joshi for *Unutterable Horror: A History of Supernatural Fiction, Volumes 1 & 2* (PS Publishing).

Notable Novels of 2013

London Falling by Paul Cornell (Tor UK 2012/Tor/Forge 2013) is an engrossing dark urban fantasy/police procedural about strange doings in contemporary London. After two undercover cops participate in the increasingly strange end game of a criminal gang and its leader, they're assigned to a special squad looking into a series of impossible and grisly slayings.

Blood Oranges by Kathleen Tierney aka Caitlín R. Kiernan (Roc) is a breezy and bloody romp about a young junky who fancies herself a monster killer and finds herself in the unlucky (and unique) position of being bitten by a werewolf and a vampire.

Red Moon by Benjamin Percy (Grand Central Publishing) is a werewolf novel that's not about werewolves. It's a political mash-up of terrorism and recent United States history. Often werewolves are partly used as metaphors for the "beast within" but, in most novels about them, this is not the "main event"—unfortunately, in *Red Moon*, the werewolf is all metaphor. In fact, the big bad master werewolf is barely in the book and is dispatched as if he's just more fodder for destruction.

American Elsewhere by Robert Jackson Bennett (Orbit) is one of my favorite novels of the year. When a burned out, divorced former cop inherits the house she didn't know her mother (dead many years from suicide) owned in a town no one has ever heard of called Wink, Mona Bright decides to check it out, hoping to learn more about the mother she barely remembers. As the story rolls on, it expertly blends elements of science fiction, dark fantasy, and horror, all folded into the primary mystery of this Bradburyesque town.

The Shining Girls by Lauren Beukes (Mulholland Books) is a riveting thriller about a time-tripping serial killer and his only survivor. The novel provides a portrait of Chicago throughout the decades from the 1929 depression on. A mysterious house gives agency to an evil sadist who we see begins by torturing animals and moves to snuffing out young women who he has visited as children in the past, chosen for their promise.

Kill City Blues by Richard Kadrey (HarperCollins) is the fifth of the author's Sandman Slim novels, about a Nephilim (half man-half angel) who has died, been resurrected, and traveled to Hell and back—more than once. Down and dirty urban dark fantasy with enough murder, mayhem, and gore to satisfy readers looking for adventure, and complicated moral/theological issues to please readers looking for a bit more. James Stark (aka Sandman Slim), is living in Los Angeles minding his own business when, as always, trouble comes a calling. Someone wants to hire him to find a missing weapon and won't take no for an answer.

Mayhem by Sarah Pinborough (Jo Fletcher Books) brings Victorian London to life in this supernatural police procedural about a brutal serial killer active during the same period as Jack the Ripper. This one dismembers and takes the heads of his victims. A pitiful male Cassandra "sees" the future, but is unable to persuade anyone to take him seriously, and a detective prone to roaming the streets of London (and partaking of opium) may be the only ones who can stop the murderer.

Murder as a Fine Art by David Morrell (Mulholland Books) is the perfect complement to Pinborough's novel. It too takes place in London, is about a serial killer, and has a character enamored of (or rather, addicted to) opium—in this case based on the historical figure Thomas de Quincy, who, in addition to writing the infamous *Confessions of an Opium Eater*, also wrote crime essays, including "On Murder Considered as One of the Fine Arts." This latter article seems to be inspiring a spate of vicious mass murders similar to a series that took place years earlier.

Accidents Happen by Louise Millar (Emily Bestler Books) is about a woman traumatized by the death of her parents in a car accident the day of her wedding, and then the murder of her husband just a few years later. Fleeing London, she takes refuge in Oxford and in the world of statistics, driving herself crazy and screwing up her son. Then she meets a Scottish professor at Oxford University who believes he can help her. Unfortunately his "cure" is almost as bad as her sickness, plus she and her son are being stalked by a nutter. Although the first half is suspenseful and creepy, the second half devolves into unconvincing territory.

Six-Gun Tarot by R. S. Belcher (Tor) is a rousing first novel taking place in the weird wild west of 1869 cattle town Golgotha, Nevada. A seemingly unkillable sheriff and his half-Indian deputy are responsible for keeping the citizenry—a mixture of Christians, Mormons, Chinese immigrants, and rough-and-tumble silver miners—safe from bad stuff happening in town (and apparently it happens with regularity). The book is an entertaining mishmash of godly infighting to control Earth, featuring Lovecraftian Elder gods vs. the Judeo Christian Gods vs. the Goddess. Title and chapter heads heralding the tarot are misleading, as the plot makes no use of it.

The Darkling by R. B. Chesterton aka Carolyn Haines (Pegasus Books) is a southern gothic taking place in 1974, about an amnesiac teenage girl discovered wandering the streets and taken in by a family in Coden, Alabama. The live-in tutor, only a few years older than the newcomer, is immediately suspicious of the young woman, not to mention fearful of being displaced from her own secure niche within this happy, loving family. Of course, the mysterious teenager seduces her way into the family and things go badly for everyone. Alas, the prologue kills any surprise before the book actually begins.

Night Film by Marisha Pessl (Random House) is, if possible, both a page-turner and a slow burn of a novel in one of my favorite subgenres: film horror. Scott McGrath is an investigative reporter intrigued by the mysterious, reclusive underground filmmaker Stanislas Cordova, whose movies are disturbing, horrifying, addictive, and often difficult to track down. There have always been dark rumors swirling about the director's working methods and when McGrath gets too close, he's set up—leaving his reputation and career shot to Hell. But he's sucked back into the world of Cordova when the director's twenty-four-year-old daughter falls to her death in a derelict building. Fuelled by anger and bent on vengeance, McGrath sets out to prove that Cordova is responsible for his daughter's death. I particularly love the visionary weirdness reminiscent of John Fowles' great novel, *The Magus*.

The Burn Palace by Stephen Dobyns (Blue Rider Press) opens strongly with the disappearance of a newborn baby and the scalping of a middle-aged man. These incidents and other frightening occurrences are making the residents of the town of Brewster jittery. There are hints of the supernatural throughout: a young boy works on developing his skills in telekinesis; local coyotes don't behave the way coyotes should; large, goat-like two-legged footprints are discovered; and a family man seemingly transforms into a rabid animal. Over the course of the novel, the sense of unease created by the non-supernatural behavior of the humans in town takes precedence over the otherworldly, but this shift doesn't decrease the suspense. Dobyns has delved in the dark with two excellent previous novels, specifically in *The Two Deaths of Senora Puccini* and *The Church of Dead Girls*.

NOS4A2 by Joe Hill (William Morrow) is rich in characterization and a terrifically satisfying read. We follow Vic through a magical girlhood during which she discovers an impossible bridge to the past where she can find lost objects. Unfortunately, she's also noticed by an evil piece of work named Charlie Manx and his sadistic lunatic sidekick named Bing who kidnap children and take them to Christmasland in a vintage Rolls Royce nicknamed The Wraith. The encounter reverberates through the rest of Vic's troubled life.

Dust Devil on a Quiet Street by Richard Bowes (Lethe Press) is a fictional memoir beautifully incorporating fourteen previously published (I originally published five) fantasy and dark fantasy stories of the ghosts—figurative and literal—that haunt us all throughout our lives. Bowes' book is a fascinating look at life in Boston and New York in the decades leading up to 9/11, an event that changed Manhattan—and the world—forever. *The Village Sang to the Sea: A Memoir of Magic* by Bruce McAllister (Aeon Press Books) is another successful incorporation of eight previously published stories into a coming-of-age story, this one about a young American boy moving with his family to a small village in Italy.

ALSO NOTED

Stephen King returned to the world of *The Shining* with *Doctor Sleep* (Scribner), a sequel starring the grown-up Danny Torrance. He also published the relatively short supernatural/crime/coming-of-age novel *Joyland* (Hard Case Crime) about a twenty-one-year-old who works at the eponymous amusement park the summer of 1973. Neil Gaiman's *The Ocean at the End of the Lane* (William Morrow), his first adult novel since *Anansi Boys*, is a dark magical fairy tale. *We are Here* by Michael Marshall (Orion) is about two couples encountering strangers who want . . . *something* from them. *Deeply Odd* by Dean Koontz (Bantam) is the sixth volume in the Odd series. *What Happens in the Darkness* by Monica O'Rourke (Sinister Grin) has a twelve-year-old girl struggling for survival in a mostly destroyed Manhattan. *Parasite* by Mira Grant (Orbit) is a near-future medical thriller about genetically engineered tapeworms. *The Year of the Ladybird* by Graham Joyce (Gollancz) is a ghost story about a young man who takes a summer job at a seaside resort in 1976, the year of a great ladybird (ladybug in the United States) invasion plus great social upheaval in England. *A Necessary End* by Sarah Pinborough and F. Paul Wilson (Shadowridge Press) is about a plague of flies that spreads a fatal auto-immune disease throughout the world and the aftermath. *The Asylum* by John Harwood (Houghton Mifflin Harcourt) is a gothic about a woman who awakens in a private asylum with no memory of the past weeks. When she can't prove who she is, she's held prisoner. *The Gospel of Z* by the prolific Stephen Graham Jones (Samhain) takes a dangerous trip into the past, ten years after zombies destroyed the world. *Anno Dracula: Johnny Alucard 1976–1991* by Kim Newman (Titan Books) is the newest novel in Newman's Anno Dracula series, this time with a new younger vampire who moves to Manhattan in the 1980s and wreaks havoc. *Kitty Rocks the House* by Carrie Vaughn (Tor) is the eleventh in this urban fantasy series about the eponymous werewolf named Kitty.

The Wolves of Midwinter by Anne Rice (Knopf) is a werewolf novel, the second in the Wolf Gift Chronicles series. *The Abominable* by Dan Simmons (Little, Brown) is about the 1924 Mt. Everest recovery expedition to bring back the corpse of an earlier climber. *Island 731* by Jeremy Robinson (St. Martin's Press/ Dunne) is a horror/thriller inspired by *The Island of Doctor Moreau*. *Long Black Coffin* by Tim Curran (Dark Fuse) is about a deadly car. *The Heavens Rise* by Christopher Rice (Gallery Books) takes place in New Orleans, where a wealthy family has finds a well with strange powers on their property. Days after the daughter and a schoolmate are immersed in the water, she and her family are presumed dead and the boy jumps from a high rise, surviving in a comatose state. It becomes apparent that despite his coma, he can psychically cause devastation in the physical world. *The Accursed* by Joyce Carol Oates (Ecco) is an account of a local curse in Princeton, New Jersey, 1905–1906, provided by an obnoxious amateur historian. *The Least of My Scars* by Stephen Graham Jones (Broken River Books) is a snappy, edgy (always with Jones), weird little novel about a deranged serial killer. *The Tale of Raw Head & Bloody Bones* by Jack Wolff (Penguin) is about a demented young man studying medicine in London in 1751. *Rivers* by Michael Farris Smith (Simon & Schuster) is about a man who has lost everything to a series of southern hurricanes and, who when migrating north, encounters a dangerous preacher and his congregation. *The Ruining* by Anna Collomore (Razorbill) is a young adult novel inspired by Charlotte Perkins Gilman's "The Yellow Wallpaper." *Daddy Love* by Joyce Carol Oates (Grove Atlantic/Mysterious Press) is about child abduction and abuse when a young boy is kidnapped by a sadistic, part-time reverend. *Gun Machine* by Warren Ellis (Mulholland Books) is a bizarre crime novel about a detective who comes upon a cache of guns all connected to unsolved crimes. *The One I Left Behind* by Jennifer McMahon (William Morrow) is about a middle-aged woman forced to confront the past when her mother, who had been abducted by a serial killer twenty-five years earlier, shows up alive. *Evil and the Mask* by Fuminori Nakamura (Soho Crime) is about a child educated by his wealthy, enigmatic father to create as much destruction and unhappiness in the world around him as a single person can. *Only the Thunder Knows* by Gord Rollo (Journalstone) is about Burke and Hare, the infamous grave robbers and murderers flourishing in late 1820s Scotland, and the possible accomplices who egged them on, for reasons of their own.

Sister Mine by Nalo Hopkinson (Grand Central) is a dark fantasy about formerly conjoined twins faced with the mystery surrounding their birth. *The 'Geisters* by David Nickel (CZP) is about a young woman haunted by the imaginary friend/poltergeist she thought she'd gotten under control as a child. *Malediction* by Lisa Morton (Evil Jester Press) is about a teenage girl who arrives in Los Angeles determined to use her psychic abilities to destroy everything in her path and the only two residents that might be able to stop her.

First novels: *Bait* by J. Kent Messum (Plume) is an ugly little book about six junkies who are strangers and find themselves on an island with no heroin. They're forced to swim to another island for their next fix. Are there sharks? Of *course* there are sharks. *The Golem and the Jinn* by Helen Wecker (HarperCollins) is about the relationship of two magical creatures that mysteriously appear in the New York of 1899. *Splintered* by A. G. Howard (Abrams/Amulet) is a young adult dark retelling of *Alice in Wonderland*. *Rage Against the Dying* by Becky Masterman (Minotaur) is about a former FBI agent drawn back into one of her unsolved cases involving a sexual predator. *The Black Fire Concerto* by Mike Allen (Haunted Stars) is the author/editor's first novel. A young harpist residing on a river boat infested by ghouls is drawn into a fight to save the world by using her music as magic—dark and light. *Stoker's Manuscript* by Royce Prouty's (Putnam) is about a manuscript and handwriting expert lured back to his native Rumania to authenticate the original draft of Stoker's *Dracula*. Longtime Lovecraft expert S. T. Joshi's first novel, *The Assaults of Chaos: A Novel About H. P. Lovecraft* (Hippocampus Press), celebrates Lovecraft's life and his work. *The Year of the Storm* by John Mantooth (Berkley) is about a young boy searching for his mother and sister after they disappeared in a violent storm. *Harrowgate* by Kate Maruyama (47 North) is about a man faced with increasingly bizarre behavior in his wife after the birth of their son.

MAGAZINES, JOURNALS, AND WEBZINES

It's important to recognize the work of the talented artists working in the field of fantastic fiction, both dark and light. The following artists created art that I thought especially noteworthy during 2013: Teresa Tunaley, Dominic Black, Dave Senecal, Yuri Kabisher, Tara Bush, Kinuko Y. Craft, David Gentry, Vincent Sammy, Tessa Chuddy, Soufiane Idrassi, Carlos Araujo, Saber Core, Sarah Emerson, Rasa Dilyte, Athine Saloniti, Brigitte-Fredensborg, Akura Pare, Linda Saboe, Nick Gucker, Ben Baldwin, John Kaaine, Mike Dominic, Eric Lacombe, Anja Millen, Kate Harrison, Lynette Watters, Stephen Upham, Melissa Gannon, Azathoth, Tais Teng, Joachim Luetke, Sam Dawson, Mikio Murakami, Richard Wagner, Tom Brown, Ed Binkley, Miles Tittle, Stephen J. Clark, Reggie Oliver, Danielle Serra, George Cotronis, Oliver Wetter, Richard Wagner, Erin Wells, Edward Miller, David Ho, Ashley Mackenzie, Szymon Siwak, David Rix, Keith Miller, Louise Boyd, Lauren Rogers, Amandine van Ray, Katerina Apostolakou, Johannes Amm, Pauline De Hoe, Martin Wydooghe, Richard Anderson, Jon Foster, Greg Ruth, Chris Buzelli, Red Nose Studio, Victo Ngai, John Jude Palencar, John Picacio, Robert Hunt, Gregory Manchess, Anna and Elena Balbusso, Goni Montes, Karla Ortiz, Nicolas Delort, Pascal Campion, Sam Wolfe Connelly, Erik Mohr, Harry Morris, and Justin Aerni.

The British Fantasy Society's *Journal* is a quarterly perk of membership in the British Fantasy Society and was edited in late 2012 throughout 2013 by Cavan Scott, Stuart Douglas, Guy Adams, and Ian Hunter. The *Journal* includes fiction, poetry, regular columns, and nonfiction articles. There were strong stories during 2013 by Clare Le May, Aliya Whiteley, and Joel Lord.

Ghosts & Scholars M.R. James Newsletter, edited by Rosemary Pardoe, continues to be published periodically. Two issues came out in 2013, and they included news of the field, articles, reviews, a letter column, and some original fiction. There were notable stories by Chico Kidd, Jane Jakeman, and Peter Bell.

The Friends of Arthur Machen is a society whose stated intention is to "encourage a wider recognition of Machen's work, foster familiarity with his work, and provide a focus for critical debate." Members receive the twice yearly newsletter, *Machenalia*, edited by Gwilym Games, and the twice yearly journal, *Faunus*, edited by James Machin, which has Machen-related material in it.

The Silent Companion, edited by António Monteiro, is an annual fiction magazine that comes as part of the subscription price to A Ghostly

Company, an informal literary society devoted to the ghost story in all its forms. The group produces a quarterly, non fiction newsletter containing articles, letters, and book reviews. The fiction magazine featured seven stories, the strongest by Mark Nicholls and Christopher Harman.

The Green Book: Writings on Irish Gothic Supernatural and Fantastic Literature, edited by Brian J. Showers, debuted with two issues and is a welcome addition to the realm of accessible nonfiction about supernatural horror. These issues include essays about the plays of Conor McPherson, Le Fanu's use of the oral tradition in his works, Lord Dunsany's connections to the Irish Arts and Crafts movement, and plenty of other interesting material, including book reviews.

Black Static, edited by Andy Cox, is one of the best horror magazines in looks and content and is well-worth your money for its fiction, book, television, and movie reviews. My favorite stories in 2013 were by Drew Rhys White, Jacob A. Boyd, Tim Casson, James Cooper, Steven J. Dines, Jason Gould, Andrew Hook, V. H. Leslie, Ray Cluley, Nina Allan, Joel Lane, Ilan Lerman, and Steve Rasnic Tem. Stories by Priya Sharma, Ray Cluley, Tim Casson, Steve Rasnic Tem, and Stephen Bacon are reprinted herein.

Shadows & Tall Trees, edited by Michael Kelly, brought out one issue in 2013 and will move to an annual anthology in print and ebook format in 2014. The eight supernatural stories were all good, but those that stood out for me were by Lynda E. Rucker, Daniel Mills, Ray Cluley, D. P. Watt, and Richard Gavin. There was also a brief essay about Charlotte Perkins Gilman's story "The Yellow Wallpaper."

Supernatural Tales, edited by David Longhorn, continues its excellent run as a digest-sized journal from England. Three issues were published in 2013, with notable stories by Christopher Harmon, Chloe N. Clark, Iain Rowen, Sam Dawson, Sean Logan, John Llewellyn Probert, Jane Jakeman, Stephen Goldsmith, and Michael Chislett. The Jakeman is reprinted herein.

Not One of Us, edited by John Benson, is published twice a year and contains stories and poetry. In 2013 there were notable stories and poetry by Mat Joiner, Patricia Russo, and Adrienne J. Odasso. In addition, Benson puts out an annual "one-off" on a specific theme. The theme for 2013 was *Lost and Lonely* and there was good fiction and poetry by Patricia Russo and K. S. Hardy.

Nightmare: Horror and Dark Fantasy, edited by John Joseph Adams, is one of only a handful of webzines dedicated to publishing horror fiction, articles on horror, and art. It had a good year in 2013 with notable stories by Tanith Lee, Marc Laidlaw, David Tallerman, Carrie Vaughn, Brit Mandelo, Brooke Bolander, Jennifer Giesbrecht, Alison Littlewood, C. S. McMullen, Sam J. Miller, Tamsyn Muir, Linda Nagata, Norman Partridge, David J. Schow, Lynda E. Rucker, and Jeff VanderMeer. The Rucker and Nagata are reprinted herein.

Innsmouth Magazine, edited by Paula R. Stiles and Silvia Moreno-Garcia, moved into print November 2013 with issue #14. During the year, there were notable stories by Steve Toase and E. Catherine Tobler. The Toase story is reprinted herein.

Primeval: A Journal of the Uncanny, edited by G. Winston Hyatt, debuted in the fall and plans to be publish in print semi-annually. The magazine is dedicated to "examining the convergence of contemporary anxiety and ancient impulse." The first issue had reprints by Harlan Ellison and Saki and a loosely structured, experimental new story by Laird Barron; plus essays and an odd screed by Adam Rose, "Artistic Director of Antibody Corporation, a non-profit organization specializing in mind-body and occult research." It also featured an interview with Jack Ketchum. The issue is interesting but with no real focus. It'll be interesting to see if it finds a large enough audience to stay afloat.

The Dark, a new bi-monthly webzine of dark fantasy and strange fiction edited by Jack Fisher and Sean Wallace, debuted in October and managed to get out a second issue before the end of the year. The two issues had notable fiction by Angela Slatter, Nnedi Okorafor, and E. Catherine Tobler.

Midnight Echo is the magazine of the Australian Horror Writers Association. The ninth issue, edited by G. N. Braun, focused on myths and legends, with non fiction and fiction. Issue 10 was edited by Craig Bezant. There was notable horror by James A. Moore, Kristin Dearborn, and Amanda J. Spedding.

Cemetery Dance, edited by Richard Chizmar, has been around for twenty-five years and has featured lots of fiction, interviews, and reviews over the years. In 2013, two issues were published with notable stories by Kealan Patrick Burke, Brian James Freeman, Kaaron Warren, P. D. Cacek, Robert Dunbar, and a collaboration by Jack Ketchum and Lucky McKee.

Lovecraft E-zine, edited by Mike Davis, is *the* online portal for everything Lovecraftian, from regularly publishing new fiction and criticism, holding video interviews (I've been on a number of times) and podcasts, a page with Lovecraftian movies available for free on YouTube, and a blog. During 2013, there were notable stories by Samantha Henderson and a good collaboration by David Conyers and John Goodrich.

Dark Moon Digest, edited by Stan Swanson, is a quarterly, which, in addition to regular issues, also published a special YA issue in 2013. There were notable stories by Steve Scott, Joe McKinney, and P. B. Kane.

Three-Lobed Burning Eye, edited by Andrew S. Fuller, has been publishing dark and weird fiction since 1999 and is currently trying to bring out two issues a year. There was a notable story by Lawrence Conquest in #23, but #24 was published too late for me to cover it.

Postscripts to Darkness, edited by Sean Moreland, calls itself an anthology, but, with interviews and a twice yearly schedule, it seems more like a magazine. One notable story by Ralph Robert Moore.

Shock Totem, edited by K. Allen Wood, had two issues out in 2013 with notable fiction by P. K. Gardner and M. Bennardo.

The Horror Zine, edited by Jeani Rector, is a monthly e-zine that has been publishing fiction, poetry, art, small press book reviews, and independent film reviews since 2009. There was an excellent poem by Joe R. Lansdale published on the site in 2013.

Mixed-Genre Magazines

Aurealis, edited by Dirk Strasser, Stephen Higgins, and Michael Pryor, is one of only a few long-running Australian genre magazines. It went to a monthly online schedule in 2011. During 2013, there was strong horror by James Bradley, Jason Franks, O. J. Cade, and C. S. McMullen. *On Spec* is Canada's premiere genre magazine and has been published quarterly by the Copper Pig Writers' Society, a revolving committee of volunteers, for a very long time. They always publish an interesting mix of sf/f/h fiction and poetry with good, dark stories in 2013 by J. D. DeLuzio, Kevin Cockle, Tyrell Johnson, and David Gordon Buresh. There are also profiles and nonfiction articles. *The Journal of Unlikely*

Entomology, edited by Bernie Mojzes and A. C. Wise, is self-described as "an online magazine of fiction that delves into the world of things that creep and crawl and explores the limits of what it means to be human." *The Journal* publishes biannually in May and November with an additional roving mini-issue some time during the year. In 2013, that special issue was *The Journal of Unlikely Architecture* (#6), which was weirder than dark. The art is always topnotch, the fiction a mixed bag, with stories told from the point of view of insects usually less successfully than those not. There were notable dark stories by Nicole Cipri, Maria Dahvana Headley, Nghi Vo, and Nicole Belte. *Electric Velocipede*, edited by John Klima, announced that it would cease publication with its twenty-seventh issue, published December 2013. That issue and the previous one had strong dark fiction by Jamie Killen, Sam J. Miller, Lisa L. Hannett, and Brooke Juliet Wonders. *Bourbon Penn*, edited by Erik Secker, is published out of Myrtle Beach, South Carolina, and has some interesting fiction of different types. In 2013, there were notable dark stories by Sean Doolittle, Rebecca Schwarz, Jessica Hilt, and Will Kaufman. *Kzine*, edited by Graeme Hurry, is published three times a year and includes horror, sf, fantasy, and crime fiction. There were notable stories in 2013 by Donald McCarthy, Nicole Tanquary, and Gregory Marlow. *Mythic Delirium*, edited by Mike Allen, has been featuring notable sf/f/h prose and poetry since 1998. Although Allen started moving the magazine to online publication in 2013, he continued to publish a separate print issue through 2013. Throughout the year, there was notable dark poetry by Bonnie Jo Stufflebeam, S. Brackett Robertson, Alexandra Seidel, Liz Bourke, Georgina Bruce, C. S. Cooney, and Jennifer Crow. *Apex* Magazine is a monthly science fiction, fantasy, horror webzine edited by Lynn M. Thomas that had notable dark fiction and poetry by Emily Jiang, Tang Fei, Sarah Monette, Shira Lipkin, and Rachel Swirsky and two very good non-horror stories by E. Lily Yu and Maria Dahvana Headley. *Ideomancer* is a quarterly webzine edited by Leah Bobet that publishes a mix of sf/f/f. There were good, dark stories in 2013 by Sunny Moraine and Michael Matheson. *The BFS Journal* is edited by Sarah Newton, Stuart Douglas, and Ian Hunter and available to all members of the British Fantasy Society for free. There were notable stories by Clare Le May, Aliya Whiteley, and Joel Lord. *Albedo One*, edited by Frank Ludlow, David Murphy, and Robert Neilson, is the only genre magazine I'm aware of that's published in Ireland. It runs sf, fantasy, and horror and regularly includes interviews and book reviews. There were two issues published in 2013 with notable dark stories by Kevin Brown and David Siddall. *Crimewave: Hurts,* edited by Andy Cox, has been missed. Issue #12, out late in 2013, was the first issue of this excellent crime/mystery magazine published in three years. The stories are rarely horror, but they're usually dark and always readable. My favorites in the new issue are by Steven J. Dines, James Cooper, Melanie Tem, Stephen Bacon, Joel Lane, Tim Lees, and Antony Mann. *Shimmer*, edited by E. Catherine Tobler, had two issues out in 2013 with notable stories by Cate Gardner, Dennis Y. Ginoza, William Jablonsky, Alex Dally MacFarlane, Sunny Moraine, and Christie Yant. *Interzone*, edited by Andy Cox, is the sf/f sister to *Black Static*, but occasionally some quite dark pieces slip into *Interzone*. During 2013, there were notable dark stories by Greg Kurzawa, Damien Walters Grintalis, and Melanie Tem. *The Magazine of Fantasy and Science Fiction*, edited by Gordon Van Gelder, is a bi-monthly magazine that publishes sf/f/h in addition to columns, book and movie reviews, and a cartoon. During 2013, there was notable dark fiction by David Gerrold, Joe Haldeman, M. K. Hobson, Ken Liu, Bruce McAllister, Chen Qiufan (translated by Ken Liu), Michael Reaves, Dale Bailey, Harry Campion, Albert E. Cowdrey, Brendon Dubois, and KJ Kabza. The Kabza is reprinted herein. *Asimov's Science Fiction Magazine* is a monthly magazine edited by Sheila Williams and, in addition to sf/f (and the occasional horror story), also includes columns and reviews. During 2013, there were notable dark stories by Gregory Frost, Garrett Ashley, Jack Dann, Nancy Kress, Kit Reed, and Leah Thomas. *Black Candies: See Through* is the 2013 edition of an annual "literary horror" journal published by So Say We All Press. Many of the stories are interesting but only a few are dark. The best of those were by Adrian Van Young, C. A. Schaefer, and Julia Evans. *Phantom Drift: A Journal of New Fabulism*, edited by David Memmott, Martha Bayliss, Leslie What, and Matt Schumacher, is an annual published in the fall. The 2013 issue has excellent dark fiction and poetry by Zoltán Komor, Julia Patt, and Jeannine Hall Gailey. The Gailey is reprinted herein. *McSweeney's Quarterly Concern*, edited by Will Georgantas, often has darker material within its pages. *Issue 45: Hitchcock and Bradbury Fist Fight in Heaven* was especially rich with classic reprints by Ray Bradbury, Roald Dahl, and Frederic Brown and new dark stories by Brian Evenson and China Miéville.

ANTHOLOGIES

Chilling Tales: In Words, Alas, Drown I, edited by Michael Kelly (Edge), is the second volume of new, non-theme horror stories in what I hope will be a series. There are some excellent stories among the twenty, including those by David Nickle, Sandra Kasturi, Catherine MacLeod, Ian Rogers, Derek Künsken, Helen Marshall, Simon Strantzas, Daniel LeMoal, and Michael Matheson. The Künsken is reprinted herein.

Dark World: Ghost Stories, edited by Timothy Parker Russell (Tartarus Press), has fourteen stories, all but one original to the anthology. There are notable stories by Steve Rasnic Tem, Anna Taborska, Jason A. Wyckoff, Mark J. Saxton, John Gaskin, Rhys Hughes, and Reggie Oliver. The book is a fundraiser for the Amala Children's Home in the Tamil Nadu region of India. For more information on the project, visit www.amalatrust.org.

The Grimscribe's Puppets, edited by Joseph S. Pulver, Sr. (Miskatonic River Press), is a tribute to weird fiction writer Thomas Ligotti with twenty-two stories, all but one published for the first time. Most of the contributors do an admirable job using Ligotti's dense, visionary, strange work to create their own weird fictions. There were notable stories by Livia Llewellyn, John Langan, Gemma Files, Jeffrey Thomas, Paul G. Tremblay, Nicole Cushing, Richard Gavin, Michael Griffin, Michael Kelly, Joel Lane, and Kaaron Warren.

Deep Cuts: 19 Tales of Mayhem, Menace, and Misery, edited by Angel Leigh McCoy, E. S. Magill, and Chris Marrs (Evil Jester Press), is a an anthology created to celebrate women horror writers and was funded by Kickstarter. It features nineteen stories (all but three original) by both men and women, and each story is introduced by a woman writer who influenced the contributor. There are notable stories by R. S. Belcher, Samael Gyre, Michael Haynes, Sandra M. Odell, Stephen Woodworth, Colleen Anderson, James Chambers, and Scathe meic Boerh.

Exotic Gothic 5 Volumes I and II, edited by Danel Olson (PS Publishing), has doubled its size to twenty-six stories, split between two volumes. There are notable stories by Nick Antosca, Kola Boof, Terry Dowling, Lucy Taylor, Reggie Oliver, Sheri Holman, Deborah Noyes, John Llewellyn Probert, and Anna Taborska.

Dead North: Canadian Zombie Fiction, edited by Silvia Moreno-Garcia (Exile Editions), is, as is evident from the title, a zombie anthology—a good one. There are five reprints and fifteen new stories, with excellent originals by Rhea Rose, Jamie Mason, Sèphera Girón, Tyler Keevil, and Simon Strantzas. The Strantzas is reprinted herein.

Turn Down the Lights, edited by Richard Chizmar (Cemetery Dance Publications), celebrates twenty-five years of *Cemetery Dance Magazine* with ten entertaining stories (all new but for the Ed Gorman) by Stephen King, Clive Barker, Peter Straub, and six other writers who have appeared in the long-running horror magazine.

Shadow Masters: An Anthology from The Horror Zine, edited by Jeani Rector (Imajin Books), presents thirty-seven previously unpublished stories. The more interesting ones are by Chris Castle, Simon Clark, Elizabeth Massie, and Yvonne Navarro. The Clark is reprinted herein.

Arcane II, edited by Nathan Shumate (Cold Fusion Media), is an unthemed anthology showcasing twenty-one stories of dark fantasy, horror, and weird fiction. There are notable stories by Harry Markov, Patrick S. McGinnity, Craig Pay, Priya Sharma, Anna Sykora, Nicole M. Taylor, Steve Toase, Andrew Bourelle, and Eric Dimbleby.

Undead & Unbound: Unexpected Tales from Beyond the Grave, edited by Brian M. Sammons and David Conyers (Chaosium, Inc), presents nineteen stories about people who return from the grave. There are notable stories by Gary McMahon, Robert Neilson, David Dunwoody, and Mercedes M. Yardley.

Tales of Jack the Ripper, edited by Ross E. Lockhart (Word Horde), is the first book out from this new California publisher and marks the 125th anniversary of one of the most famous serial killers of all time. Most of the nineteen stories and poems are original to the anthology, and the most interesting ones are by T. E. Grau, Laird Barron, Orrin Grey, Joseph S. Pulver, Jr., and E. Catherine Tobler.

Fearie Tales: Stories of the Grimm and Gruesome, edited by Stephen Jones and illustrated by Alan Lee (Jo Fletcher Books), takes the retold fairy tale sub genre, already claimed and used exquisitely in fantasy and dark fantasy fiction, deep into horror territory. Each of the fifteen stories has a précis of the original story and a black-and-white illustration by Lee.

There are notable stories by Ramsey Campbell, Peter Crowther, Brian Hodge, Tanith Lee, John Ajvide Lindqvist, Brian Lumley, Garth Nix, Reggie Oliver, Angela Slatter, Robert Shearman, and Michael Marshall Smith.

A Killer Among Demons, edited by Craig Bezant (Dark Prints Press), has ten new stories mixing crime and horror. The strongest are by Angela Slatter, Chris Large, William Meikle, and S. J. Dawson.

Second City Scares: A Horror Express Anthology, edited by Marc Shemmans (Horror Express Publications), features twelve horror stories that take place in Birmingham, England, including two by members of the editor's family. There are notable stories by Mike Chinn, Joel Lane, John Howard, and David A. Sutton.

Vampires Don't Sparkle, edited by Michael West (Seventh Star Press), has fifteen anti-*Twilight* vampire stories, all but three new. The strongest are by Lucy A. Snyder, Maurice Broaddus, and Douglas F. Warrick.

Gay City 5 Ghosts in Gaslight, Monsters in Steam, edited by Vincent Kovar and Evan J. Peterson (A Minor Arcana Press Incantation), is an interesting anthology of gay and lesbian horror. The title is misleading—few, if any of the thirty-seven stories, poems, and graphic novel are steampunk. There's notable work by Ocean Vuong, Steve Berman, Gregory L. Norris, and Anthony Rella.

Anatomy of Death: In Five Sleazy Pieces, edited by Mark West (Hersham Horror Books), is an original anthology intended to provide a taste of the old lurid horror of the '70s. It does, for better or worse, and while some of the stories are entertaining, most don't stay with the reader longer than it takes to read them. There are notable stories by Stephen Bacon and John Llewellyn Probert, plus one by Stephen Volk that rivals the movie *The Human Centipede* for repulsiveness.

The Haunted Mansion Project Year Two, presented by Rain Graves and edited by Loren Rhoades (Damnation Books), is the end result of a writers retreat attended by seventeen horror writers in the fall of 2012. It includes essays, poems, and stories inspired by the weekend. The strongest stories and poems are by Weston Ochse, Sèphera Girón, Rain Graves, and Dan Weidman.

The Book of the Dead, edited by Jared Shurin (Jurassic London in partnership with the Egypt Exploration Society), has nineteen stories about mummies. The best are by Maria Dahvana Headley and Maurice Broaddus.

Eulogies II: Tales from the Cellar, edited by Christopher Jones, Nanci Kalanta, and Tony Tremblay (HW Press), contains thirty-two stories, with proceeds going to Tom and Michelle Piccirilli. There were strong stories by Michael Boatman, Gary McMahon, Gary A. Braunbeck, Eric J. Guignard, Malcolm Laughton, Thad Linson, and Monica O'Rourke.

Halloween: Magic, Mystery, and the Macabre, edited by Paula Guran (Prime Books), is a varied mix of seventeen original (and one reprint) stories about Halloween. All of the stories are readable, most are dark, a few are dark enough to consider horror. The strongest stories are by Brian Hodge, A. C. Wise, Lawrence C. Connolly, Maria V. Snyder, Stephen Graham Jones, Laird Barron, and Laure Bickle. There's also a very fine horror novella by Norman Partridge.

The Burning Circus: BFS Horror 1, edited by Johnny Mains, is one of two special anthologies intended for members of the British Fantasy Society. The other is *Unexpected Journeys*, a fantasy anthology edited by Juliet E. McKenna. *The Burning Circus* is short, with no apparent theme, despite the title and includes eight stories, one a reprint. Ramsey Campbell provides the introduction. The strongest stories were by Stephen Volk, Adam Nevill, Lynda E. Rucker, and Angela Slatter.

The Mountains of Madness, edited by Robert M. Price (Dullahan Press), is an entertaining theme anthology of twelve stories centering and/or inspired by the H. P. Lovecraft's novella of the same title. Some notable stories by Stephen Mark Rainey, Edward Morris, and Brian M. Sammons.

Bad Seeds: Evil Progeny, edited by Steve Berman (Prime), has twenty-seven horror stories about really nasty kids. With reprints by Stephen King, Peter Straub, Cassandra Clare, Holly Black, Joe R. Lansdale, and others. The best of the five originals is by Joel D. Lane.

Shadows Edge, edited by Simon Strantzas (Gray Friar Press), takes as its theme the edges between nightmare and reality, and although individually each story is quite good, unfortunately, as a group of fifteen, they seem awfully desolate/static. The standouts are those by Richard Gavin, Gary McMahon, Lisa Hannett, Simon Strantzas, Peter Bell, R. B. Russell, and John Langan.

Impossible Monsters, edited by Kasey Lansdale (Subterranean Press), is an entertaining anthology of twelve (all but one new) stories about new monsters. The meatiest stories are Chet Williamson's tour de force that will make anyone who stays in hotel rooms totally paranoid and Joe R. Lansdale's new adventures about supernatural sleuth Dana Roberts.

There were two volumes in the Terror Tales anthology series, edited by Paul Finch (Gray Friar Press): *Terror Tales of the Seaside* has fourteen horror stories taking place in the seaside towns of England. All but two stories are new. The strongest were by Gary Fry, Paul Kane, Reggie Oliver, Sam Stone, and Stephen Volk. *Terror Tales of London* features thirteen stories, ten published for the first time. The best were by Barbara Roden, Mark Morris, Nina Allan, Adam Nevill, and Rosalie Parker. The Allan is reprinted herein.

Barbers & Beauties, edited by Michael Knost and Nancy Eden Siegel (Hummingbird House Press), is a clever concoction. Created as a double book, with one half dubbed Beautyshop Quartet, consisting of four original stories by women, and the other half dubbed Barbershop Quartet, consisting of four original stories by men. The stories all take place within either a barbershop or beautyshop. The strongest stories are by Lee Thomas, Tim Lebbon, and Rhodi Hawks.

Weirder Shadows over Innsmouth, edited by Stephen Jones (Fedogan & Bremer), is the third in a trilogy of anthologies inspired by the H. P. Lovecraft novella *The Shadow over Innsmouth*. The volume contains a poem by Lovecraft, sixteen reprints by various writers, and seven originals, including notable work by Conrad Williams, Michael Marshall Smith, Angela Slatter, and Brian Hodge. The Hodge is reprinted herein.

Psycho-Mania, edited by Stephen Jones (Robinson), features thirty-four stories, a little more than half of them new, with interstitial material by John Llewellyn Probert pulling the anthology together (so that all the stories are seen as "case histories" of patients in Crowsmoor asylum for the criminally insane), and an introduction by Robert Bloch (a previously unpublished essay). While all the originals are good, the strongest are by Brian Hodge, Robert Shearman, Rio Youers, Michael Marshall, and Kim Newman. The Shearman and Newman are reprinted herein.

Zombies: Shambling through the Ages, edited by Steve Berman (Prime), has more than thirty zombie stories, eight of them reprints, all taking place from pre-history through the early twentieth century. There are notable originals by Paul M. Berger, Samantha Henderson, Carrie Laben, Livia Llewellyn, L. Lark, and Aimee Payne.

Appalachian Undead, edited by Eugene Johnson and Jason Sizemore (Apex Publications), features twenty all new zombie stories. There are notable ones by Maurice Broaddus, Michael Paul Gonzalez, Paul Moore, Steve Rasnic Tem, and a good collaboration by John Skipp and Dori Miller. *Mountain Dead*, edited by Jason Sizemore and Eugene Johnson (Apex Publications), is a chapbook extension of the anthology (ebook only) with four more zombie stories.

Zippered Flesh 2: More Tales of Body Enhancement Gone Bad!, edited by Weldon Burges (Smart Rhino), has twenty-two stories, all but three new. The best are by Shaun Meeks, Lisa Mannetti, Christine Morgan, and Michael Bailey.

Space Eldritch II: The Haunted Stars, edited by Nathan Shumate (Gold Fusion Media), is an all original anthology of eleven Locraftian space operas.

For the Night is Dark, edited by Ross Warren (Crystal Lake Publishing), has twenty original stories about fear of the dark, and the best stories are by Ray Cluley, Benedict J. Jones, and Carole Johnstone. One story is by publisher Joe Mynhardt, something I've never before encountered. Sometimes editors include their own stories—in the case of big name author-editors, occasionally they are required by their publisher to include their own stories for marketing purposes—*because* they're a big name. I personally think it's a lousy idea because it means there's no editorial *choice* at play and that's one of the most crucial jobs of editing an anthology. There's no excuse for a non-name to do so. But for the *publisher* to force his editor to include that publisher's story? That's a conflict of interest.

Ill at Ease II (Penman Press, no editor) is a short anthology of seven stories, following up from the 2011 three-writer chapbook *Ill at Ease*. The most interesting stories this time around are by Mark West and Robert Mammone.

Mister October: An Anthology in Memory of Rick Hautala volumes I and II (Journalstone Publishing) is an all-reprint anthology with 100 percent of the profits going to the Hautala family. Rick Hautala, a well-known figure in horror circles, died suddenly in March 2013. Some of the contributors include Peter Straub, Neil Gaiman, Sarah Langan, F. Paul Wilson, Sarah Pinborough, Joe Lansdale, Elizabeth Massie, and other prominent names in horror.

His Red Eyes, Again, edited by Julia Kruk and Tracy Lee (CreateSpace), celebrates the fortieth anniversary of The Dracula Society with thirteen stories, twelve by members. The best stories are by Chris Priestley and Laura Miller.

Chiral Mad 2, edited by Michael Bailey (CreateSpace), is a mix of twenty-eight new and reprinted psychological horror stories. The best of the originals are by Emily B. Cataneo, James Chambers, Patrick O'Neill, Andrew Hook, and Usman T. Malik.

The Tenth Black Book of Horror, edited by Charles Black (Mortbury Press), has fifteen stories, the strongest by Andrea Janes. This volume in the series is a bit too pulpy for my taste.

Hauntings, edited by Ellen Datlow (Tachyon Publications), is a reprint anthology of twenty-four stories of ghosts and other types of hauntings originally published between 1983 and 2012. Included are stories by Neil Gaiman, Peter Straub, Connie Willis, Lucius Shepard, Joyce Carol Oates, and nineteen other writers.

The Transfiguration of Mister Punch by D.P. Watt, Charles Schneider, and Cate Gardner (Egaeus Press) is an anthology of three works commissioned (by publisher Mark Beech) to reinvent the Punch and Judy mythos. The first by Charles Schneider is a fictitious essay interspersed with macabre vignettes about the history and various aspects of the show. The second grouping, by D. P. Watt, has stories within stories, all very dark. And the third is a disturbing novella by Cate Gardner in which Punch and Judy and another character start out in Hell. The book is profusely illustrated (with drawings and black-and-white photographs) throughout.

Limbus, Inc., edited by Anne C. Petty (Journalstone), is a shared world anthology about an employment agency that uses sketchy methods of hiring employees for unique jobs that might not be survivable. Contributions by Jonathan Maberry, Joseph Nassise, Benjamin Kane Ethridge, Brett J. Talley, and Anne C. Petty.

Suffered from the Night: Queering Stoker's Dracula, edited by Steve Berman (Lethe Press), is an anthology of fourteen new stories, but unfortunately the narrow focus (in contrast to a broader one of "vampires" or the editor's *Where Thy Dark Eye Glances: Queering Edgar Allan Poe*—see mention below—which would be/is more successful because it's not concentrated on one work by Poe) limits the variety and imagination of most of the contributors. Few do more than adding a gay character or changing one of the character's sexual preferences. Notable exceptions are the stories by Laird Barron, David Shaw, Livia Llewellyn, Seth Cadin, Traci Castleberry, and editor Steve Berman.

Dark Fusions: Where Monsters Lurk!, edited by Lois H. Gresh (PS Publishing), is an entertaining all original anthology of eighteen supernatural, sf/horror, dark fantasy, and horror stories, many containing monsters. The most interesting are by Cody Goodfellow, Nicholas Kaufmann, Nancy Kilpatrick, Lisa Morton, Norman Prentiss, David Sakmyster, Darrell Schweitzer, and Ann K. Schwader.

In *Four Summoner's Tales* by Kelly Armstrong, Christopher Golden, David Liss, and Jonathan Maberry (Gallery Books), each contributor takes a crack at the premise: what if the dead could be summoned from their graves.

Dueling Minds, edited by Brian James Freeman (CD), is #10 in the publisher's signature series. Six stories, two original, with jacket art by Alan M. Clark, and interior illustrations throughout by Erin S. Wells. There, a notable story by Gerard Houarner

All-American Horror of the 21st Century: The First Decade: 2000–2010, edited by Mort Castle (Wicker Park Press), is a volume of thirty stories by American writers dealing with "uniquely American" themes and written in an "equally unique style." Two of the stories were actually published in the late Nineties. And while I've always appreciated editors using a few unknowns in anthologies, it seems counter to the spirit of the showcase that this volume intends to be because several writers are missing—influential and flat-out brilliant new horror writers who started publishing in the late ought's and are currently flowering during this second decade of the twenty-first century.

MIXED-GENRE ANTHOLOGIES

ISF 2012 Annual Anthology, edited by Roberto Mendes and Ricardo Loureiro (International Speculative Fiction in association with Hipper Tiger Books and IndieBookLauncher.com), is the first anthology of science fiction, fantasy, and horror published by this international organization promoting speculative fiction from around the world. The stores are all reprints from various magazines and the organization's webzine. *Weird*

Detectives: Recent Investigations, edited by Paula Guran (Prime), features twenty-three dark reprints published between 2004 and 2011 by writers such as Neil Gaiman, Charlaine Harris, Jim Butcher, Joe R. Lansdale, Ilsa J. Bick, and many others. *After Death…*, edited by Eric J. Guignard (Dark Moon), has thirty-four original stories about death, some but not all dark. The more interesting ones are by Lisa Morton, Joe McKinney, and Ray Cluley. *After the End: Recent Apocalypses*, edited by Paula Guran (Prime), presents twenty previously published dark, mostly sf tales of what might happen after the world as we know it ends—for whatever reason. *In Heaven, Everything is Fine: Fiction Inspired by David Lynch* (Eraserhead Press) features thirty-nine intriguing original and reprinted (nine of the latter) stories, vignettes, and dreamscapes. Most of the pieces are surreal and very effective. Some don't work at all. A few are laced with horror. The original dark pieces I liked the best are by Edward Morris, Cody Goodfellow, Jeffrey Thomas, Matthew Revert, Andrew Wade Adams, and Garrett Cook. *Where Thy Dark Eye Glances: Queering Edgar Allan Poe*, edited by Steve Berman (Lethe Press), presents twenty-six fantasy, dark fantasy, and horror stories and poems about or influenced by Poe, all involving gay or lesbian relationships. There are notable pieces by John Mantooth, Richard Bowes, Ray Cluley, Ed Madden, Tansy Rayner Roberts, and Cory Skerry. *End of the Road*, edited by Jonathan Oliver (Solaris), mixes sf/f/h in fifteen new stories about travel along the road. There are notable horror stories by Jay Caselberg, Helen Marshall, Paul Meloy, Benjanun Sriduangkaew, S. L. Grey, and Adam Nevill. *Rustblind and Silverbright*, edited by David Rix (Eibonvale), is a terrific anthology comprised of twenty-three stories and one poem about railways. Several of the stories treat the theme obliquely, to marvelous effect. Although not all the stories held my interest, most did, and some were excellent, including those by Andrew Coulthard, Christopher Harman, Andrew Hook, John Howard, Joel Lane, Danny Rhodes, Steve Rasnic Tem, Aliya Whiteley, and Charles Wilkinson. There's also a notable poem by Gavin Salisbury and a brilliant novella by Nina Allan. In addition, the interstitial material by editor David Rix is consistently fascinating. *One Small Step: An Anthology of Discoveries*, edited by Tehani Wessely (Fablecroft Publishing), features sixteen original stories by Australian women on the theme of exploration and discovery. There are notable dark stories by Kathleen

Jennings and the collaborative teams of Joanne Anderton and Rabia Gale and Lisa L. Hannett and Angela Slatter. *Shades of Blue & Gray*, edited by Steve Berman (Prime), has twenty-two original and reprinted fantasy and dark fantasy (with a bit of horror) stories about American Civil War ghosts. Of the fifteen new stories, there were notable dark stories by Ed Kurtz, Chaz Brenchley, Melissa Scott, Laird Barron, Christopher Cevasco, and Cindy Potts. *Rags & Bones*, edited by Melissa Marr and Tim Pratt (Little, Brown), has twelve new stories inspired by classic tales of various types ranging from "The Monkey's Paw" and "Carmilla" to "Sleeping Beauty," *The Man Who Would Be King*, and *The Awakening*. The strongest of the dark tales are by Holly Black, Gene Wolfe, and Kami Garcia. *Horror Without Victims*, edited by D. F. Lewis (Megazanthus Press), is an interesting all-original anthology with twenty-five stories: some horror, some just weird. And despite the title, there are indeed occasional victims. With notable dark stories by DeAnna Knipling, Katie Jones, Gary McMahon, David Murphy, John Travis, Charles Wilkinson, and L. R. Bonehill. *Shadows of the New Sun*, edited by J. E. Mooney and Bill Fawcett (Tor), features eighteen original stories in honor of the great sf/fantasist (including one by Wolfe himself). There are notable dark stories by Neil Gaiman and Nancy Kress. *Beyond Rue Morgue: Further Tales of Edgar Allan Poe's 1st Detective*, edited by Paul Kane and Charles Prepolec (Titan), features eight new stories, the original "Murder in the Rue Morgue" by Poe, plus a reprint by Clive Barker. There are notable stories by Lisa Tuttle, Stephen Volk, Elizabeth Massie, and Joe R. Lansdale. *Red Spectres: Russian Gothic Tales from the Twentieth Century*, selected and translated by Muireann Maguire (The Overlook Press/Ardis), features eleven stories, all but two translated from Russian into English for the first time—subtlety creepy and weird. *Queen Victoria's Book of Spells: An Anthology of Gaslamp Fantasy*, edited by Ellen Datlow and Terri Windling (Tor Books), is a mixture of fantasy and dark fantasy with the darkest stories by Kaaron Warren, Veronica Schanoes, Maureen F. McHugh, Leanna Renee Hieber, and Dale Bailey. The Bailey is reprinted herein. *By Faerie Light*, edited by Scott Gable, Caroline Dombrowski, and Dora Wang (Broken Eye Books), is a charming anthology of dark fantasy tales about faeries. A few stories, such as the fine one by Andrew Penn Romine, verge on horror. *The Farthest Shore: An Anthology of Fantasy Fiction from the Philippines*, edited by Dean Francis

Alfar and Joseph Frederic F. Nacino (the University of the Philippines Press), showcases twelve stories of fantasy and dark fantasy. The volume is also an homage to the third book in Ursula K. Le Guin's Earthsea trilogy, which is set on a fantastical world made of islands, as is the Philippines. *Sorcery & Sanctity: A Homage to Arthur Machen* (Hieroglyphic Press) is a tribute featuring twenty stories inspired by Machen's writing from different periods of his life. Most of the stories are more weird than horrific but would likely appeal to connoisseurs of Machen. *Encounters with Enoch Coffin*, by W. H. Pugmire and Jeffrey Thomas (Dark Regions Press), has twelve stories (six by each author) that follow an artist on his quest to paint, illustrate, or create in pottery sights that no one has ever seen before—Lovecraftian and weird. *Horror: Filipino Fiction for Young Adults*, edited by Dean Alfar and KennethYu (University of Philippines Press), has fourteen stories. Unfortunately, as an adult, I find most horror anthologies and single-author collections aimed at kids not very creepy. This is no exception but still, there are a couple of notable darker stories by Renelaine Bontol-Pfister and Fidelis Tan. *Memoryville Blues*, edited by Peter Crowther and Nick Gevers (PS), is volume 30/31 of the PS Publishing anthology series and has some excellent horror among its twenty-five offerings. The best were by Alastair Reynolds, James Cooper, Lynda E. Rucker, John Grant, Peter Hardy, and a collaboration by Allen Ashley and Douglas Thompson.

The Year's Best Dark Fantasy & Horror 2013, edited by Paula Guran (Prime), features thirty-five stories and novellas of dark fantasy and horror. One story overlapped with my own *The Best Horror of the Year Volume Five*. *The Mammoth Book of Best New Horror 24*, edited by Stephen Jones (Robinson), features twenty-two reprints published during 2012. There was one overlap with my Volume Five, two with Guran's. *Wilde Stories 2013: The Year's Best Gay Speculative Fiction*, edited by Steve Berman (Lethe Press), reprinted twelve mixed-genre stories originally published in diverse publications such as *Strange Horizons, Shadows and Tall Trees, Subterranean*, and several anthologies. *Imaginarium 2013: The Best Canadian Speculative Fiction Writing*, edited by Sandra Kasturi and Samantha Beiko (Chizine Publications), is the second in this series showcasing sf/f/h first published in 2012. This year's volume includes thirty-six stories and poetry by Canadians such as Gemma Files, Angela Slatter and Lisa Hannett (a collaboration allowing Aussie Slatter into the anthology), Helen Marshall, Ian Rogers, and Silvia Moreno-Garcia. *The Best of Philippine Speculative Fiction 2005–2010*, edited by Dean Francis Alfar and Nikki Alfar (The University of Philippines Press), is an important addition to world genre literature, presenting thirty science fiction, fantasy, and horror stories selected from the first five years annual *Philippine Speculative Fiction* anthologies.

COLLECTIONS

There is a triumvirate of American male, dark fiction writers who have sprung up within the past several years and been creating brilliant work: Laird Barron, John Langan, and Nathan Ballingrud. All three have new collections out in 2013.

North American Lake Monsters by Nathan Ballingrud (Small Beer Press) is the author's first collection. Some of the nine stories are *almost* mainstream, I guess you could say mainstream in sensibility, but there's always a touch of the weird in them. Since publishing his first story in *SciFiction* in 2003, I've been astounded by his range. There's one original story is a knockout, and it's reprinted herein.

The Wide, Carnivorous Sky and Other Monstrous Geographies by John Langan (Hippocampus Press) is the author's second collection of marvelously creepy short fiction. Langan especially shines at the novelette and novella length, and almost everything in the new book is those lengths. Eight were originally published between 2008 and 2010, one on the author's blog. "Mother of Stone," the one original, is an excellent novella. It features an introduction by Jeffrey Ford and an afterword by Laird Barron.

The Beautiful Thing That Awaits Us All by Laird Barron (Night Shade) was published a few months later than scheduled because it was caught in the sale of Night Shade's assets to Skyhorse. It's Barron's third collection and has eight stories originally published between 2010 and 2012, plus one new one. Barron's writing might be described as an amalgam of Lovecraftian themes and paranoia with the language and characterizations of tough men laid low (sometimes by women) of Lucius Shepard. Critics talk about Thomas Ligotti as an inheritor of Lovecraft's mantel, and that might be, but Barron at his best has pushed cosmic horror through to the twenty-first century. It has an introduction by Norman Partridge. The original story is reprinted herein.

Everything You Need by Michael Marshall Smith (Earthling Publications) is a welcome new collection of seventeen stories by one of the contemporary masters of the form. Smith's range is extraordinary, roaming equally smoothly among horror, dark fantasy, science fiction, and mainstream. There are three new stories, one of them mainstream and heartbreaking.

The Moment of Panic by Steve Duffy (PS Publications) is a the author's fourth collection and has twelve stories and novelettes, five of them new. The novelette "The A-Z" is particularly good as the weirdness creeps up on the reader, but all are enjoyable.

Like Light for Flies by Lee Thomas (Lethe Press) is a fine, second collection by Thomas. In it are twelve stories, three new, one of those three a powerful novella about a South Florida government work camp built during the depression affected by a hurricane in 1935. The reprints were originally published in a variety of anthologies and magazines. Sarah Langan provides an introduction. The title story is reprinted herein.

The Ape's Wife and Other Stories by Caitlín R. Kiernan (Subterranean Press) is Kiernan's twelfth collection, containing stories written between 2001 and 2012 (plus *Black Helicopters,* an ambitious and dense new sf/horror novella hardcover chapbook, included with the limited edition). She's one of the few contemporary writers of dark fiction today writing science fiction/horror with a Lovecraftian tinge to it. Her writing continues to get better and better.

Holes for Faces by Ramsey Campbell (Dark Regions Press) contains fourteen stories published between 2005 and 2013 by this master of the short story. Campbell is great at conveying a creeping dread in the vulnerable, whether children or the elderly, something he does quite powerfully in the two stories first published in 2013.

There were two prose collections by British author Mark Valentine published in 2013: *Herald of the Hidden and Other Stories* (Tartarus Press) features ten entertaining dark fantasy stories (two new) about the occult detective Ralph Tyler, plus six early stories by the author. *Seventeen Stories* (The Swan River Press) includes both weird and darkly supernatural tales, two published in 2013, one of those appearing in the collection for the first time. There's no overlap between the two volumes.

Monsters in the Heart by Stephen Volk (Gray Friar Press) is the author's powerful second collection, with fifteen stories, all published since 2006 and two of them new. It contains story notes.

The Sea Change & Other Stories by Helen Grant (The Swan River Press) is the first collection of a very talented author of four novels. The stories were originally published between 2005 and 2012.

The Condemned by Simon Bestwick (Gray Friar Press) has six novelettes and novellas, two of them reprints. Grim, powerful, hard-edged, well-written.

Paul Kane had two new collections out in 2013: *Ghosts* (Spectral Press) with sixteen supernatural stories—four first published in 2013, one poem, and a script written for the short film *Wind Chimes*. Nancy Kilpatrick wrote the introduction. Also, *The Spaces Between* (Dark Moon Books) with eight longer stories, three published for the first time. It has an introduction by Kelley Armstrong.

The Moon Will Look Strange by Lynda E. Rucker (Karōshi Books) is the debut collection of a writer who amply demonstrates her chops with eleven stories (three published for the first time). It contains an introduction by Steve Rasnic Tem and an author's note, discussing some of the stories.

Elegies & Requiems by Colin Insole (Side Real Press) is an excellent collection of ghostly stories and weird, dark tales and novellas. Traditional but fresh in feel. Nine of the eighteen stories are new.

Remorseless: Tales of Cruelty by Thomas Tessier (Sinister Grin Press) is the second collection by an author better known for his novels than his short fiction. This volume, with cover art by Alan M. Clark, features fifteen stories published between 1998 and 2011 in various magazines, anthologies, and websites.

Five Autobiographies and a Fiction by Lucius Shepard (Subterranean Press) showcases six powerful horror novellas by a writer utterly at home in any genre (not to mention mainstream), five of which have some autobiographical elements in them.

For Those Who Dream Monsters by Anna Taborska (Mortbury Press) is a debut collection with eighteen stories, two new. Included in the book is the powerful "Little Pig," which was reprinted in *The Best Horror of the Year Volume Four*. It has black-and-white illustrations throughout by Reggie Oliver.

Bone Whispers by Tim Waggoner (Post Mortem Press) has eighteen stories, all reprints, published between 2007 and 2012.

The Tears of Isis by James Dorr (Perpetual Motion Publishing Machine) brings together sixteen stories and a poem published between 1992 and 2012. It also includes one new story.

Looking Back in Darkness by Kathryn Ptacek (Wildside Press) is a retrospective of nineteen fantasy and horror stories originally published between 1987 and 2012.

Ten Minute Stories / Day and Night Stories by Algernon Blackwood (Stark House Press) are two short story collections of hauntings, strange nature tales, weird events, and dark fantasy by one of the major writers of supernatural fiction in the twentieth century. It includes a new introduction by Mike Ashley, plus a rare early story, "The Farmhouse on the Hill," originally published in an Australian newspaper back in 1907.

The Heaven Tree & Other Stories by Christopher Harman (Sarob Press) is a short but excellent introduction to this writer's supernatural tales. It includes reprints of five recent stories plus two new novelettes.

The Bohemians of Sesqua Valley by W. H. Pugmire (Miskatonic Books) collects six novelettes (one reprint) paying homage to H. P. Lovecraft about the haunted valley in the Pacific Northwest.

Where You Live by Gary McMahon (Crystal Lake Publishing) is a revised edition of the one hundred copy signed, limited hardcover published as *It Knows Where You Live* in 2012 by Gray Friar Press. Three stories have been deleted, but five new stories have been added to this trade paperback edition.

Worse Things Than Spiders by Samantha Lee (Shadow Publishing) is the author's first collection of dark fiction. Included are thirteen stories and an introduction by David A. Sutton.

Shades of Nothingness by Gary Fry (PS Publishing) has seventeen stories, twelve published between 2008 and 2012, and five of them—all pretty grim—appearing for the first time.

From the Dusklands: Dark Fiction from the Pen of Aaron Gudmunson (Hazardous Press) is a debut collection featuring ten pieces of fiction, two reprinted essays, and one new novella.

In a Season of Dead Winter by Mark Fuller Dillon (Smashwords) is an interesting collection of seven stories, most published for the first time.

Several of the stories are open to interpretation as to whether anything supernatural occurs or if all the events are in the minds of the protagonists.

Rose of Sharon and Other Stories by Gary A. Braunbeck (Creative Guy Publishing) is available as an e-book only. The twenty-nine stories provide a good overview of the author's work. Three of them are new.

Your Place is in the Shadows by Charlie Williams (Gibbous Moon) is a very good collection of six edgy dark crime stories, available only for Kindle. One story is new.

The Dragonfly and the Siren: A Collection by Jay Wilburn and T. Fox Dunham (Hazardous Press) has eleven stories, six by Dunham, five by Wilburn, all but two (by Dunham) published for the first time.

Dark Renaissance Books is a new publishing venture by Joe Morey, intended to produce beautiful, limited edition, illustrated hardcover books. Three of the first books are prose collections and the fourth is a poetry collection (see under "Poetry" for this last): *Worship the Night* by Jeffrey Thomas (Dark Renaissance Books) has eight stories, two new. It has black-and-white interior illustrations by Erin Wells. *The Universal and Other Terrors* by Tony Richards (Dark Renaissance Books) has twelve stories, five of them new. The best of these is the title story, a nicely wrought sf/horror tale. William Meikle's entertaining *Sherlock Holmes: The Quality of Mercy and Other Stories* has ten Holmesian adventures, six of them new. The book is a treat for those fans who don't mind supernatural outcomes for the character. Frontispiece and interior illustrations are by M. Wayne Miller.

Twisted Fairy Tales by Maura McHugh (Barron's) is a gorgeous package of twenty dark, retold fairy and folk tales illustrated by Jane Laurie. Included are some adult and/or grisly takes on "Snow White," "The Red Shoes," "Rapunzel," and seventeen others. McHugh had a second book out from Barron's, this one *Twisted Myths*, with many of the stories sporting more feminist and positive outcomes for the characters. The stories were inspired by Greece and Norse myths and legends from Asia, Africa, and the Americas. Again, it is beautifully illustrated by Jane Laurie.

Their Hand Is at Your Throats by John Shire (Invocations Press) is an interesting collection of ten Lovecraftian stories, six originally published in small press journals between 1997 and 2007, four appearing for the first time. The new stories are surprisingly good, mostly rising above pastiche.

Three Miles Past by Stephen Graham Jones (Nightscape Press) is a powerful and disturbing three-story collection (two are new novelettes) that leaves the reader wanting more. Jones provides extensive story notes with each story.

Darkscapes by Anne-Sylvia Salzberg translated from the French by William Charlton (Tartarus Press) features fifteen weird and usually darkly fantastic tales, most appearing in English for the first time. Although some of the stories are overly oblique, most of them are effective.

Staring into the Abyss by Richard Thomas (Kraken Press) is the author's second collection—made up of twenty reprints—most of which pack a surprisingly powerful punch at very short length.

Dead Clown Barbecue by Jeff Strand (Dark Regions Press) features twenty-nine stories, including seven new ones.

Fresh Cut Tales by Kenneth W. Cain (Distressed Press) is the second collection by the author and has sixteen stories, half of them appearing for the first time.

Unfortunately, I only got hold of *Let the Old Dreams Die and Other Stories*, John Ajvide Lindquist's 2012 horror collection (Quercus) in 2013. The eleven stories were translated from the Swedish by Marlaine Delargy and includes a story that might be considered a tangential sequel to his brilliant vampire novel, *Let the Right One In*. There's also an afterword about the Swedish and US film versions of his novel (he enjoyed both very much) stating that the implied ending of both versions don't reflect his intent at all.

How to Die Well by Bill Breedlove (Bad Moon Books) features twenty effective humorous horror stories.

The Tightening Spiral by Tara Fox Hall (Hazardous Press) has nineteen stories, some new and some reprints.

Dead Reflections by Carol Weekes (Journalstone) contains a short novel, five short stories, and two poems.

Cravings by Joan VanderPutten (Necon E-Books) is a ten-story reprint collection.

David A. Riley had two new collections out in 2013: *His Own Mad Demons* (Hazardous Press), with five stories published between 2007 and 2010; and *The Lurkers in the Abyss and Other Tales of Terror* (Shadow Publishing), a more substantial collection with seventeen stories, the first published in 1974 and one appearing for the first time in this volume. The introduction to the latter is written by David Sutton.

Tricks, Mischief and Mayhem by Daniel I. Russell (Crystal Lake Publishing) has twenty-two stories, almost half published for the first time in 2013.

Bible Stories for Secular Humanists by S. P. Somtow (Diplodocus Press) features nine reprinted stories and an essay that was originally published in *Iniquities* Magazine.

Lovecraft's Pillow and Other Strange Stories by Kenneth W. Faig, Jr. (Hippocampus Press), who is best-known as a Lovecraftian scholar, but this is a collection of his fiction, mostly stories previously published in the Esoteric Order of Dagon (EOD) and Necronomicon amateur press associations between 1977 and 2006.

Black Tea and Other Stories by Samuel Marolla (Mezzotints) is a mini-collection of three dark tales published for the first time in English. The stories are translated from the Italian by Andrew Tanzi, and Gene O'Neil supplies an introduction.

Absinthe & Arsenic: Tales of Victorian Horror by Raven Dane (Telos) has sixteen mostly supernatural tales, of which all but a couple are new.

The Whispering Horror by Eddy C. Bertin (Shadow Publishing) has fourteen mostly Lovecraftian horror stories originally published between 1968 and 2013. One is new to the collection.

Not to Be Taken at Bed-Time & Other Strange Tales by Rosa Mulholland (Sarob Press) contains seven of what are considered this Victorian writer's best supernatural and weird stories. This is the first time they're collected in one volume. It features an introduction by Richard Dalby.

Bleeding Shadows by Joe R. Lansdale (Subterranean Press) is a big, beautiful, 150,000-word collection of thirty stories, novellas, and poems in all the genres Lansdale excels: crime, dark fantasy, and horror. It contains story notes.

MIXED-GENRE COLLECTIONS

Across the Event Horizon by Mercurio D. Rivera (Newcon Press) is an excellent showcase for this relatively new author of science fiction, who is not afraid of delving into the dark aspects of future behavior. The thirteen stories within were originally published in *Interzone*, *Black*

Static, Asimov's Science Fiction Magazine, Electric Velocipede, Sybil's Garage, and some anthologies. Some of the stories are sf/horror. Steve Rasnic Tem had two impressive mixed-genre collections out in 2013: *Onion Songs* (Chomu Press) is a retrospective of this prolific short story writer's career, with forty-two stories of varying lengths, including several new short-shorts. As always with Tem, this is a mix of existential horror about relationships, weird fictions, and disturbing meditations. And *Celestial Inventories* (CZP) with twenty-two stories from obscure venues, plus one new story. Several stories from this latter collection were reprinted in the *Year's Best Fantasy and Horror*. *Kabu Kabu* by Nnedi Okorafor (Prime) is the author's first collection and features twenty-two stories, several published for the first time, a few of them dark. *Caution: Contains Small Parts* by Australian Kirstyn McDermott (Twelve Planets) is volume 9 of the Twelve Planets series of short collections. It has four original stories and novellas by the award-winning writer, a couple of them horror. Nina Allan had two collections out in 2013: *Stardust: The Ruby Castle Stories (PS Showcase 11)*, containing a mix of six horror and mainstream stories and novellas and one poem (all but one new) and *Microcosmos* (Newcon Press), containing five reprints and two originals by this up-and-coming British writer. *Jewels in the Dust* by Peter Crowther (Subterranean Press) collects thirteen fantasy and dark fantasy stories by the British author. *Ghost Stories and Mysteries* by Ernest Favenc, edited by James Doig, (Borgo Press) collects thirty-one gothic and supernatural stories by a prolific but now almost forgotten Australian journalist and non fiction writer. The stories span the period 1875–1907 and are reprinted for the first time since their original publications. *Revenge* by Yoko Ogawa (Picador), translated from the Japanese by Stephen Snyder, is an intertwined series of eleven weird, sometimes dark stories, all but three published in English for the first time. *Simulacrum and Other Possible Realities* by Jason V. Brock (Hippocampus Press) contains sixteen stories and thirteen poems of sf/f/dark fantasy and horror. *The Bride Price* by Cat Sparks (Ticonderoga Publications) features thirteen sf/f and dark fantasy stories by this Australian writer—three of the stories won awards and two appear for the first time. *Everything is a Graveyard* by Jason Fischer (Ticonderoga Publications) has fourteen sf/f/dark fantasy stories published since 2008. Three of the stores are new. *This Strange Way of*

Dying by Silvia Moreno-Garcia (Exile Editions) is the first collection by a Mexican-Canadian who is probably better known within horror for her editorship of Innsmouth Free Press. The fifteen stories (four, first published in 2013) are science fiction, fantasy, and horror. A few of them, rather than hinting at something inconclusive beyond the "ending," simply trail off. But others are quite effective, and my favorite of the originals is a well-told zombie story. *Plow the Bones* by Douglas F. Warrick (Apex Publications) is Book 01 of Apex Voices, a new series of collections to be published several times a year. The idea is to introduce mostly newer voices to the reading public. Warrick is an excellent choice—his work includes science fiction, horror, and just plain weird stories. Four of the fourteen appear for the first time (and one was in a vampire anthology earlier this year). Gary A. Braunbeck supplies an introduction. *13 Conjurations* by Jonathan Thomas (Hippocampus Press) is the author's third collection and all but four of the stories are new. Some of the stories are Lovecraftian, others about weird occurrences. *Of Eggs and Elephants* by Darren Speegle (Gallows Press) is a fine third collection of sixteen stories, with four originals, including the powerfully weird eponymous novella. *In Search Of and Others* by Will Ludwigsen (Lethe Press) has some excellent dark stories among the fifteen in his second collection. Six appear for the first time and there is an introduction by Jeffrey Ford. *The Girlfriend Game* by Nick Antosca (Word Riot) collects twelve dark tales by a writer who won the Shirley Jackson Award for his short novel, *Midnight Picnic*. *The Bone Chime Song and Other Stories* by Joanne Anderton (Fablecroft) is an excellent debut collection of science fiction and horror, often with the two mixed. A few appear for the first time. *Flowers of the Sea* by Reggie Oliver (Tartarus press) includes sixteen weird and often dark stories and novellas, including three published for the first time. As always, Oliver's experiences and enthusiasms shine through this excellent collection. The introduction is by Michael Dirda. *What the Doctor Ordered* by Michael Blumlein (Centipede Press) is a beautiful looking collection illustrated throughout by Brian McCarty. Of the fifteen stories, two are new, a few are dark. There's an introduction by Rudy Rucker. *An Emporium of Automata* by D. P. Watt (Eibonvale Press) is an expanded version of the author's first, hard to find collection. In this edition, there are twenty strange tales. *Rumbullion* by Molly Tanzer

(Egaeus Press) is the second collection by this up-and-coming writer. Included are seven stories, one a new novella. *Tell My Sorrows to the Stones* by Christopher Golden (CZP) brings together twelve stories in different genres. All but two were published in anthologies. The other two have appeared online. *Written by Daylight* by John Howard (The Swan River Press) is a beautiful little hardcover volume of eleven weird, sometimes dark stories originally published between 2003 and 2013. *Defeated Dogs* by Quentin S. Crisp (Eibonvale Press) is the author's fifth collection of weird and dark fiction. Of the ten stories, four appear for the first time. *Growing Pains* by Ian Whates (PS Publishing) is the author's debut collection, containing nine science fiction and dark fantasy/horror stories, two published for the first time. *Psychedelia Gothique* by Dale Sproule (Arctic Mage) is an overview of the author's short fiction published between 1984–2013. Five of the stories appear for the first time. *They Might be Demons: A Collection of Flash Fiction Bizarro* by Max Booth III (Dark Moon) is filled with strange, often dark (and sometime funny) short-shorts. *Vampires in the Lemon Grove* by Karen Russell (Knopf) is the excellent second collection by a writer embraced by the literary despite her fantasy/horror writing. Among the eight stories in the new collection are the very dark title story and "Reeling for the Empire." *The Inner City* by Karen Heuler (CZP), the author's second collection, has fifteen weird, sometimes dark stories, one published for the first time. *The Miniature Wife and Other Stories* by Manuel Gonzalez (Riverhead Books) is an interesting fantasy and dark fantasy-tinged debut collection. *The Story So Far* by Kit Reed (Wesleyan University Press) is a great overview of Reed's short fiction, with a selection of thirty-five of her stories published between 1959 and 2013. Prescient, vicious, funny, creepy—she's written everything during her (so-far) fifty-five-plus year long career. *The Oblivion Room* by Christopher Conlon (Evil Jester Press) is a fine collection of four stories and one novella, all published for the first time. *Masquerade* by Marija Elektra Rodriquez (Huntress Ink) has twenty-eight erotic horror stories and vignettes (most vignettes). Three appear for the first time. *Unseen Moon* by Eliza Victoria (CreateSpace) is a five-story collection with one new story by this award-winning Filipino writer. *Mouths to Speak, Voices to Sing* by Kenneth Yu (self-published) is the first collection of a Filipino writer, showcasing fifteen stories originally published in a variety of genre magazines, webzines, and anthologies. *Antiquities and Tangibles and Other Stories* by Tim Pratt (The Merry Blacksmith Press) is the third collection of the Hugo Award–winning author. There are twenty-three science fiction, fantasy, and dark fantasy stories here, including three new ones. *Before and Afterlives: Stories* by Christopher Barzak (Lethe Press) has seventeen fantasy/dark fantasy, gothic, and ghostly stories. One is original. *Rabbit Pie and Other Tales of Intrigue* by Brian Clemens (PS Publishing) collects fifteen oddball stories by a writer best known for his screen and television work, particularly for writing the pilot and most of the scripts for *The Avengers* television series. *The Year of Ancient Ghosts* by Kim Wilkins (Ticonderoga Publications) presents five fantasy and dark fantasy novellas by the multi award–winning Australian. Two of the novellas are new, one a horrific story about a vengeful ghost's incursion into the contemporary world. *The Man Who Noticed Everything* by Adrian Van Young (Black Lawrence Press) is the author's first collection and has seven stories, five new. Although none of the stories is actually horror, most of them dwell on the fringes of the dark and might appeal to horror readers. *If Angels Fight* by Richard Bowes (Fairwood Press) showcases a dozen stories written over twenty-five years, all originally published in anthologies, magazines, and webzines. Some of them are very dark indeed. Two new pieces of flash fiction are included. *The Tenth of December* by George Saunders (Random House) has ten stories, and while generally considered a mainstream writer, Saunders's work—usually satire—slops over into the fantastical (and to the dark) enough to be of interest to aficionados of the dark. (His 2009 story, "The Red Bow" was chosen by me for *The Year's Best Fantasy and Horror: Seventeenth Annual Collection*).

POETRY JOURNALS, WEBZINES, AND CHAPBOOKS

Goblin Fruit, a quarterly webzine edited by Amal El-Mohtar, Jessica P. Wick, Caitlyn Paxson, Oliver Hunter, and Dmitri Zagidulin remains the best publisher of fantasy and dark fantasy poetry, consistently publishing varied, quality material. Some of the darkest poems in 2013 were by Laura Lee Washburn, Jennifer Jerome, Bonnie Jo Stufflebeam, Samantha Henderson, Liz Bourke, Mike Allen, Yumi Dineen Shiromi, Shweta Narayan, C. S. E. Cooney, and Andy Humphrey. The fall issue, in addition to its usual great line up of poetry, featured an interview and series of poems by Mike Allen. *Star*Line,* edited by F. J. Bergmann, is the bi-monthly journal of the Science Fiction Poetry Association and publishes science fiction, fantasy, and horror poetry. During 2013, it published notable dark poems by Ann K. Schwader, Wade German, and Ian Hunter. *Paper Crow* (no editor listed) is meant to be bi-annual, but only had one issue out in 2013. There were notable dark poems by Bruce Boston and Jill Crammond.

POETRY COLLECTIONS AND ANTHOLOGIES

Dreams of Fear: Poems of Terror and the Supernatural, edited by S. T. Joshi and Steven J. Mariconda (Hippocampus Press), is, according to the publisher, the first comprehensive historical anthology of weird, horrific, and supernatural poetry in more than fifty years. The survey begins with *The Odyssey* and ends with contemporary weird poets Richard L. Tierney, Bruce Boston, W. H. Pugmire, and Ann K. Schwader. *The Sex Lives of Monsters* by Helen Marshall (Kelp Queen Press) is the prose writer and poet's strong second collection, the first of which won Canada's Aurora Award. Much of Marshall's poetry uses fairy tale, myth, and urban legends. Six of the seventeen poems are new. *Letting Out the Demons and Other Poems* by Terrie Leigh Relf (Elektrik Milk Bath Press) has forty poems, most brief, some published for the first time. *Death Poems* by Thomas Ligotti (Bad Moon Books) is the first collection of poetry by the author of much strange, dark prose. Nine of the almost fifty poems have never before been published. *The First Bite of the Apple* by Jennifer Crow (Elektrik Milk Bath Press) is an excellent collection of dark fantasy/ horror poetry. Many of the poems use fairy-tale motifs. Among the more than fifty poems are several new ones. *Scenes Along the Zombie Highway* by G. O. Clark (Dark Regions Press) is an entertaining collection of more than forty pieces of zombie poetry, most appearing for the first time. *Dark Roads: Selected Long Poems 1971–2012* by Bruce Boston (Dark Renaissance Books) is a substantial overview of this popular dark poet's work. It features illustrations by M. Wayne Miller. *Four Elements* by Charlee Jacob, Marge Simon, Rain Graves, and Linda Addison is an entertaining volume of all new poetry and prose with each writer taking a season and running with it. *Demonstra* by Bryan Thao Worra (Innsmouth Free Press) collects about seventy poems written over twenty years by this award-winning Laotian-American poet. Most are new. *The 2013 Rhysling Anthology: The Best Science Fiction, Fantasy, and Horror Poetry of 2012*, selected by the Science Fiction Poetry Association and edited by John C. Mannone (Science Fiction Poetry Association/Hadrosaur Productions), is used by members to vote for the best short poem and the best long poem of the year. Its sister publication *Dwarf Stars 2013,* edited by Stephen M. Wilson and Linda D. Addison (Science Fiction Poetry Association), features the best very short speculative poems published in 2012 and is used by members to vote for the best poem of the year ten lines or fewer. *Star Kites: Poems & Versions* by Mark Valentine (Tartarus Press) is the author's first book of poems, many drawing on the same inspirations of his short stories. *Dangerous Dreams* by Marge Simon and Sandy DeLuca (Elektrik Milk Bath Press) is a collaboration of erotic dark poetry and art created by both women.

Nonfiction

Telling Tales of Terror: Essays on Writing Horror and Dark Fiction, edited by Kim Richards (Damnation Books), presents advice by Lisa Morton, Sephera Giron, and other practitioners of the craft. *Devil's Advocates* is a series of single-film books published by Auteur Press (an imprint of Columbia University Press) and edited by John Atkinson. Begun in 2011, the 2013 titles are: *Witchfinder General* by Ian Cooper, *The Descent* by James Marriott, *The Texas Chainsaw Massacre* by James Rose, and *The Silence of the Lambs* by Barry Forshaw. *New Critical Essays on H. P. Lovecraft* edited by David Simmons (Palgrave Macmillan) contains twelve entries about Lovecraft and his work. *The Women of Hammer Horror* by Robert Michael "Bobb" Cotter (McFarland) is a reference book featuring every known actress who worked with the studio. *Nolan on Bradbury,* edited by S. T. Joshi (Hippocampus Press), provides an entertaining personal perspective on the late Ray Bradbury by his friend of sixty years, William F. Nolan.

Included are twenty articles published between 1952 and 2013, eight stories by Nolan that were influenced by Bradbury, and several tributes to Bradbury. *H. P. Lovecraft in the Merrimack Valley* by David Goudsward (Hippocampus Press) traces Lovecraft's visits to coastal Massachusetts and New Hampshire from the 1920s on, analyzing the impact of those visits on his fiction. *H. P. Lovecraft: Art, Artifact, and Reality* by Steve J. Mariconda (Hippocampus Press) collects almost thirty years of articles and criticism about Lovecraft's prose style, the literary sources of some of his work and how the Cthulhu Mythos developed as Lovecraft responded to the reactions of his readers and other writers to the tales as they were published. *Fear and Learning: Essays on the Pedagogy of Horror,* edited by Aalya Ahmad and Sean Moreland (McFarland), collects new essays about the teaching of horror. These can be read and enjoyed by non-academics. *The Modern Literary Werewolf: A Critical Study of the Mutable Motif* by Brent A. Stypczynski (McFarland) considers the treatment of werewolves in fiction by Jack Williamson, J. K. Rowling, Charlaine Harris, Charles deLint, and other writers. *Fractured Spirits: Hauntings at the Peoria State Hospital* by Sylvia Shults (Dark Continents Publishing) is a historical overview of one of the premiere mental health facilities of the first half of the twentieth century. It was considered a model for the care of the mentally ill. This is an entertaining combination of nonfiction and fiction-history and ghostly reports. *Who Was Dracula?: Bram Stoker's Trail of Blood* by Jim Steinmeyer (Jeremy P. Tarcher/Penguin) explores Bram Stoker's life for clues to the inspiration for one of the greatest fictional characters, going beyond the usual. *The Horror Show Guide: The Ultimate Frightfest of Movies* by Mike Mayo (Visible Ink) features mini-reviews of over one thousand horror movies. There's also an appendix of credits for each movie.

CHAPBOOKS

There are now three UK publishers regularly bringing out single author chapbook. This Is Horror published an excellent novelette by Pat Cadigan titled *Chalk* about the relationship between two girls who chafe against the restrictions of their parents. Also, Joseph D'Lacey's *Roadkill* is a sf/horror story taking place over a period of one hundred seconds as a man races a machine that's fused with his body. Nicholas Royle's Nightjar Press continues its run of high quality horror with Elizabeth Stott's creepy tale of a man, a woman, and a manikin in *Touch Me with Your Cold, Hard Fingers*; a weird, mysterious story called *Getting Out There* by M. John Harrison; and *The Jungle*, a weird tale by Conrad Williams. Spectral Press's Simon Marshall-Jones presented four chapbooks in 2013: Terry Grimwood's *Soul Masque*, an effective dark fantasy about the war between Heaven and Hell and the humans caught up in the battle; *Whitstable*, a marvelous novella by Stephen Volk using the late Peter Cushing who, while in mourning for his beloved wife, attempts to help a young boy in need of a hero. A moving and apt homage to a movie legend, *Creakers* by Paul Kane is a haunting tale about a man who returns to his childhood home upon his mother's death in order to prepare it for sale; *Still Life* by Tim Lebbon is a chilling sf/horror story about mysterious alien invaders who keep villages under their sway by giving a few turncoats special powers. *Milton's Children* by Jason V. Brock (Bad Moon Books) is an homage to King Kong and other lost world fictions, in which a crew of explorer-scientists end up on a mysterious island on which everything living is out to kill them. *Waiting for Mister Cool* by Gerard Houarner (Crossroads Press) features the author's ongoing character, Max, an assassin with an internal demon that when let loose destroys anyone around in graphically violent ways. In this novella, Max is sent by the US government to break up a cult. *The Rolling Darkness Revue 2013: The Imposter's Monocle* by Peter Atkins and Glen Hirshberg (Earthling Publications) is the chapbook created for the two authors' annual autumn reading series. This year there is a playlet and three excellent stories by the authors. The wonderful cover art and design is by Deena Warner. *Astoria* by S. P. Miskowski (Omnium Gathering) is about a woman who flees her hometown after a tragedy only to discover it's not that easy to escape her past. *The Madman of Toserglope* by Louis Marvick (Les Éditions de L'Oubli) is a beautiful oblong hardcover artifact of a book. A man visits a town in Saxony to research the life and the disappearance of a pianist possessed of an extra thumb. A strange tale filled with paranoia. *The Gist* by Michael Marshall Smith (Subterranean Press) is a marvelous experiment in addition to an absorbing story. Smith wrote the story about a man hired by a dealer in old and lost books to extract the meaning of one such item. The story was then translated into

French by Benoît Domis and re-translated from the French back into English by Nicholas Royle. Not a reader of French, I can't judge how closely that version is to the original, but the slight alterations in the English translation are fascinating. *Love in the Time of Metal and Flesh* by Jay Lake (Prime) takes place in San Francisco's sexual underground and is about extreme body modification. Earthling Publications published two substantial hardcover chapbooks: *The Bones of You* by Gary McMahon is about a divorced father who moves next door to an abandoned house in the suburbs. The ghostly residue of the evil done in the house endangers both him and his daughter. *It Sustains* by Mark Morris packs a wallop from its beginning, as a teen and his father leave their home, hoping to escape from personal trauma by moving away. Unfortunately, starting a new life is harder than they think. Morris ratchets up the suspense as the son begins to see unexplained images and becomes involved with some troublesome local boys. *Tyler's Third Act* by Mick Garris (CD) is number 12 in the signature book series of novella chapbooks. This one treads familiar territory by showing how awful the media is and how far both viewer and viewed are willing to go in the name of entertainment. *I Travel by Night* by Robert McCammon (Subterranean Press) is about a Civil War soldier turned into a vampire during the Battle of Shiloh. For twenty-five years, he's fought to retain his humanity and now he searches for the vampire who turned him to kill her and save himself. *Summer's End* by Lisa Morton (Journalstone) is about a woman hired as a consultant on an ancient text that might shed light on Samhain, the Celtic precursor to Halloween. But nasty things start happening around her.

ODDS AND ENDS

Steampunk H. G. Wells illustrated by Zdenko Basic (RP Classics) is a beautifully illustrated omnibus of *The Time Machine*, *The War of the Worlds*, and "The Country of the Blind." The award-winning Croatian artist has illustrated a number of children's classics.

The Resurrectionist by E. B. Hudspeth (Quirk) is a fascinating and imaginative fictional biography of a surgeon studying at The Philadelphia Academy of Medicine in the last 1870s who had some radical ideas about mythological creatures and their relationships to humanity, leading him to radical "creative" surgery exhibitions and finally to his mysterious disappearance. It's also a compendium of the detailed anatomical illustrations the surgeon made of mythical creatures of those mythical creatures.

The Lady and Her Monsters: A Tale of Dissections, Real-Life Dr. Frankensteins, and the Creation of Mary Shelley's Masterpiece by Roseanne Montillo (William Morrow) is an entertaining almost pop-biography of Mary Shelley (with all the scandal) entwined with a study of the anatomists whose work in the 1700s helped inspire her to create her great novel.

APPORTS

STEPHEN BACON

They met at a café on the corner of Mulberry Street. It was a fairly nondescript place—greasy net curtains, laminated menus, chipped formica tables. Probably bustling with overweight truckers first thing in the morning, but at this hour it was almost deserted. Casual patrons had possibly been deterred by the rain. Or maybe the poor hygiene.

Cowan spotted Jimenez as soon as he stepped inside. He was sitting at a table in the corner, and he glanced up and waved at the sound of Cowan's entrance. The only other customer was an elderly man slurping noisily from a mug, a mangy dog lying at his feet. Despite the ban, the air was thick with cigarette smoke.

Cowan slid into the plastic chair opposite Jimenez. At first he thought the older man's hair was wet, but then realised the greying locks were actually slicked back with Brylcreem. Dandruff dusted his shoulders. The lines around his mouth were deeply ingrained with age, greying whiskers indicating several days' growth. He drew out a manila envelope from beneath the table and patted it with his nicotine-stained fingers. "Got what you wanted, Mr. Campbell."

Cowan licked his lips. "Good." He squirmed inside his tight collar. "Got the money?"

Cowan took an envelope from his pocket and passed it quickly across to Jimenez, who accepted it and transferred it into his own. There was a layer of dirt beneath the man's cracked fingernails, so ingrained it looked like wood-varnish.

"Five hundred—like you said." Cowan cleared his throat and glanced at the counter. The owner—an Asian woman in a stained apron—was wiping down the wall-tiles with a dishcloth. Behind her, a tinny speaker blared out the insipid blandness of local radio.

Jimenez began to speak. "I managed to locate him. . . . Before I run through what I found, though, I need to ask you one question—why're you looking for Mark Fisk?"

Cowan continued to shift his gaze round the café. "I told you—we were at school together. He was a mate of mine. I just wanted to see him again. You know—catch up." His eyes were restless. "Old time's sake and all that."

"Ah yes, I remember now." He flexed his fingers and rubbed the back of his left hand. "Took quite an effort to find him. Our Mr. Fisk did not want to be found."

"Really?"

"Hmmm. You see, he's going under an assumed name now—Peter Feltham. Been living under that name for several months, in fact." His eyes searched the younger man's face. "I had to call in some extra favours to discover this, believe me."

Cowan blinked. "I thought we'd agreed the fee—"

"We did, we did. Don't worry—no extra." Jimenez waved a hand. "No, I meant I know a few contacts in the criminal justice system, the legal profession. And the police, for that matter. Had to go to them to get the info. Quite interesting really."

"Oh?"

"Well you know the first part of the story—up till he left school, right? Well after that, Fisk got a job in the steelworks. Worked for a Sheffield company. He inherited his mother's house when she died in 1994. Lived there for a couple of years. Then in '97 he married a Rosemary Willows. They sold his house and moved to Stannington. He was still at the steel company. She was a secretary at a firm of insurance brokers. They had a son, Alex, in 2002. This is where it takes a turn."

He leaned forward in his chair. "In 2006 they separated. The wife left him and got custody of the kid. He was pretty cut-up about it, apparently. As you would be. Had to move into a council flat. For a few months he was just getting access to the lad every other weekend. The missus starts seeing another bloke. Looks like Fisk then gets edgy—thinking he's going to lose the kid; reckons the lad's going to start calling another bloke '*Dad.*'

"Then in the summer of 2008 he picks little Alex up as usual. Takes him to the top of the towerblock and they both jump off."

"Jump off?"

"Well, Fisk jumped and dragged the kid with him. Even left a suicide note for the ex, saying if *he* couldn't have his son, no one would."

Cowan swallowed and glanced away from the scrutiny of the older man's gaze. He watched the Asian woman browsing a magazine, licking her fingers as she turned the pages.

"I remember it in the news, actually," said Jimenez. "There was a public outcry. Front-page shit."

Cowan nodded noncommittally.

"But here's the best part—although the kid died, *Fisk survived.* Just snapped his fucking legs. The kid broke his fall."

Cowan looked out of the window. Mid-morning traffic crawled past, glistening in the rain. Pensioners shuffled along the pavement laden with carrier bags. He shook his head. "What a bastard."

"Bastard indeed." Jimenez pursed his lips. "He was charged with murder but the judge let him off—diminished responsibility. He got five years in a nuthouse. The ex-wife killed herself a few months later. Overdose."

Cowan watched the older man remove a cigarette and light it, taking a deep drag and blowing the smoke out almost provocatively, his eyes narrowing. "The judge said Fisk *was* remorseful afterwards—he'd just cracked under the pressure of the divorce, that's all."

"So he's—what? Locked up still?"

Jimenez shook his head. "Got released after four years. Since last summer he's been living *here* under the name Peter Feltham." He opened the envelope and took out a folded sheet of A4 paper. His fingers hesitated on it for a second before he slid it across the table.

Cowan unfolded the paper and looked at the address. "Leeds?"

"Yeah. As part of the rehabilitation process he was given a new identity. That's why I asked why you were looking for him." Jimenez paused. "This info can't be traced back to my contact—it's now a matter of public record anyway, if you can be arsed to wade through enough paperwork—but I wanted to make sure you'd be . . . *discreet* with it."

Cowan forced himself to maintain eye contact. "So you think—what? That I'll grass to the papers?"

"I don't know, son." His hand gripped Cowan's wrist. "But if you go through with what I think you're planning, I'd urge you to be careful."

Cowan released his hand, on the pretence of scratching his nose. "Mr. Jimenez, I just wanted to see him—to talk. I won't mention it to anyone else."

Jimenez shrugged. "Look, I couldn't give a shit. Just don't bring my name into it if he gets itchy feet and scarpers. The authorities'll have your arse for an ashtray." His laughter sounded ugly and coarse.

"I just want to say hello—that's all. Maybe he'll be pleased to see an old face." Cowan slipped the address into his pocket.

Jimenez smiled wanly and began packing the envelope away. "Aye, Mr. Campbell—or whatever your real name is—maybe he will."

◄◦►

The rain hadn't let up all week. Cowan tried to concentrate as he peered through the windscreen, the wipers doing their best to distract him. Rows of sagging shops blurred into one continuous line as he negotiated the ceaselessly spiralling roads. Leeds appeared to be a labyrinth of narrow streets choked by parked cars. The bricks of the buildings were a strange shade of ochre. It was quite unlike anything he'd seen before, certainly different to the houses in Sheffield.

He'd stumbled across a Tesco on the ring road. He'd been queuing at the checkout, clutching a Leeds A-Z, when the enormity of what he was about to do engulfed him. He quickly paid and rushed to the toilet, his legs almost buckling with nerves.

Outside, the cool air helped revive him. He waited in the car and browsed the A-Z, taking time to familiarise himself with his destination. He took a carrier bag from the glove box, gauging its weight in his hand. He drew back the plastic opening and admired the pistol inside, careful not to touch it with his fingers. The two-inch barrel looked deceptively harmless. It had been originally manufactured in Brazil; standard issue for the Singapore Police Force. The serial number had been filed down. This particular model—the Taurus 85—had an ornate pearl handgrip. He'd paid £600 for it from a man in his local, a transaction that had come with unspoken conditions attached: the weapon was untraceable—there would be no incriminating trail—*but Cowan better keep his mouth shut if things went wrong.* He swallowed and wrapped it back up.

Soon Cowan was back on the road, Fisk's address seared indelibly into his mind. He was headed for a tower-block in Gipton called Coldcote Heights. He pushed other thoughts away and tried to concentrate on driving.

Eventually he spotted an ugly, brooding building on the corner of Beech Lane—the Church of the Epiphany—and realised his destination was close by. He parked on the roadside and switched off the ignition, listening to the patter of rain on the roof as it synchronised with the ticks of the cooling engine. The wipers—frozen in the act of clearing the windscreen—helped to divert him as the raindrops obliterated his view.

He removed the carrier bag from the glove box and tucked it into his jacket pocket. Then he paused for a few moments to gather his nerves before climbing out of the car and locking it.

A row of shops slouched to his left, rendered almost identical by the metal grilles obscuring their windows. Two elderly women in headscarves stood chatting outside the off-licence. An Asian man was talking loudly on his mobile phone, glaring through the window of the bookies. Cowan drew up his hood and set off across the grassy incline towards the kids' playground.

The squat, redbrick council houses surrounding the muddy expanse seemed to stare at him reproachfully. The play area was in a poor state. Cowan stepped between used condoms and rusting syringes. The rungs of the slide's ladder were blackened with fire. Spray-painted obscenities adorned the side of the toddlers' climbing frame. Nearby, a heavily-muscled skinhead waited patiently as his Staffordshire Bull Terrier shivered a pale turd onto the grass. Cowan glanced away.

Ahead, his destination loomed like a beacon for the destitute. He hurried up the slope. Coldcote Heights towered broodingly above the roofs of the surrounding houses, seeming to watch over Gipton like a guardian. The cold impassive building almost made him shudder.

A chain-link fence at the top of the grassy square had been breached, its posts skewed by force. Empty cigarette packets and McDonald's cartons wilted in the rain. The sign on the Bangladeshi community centre had been vandalised, clearly by someone lacking the use of a spell-check. Youths loitered around the industrial bins at the rear.

Soon he had negotiated the warren of faceless tenements and found himself approaching the tower-block. He crossed the quadrangle of concrete, suddenly feeling exposed by the countless windows that watched his progress. A burnt-out car stood in the centre, rusting on four flat tyres. From somewhere nearby came the frantic barking of a dog. He pushed open the door of the building and entered the dark foyer.

The smell of piss was overpowering. To the left, a flight of concrete steps rose out of sight. A CCTV camera was positioned at a weird angle—possibly made ineffective by some wrong-doer. Signs on the walls promised direction but did nothing more than bewilder him. He scanned for the address that Jimenez had supplied, seeing that he needed to trek to the ninth floor.

The steel door of the lift was so scratched it looked as if ancient runes had been etched into its surface. Someone had smeared a foul-smelling substance over the call button. Wrinkling his nose, Cowan glanced down and spotted the neck of a broken beer bottle discarded in the corner. He picked it up and used the lip of the glass to press the button. The noise of the lift's approach sounded ominous, as if the action had tripped some unseen signal.

Inside the lift, the smell of piss was just as strong. He used the glass shard to press the number 9 on the panel. A furry patch of mould stained the floor and a lower section of the compartment. Cowan stood as far away as possible from it as the lift bounced its ascent. The red LED above the panel flickered aggressively. Presently the door opened and he stepped out onto the ninth floor, taking time to carefully deposit the glass in the corner where he might later retrieve it.

A narrow corridor led into the heart of the building. Cowan wandered down it, glancing at the door numbers to check he was headed in the right direction. The light was meagre. Shadows scuttled in the corners. Windows at evenly spaced intervals looked down into the quadrangle, accentuating his dizzying height. From further down the landing, he heard the sound of someone singing in a foreign language, the staccato rhythm of the words suggesting a football chant. Cowan hurried along until he reached an intersection, heading to the left according to the door numbers.

He could feel his heart pounding as he drew close. The bag in his pocket felt like it was getting heavier. He stopped outside a door and stared at the plastic numbers screwed to the wood, licking his lips to alleviate the dryness. A quick glance both ways up the corridor eased his nerves. He pressed his ear to the door and listened.

Indistinct music was playing inside. Somewhere beyond the sound, a child was crying. Cowan considered the two bullets loaded in the pistol; for the first time worried that he ought to have requested more. The original intention had been for one bullet for Fisk and one for himself. The bloke in the pub had warned that it was difficult to silence this type of weapon; he'd need to make every shot count. He took a deep breath and tried the door handle.

He peered into a deserted hallway. The music was now recognisable— The Style Council—and he slipped inside the flat and closed the door.

From this angle, he had a narrow vantage point into the living room. He could see the crown of someone's head as they sprawled on the sofa. The weeping child now sounded like it was coming from next door. He crept closer. As he drew near, he could see that the prone figure was indeed Fisk. But not as he'd remembered him.

The man had his eyes closed tight, his face screwed up like a wrinkled cloth. His forehead looked unnaturally pock-marked. Sallow. The skin was pale and gaunt, stretched over the bones like tissue. His thinning hair barely covered the skull. His hands clutched the side of his head, accentuating the tendons in his rail-thin arms. He looked depleted.

Cowan swept a quick glance around, noting the signs of disarray. Empty beer bottles and cans littered the floor. Discarded pizza boxes and the misshapen trays from microwave-ready meals. Boxes were stacked in the corners, filled with brightly coloured objects. Light was pouring through the curtainless window. There was a powerful odour of stale sweat and booze. Relief surged. The pokey flat seemed otherwise empty. Cowan's fingers curled around the handle of the gun.

"Fisk." He stood over the emaciated wreck of a man, staring, daring him to look.

Fisk's eyes opened slowly. They looked blurred and bloodshot. He widened them, trying to focus, shuffling into an upright position.

"Remember me?" Cowan tried to keep his voice low and threatening, but he was afraid it just sounded weak.

Fisk blinked slowly. He appeared to be under the influence of something; probably drink, by the smell. He pulled a sour face.

"I've come to kill you," Cowan said quietly. He shuffled his feet.

Fisk smiled wanly and rolled onto his side, moved to a sitting position. "You were Rosie's bit on the side. I remember you." His voice sounded dead. Listless.

"I wasn't *a bit on the side*. I tried to help her after you two split up."

"So you say." Fisk laughed hollowly. "How'd you find me?"

Cowan made a fist. "I made a promise to Rose before she died."

Fisk shrugged. It was an unsightly gesture. Cowan marvelled again at the man's appearance. He looked ravaged. Close to death.

"Go on then." He sat up and put his head in his hands. "You'll be doing me a favour."

Cowan stared at him, clenching his teeth. He fought to suppress the rage that ached inside. "You piece of shit. He was six years old, for fuck's sake. A good kid."

"Should I tell you something . . . what's your name?"

"Cowan."

"Cowan, that's right. Cowan." He rolled the word around his mouth. "Let me tell you something—he's not a *good kid* anymore."

"You selfish bastard. Why couldn't you just kill yourself and leave him with his mum?"

"With *you* and Rosie, you mean? That would've been nice." His breath hitched. A change seemed to come over him. He looked detached. "Don't you think I'm sorry for what I done? Don't you think I wished I'd died that day? I'd end it tomorrow if I thought it would all stop."

"This place is a shithole. Why'd you move here?"

Fisk shrugged. "Why not? I lived 'round here as a kid. Till we moved to Sheffield when I left school."

Shit. Jimenez must have known about the lies. He must have known Fisk hadn't attended school in Sheffield.

Cowan glanced around. There was a cushion on the sofa. He could hold the gun against it and shoot through. It should muffle the shot. The crying kid nextdoor might mask the noise. It could give him sufficient time to get away.

Fisk looked up, wrongly interpreting the pause. "*You* can hear him too, can't you?"

"That kid?"

Fisk nodded and grimaced, revealing yellow teeth. His next words chilled Cowan to the core. "That's Alex."

Cowan peered in the direction of the sound. He'd assumed it had been from the neighbouring flat, but he realised it was coming from the next room. Heart hammering in his throat, he approached the door and pushed it open.

The sound stopped instantly. He could see similar signs of disorder in the room—an unmade bed, clothes strewn on the floor, boxes of things stored in the corner.

"It's not so bad in the day," Fisk said. "The nights are worst. I can't get away. He's changed. He doesn't love his dad no more."

Cowan turned back.

"You should see his face at night. Fucking terrifying." Fisk stood with a groan and switched off the music. "That's why I have *that* on—drowns him out a bit." His foot knocked an empty can of Tennent's Super across the floor. He slumped back onto the sofa, the movement causing a hole in the upholstery to gape like a hungry mouth. He stared at a spot in the corner of the ceiling.

"Sometimes at night I see him watching me from up there." He motioned with his hand.

Despite himself, Cowan glanced into the empty, mildew-stained corner.

"He grows spindly legs like a spider. He creeps around quiet, daring me to watch. If I close my eyes, he'll pounce. It's just a game to him. Without the booze, I can't sleep."

Cowan rolled his eyes. "Maybe the booze makes you imagine things."

"The fuck it does." He suddenly lifted the sleeve of his t-shirt, revealing a pattern of angry scabs. "Trouble is, I'm so out of it, I can't feel him slashing me."

Cowan winced at the rawness of the wounds.

"Stanley knife," Fisk said. "Fucker likes to have his fun."

Cowan studied the boxes for the first time. They were stuffed with children's toys, videos, wooden jigsaws. "You need help."

Fisk laughed again, that horrible sound. "I'm past help." He slumped back onto the sofa. "I need to *drink*—that's what keeps me from seeing him. That or the gear." He ran his fingers through his hair and belched. Cowan could see the forearm was scarred with circular marks like burns. The man looked wrecked with exhaustion.

His anger was beginning to dissipate, replaced by a modicum of pity. It seemed like Fisk was existing in his own self-induced hell. Tormenting himself. The guilt must have tipped his mind. That or the booze.

"If I carry on drinking, I know I'll die. I've already seen signs. Liver's knackered. Be a blessing when it comes." He motioned with his hand. "Benny from over the way brought me a couple of bottles of absinthe back from his last trip. That's good stuff, let me tell you. Good stuff."

"Why do you keep these?" Cowan tapped the side of one of the cardboard boxes. "You should let it go. You're just torturing yourself."

Fisk shook his head. "You don't get it, do you? *He* brings them."

"You think Alex brought this stuff?"

"Uh-huh. He leaves me . . . little gifts. From the other side."

Cowan felt the skin on the back of his neck prickling. He lifted a soft toy out of the box. It was a cloth mouse wearing a gingham shirt—*something from Bagpuss?* Cowan's memory faltered. It looked old. Some of the stitching had come loose. One of its eyes looked wonky. As he held the object, a foul stench seemed to emanate from it. An intense feeling of revulsion struck. He tossed the toy back into the box, almost recoiling.

Little gifts. Cowan knew enough to understand the correct word even if Fisk didn't—*apports.* Fisk believed the toys were reminders from his dead son. Reminders of what damage he'd done. He had clearly lost his mind. The self-harming was just another symptom of the madness. Cowan supposed guilt could do that.

Fisk was speaking. "Remember that film with Bruce Willis's wife and the crazy black woman? And him—Lundgren?"

"Swayze."

"Yeah, that's it. Well that's what it's like. Twenty-four hours a day. He's there taunting me, trying to hurt me. Reminding me that he's angry.

At night he sometimes burns my skin." He rested his head back on the sofa. "And he set fire to my hair once. But it's no more than I deserve." His voice seemed stronger now, less slurred. Maybe he was sobering up.

Cowan became aware of the gun's weight again. He looked around the squalor, considering Fisk's situation. His physical condition was pathetic. Dishevelled. The mementoes, the cans of booze, the state of his mind. Ending Fisk's life would be doing him a favour, and that was the last thing he wanted to do.

"Why not kill yourself then? Proper this time though."

Fisk blinked slowly. "You a religious man?"

Cowan shook his head.

"Neither was I before all this shit." He swallowed. "But in hospital I was encouraged to find God. So I'm hedging my bets—this might be His test. I need to endure my punishment. Anything else would be to face eternal damnation. And—like I said—my liver's on its way out anyway."

Cowan shook his head. "You sick fuck. You committed a wicked act. For that you'll rot in hell when your time comes." He fought to keep his composure. "You ruined Rose's life—and mine. And you took poor Alex. But the judge was right—you're fucked up in the head. That's no excuse for what you did, but I think you're suffering in your own hell."

He shook his head and left the flat, slamming the door behind him. Almost instantly the crying kid started up again. It really did sound like it was coming from inside Fisk's flat. The music recommenced straight away.

Cowan made his way back to the lift. Turning back, he glanced into the throat of the corridor. An indistinct shape loitered in the shadows. The singsong tone of a nursery rhyme echoed along the passage, followed by the sound of children's laughter.

"Hello?" Cowan's voice was taut. "Who's there?"

The laughter rang again, this time with a malevolent edge. Brittle.

Cowan turned back to the lift. He flared his nostrils at the panel and shouldered open the door to the stairs. The air was cool. He began his descent. Raindrops on the windows warped his view. Someone was kicking a football in the stairwell far below. A child's echoing voice recited "Baa Baa Black Sheep." The noise felt like it was swirling around him. Monochrome colours of the décor matched his headache. He was gasping by the time he reached the ground floor, bursting from the foyer into the quadrangle. It had stopped raining.

He strode back to his car, feeling uncomfortably warm beneath his coat. Shafts of sunlight were fighting to break through the clouds. He uttered silent apologies to Rose as he crossed the playground, reminding himself that Fisk's suffering justified the broken promise. It made him feel no better.

As he drew near to the car, he clicked his remote control. The alarm squealed its short burst and unlocked the doors. He was desperate to get back to Sheffield. He was tired of this world of graffiti and decay, of litter and filth. He took off his coat and tossed it into the back. The key slid into the ignition and he turned it, firing the engine. And it was just as he was reaching over to fasten his seatbelt that he spotted the toy mouse on the dashboard.

He picked it up carefully and studied it. The faded gingham, the worn seams, the wonky eye—all identical to the one in Fisk's flat.

Cowan clicked the seatbelt in and released the handbrake.

◄◦►

He stopped in a lay-by several miles outside Leeds. A stone bridge spanned the road, under which flowed a deep waterway identified by a wooden sign as the River Aire. Cowan paused for a moment and peered at the brown water as it flowed languidly beneath. The road was deserted. He removed the plastic bag from his pocket and paused for a second before dropping it over the side. The splash was deep and satisfying. For several minutes, he watched the ripples until they died away and the surface returned to its flat, constant motion. Then he walked back to the car.

MR. SPLITFOOT

DALE BAILEY

Modern Spiritualism as a popular movement began with the Hydesville raps. . . . Whether by the design of the spirits or inadvertently, Kate and Maggie Fox served as the catalyst for what believers in spiritual communication call the dawning of a new era.

Barbara Weisberg
Talking to the Dead
2004

That I have been chiefly instrumental in perpetrating the fraud of Spiritualism upon a too-confiding public, most of you doubtless know. The greatest sorrow in my life has been that this is true, and though it has come late in my day, I am now prepared to tell the truth. . . . I am here tonight as one of the founders of Spiritualism to denounce it as an absolute falsehood . . . the most wicked blasphemy known to the world.

Maggie Fox
New York World
1888

1893

They have taken me to Emily Ruggles's house to die.

I had hoped to die in my little apartment in the city, but Emily's house is very pleasant, and will serve as well, I suppose. The March sunlight illuminates my room in the morning, and Emily is kind enough to sit up with me at night. The nights are hardest. The follies and illusions of childhood re-assert themselves at night, and it is reassuring to see a human face when you open your eyes in the gloom, in an unfamiliar house, thinking that perhaps you are already dead. Last night—was it last night?—I woke from a dream of Hydesville and Emily looked like Kate, bending to her needlework by the light of a guttering taper. For a moment, we were girls, all undone between us. Kate, I cried, Kate—then Emily took my hand and became just plain Emily once more. So I remembered that Kate was dead and had to mourn her all over again. The mind is a funny thing, playing tricks like that.

You were always playing tricks on me, too, weren't you, Kate? Full of tricks from the day you were born. Remember how we held the stage when Leah paraded us from city to city like a pair of trained lovebirds, tapping and preening? Every girl's dream to be a bird, feted on every side, and oh, we were feted Kate, how our names did ring upon every tongue! And even then you were a tapping, preening little thing, all dressed up in your skirts of robin's-egg-blue. Do you remember how the people used to gather before a sitting, how they would come from near and far, crying your name aloud and reaching out to touch you? Do you remember how easy it all was, how eager they were to believe? What a glorious trick that was, Kate! That was the best trick of all! Who could have seen that it would all turn out as it has? *We were children, Maggs.* I can hear you say it. *We didn't know. Surely that's something. Surely that's enough—*

You were at them again, your tricks, last night, weren't you? Emily dozed—even the most faithful watchers doze—and as she nodded over her needlework, you were up to your old tricks, rapping and tapping and knocking oh so quietly, so only I could hear. It got cold in the room then, just like it used to when we were girls, all those years ago. Do you remember the cold, Kate? The cold of the grave, so black and deep it prickled up the hairs along the back of your neck and turned your breath to vapor?

The Summerland indeed.

And here you are with another blanket to comfort me. Look at me, Kate! Look how frail I've become. I've become *old*, I say, and a young girl's melancholy creeps into my breast. How funny it is, the way we never age inside our hearts, whilst outwardly this catastrophe every day renews itself. Tutting—

—*you must calm yourself, Mrs. Maggie*—

—Emily—it *is* Emily, isn't it? In the gloom it's hard to see—tucks the blanket in tight around me. She means kindness, I know, dear Emily. Why, I remember when she came to us, how dumbfounded she was to be among us at last: the mothers of Spiritualism! I remember her first sitting and afterward teaching her the secrets of material manifestations. How shocked she was at this cheerful fraud! Yet I'll admit, and I admitted then, that there is something of the illusionist's craft in our art; it helps the sitters to suspend their disbelief, to quote Mr. Coleridge.

But there is truth, as well.

There is the matter of the cold. And of Hydesville.

That was March, too, wasn't it? More than forty years have passed since then—I was sixteen that year, and you still a slip of a girl—yet I still remember the winter of 1848, spilling right over into spring, such a fierce year it was. At first, I thought that no one noticed the cold because it was already so cold in that house, with the wind tearing down off Lake Ontario and rattling the timbers like bones. *Pop, pop, pop,* went that house, like an old man cracking his joints, and it wasn't much warmer in the house than it was standing in the street. What was a little tapping to me?

That's what I said in New York, Katie, remember that? The biggest stage of all, right there in New York City, and you stuck in the audience whilst I held the spotlight. How that must have chafed, you always so loved the stage. But there you sat with your face of stone. I saw you! I saw you when I peeked between the curtains before the show. You and the whole house, and what a house it was! A hundred people, all of them in their Sunday best, and the house all shining and gilt by the gaslight chandeliers, and me there to say our whole lives had been a lie.

Leah—the third Fox sister, she styled herself, as if she ever had any traffic with the dead—the way she made us back in Rochester. That's what she always said. I made you! I was the one who booked the Corinthian Hall in Rochester, I was the one who made you! *The Fox Sisters of the Famous Events in Hydesville, that Occurred in the Spring of 1848,* tapping and preening like little birds, always her little birds, and we hardly knowing her before Hydesville, her seventeen years our senior, a grown woman and a family of her own. The Queen of Lies! Our sittings with the great and small alike. Oh, Katie, how grand they all were! Mr. Cooper and Mrs. Stowe, the great Sojourner Truth and Mr. Horace Greeley himself, our patron and protector, to them all delivering, each and every one—Lies! And most of all the hundreds, the thousands! that followed, innumerable to count, with their sittings and their gauzy apparitions, their spirit lights, their automatic writing: Lies, all lies. And we the Sisters of the Lie, who birthed a monstrous truth.

"Our whole lives," you said backstage, your voice quavering with resentment.

"Our whole goddamn lives, Maggs," you said. "You with your toes popping and your knuckles cracking, all the tricks of the trade. The spirit hands and the voices and the Summerland itself." All a lie—though it didn't keep you from taking your half of the money, did it? Seven hundred and fifty dollars each, a small fortune in 1888, like sand through our fingers, it went. You folded it away in your purse with an edge of fierce defiance in your voice. I can hear it now, your fury at all my lies, saying, "But it wasn't all a lie. Not all of it, Maggs."

Even lies have some truth inside them, and truth some lies. The Summerland is a cold, hard place. It's a cold, hard place we go when we die. And there are voices, there is a voice to make you shudder and run all cold inside. Nobody's going to pay their good, hard-earned money to hear such a monstrous truth—or believe it when they do. Some things cannot be countenanced or believed, not if you want to go on living or crawl inside a bottle where the voice goes silent for a while. Not unless. So we lied. Our whole career a lie built upon a truth, and our renunciation of it a truth built upon a lie.

I sleep a little then, a little slice of death somebody once told me, but I know that it's not true. Not the sleep of oblivion, but the sleep of nightmare, breeding monsters—

Then Emily is bending over me. It's morning, a bright shining March morning to make you forget all these truths—

—that awful voice—

—for a while. The confusion has lifted. I'm clearest in the mornings.

"Here, Mrs. Maggie, take some broth," she says. "I made it special."

So I take a sip to please her. You have to please people, that's what we do, you know. But the truth is I don't want it, I haven't any appetite any more. Then it's dark, and here you come bending over me again, saying Mrs. Maggie, Mrs. Maggie, are you there. Your voice is coming from far away, like a voice from the bottom of a well. Why you should call me Mrs. Maggie I don't know. Plain old Maggs has always been good enough for all these years. I can hear you say it now—*Maggs, Maggs, Maggs,* your voice dripping with scorn.

You always scorned me so, saying I couldn't summon the spirits, not the way you could. Yet I never denied it. I never denied the ascendancy of your gift. Why, I remember a time when you said as much, as though I had denied it. We were mere girls then. I wasn't yet twenty and you just then fifteen-years-old, in your dress of robin's-egg blue and your hair done up so pretty, with some stray wisps falling down around your eyes, as if they'd just worked loose and you hadn't planned it that way from the first, so artful, to frame your face just so. In a fine hotel room in New York City, that was. How rich it had seemed, the fine velvet upholstery and the gilt moldings and the golden and red brocade on the curtains, that new smell on everything, as if it was fresh made. Leah said we could afford such fine things by then, the very best, I remember the way she said it: *We can afford the very best now, girls,* as though she had anything to do with it. That was Leah for you. She was out at the shops, I remember. We had just arrived in the city—where was it we had been before that? I wonder—and she was always out at the shops. *We have to look the part, girls,* she always said so cheery, but why she should have to look it, I never did understand. I sometimes think that it was just to spite Leah that we renounced it all, and condemned it as a sin and blasphemy.

But that day, that day the sky was clear and blue as the blue in your dress, as though they'd been special made to match. You had tied back the heavy curtains and posed yourself in the most flattering fall of light, as though there were anyone there to see it but me. You were always on stage. Every time in my life I ever saw you, you were on stage.

You said, "Come to the window, Sister. It's so pretty out."

So I did. For a time we were quiet, just looking out the window. Fine carriages rolled by three stories below, full of the richest sort—who could say, some of them might have paid for private sittings, we were that well loved in that day. And cabs too, and dray carts rattling over cobbles and flinging up horse apples, which was what our father always called them, remember that? People pushing and shoving on the sidewalks, and newspaper boys, and ballad-sellers singing out the titles of the latest songs, a penny each for the sheet music so that pretty girls in pretty parlors could play them for their pretty boys. We never learned to play, of course, that was not our station in the world, but our station had changed, hadn't it? And I could almost smell the street below—the hay scattered out across the cobbles, and the horse apples, too, and the smell of perfumes and the like in the press—I could smell it in my mind, the way you can, you know.

And you, whispering right in my ear, "I can do it better, Maggs."

For some reason that made me feel so ashamed. "Do what?" I said, all innocent, though of course I knew.

I always knew. Both of us knew.

"Why I can call the spirits better," you said, all innocent, flouncing across the room to pose yourself on a little loveseat they had sitting there, arranging your dress just so.

"You can't," I said. I said, "I can do it twice as good as you. I'm older," the only card I had to play.

"Then do it," you said.

But I didn't want to, that's what I said. I couldn't, of course, not then and only sometimes later. The spirits came to me of their own accord, I couldn't summon them. I just wanted to sit at the window and watch the street, I always liked the city so. It reminded me of how far we'd come from Hydesville, where it had always seemed dark to me, and cold. And how we didn't have to be there anymore, not ever again. That's what I thought in that day—that we'd never be poor again—not knowing the miseries to come. I was just a girl, so young.

Even then I liked the lie better than the truth. I liked the toe cracking and the finger popping and all the other tricks Leah had taught us, she was as tricksy as you were, almost.

The truth scared me.

"Because you can't," you said, and I feigned not to care.

I remember your face then, the way you'd posed so that the shadow cut your face right in half. I remember the look in your eyes in that moment, the way they got hard and like a set of mirrors, like you weren't there anymore or you'd gone way down deep inside yourself.

"Katie, don't—" I cried, but it was too late.

Already the light seemed to have gone all watery and pale, like it was shining down from a faraway star. And a minute after that came the cold, a black hateful kind of cold that made your breath frost the air, and that on a summer day.

That's how you know. The cold. Like vapors from the grave. The rest is just tricks without the cold.

And you were always a tricky one, weren't you, Kate?

Tricksy, tricksy, tricksy. But not everything was tricks. Not Hydesville. And not that day in the hotel, either. Not when all that light went out of the room, and the cold started up and the tap, tap, tapping began, like a man with claw hammer deep buried in a mine.

Oh, I remember. It was a terrible thing, Katie, a terrible thing, your eyes rolling up to whites like that and you sitting straight like a rod had been driven down your spine, your hands upturned upon your crossed knees, giggling as the room grew darker and darker still, until I could not see to see. The tapping got louder and this time there was no playacting. This time there were no tricks, were there, Katie?

How used to them I had become by then, all the posing and the playacting, all the tricks! I could summon up the taps myself, Katie—sometimes anyway. I won't deny that, no matter how much it would please you. I had a touch of the gift myself—

But you—

I remember. I remember it all so clearly. The way the room seemed to fall away into a black void. The way that blackness seized us up so careless, like a pair of rag dolls, boneless and limp, and carried us off. Like being caught in an undertow and swept out to sea, it was, the black stuff pouring in at your mouth and your nostrils, shoving aside everything that was you, until you drowned in it and there was nothing left but void and darkness. Yes, and I remember the way the tapping became a knocking, the knocking a thunderous *boom boom boom boom,* so that I cried aloud for the terror of it and clapped my hands over my ears. And between the booms, the voice. That cold and creeping voice, whispering at me, coaxing and wheedling, saying—

—*wake up Mrs. Maggie wake up*—

—and Emily Ruggles bends over me in the gloom.

"You were dreaming," she says, and here it is March and I can see her breath in the air.

My mouth is parched. All I can manage to croak is a single word. "Water."

She cradles my head and lifts a cup to my lips, ice crackling against my tongue.

"What were you dreaming of?" Her mouth twitchy and eager, hungry like the crowds who turned out to see us all those years ago, when I was a girl. That was the one part I had never expected, that hunger, the way they looked at you just like they could eat you up.

Just you remember, Leah used to say. *It's not you they want. It's what you do.* And so she held her power over us, with the clever tricks she taught us and the thought of those hungry crowds, and how she alone stood between us.

"What were you dreaming of?" Emily prompts me again, and maybe she senses it, too, that hunger and how unseemly it is, here in my final hours, for she goes on to add, "I only want to help you, Mrs. Maggie."

It's hard to be sure. But I know that hunger when I see it—I've seen it so many times—and what I feel is a rush of pity for the girl. I've done her a great disservice, showing her all our tricks like that, and letting her catch a glimpse of the bigger truth inside the lie at the same time. It's the truth she's so hungry to possess, and never will; Emily doesn't possess so much as a jot of the gift. Or it doesn't possess her. Because that's what it is—possession. We've been possessed since we were girls, Katie and I, and now it draws to a close at last. Now I stand for the last time on the threshold where I've spent a lifetime lingering, and on the other side there are worse things waiting. That voice, whispering, always whispering.

A lie's the thing, it always has been. I try to work up the moisture to spit it out. Once again the ritual with the cup. The rime of ice is gone. The water is cool, salving to the lips. The room has warmed. I kick at the covers. Emily folds back the counterpane, neat as a pin. She's a kind girl, Emily. She deserves the lie.

And how easy it comes to the lips, the habit of a lifetime. "Tis only the Summerland," I whisper, gasping for a breath of the March air that billows out the sheers. "I see it now, all stretched out before me, green and lovely as a day in June. The passage draws near, Emily, dear." For a lie goes down easier with a taste of the truth inside it.

And then here you are again, Katie, leaning over me, your face so white in the moonlight, saying, "Mrs. Maggie, Mrs. Maggie, Mrs.—"

—*Maggs*—

"It's always half measures with you, isn't it, Maggs? Not the lie and not the truth either, but some misbegotten thing in between, monstrous and malformed."

Such nerve, you have, calling me the monster, you so handy with the lie from the start. From the start, Katie, from Hydesville. Remember Hydesville, Katie, that ramshackle old house popping its joints in the wind screaming down off the lake? March it was, and no man had ever seen such a winter: snow piled as high as a tall man's shoulder on the north face of the house, the cramped rooms inside stinking of ash and rancid fatback, and in the bedroom we all shared the reek of tapers dipped in animal fat. It had been a long time since Daddy could afford candles, and if it hadn't been for Leah sweeping us off like a couple of performing birds, it might have been longer still.

Eighteen-forty-eight, that was, you just a girl with your first blood upon you and right away the tapping commences, just a faraway sound at first, like the door rattling its hinges in the wind. Like the time my blood had come in three years before that—a whisper in my ears upon the edge of sleep, a tap, tap, tapping, quiet as my heart against my ribs. Then nothing, and when I think about that time now, a lifetime gone, I wonder if I might have escaped the whole thing, if my piddling gift might have slept forever. Such a happy life that would have been, I sometimes think, a husband and a houseful of little ones, neither the riches of a king nor the crumbs off a poor man's table—and I've had both, haven't I?—but something steady and standing in between.

Then your blood came in, and me trying to sleep, huddled close against you as the room grew colder and then colder still, no natural cold, but something deeper and blacker, with iron in its bones and hatred in its heart. The darkness deepened so that I could hardly see my hand before my face, and the real knocking commenced—not from one of your childish tricks either, was it, Katie? Not from an apple bobbing on a string to bang against the floor, or your toes and fingers cracking, but a spirit knocking and more, scurrying like footsteps across the ceiling and banging the furniture around the room like a housewife banging on her pans.

A light guttered to life. A wavering taper pushed back the dark, and in that flickering glow I saw my father's face. If I live a thousand years, I hope never to see another man's face like that one. All drawn and pale, it was. Why, it was as white as a freshly laundered sheet, and his eyes the size of saucers, shot through with blood and the pupils so round and black that you could hardly see the color at all, and such a pretty blue they were. My mother clutched at him, crying aloud, "What is it, John? What is it?"

But he doesn't answer, just stumbles out of bed in his nightshirt, him so prayerful and wary of his modesty.

"Girls?" he cries. "Girls?"

And, oh, how you shrieked with laughter, a high-pitched screech so unlike you that it's a marvel your mouth could produce such an awful sound. All erect you sat, with your nightdress draped across your crossed knees and your hands turned up atop your thighs. I could feel that piercing shriek run all through me like the horrors.

Great fists hammered the walls, shivering the boards. In the kitchen, the table danced like a drunken man on a Saturday night—you could hear it—and the chairs dashed themselves to kindling against the walls. But that wasn't the worst of it. The worst of it was that I heard all this as through a veil. Someone had flung a veil over me, and everything came through to me all blurry, only it was a veil of whispers, it was a veil of words.

As the knocking grew more violent, that voice grew louder, until it was screaming inside my head, guttural and hateful. It scoured out the inside of my skull, it erased everything I ever thought I was, and it knew me. It *knew me*, Katie. Knew every lie I'd ever told, every grudge and secret thought I'd nursed inside my crooked heart, no matter how base and hateful. It knew me. What do you think Emily Ruggles would think of *that*, Katie? What would she think of the blood-red hatred that seized me then, and of the awful things it asked me to do. To my father, as he stumbled from the room in search of that awful knocking's source. To my mother, huddled under the bedclothes against that hateful cold, her breath a flag of vapor in the dark. And to you, Katie. To you most of all. Oh such horrible red thoughts that I weep to recall them. Such red, red thoughts.

How long it lasted, how long I wrestled with that awful spirit like Jesus in the desert, I cannot say. Only that a time came when it was over—when a bright sun dawned glittering off the snow outside the window. The stink of sweat and terror faded. Even our father slept then, giving up at last, unable to locate the origin of all that terrible racket.

Three nights.

On the second night our neighbors crowded into the room, disbelievers every one—Mary and Charles Redfield and the Dueslers and the Hydes and others too, that old house rocking around them. Every one they came in doubt and every one they left believers, that unearthly cold shivering their bones, their faces scrubbed clean with terror, pale and blank as eggs.

The next night, hundreds. It was them that brought Leah, those hundreds, and the chance they represented. Hundreds crowding into the bedroom shoulder to shoulder, rank with the stench of unwashed bodies, hundreds spilling out into the kitchen and beyond, into the street itself, where a raw wind came tearing off the lake, chilling everyone to the bone. How I envied them that warmth. For inside the bedroom, it was colder still. How can I convey it, that cold? Like being buried to your shoulders in ice, it was, or worse, the cold of all dead things and dead places on this earth, the cold of the grave yawning open to receive you.

And you, Katie, with your hands upturned upon your knees and your hair hanging over your eyes, in a night dress thin as gossamer, all untouched. Your crowning moment that was, your best trick of all, breathing in the stillness, "Do as I do, Mr. Splitfoot," and the spirit did. One two three you snapped your fingers and one two three the spirit rapped in answer.

Gasps of disbelief and wonder. Do you remember that, Katie? Gasps of wonder and disbelief—proof incontestable of this raging spirit that hurled furniture around like kindling and responded to the quiet admonition of a little girl. Do you remember that?

And all this time in my head, that rageful voice, entreating, wheedling, screaming in frustration, for I would not do as it demanded. I would not take up the knife in the kitchen or lift a leg from a dismembered chair. I would not turn my home into an abattoir. But oh such effort did I have to exert to resist. Sweat sprang out on my forehead despite that glacial cold, and by the guttering flame of the taper I could see that my hands, all of their own accord, had clenched themselves into white-knuckled fists and so it would be ever after. That hateful voice whispering and cajoling in my head, my constant attendant, and when Katie called the spirits, a spiteful and powerful spirit it became. In those moments it took every ounce of strength I possessed to resist it. A life embattled we have shared, Katie and I, a life that enriched us beyond measure one moment and plunged us into poverty the next, always the voice beyond the rappings, urging us to horrors that we must struggle to resist. Two husbands we have known between us, but Mr. Splitfoot was our one and only true betrothed. Many nights I stood over my own dear husband's bed, clutching a knife in my hand, my whole body wracked with the effort of turning Mr. Splitfoot away.

We were children, Maggs, I can hear you say it now. *We didn't know. Isn't that enough?*

But it is not. For a time came, and early, when we *did* know, and even then we did not, could not, stop. There was too much of fortune in it, and too much of pleasure as well, in giving yourself over to something larger than you had ever known, something sinewy and vast. Even from the start, Mr. Splitfoot ruled our hearts.

Mr. Splitfoot, Mr. Splitfoot—

—and here is a figure leaning over me, its face cast in shadow by the candle it holds aloft.

"Katie," I cry, "Katie—"

But it's only Emily, leaning over to smooth the hair from my brow.

"You were talking in your sleep, Mrs. Maggie." So gentle-like. "What was it you were dreaming?" That hunger in her eyes.

But what shall I say? Some truths are better left unsaid. Sometimes the lie is kinder. "I miss Katie, dear"—taking her hand—"I miss her so much."

And here is the truth inside the lie. I miss you, Kate. Every morning I wake afresh to find you gone away from me. Every morning I grieve you like the first. Gone, gone, gone—and who else to confide in here at the end of all days, about matters so fraught and fearsome?

"We all miss her, dear," Emily says, withdrawing to her needlework, and after a time I'm not sure who it is I'm looking at anymore, time seems so slippy and uncertain. Only there is a chill in the room, a faraway rapping, and you're sitting here beside me once again, your strong hand in my own, bony as a bird's and heavy-veined. You were always so strong, and I the weak one. Why, see how old I've become, and still a sixteen-year-old in Hydesville in my heart, before it all began. Or so I could believe but for the whisper in my ears, but for my one true love and paramour, goading me, always goading me to blood and madness.

Blood and madness. For once it came to me, it never fully departed, that voice. It lingered, whispering, insinuating, urging me on to bloodshed and hatred. But only once did I succumb.

I begged you not to do it. How I begged you.

Nineteen, I was, and you just fifteen—mere girls with the petty jealousies of sisters, the thoughtless malice and spite. There in that lush hotel room, with the sounds of the street rising to us in a hushed murmur, muffled by the heavy velvet curtains that draped the windows. And the taps at first, the raps and knocks, the *boom boom boom,* so loud that floor itself seemed to rock, and I marveled that no one else could hear it. Those heavy curtains billowed out like the thinnest sheers. A great wind filled the room, like the rank breath of the dead, and in it the voice, such a voice it was, guttural and full of hate, and then worse—wheedling, insinuating, flattering. And promising. Yes, promising.

What was yours mine, your vast gift in exchange for my paltry one. You with your eyes rolled back, your legs crossed, your palms face up on your thighs, beneath your dress of robin's-egg blue.

And that voice, whispering now, conniving and entreating. It drew me across the room to the loveseat, my arms outstretched, and how it thrilled me to take your neck between my hands, to feel my fingers dig into the soft, pale flesh beneath your high-necked dress, and *squeeze.* Squeeze and squeeze, nails biting, fingers gouging. Who knew then how thin and high it was, that neck, as delicately boned as a bird's. Bones creaked beneath the pressure.

And then you were there again. Your eyes snapped open with dread of the terrible thing that was death, the cold of the grave and the voice that lived on the other side and the hatred everlasting. Your hands flew up to pry my hands away, weak, too weak. I had gifts of my own, you see: the strength of my hands and purpose, and that voice capering inside my head in joy.

You gasped.

"Maggie," you croaked. "Maggs, Maggie, please—"

And then there were no words, just struggle. Your legs kicking. Your hands tearing at my own, your body heaving. Second by second, your strength left you. Your body fell still. Your hands fell away. Your body went limp. And gradually, gradually, your face took on a deepening blue cast.

You might have died then—the one true person I ever loved, and I would have exulted in it.

But the door flew open, and here was Leah, laden with packages, saying, "Oh, girls, you won't believe such finery I got, and at a poor man's cost—" Her voice breaking off like that. Hatboxes and shoeboxes and dresses on their woolen-cloaked hangers, fumbled from her hands.

She found her voice then, a rising note of panic, edged in hysteria.

"Maggs, Maggie! You let your sister go!"

And just that easily the spell was broken. I sagged, my hands as of their own accord unfolding from your neck, that terrible, alluring voice dwindling—but never fading—from my mind. I stumbled away in tears, retching as your own hands came up to your neck in wonder and dismay.

Silence reigned. Even Leah, gathering her packages, could find no words to speak. And as for Katie and me, we knew. No words were necessary. We knew what had happened—we had heard that hating voice—and though it remained with us for the rest of our days, never again would we speak of what had happened that afternoon, never again would we risk so deep a trance, never again surrender ourselves so wholly to the thing that lay in wait for us upon the other side.

Until now.

Emily sleeps over her needlework, the darkness deepens, the room grows cold. I hear a knocking in the distance, growing louder. And worse yet, a voice, guttural and full of hate, and growing louder.

Katie, I want to say, Katie, is that you.

But I know it is not. Mr. Splitfoot slouches toward us, battening upon half a century of belief and blood, waiting to be born.

My lifetime draws to a close. The year is 1893. A new era draws nigh.

We were girls. How could we know? Surely that is enough.

God forgive us both. God help us all.

What manner of doorway have we opened? What awful beast have we unleashed upon the world?

I foresee a century of blood.

THE GOOD HUSBAND

NATHAN BALLINGRUD

The water makes her nightgown diaphanous, like the ghost of something, and she is naked underneath. Her breasts are full, her nipples large and pale, and her soft stomach, where he once loved to rest his head as he ran his hand through the soft tangle of hair between her legs, is stretched with the marks of age. He sits on the lid of the toilet, feeling a removed horror as his cock stirs beneath his robe. Her eyes are flat and shiny as dimes and she doesn't blink as the water splashes over her face. Wispy clouds of blood drift through the water, obscuring his view of her. An empty prescription bottle lies beside the tub, a few bright pills scattered like candy on the floor.

He was not meant to see this, and he feels a minor spasm of guilt, as though he has caught her at something shameful and private. This woman with whom he had once shared all the shabby secrets of his life. The slice in her forearm is an open curtain, blood flowing out in billowing dark banners.

"You're going to be okay, Katie," he says. He has not called her Katie in ten years. He makes no move to save her.

—◦—

Sean shifted his legs out of bed and pressed his bare feet onto the hardwood floor; it was cold, and his nerves jumped. A spike of life. A sign of movement in the blood. He sat there for a moment, his eyes closed, and concentrated on that. He slid his feet into his slippers and willed himself into a standing position.

He walked naked across the bedroom and fetched his robe from the closet. He threw it around himself and tied it closed. He walked by the vanity, with its alchemies of perfumes and eyeshadows, ignoring the mirror, and left the bedroom. Down the hallway, past the closed bathroom door with light still bleeding from underneath, descending the stairs to the sunlit order of his home.

He was alert to each contraction of muscle, to each creak of bone and ligament. To the pressure of the floor against the soles of his feet, to the slide of the bannister's polished wood against the soft white flesh of his hand.

His mind skated across the frozen surface of each moment. He pushed it along, he pushed it along.

◄◦►

They'd been married twenty-one years, and Katie had tried to kill herself four times in that span. Three times in the last year and a half. Last night, she'd finally gotten it right.

The night had started out wonderfully. They dressed up, went out for dinner, had fun for the first time in recent memory. He bought her flowers, and they walked downtown after dinner and admired the lights and the easy flow of life. He took her to a chocolate shop. Her face was radiant, and a picture of her that final night was locked into his memory: the silver in her hair shining in the reflected light of an overhead lamp, her cheeks rounded into a smile, the soft weight of life turning her body beautiful and inviting, like a blanket, or a hearth. She looked like the girl she used to be. He'd started to believe that with patience and fortitude they could keep at bay the despair that had been seeping into her from some unknown, subterranean hell, flowing around the barricades of antidepressants and anxiety pills, filling her brain with cold water.

When they got home they opened up another bottle and took it to the bedroom. And somehow, they started talking about Heather, who had gone away to college and had recently informed them that she did not want to come home for spring break. It wasn't that she wanted to go anywhere special; she wanted to stay at the dorm, which would be nearly emptied of people, and read, or work, or fuck her new boyfriend if she had one, or whatever it was college girls wanted to do when they didn't want to come home to their parents.

It worked away at Kate like a worm, burrowing tunnels in her gut. She viewed Sean's acceptance of Heather's decision as a callous indifference. When the subject came up again that night, he knew the mood was destroyed.

He resented her for it. For spoiling, once again and with what seemed a frivolous cause, the peace and happiness he was trying so hard to give her. If only she would take it. If only she would believe in it. Like she used to do, before her brain turned against her, and against them all.

They drank the bottle even as the despair settled over her. They ended the night sitting on the edge of the bed, she wearing her sexy nightgown, her breasts mostly exposed and moon-pale in the light, weeping soundlessly, a little furrow between her eyebrows but otherwise without affect, and the light sheen of tears which flowed and flowed, as though a foundation had cracked; and he in the red robe she'd bought him for Christmas, his arm around her, trying once again to reason her away from a precipice that reason did not know.

Eventually he laid back and put his arm over his eyes, frustrated and angry. And then he fell asleep.

He awoke sometime later to the sound of splashing water. It should have been too small a sound to reach him, but it did anyway, worming its way into the black and pulling him to the surface. When he discovered that he was alone in the bedroom, and sensed the deepness of the hour, he walked to the bathroom, where the noise came from, without urgency and with a full knowledge of what he would find.

She spasmed every few seconds, as though something in the body, separate from the mind, fought against this.

He sat down on the toilet, watching her. Later he would examine this moment and try to gauge what he had been feeling. It would seem important to take some measure of himself, to find out what kind of man he really was.

He would come to the conclusion that he'd felt tired. It was as though his blood had turned to lead. He knew the procedure he was meant to follow here; he'd done it before. Already his muscles tightened to abide by the routine, signals blew across his nerves like a brushfire: rush to the tub, waste a crucial moment in simple denial brushing the hair from her face and cradling her head in his warm hands. Hook his arms underneath her body and lift her heavily from the water. Carry her streaming blood and water to the bed. Call 911. Wait. Wait. Wait. Ride with her, and sit unmoving in the waiting room as they pump her stomach and fill her with a stranger's blood. Answer questions. Does she take drugs? Do you? Were you fighting? Sir, a social worker will be by to talk to you. Sir, you have to fill out these forms. Sir, your wife is broken, and you are, too.

And then wait some more as she convalesces in the psych ward. Visit her, try not to cry in front of her as you see her haunting that corridor with the rest of the damned, dwelling like a fading thought in her assigned room.

Bring this pale thing home. This husk, this hollowed vessel. Nurse her to a false health. Listen to her apologize, and accept her apologies. Profess your reinvigorated love. Fuck her with the urgency of pity and mortality and fear, which you both have come to know and to rely on the way you once relied on love and physical desire.

If they could save her.

And if, having saved her, they decided to let her come home at all.

She will never be happy.

The thought came to him with the force of a revelation. It was as though god spoke a judgement, and he recognized its truth as though it had been with them all along, the buzzard companion of their late marriage. Some people, he thought, are just incapable of happiness. Maybe it was because of some ancient trauma, or maybe it was just a bad equation in the brain. Kate's reasons were mysterious to him, a fact which appalled him after so many years of intimacy. If he pulled her from the water now, he would just be welcoming her back to hell.

With a flutter of some obscure emotion—some solution of terror and relief—he closed the door on her. He went back to bed and, after a few sleeping pills of his own, he fell into a black sleep. He dreamed of silence.

In the kitchen, light streamed in through the bay window. It was a big kitchen, with a stand-alone chopping table, wide crumb-flecked counters, ranks of silver knives agleam in the morning sun. Dirty dishes were stacked in the sink and on the counter beside it. The trash hadn't been taken out on time, and its odor was a dull oppression. The kitchen had once been the pride of their home. It seemed to have decayed without his noticing.

A small breakfast nook accommodated a kitchen table in a narrow passage joining the kitchen to the dining room. It still bore the scars and markings of the younger Heather's attentions: divots in the wood where she once tested the effectiveness of a butter knife, a spray of red paint left there during one of her innumerable art projects, and the word *kichen* gouged into the side of the table with a ballpoint pen, years ago, when she thought everything should carry its name. It had become an inadvertent shrine to her childhood, and since she'd left, Kate had shifted their morning coffee to the larger and less welcoming dining room table in the adjoining room. The little breakfast nook had been surrendered to the natural entropy of a household, becoming little more than a receptacle for car keys and unopened mail.

Sean filled the French press with coffee grounds and put the water on to boil.

For a few crucial minutes he had nothing to do, and a ferocious panic began to chew at the border of his thoughts. He felt a weight descending from the floor above him. An unseen face. He thought for a moment that he could hear her footsteps. He thought for a moment that nothing had changed.

He was looking through the bay window to the garden out front, which had ceded vital ground to weeds and ivy. Across the street he watched his neighbor's grandkids tear around the corner of their house like crazed orangutans: ill-built yet strangely graceful, spurred by an unknowable animal purpose. It was Saturday; though winter still lingered at night, spring was warming the daylight hours.

Apparently it was a beautiful day.

The kettle began to hiss and he returned to his rote tasks. Pour the water into the press. Stir the contents. Fit the lid into place and wait for the contents to steep. He fetched a single mug from the cabinet and waited at the counter.

He heard something move behind him, the soft pad of a foot on the linoleum, the staccato tap of dripping water. He turned and saw his wife standing at the kitchen's threshold, the nightgown still soaked through and clinging intimately to her body, streams of water running from the gown and from her hair, which hung in a thick black sheet, and pooling brightly around her.

A sound escaped him, a syllable shot like a hard pellet, high-pitched and meaningless. His body jerked as though yanked by some invisible cord and the coffee mug launched from his hand and shattered on the floor between them. Kate sat down in the nook; the first time she'd sat there in almost a year. She did not look at him, or react to the smashed mug. Water pit-patted from her hair and her clothes onto the table. "Where's mine?" she said.

"Kate? What?"

"Where's my coffee? I want coffee. I'm cold. You forgot mine."

He worked his jaw, trying to coax some sound. Finally he said, "All right." His voice was weak and undirected. "All right," he said again. He opened the cabinet and fetched two mugs.

She'd had a bad dream. It was the only thing that made sense. She was cold and wet and something in her brain tried to make sense of it. She remembered seeing Sean's face through a veil of water. Watching it recede from her. She felt a buckle of nausea at the memory. She took a drink from the coffee and felt the heat course through her body. It only made her feel worse.

She rubbed her hands at her temples.

"Why am I all wet?" she said. "I don't feel right. Something's wrong with me. Something's really wrong."

Sean guided her upstairs. She reacted to his gentle guidance, but did not seem to be acting under any will of her own; except when he tried to steer her into the bathroom. She resisted then, turning to stone in the hallway. "No," she said. Her eyes were hard and bright with fear. She turned her head away from the door. He took her wrist to pull her but she resisted. His fingers inadvertently slid over the incision there, and he jerked his hand away.

"Honey. We need to fix you up."

"No."

He relented, taking her to the bedroom instead, where he removed her wet nightgown. It struck him that he had not seen her like this, standing naked in the plain light of day, for a long time. They had been married for over twenty years and they'd lost interest in each other's bodies long ago. When she was naked in front of him now, he barely noticed. Her body was part of the furniture of their marriage, utilized but ignored, with occasional benign observations from them both about its declining condition.

In a sudden resurgence of his feelings of the previous night, he became achingly aware of her physicality. She was so pale: the marble white of statues or of sun-bleached bones. Her flesh hung loosely on her body, the extra weight suddenly obvious, as though she had no muscle tone remaining at all. Her breasts, her stomach, her unshaven hair: the human frailty of her, the beauty of a lived-in body, which he knew was reflected in his own body, called up a surge of tenderness and sympathy.

"Let's put some clothes on," he said, turning away from her.

He helped her step into her underwear, found a bra and hooked her into it. He found some comfortable, loose-fitting clothes for her, things he knew she liked to wear when she had nowhere special to go. It was not until he was fitting her old college reunion t-shirt over her head that he allowed himself to look at her wrist for the first time, and the sight of it made him step back and clasp a hand over his mouth.

Her left arm bore a long incision from wrist to elbow. The flesh puckered like lips, and as she bent her arm into the shirt, he was afforded a glimpse at the awful depth of the wound. It was easily deep enough to affect its purpose, and as bloodless as the belly of a gutted fish.

"Katie," he said, and brought her wrist to his lips. "What's happening to you." He pressed her fingers to her cheek; they were cool, and limp. "Are you okay?" It was the stupidest question of his life. But he didn't know what else to ask. "Katie?"

She turned her face to him, and after a few moments he could see her eyes begin to focus on him, as though she had to travel a terrible span to find him there. "I don't know," she said. "Something doesn't feel right."

"Do you want to lie down?"

"I guess."

He eased her toward her side of the bed, which was smooth and untroubled: she had slept underwater last night, not here. He laid her there like folded laundry.

He sat beside her as she drifted off. Her eyes remained open but she seemed gone; she seemed truly dead. Maybe, this time, she was.

Does she remember? he thought. *Does she remember that I left her?*

He stretched himself out beside her and ran his hand through her hair, repetitively, a kind of prayer.

Oh my god, he thought, *what have I done? What is happening to me?*

Eventually she wanted to go outside. Not at first, because she was scared, and the world did not make any sense to her. The air tasted strange on her tongue, and her body felt heavy and foreign—she felt very much like a thought wrapped in meat. She spent a few days drifting through the house in a lethargic haze, trying to shed the feeling of unease, which she had woken with the morning after her bath and which had stayed rooted in her throat and in her gut the whole time since. Sean came and went to work. He was solicitous and kind; he was always extra attentive after she tried to kill herself, though; and although she welcomed the attention she had learned to distrust it. She knew it would fade, once the nearness of death receded.

She watched the world through the window. It was like a moving picture in a frame; the details did not change, but the wind blew through the grass and the trees and the neighbors came and went in their cars, giving the scene the illusion of reality. Once, in the late afternoon before Sean came home, she was seen. The older man who lived across the street, whose cat she fed when he went out of town and who was a friend to them both, caught sight of her as he stepped out of his car and waved. She only stared back. After a moment, the man turned from her and disappeared into his own house.

The outside world was a dream of another place. She found herself wondering if she would fit better there.

On the evening of the third day, while they were sitting at dinner—something wretched and cooling that Sean had picked up on his way home—she told him.

"I want to go outside."

Sean kept eating as though he didn't hear her.

This was not new. He'd been behaving with an almost manic enthusiasm around her, as though he could convince her that their lives were unskewed and smooth through sheer force of will. But he would not look at her face; when he looked at her at all he would focus on her cheek, or her shoulder, or her hairline. He would almost look at her. But not quite.

"I don't know if that's a good idea," he said at last. He ate ferociously, forking more into his mouth before he was finished with the last bite.

"Why not?"

He paused, his eyes lifting briefly to the salt and pepper shakers in the middle of the table. "You still don't seem . . . I don't know. Yourself."

"And what would that be like?" She had not touched her food, except to prod it the way a child pokes a stick at roadkill. It cooled on the plate in front of her, congealing cheese and oils. It made her sick.

His mood swung abruptly into something more withdrawn and depressed; she could watch his face and see it happen. This made her feel better. This was more like the man she had known for the past several years of their marriage.

"Am I a prisoner here?"

He finally looked at her, shocked and hurt. "What? How could you even say that?"

She said nothing. She just held his gaze.

He looked terrified. "I'm just worried about you, babe. You don't— you're not—"

"You mean this?" She raised her left arm and slipped her finger into the open wound. It was as clean and bloodless as rubber.

Sean lowered his face. "Don't do that."

"If you're really worried about me, why don't you take me to the hospital? Why didn't you call an ambulance? I've been sleeping so much the past few days. But you just go on to work like everything's fine."

"Everything *is* fine."

"I don't think so."

He was looking out the window now. The sun was going down and the light was thick and golden. Their garden was flowering, and a light dusting of pollen coated the left side of their car in the driveway. Sean's eyes were unblinking and reflective as water. He stared at it all. "There's nothing wrong with you," he said.

Silence filled the space between them as they each sat still in their own thoughts. The refrigerator hummed to life. Katie finally pushed herself away from the table and headed toward the door, scooping up the car keys on her way.

"I'm going out," she said.

"Where?" His voice was thick with resignation.

"Maybe to the store. Maybe no where. I'll be back soon."

He moved to stand. "I'll come with."

"No thanks," she said, and he slumped back into his chair.

Once, she would have felt guilty for that. She would have chastised herself for failing to take into account his wishes or his fears, for failing to protect his fragile ego. He was a delicate man, though he did not know it, and she had long considered it part of her obligation to the marriage to accommodate that frailty of spirit.

But she felt a separation from that now. And from him too, though she remembered loving him once. If anything inspired guilt, it was that she could not seem to find that love anymore. He was a good man, and deserved to be loved. She wondered if the ghost of a feeling could substitute for the feeling itself.

But worse than all of that was the separation she felt from herself. She'd felt like a passenger in her own body the last three days, the pilot of some arcane machine. She watched from a remove as the flesh of her hand tightened around the doorknob and rotated it clockwise, setting into motion the mechanical process that would free the door from its jamb and allow it to swing open, freeing her avenue of escape. The flesh was a mechanism too, a contracting of muscle and ligament, an exertion of pull.

There's nothing wrong with you, he'd said.

She opened the door.

The light was like ground glass in her eyes. It was the most astonishing pain she had ever experienced. She screamed, dropped to the floor, and curled into herself. Very distantly she heard something heavy fall over, followed by crashing footsteps that thrummed the floor beneath her head, and then the door slammed shut. Her husband's hands fell on her and she twisted away from them. The light was a paste on her eyes; she couldn't seem to claw it off of them. It bled into her skull and filled it like a poisonous radiation. She lurched to her feet, shouldering Sean aside, and ran away from the door and into the living room, where she tripped over the carpet and landed hard on her side. Her husband's hysterical voice followed her, a blast of panic. She pushed her body forward with her feet, wedged her face into the space beneath the couch, the cool darkness there, and tried to claw away the astounding misery of the light.

⊶◦⊶

That night she would not come to bed. They'd been sleeping beside each other since the suicide, though he was careful to keep space between them and had taken to wearing pajamas to bed. She slept fitfully at night, seeming to rest better in the daylight, and this troubled his own sleep, too.

She would be as still as stone and then struggle elaborately with the sheets for a few moments before settling into stillness again, like a drowning woman. He turned his head toward the wall when this happened. And then he would remember that he'd turned away from her that night, too. And he would stay awake into the small hours, feeling her struggle, knowing that he'd missed his chance to help her.

The incident at the door had galvanized him, though. Her pain was terrifying in its intensity, and it was his fault. He would not let his guilt or his shame prevent him from doing whatever was necessary to keep her safe and comfortable from now on. Love still lived in him, like some hibernating serpent, and it stirred now, it tasted the air with its tongue.

It took her some time to calm down. He fixed her a martini and brought it to her, watched her sip it disinterestedly as she sat on the couch and stared at the floor, her voice breaking every once in a while in small hiccups of distress. Long nail marks scored her skin; her right eye seemed jostled in its orbit, angled fractionally lower than the other. He had drawn the curtains and pulled the blinds, though by now the sun had sunk and the world outside was blue and cool. He turned off all but a few lights in the house, filling it with shadows. Whether it was this, or the vodka, or something else that did it, she finally settled into a fraught silence.

He eased himself onto the couch beside her, and he took her chin in his fingers and turned her face toward him. An echo of his thought from the night of the suicide passed through his mind: *she will never get better.*

He felt his throat constrict, and heat gathered in his eyes.

"Katie?" He put his hand on her knee. "Talk to me, babe."

She was motionless. He didn't even know if she could hear him.

"Are you all right? Are you in any pain?"

After a long moment, she said, "It was in my head."

"What was?"

"The light. I couldn't get it out."

He nodded, trying to figure out what this meant. "Well. It's dark now."

"Thank you," she said.

This small gratitude caused an absurd swelling in his heart, and he cupped her cheek in his hand. "Oh baby," he said. "I was so scared. I don't know what's going on. I don't know what to do for you."

She put her own hand over his and pressed her cheek into his palm. Her eyes remained unfocused though, one askew, almost as if this was a learned reaction. A muscle memory. Nothing more.

"I don't understand anything anymore," she said. "Everything is strange."

"I know."

She seemed to consider something for a moment. "I should go somewhere else," she said.

"No," Sean said. A violence moved inside him, the idea of her leaving calling forth an animal fury, aimless and electric. "No, Katie. You don't understand. They'll take you away from me. If I take you somewhere, if I take you to see someone, they will not let you come back. You just stay here. You're safe here. We'll keep things dark, like you like it. We'll do whatever it takes. Okay?"

She looked at him. The lamplight from the other room reflected from her irises, giving them a creamy whiteness that looked warm and soft, incongruous in her torn face, like saucers of milk left out after the end of the world. "Why?"

The question shamed him.

"Because I love you, Katie. Jesus Christ. You're my wife. I love you."

"I love you too," she said, and like pressing her cheek into his hand, this response seemed an automatic action. A programmed response. He ignored this, though, and chose to accept what she said as truth—perhaps because this was the first time she'd said it to him since the suicide, when her body had stopped behaving in the way it was meant to and conformed to a new logic, a biology he did not recognize and could not understand and that made a mystery of her again. It had been so long since she'd been a mystery to him. He knew every detail of her life, every dull complaint and every stillborn dream, and she knew his; but now he knew nothing. Every nerve ending in his body was turned in her direction, like flowers bending to the sun.

Or perhaps he only accepted it because the light was soft, and it exalted her.

His free hand found her breast. She did not react in any way. He squeezed it gently in his hand, his thumb rolling over her nipple, still soft under her shirt. She allowed all of this, but her face was empty. He pulled away from her. "Let's go upstairs," he said.

He rose and, taking her hand, moved to help her to her feet. She resisted.

"Katie, come on. Let's go to bed."

"I don't want to."

"But don't you. . ." He took her hand and pressed it against his cock, stiff under in his pants. "Can you feel that? Can you feel what you do to me?"

"I don't want to go upstairs. The light will come in in the morning. I want to sleep in the cellar."

He released her hand, and it dropped to her side. He thought for a minute. The cellar was used for storage and was in a chaotic state. But there was room for a mattress down there, and tomorrow he could move things around, make some arrangements, and make it livable. It did not occur to him to argue with her. This was part of the mystery, and it excited him. He was like a high school boy with a mad new crush, prepared to go to any length.

"Okay," he said. "Give me a few minutes. I'll make it nice for you."

He left her sitting in the dark, his heart pounding, red and strong.

He fucked her with the ardor one brings to a new lover, sliding into the surprising coolness of her, tangling his fingers into her hair and biting her neck, her chin, her ears. He wanted to devour her, to breathe her like oxygen. He hadn't been so hard in years; his body moved like a piston and he felt he could go on for hours. He slid his arms beneath her and held her shoulders from behind as he powered into her, the mattress silent beneath them, the darkness of the cellar as gentle and welcoming as a mother's heart. At first she wrapped her legs around his back, put her arms over his shoulders, but by the time he finished she had abandoned the pretense and simply lay still beneath him, one eye focused on the underbeams of the ceiling, one eye peering into the black.

Afterwards he lay beside her, staring up at the underside of his house. The cellar was cold and stank of mildew. The piled clutter of a long and settled life loomed around them in mounted stacks, tall black shadows that gazed down upon them like some alien congress. The mattress beneath them came from their own bed; he'd resolved to sleep down here with her, if this was where she wanted to be. Three candles were gathered in a little group by their heads, not because he thought it would be romantic— though he felt that it was—but because he had no idea where the outlets were down here to set up a lamp, and he didn't want to risk upsetting her by turning on the bare bulb in the ceiling. The candlelight didn't seem to bother her at all, though; maybe it was just the sun.

He turned his head on the pillow to look at her and ran his hand along the length of her body. It was cool to the touch, cool inside and out.

"This other light doesn't bother you, does it, babe?"

She turned her head too, slowly, and looked at him. Her wounds cast garish shadows across her face in the candlelight. "Hm?"

"The light?"

". . . Oh, I know you," she said, something like relief in her voice. "You're the man who left me in the water."

Something cold flowed through his body. "What?"

She settled back against the mattress, closing her eyes and pulling the sheet up to her chin. She seemed very content. "I couldn't remember you for a minute, but then I did."

"Do you remember that night?"

"What night?"

". . . You said I'm the man who left you in the water."

"I looked up and I saw you. I was scared of something. I thought you were going to help, but then you went away. What was I scared of? Do you know?"

He shook his head, but her eyes were closed and she couldn't see him. "No," he said at last.

"I wish I could remember."

She climbed off the mattress, leaving the man to sleep. He snored loudly, and this made her think of machines again. His was a clumsy one, loud and rattling, and its inefficiency irritated her. It was corpulent and heavy, uncared for, and breaking down. She decided at that moment that she would not let it touch her again.

She slipped her nightgown on over her head and walked upstairs. Cautiously, she opened the door at the top and peered into the ground floor of the house. It was welcomingly dark. Crossing the living room floor and parting the curtains, she saw that night had fallen.

Within moments she was outside, walking briskly along the sidewalk, crackling with an energy she hadn't felt in as long as she could remember. The houses on either side of the street were high-shouldered monsters, their windows as black and silent as the sky above her. The yawn of space opened just beneath the surface of her thoughts with a gorgeous silence. She wanted to sink into it, but she couldn't figure out how. Each darkened building held the promise of tombs, and she had to remind herself that she could not go inside them because people lived there, those churning, squirting biologies, and that the quietude she sought would not be there.

She remembered a place she could go, though. She quickened her pace, her nightgown—the one she had worn that night, when the man had left her in the water, now clean and white—almost ephemeral in the chilly air and trailing behind her like a ghostly film. The narrow suburban road crested a hill a few hundred feet ahead, and beyond it breached a low dome of light. The city, burning light against the darkness.

Something lay on the sidewalk in front of her, and she slowed as she approached. It was a robin, its middle torn open, its guts eaten away. A curtain of ants flowed inside it, and lead away from it in a meandering trail into the grass. She picked it up and cradled it close to her face. The ants seethed, spreading through its feathers, over her hand, down her arm. She ignored them.

The bird's eyes were glassy and black, like tiny onyx stones. Its beak was open and in it she could see the soft red muscle of its tongue. Something moved and glistened in the back of its throat.

She continued on, holding the robin at her side. She didn't feel the ants crawling up her arm, onto her neck, into her hair. The bird was a miracle of beauty.

The suburbs stopped at the highway, like an island against the sea. She turned east, the city lights brighter now at her right, and continued walking. The sidewalk roughened as she continued along, broken in places, seasoned with stones and broken glass. She was oblivious to it all. Traffic was light but not incidental, and the rush of cars blowing by lifted her hair and flattened the nightgown against her body. Someone leaned on the horn as he drove past, whooping through an open window.

The clamor of the highway, the stink of oil and gasoline, the buffeting rush of traffic, all served to deepen her sense of displacement. The world was a bewildering, foreign place, the light a lowgrade burn and a stain on the air, the rushing cars on the highway a row of gnashing teeth.

But ahead, finally, opening in long, silent acres to her left, was the cemetery.

It was gated and locked, but finding a tree to get over the wall was no difficulty. She scraped her skin on the bark and then on the stone, and she tore her nightgown, but that was of no consequence. She tumbled gracelessly to the ground, like a dropped sack, and felt a sharp snap in her right ankle. When she tried to walk, the ankle rolled beneath her and she fell.

Meat, getting in the way.

Disgusted by this, she used the wall to pull herself to a standing position. She found that if she let the foot just roll to the side and walked on the ankle itself, she could make a clumsy progress.

Clouds obscured the sky, and the cemetery stretched over a rolling landscape, bristling with headstones and plaques, monuments and crypts, like a scattering of teeth. It was old; many generations were buried here. The sound of the highway, muffled by the wall, faded entirely from her awareness. She stood amidst the graves and let their silence fill her.

The flutter of unease that she'd felt since waking after the suicide abated. The sense of disconnection was gone. Her heart was a still lake. Nothing in her moved. She wanted to cry from relief.

Still holding the dead robin in her hand, she lurched more deeply into the cemetery.

She found a hollow between the stones, a trough between the stilled waves of earth, where no burial was marked. She eased herself to the ground and curled up in the grass. The clouds were heavy and thick, the air was cold. She closed her eyes and felt the cooling of her brain.

Sounds rose from the earth. New sounds: cobwebs of exhalations, pauses of the heart, the monastic work of the worms translating flesh to soil, the slow crawl of rock. There was another kind of industry, somewhere beneath her. Another kind of machine.

It was new knowledge, and she felt the root of a purpose. She set the robin aside and tore grass away, dug her nails into the dark soil, pushed through. She scooped aside handfuls of dirt. At some point in her labors she became aware of something awaiting her beneath the earth. Moving silences, the cloudy breaths of the moon, magnificent shapes unrecognizable to her novice intelligence, like strange old galleons of the sea.

And then, something awful.

A rough bark, a perverse intrusion into this quiet celebration, a rape of the silence.

Her husband's voice.

She was alone again, and she felt his rough hands upon her.

It had been nothing more than instinct that guided him to her, finally. He panicked when he awoke to her missing, careened through the house, shouted like a fool in his front yard until lights began to pop on in the neighbors' houses. Afraid that they would offer to help, or call the police for him, he got into the car and started driving. He criss-crossed the neighborhood to no avail, until finally it occurred to him that she might go to the cemetery. That she might, in some fit of delirium, decide that she belonged there.

The thought tore at him. The guilt over leaving her to die in the bathtub threatened to crack his ribs. It was too big to contain.

He scaled the cemetery wall and called until he found her, a small white form in a sea of graves and dark grass, huddled and scared, clawing desperately in the dirt. Her ankle was broken and hung at a sickening angle.

He pulled her up by her shoulders and wrapped his arms around her, hugged her tightly against him.

"Oh Katie, oh baby," he said. "It's okay. It's okay. I've got you. You scared me so bad. You're going to be okay."

An ant emerged from her hairline and idled on her forehead. Another crawled out of her nose. He brushed them furiously away.

She returned to the cellar. He spent a few days getting it into some kind of order, moving precarious stacks into smaller and sturdier piles, and giving her some room to move around in. While she slept in the daytime, he brought down the television set and its stand, a lamp, and a small box where he kept the books she had once liked to read. He left the mattress on the floor but changed the sheets regularly. When he was not at work he spent all his time down there with her, though he had taken to sleeping upstairs so that he could lock her in when she was most likely to try to wander.

"I can't risk you getting lost again," he told her. "It would kill me." Then he closed the door and turned the lock. She heard his steps tread the floor above her.

She had taken the dead robin and nailed it to one of the support beams beside the mattress. It was the only beautiful thing in the room, and it calmed her to look at it.

Her foot was more trouble than it was worth so she wrenched it off and tossed it into the corner.

⊸◦⊱

"That was Heather," Sean said, closing the cellar door and tromping down the stairs. He sat beside her on the mattress and put his arm around her shoulders. She did not lean into him the way she used to do, so he gave her a little pull until it seemed like she was.

When he'd noticed her missing foot the other night, he'd quietly gone back upstairs and dry heaved over the sink. Then he came back down, searched until he located it in a corner, and took it outside to bury it. The crucified bird had not bothered him initially, but over the days it had gathered company: two mice, three cockroaches, a wasp, some moths. Their dry little bodies were arrayed like art. She had even pulled the bones from one of the mice, fixing them with wood glue onto the post in some arcane hieroglyph.

He was frightened by its alienness. He was frightened because it meant something to her and it was indecipherable to him.

She was watching something on tv with the sound off: men in suits talking to each other across a table. They seemed very earnest.

"She wants to come home for the weekend," he said. "I said it would be okay."

She pulled her gaze from the screen and looked at him. The light from the television made small blue squares in her eyes, which had begun to film over in a creamy haze. It was getting hard to tell that one eye was askew, which made him feel better when he talked to her. "Heather," she said. "I like Heather."

He put his fingers in her hair, hooked a dark lock behind her ear. "Of course you do, baby. You remember her, don't you."

She stared for a moment, then her brow furrowed. "She used to live here."

"That's right. She went to college, and she lives there now. She's our daughter. We love her."

"I forgot."

"And you love me, too."

"Okay."

She looked back at the television. One of the men was standing now and laughing so hard his face was red. His mouth was wide open. He was going to swallow the world.

"Can you say it?"

"Say what?"

"That you love me. Can you say that to me? Please?"

"I love you."

"Oh baby," he said, and leaned his head against hers, his arm still around her. "Thank you. Thank you. I love you too." They sat there and watched the silent images. His mind crept ahead to Heather's visit. He wondered what the hell he was going to tell her. She was going to have a hard time with this.

What is the story of our marriage?

He went back to that night again and again. He remembered standing over her, watching her body struggle against the pull of a death she had called upon herself. It is the nature of the body to want to live, and once her mind had shut down her muscles spasmed in the water, splashing blood onto the floor as it fought to save itself.

But her mind, apparently, had not completely shut down after all. She remembered him standing over her. She looked up as the water lapped over her face and saw him staring down at her. She saw him turn and close the door.

What did she see behind his face? Did she believe it was impassive? Did she believe it was unmoved by love? How could he explain that he had done it because he could not bear to watch her suffer anymore?

On the rare occasions that he remembered the other thoughts—the weariness, the dread of the medical routine, and especially the flaring anger he'd felt earlier that same night, when the depression took her and he knew he'd have to steer her through it *yet again*—he buried them.

That is not the story of our marriage, he thought. *The story is that I love her, and that's what guided my actions. As it always has.*

He was losing her, though. The change that kindled his interest also pulled her farther and farther away, and he feared that his love for her, and hers for him, would not be enough to tether her to this world.

So he called Heather and told her to come home for spring break. Not for the whole week, he knew that she was an adult now, she had friends, that was fine. But she had family obligations and her mother was lonely for her, and she should come home for at least the weekend.

Is she sick? Heather asked.

No. She just misses her girl.

Dad, you told me it was okay if I stayed here spring break. You told me you would talk to Mom about it.

I did talk, Heather. She won. Come on home, just for the weekend. Please.

Heather agreed, finally. Her reluctance was palpable, but she would come.

That was step one.

Step two would be coaxing Katie out of the cellar for her arrival. He'd thought that being locked down there at night, and whenever he was out, would have made coming upstairs something to look forward to. He'd been wrong; she showed no signs of wanting to leave the cellar at all, possibly ever again. She had regressed even further, not getting up to walk at all since losing her foot, and forsaking clothing altogether; she crawled palely naked across the floor when she wanted to move anywhere—a want that rarely troubled her mind anymore. She allowed him to wash her when he approached her with soap and warm water, but only because she was passive in this as she had become in all things.

Unless he wanted to touch her with another purpose.

Then she would turn on him with an anger that terrified him. Her eyes were pale as moon rocks. Her breath was cold. And when she turned on him with that fury, he would imagine her breathing that chill into his lungs, stuffing it down into his heart. It terrified him. He would not approach her for sex anymore, though the rejection hurt him more than he would have dreamed.

He decided to woo her. He searched the roads at night, crawling at under twenty miles an hour, looking for roadkill. The first time he found some, a gut-crushed possum, he brought the carcass into the house and dropped it onto the floor in front of the cellar door, hoping the smell would lure her out. It did not; but he did not sulk, nor did he deprive her of her gift. He opened the door and rolled the animal wreckage down the stairs.

On the night he told her about Heather, he was propelled by romantic impulse to greater heights. He poisoned the cat that lived across the street, the one she watched over when its owner left town, and brought it to her on a pillow; he'd curled it into a semblance of sleep, and laid it at the foot of her mattress. She fixed her flat, pale eyes on it, not acknowledging his presence at all. Slowly she scooped it into her arms, and she held it close to her body. Satisfied, he sat beside her on the bed. He smiled as she got to work.

-◦-

The floor was packed dirt. It seemed as hard as concrete, but ultimately it was just earth. It could be opened. She bent herself to this task. She found a corner behind some boxes of old china, where her work would not be obvious to the man when he came down to visit, and picked at the ground with a garden spade. It took a long time, but finally she began to make serious progress, upturning the packed ground until she got to the dark soil beneath it, bringing pale earthworms and slick, black insects to their first, shocked exposure to the upside world. When she got deep enough, she abandoned the small spade and used her hands. Her fingernails snapped off like little plastic tabs, and she examined her fingers with a mild curiosity.

Staring at the ruined flesh reminded her of how the man's face would sometimes leak fluid when he came down here and of his occasional wet cough.

It was all so disgusting.

She took one of the cat's bones from its place on the wall and snapped it in half. The end was sharp and she scraped the flesh from her fingers until hard bone gleamed. Then she went to work again, and was pleased with the difference.

"Hey, Dad." Heather stood in the doorway, her overnight bag slung over her shoulder. Considering how little she wanted to be here, Sean thought she was doing a good job of putting up a positive front.

"Hey, kiddo." He looked over her shoulder and saw that she had parked directly behind his car again, like she always used to do, and like he had asked her not to do a million times. He actually felt a happy nostalgia at the sight of it. He kissed her cheek and took the bag from her shoulder. "Come on in."

She followed him in, rubbing her arms and shuddering. "Jeez, Dad, crank up the AC why don't you."

"Heh, sorry. Your mother likes it cold."

"*Mom?* Since when?"

"Since recently I guess. Listen, why don't you go on up to your room and get changed or whatever. I'll get dinner started."

"Sentimental as always, Dad. I've been in the car all day and I *really* need a shower. Just call me when you're ready." She brushed past him on her way to the stairs.

"Hey," he said.

She stopped.

He held an arm out. "I'm sorry. Come here." She did, and he folded his arm around her, drawing her close. He kissed her forehead. "It means a lot that you came."

"I know."

"I'm serious. It matters. Thank you."

"Okay. You're welcome." She returned his hug and he soaked it in. "So where is she?"

"Downstairs. She'll be up."

She pulled back. "In the *cellar?* Okay, weird."

"She'll be up. Go on now. Get yourself ready."

She shook her head with the muted exasperation of a child long-accustomed to her parents' eccentricities and mounted the stairs. Sean turned his attention to the kitchen. He'd made some pot roast in the crock pot, and he tilted the lid to give it a look. The warm, heavy smell of it washed over his face and he took it into his lungs with gratitude. He hadn't prepared anything real to eat in a month, it seemed, living instead off of frozen pizzas and tv dinners. The thought of real food made him lightheaded.

He walked over to the basement door and slid open the lock. He paused briefly, resting his head against the doorjamb. He breathed deeply. Then he cracked it open and poked his head in. A thick, loamy odor rode over him on cool air. There was no light downstairs at all.

"Katie?"

Silence.

"Katie, Heather's here. You remember, we talked about Heather."

His voice did not seem to carry at all on the heavy air. It was like speaking into a cloth.

"She's our daughter." His voice grew small. "You love her, remember?"

He thought he heard something shift down there, a sliding of something. Good, he thought. She remembers.

Heather came downstairs a little later. He waited for her, ladling the pot roast into two bowls. The little breakfast nook was set up for them both. Seeing her, he was struck, as he was so often, by how much she looked like a younger version of Katie. The same roundness in her face, the same way she tended to angle her shoulders when she stood still, even the same bob to her hair. It was as though a young Katie had slipped sideways through a hole in the world and come here to see him again, to see what kind of man he had become. What manner of man she had married.

He lowered his eyes.

I'm a good man, he thought.

"Dad?"

He looked up, blinking his eyes rapidly. "Hey you."

"Why isn't there a mattress on your bed? And why is there a sleeping bag on the floor?"

He shook his head. "What were you doing in our bedroom?"

"The door was wide open. It's kind of hard to miss."

He wasn't expecting this. "It's . . . I've been sleeping on the floor."

She just stared at him. He could see the pain in her face, the old familiar fear. "What's been going on here, Dad? What's she done this time?"

"She uh . . . she's not doing very well, Heather."

He watched tears gather in her eyelids. Then her face darkened and she rubbed them roughly away. "You told me she was fine," she said quietly.

"I didn't want to upset you. I wanted you to come home."

"You didn't want to *upset me?*" Her voice rose into a shout. Her hand clenched at her side and he watched her wrestle down the anger. It took her a minute.

"I'm sorry, Heather."

She shook her head. She wouldn't look at him. "Whatever. Did she try to kill herself again? She's not even here at all, is she. Is she in the psych ward?"

"No, she's here. And yes, she did."

She turned her back to him and walked into the living room, where she dropped onto the couch and slouched back, her arms crossed over her chest like a child. Sean followed her, pried loose one of her hands and held onto it as he sat beside her.

"She needs us, kiddo."

"I would *never* have come back!" she said, her rage cresting like a sun. "God *damn* it!"

"Hey! Now listen to me. She needs us."

"She needs to be committed!"

"Stop it. Stop that. I know this is hard."

"Oh do you?" She glared at him, her face red. He had never seen her like this; anger made her face into something ugly and unrecognizable. "*How* do you know, Dad? When did you ever have to deal with it? It was always me! I was the one at home with her. I was the one who had to call the hospital that one time I found her in her own blood and then call you so you could come! I was the one who—" She gave in then, abruptly and catastrophically, like a battlement falling; sobs broke up whatever else she was going to say. She pulled in a shuddering breath and said, "I can't believe you *tricked* me!"

"*Every night!*" Sean hissed, his own large hands wrapped into fists, cudgels on his lap. He saw them there and caught himself. He felt something slide down over his mind. The emotions pulled away, the guilt and the horror and the shame, until he was only looking at someone having a fit. People, it seemed, were always having some kind of breakdown or another. Somebody had to keep it together. Somebody always had to keep it together.

"It was not just you. Every night I came home to it. Will she be okay tonight? Will she be normal? Or will she talk about walking in front of a bus? Will she be crying because of something I said, or she thinks I said, last fucking week? Every night. Do you think it all just went away when you went to sleep? Come out of your narcissistic little bubble and realize that the world is bigger than you."

She looked at him, shocked and hurt. Her lower lip was trembling, and the tears came back in force.

"But I always stood by her side. Always." He took her lightly by the arm and stood with her. "Your mother needs us. And we're going to go see her. Right now."

He led her toward the basement door.

What is the story of our family?

He led her down the stairs, into the cool, earthy musk of the basement, the smell of upturned soil a dank bloom in the air. His grip on her arm was firm as he descended one step ahead of her. The light from the kitchen behind them was an ax blade in the darkness, cutting a narrow wedge. It illuminated the corner of the mattress, powdered with a layer of dirt. Beside it, the bottom two feet of the support beam she had nailed the bird to; something new was screwed into place there, but he could intuit from the glistening mass only gristle and hair, a sheet of dried blood beneath it.

"What's going on here? Oh my god, Dad, what's going on?"

"Your mom's in trouble. She needs us."

Heather made a noise and he clamped down harder on her arm.

"Katie?" he said. "Heather's here." His voice did not carry, the words dropping like stones at his feet.

Our family has weathered great upheaval. Our family is bound together by love.

They heard something shift, in the darkness beyond the reach of the light.

"Mom?"

"Katie? Where are you, honey?"

"Dad, what happened to her?"

"Just tell me where you are, sweetheart. We'll come to you."

They reached the bottom of the steps and as he moved out of the path of the kitchen light it shone more fully on the thing fixed to the post: a gory mass of scrambled flesh, a ragged web of graying black hair. Something moved in the shadows beyond it, small and hunched and pale, its back buckling with each grunted effort, like something caught in the act of love.

Our family will not abandon itself.

Heather stepped backward; her heel caught on the lowest step and she fell onto the stairs.

Sean approached his wife. She labored weakly in the bottom of a small declivity, grave-shaped, worm-spangled, her dull white bones poking through the parchment skin of her back, her spine bending as she burrowed into the earth. Her denuded skull still bore the tatters of its face, like the flag of a ruined army.

"Daddy, come on." Sean turned to see his daughter crawling up the stairs. She reached the top and crawled through the doorway, pulling her legs in after her. In the light, he could see the tears on her face, the twist of anguish. "Daddy, please. Come on. Come on."

Sean put his hand on Katie's back. "Don't you remember me? I'm your husband. Don't you remember?"

She continued to work, slowly, her arms like pistons powered by a fading battery.

He lifted her from her place in the earth, dirt sifting from her body like a snowfall, and clutched her tightly to his chest. He rested his head against the blood-greased curve of her skull, cradled her forehead in his hand. "Stay with me."

Heather, one more time, from somewhere above him: "Daddy, oh no, please come up. Please."

"Get down here," Sean said. "Goddamn you, get down here."

The door shut, cutting off the wedge of light. He held his wife in his arms, rocking her back and forth, cooing into the ear that still remained.

He pulled her away, but she barely knew it. Everything was quiet now. Silence blew from the hole she had dug like smoke. She could feel what lay just beyond. The new countryside. The unspeaking multitude. Steeples and arches of bone; temples of silence. She felt the great shapes that moved there, majestic and unfurled, utterly silent, utterly dark.

He held her, breathing air onto the last cinder in her skull.

Her fingers scraped at empty air, the remains of her body engaged in this one final enterprise, working with a machine's unguided industry, divorced at last from its practical function. Working only because that was its purpose; its rote, inelegant chore.

THE TIGER

NINA ALLAN

There is a bed, a wardrobe with a large oval mirror, a built-in cupboard to one side of the chimney breast. The boards are bare, stained black. There is a greyish cast to everything. Croft guesses the room has not been used in quite some time.

"It's not much, I'm afraid," the woman says. Her name is Sandra. Symes has told him everyone including her husband calls her Sandy, but Croft has decided already that he will never do this, that it is ugly, that he likes Sandra better. "I've been meaning to paint it, but there hasn't been time."

She is too thin, he thinks, with scrawny hips and narrow little birdy hands. Her mousy hair, pulled back in a pony tail, has started to come free of its elastic band. Croft cannot help noticing how tired she looks.

"Don't worry," he says. "If you can let me have the paint, I'll do it myself."

"Oh," she says. She seems flustered. "I suppose we could take something off the rent money. In exchange, I mean."

"There's no need," Croft says. "I'd like to do it. Something to keep me out of mischief." He smiles, hoping to give her reassurance, but she takes a step backwards, just a small one, but still a step, and Croft sees he has made a mistake already, that the word *mischief* isn't funny, not from him, not now, not yet.

He will have to be more careful with what he says. He wonders if this is the way things will be for him from now on.

"Well, if you're sure," Sandra says. She glances at him quickly, then looks down at the floor. "It would brighten up the walls a bit, at least."

She leaves him soon afterwards. Croft listens to her footsteps as she goes downstairs, past the entrance to the first floor flat where she and Angus McNiece and their young son live, and into the pub where she works ten hours each day behind the bar. Once he feels sure she won't come back again, Croft lifts his luggage—a canvas holdall—from where he has placed it just inside the door and puts it down on the bed. As he tugs open the zip, an aroma arises, the scent of musty bedsheets and floor disinfectant, a smell he recognises instantly as the smell of the prison, a smell he has grown so used to that he would have said, if he'd been asked, that the prison didn't have a smell at all.

No smell, and no texture. Being outside is like being spun inside a centrifuge. He keeps feeling it, the enthralling pressure on his ribs and abdomen, the quickfire jolts to his brain as he tries to accustom himself to the fact that he is once more his own private property. Just walking from the station to the pub—the long, straight rafter of Burnt Ash Road, the blasted concrete triangle that is Lee Green—gave him a feeling of exhilaration so strong, so bolt upright it still buzzes in his veins like neat whisky, like vertigo.

The pub is called The Old Tiger's Head. Croft has read it was once a coaching halt, a watering hole for soldiers on their way to the Battle of Waterloo. More recently it was a tram stop, where trams on their way down from Lewisham Junction would switch from the central conduit to overhead power. Photographs of Lee Green in the early 1900s show the place when it was still a village, a busy crossroads between Lewisham and Eltham, creased all along its corners, faded, precious.

He begins to remove his clothes and books from the canvas holdall. The clothes will go in the wardrobe. He tries the door to the built-in cupboard, but it appears to be locked. Croft wishes the woman, Sandra, had felt able to stay with him in the room for just a few minutes longer.

Why would she, though? What is he to her, other than the sixty pounds each week she will get from him in rent money?

Croft wonders what, if anything, she has heard or read or been told about his case.

The child, Rebecca Riding, lived less than two miles from the place where he is now standing. A decade has passed since she died. In an alternate world, she would now be a young woman. Instead, she went to pick flowers in Manor Park on a certain day, and that was that.

Abducted and raped, then murdered. Her name had joined the register of the lost.

Did Croft kill Rebecca Riding? The papers said he had, for a while they did anyway. He has served a ten-year prison sentence for her murder. Even now that the charges have been overturned, the time he has spent living as a guilty man is still a part of reality.

He is free, but is he truly innocent?

Croft cannot say yet. There are too many things about that day that he cannot remember.

⟶

His first meeting with Symes consists mainly of Symes cross-examining him on the subject of how things are going.

"Did you manage to sign on okay?" As if penetrating the offices of the Lewisham DSS was a significant accomplishment, like shooting Niagara Falls in a barrel, or scaling Everest.

Perhaps for some it is. Croft thinks of the faces, the closed and hostile faces of free people who through their freedom were unpredictable and therefore threatening. In prison, you became used to people doing the same thing, day after day. Even insane actions came to make sense within that context. In the offices of the Lewisham DSS, even getting up to fetch a cup of water from the cooler might turn out to be a prelude to insurrection.

All the people he encounters make him nervous. He tells Symes everything is fine.

"It was lucky about the room," he adds, as a sweetener. "I'm grateful to you."

The room at The Old Tiger's Head was Symes's idea. He knows Angus McNiece, apparently. Croft dislikes Symes intensely without knowing why. In prison, you come to know a man's crime by the scent he gives off, and to Croft, Richard Symes has about him the same moist and fuggy aroma as the pathetically scheming lowlifes who always sat together in the prison canteen because no one else would sit near them, suffering badly from acne and talking with their mouths full.

Symes wears a lavender-coloured, crew-necked jersey and loose brown corduroys. He looks like an art teacher.

That Symes has been assigned to him by the probation service to help him "re-orientate" seems to Croft like a joke that isn't funny.

Symes is telling Croft about a group he runs, once a week at his home, for newly released offenders.

"It's very informal," Symes says. "I think you'd enjoy it."

Offenders, Croft thinks. *That's what we are to people. We offend.* The idea of being in Symes's house is distasteful to him, but he is afraid that if he refuses, Symes will see it as a sign of maladjustment and use it against him.

Croft says yes, he would like to attend, of course. It would be good to meet people.

"Here's my address," Symes says. He writes it down on one of the scraps of paper that litter his desk and hands it across. "It's in Forest Hill. Can you manage the bus?"

"I think so," Croft says. For a moment, he imagines how good it would feel to punch Symes in the face, even though Croft isn't used to fighting. He hasn't hit anyone since he was fifteen and had a dust-up in the school-yard with Roger Burke by name, Burke by nature. Croft has forgotten what it was about now but everyone had cheered. He imagines the blood spurting from Symes's nose the way it had from Roger Burke's nose, the red coating the grooves of his knuckles, the outrage splayed across his face (how fucking dare you, you little turd), the pain and surprise.

Symes is finally getting ready to dismiss him.

"Tuesday at eight, then. Are you sure you don't want me to email you directions?"

"There's no need." Croft isn't online yet, anyway, but he doesn't tell Symes that. "I'm sure I can find you."

◦►

"I'm just popping to Sainsbury's," Sandra says. "Can I fetch you anything?"

The supermarket is only across the road. Croft can see the car park from his window. Sandra knows Croft could easily go himself, if he needed to, but she asks anyway because she's like that, kind, so different from her husband, McNiece, who hasn't addressed a single word to Croft since he moved in.

Sandra has her boy with her, Alexander. He gazes around Croft's room with widening eyes.

"You're *painting*," the boy says.

White, Sandra bought. A five-litre can of matt emulsion and a can of hi-shine gloss for the woodwork.

The smell of it: bright, chemical, clean, the scent of new. It reminds Croft of the smell of the fixative in his old darkroom.

"That's right," Croft says. "Do you like it?"

The boy stares at him, open-mouthed.

"Don't bother Mr. Croft, Alex," Sandra says. "He's busy."

"It's no bother," Croft says. "And it's Dennis." The presence of the boy in his room makes him more than ever certain that Sandra McNiece does not know what Croft was in prison for. If she knew, she would not have brought her son up here. If she knew, she would not have allowed Croft within a mile of the building.

She will know soon though, because someone will tell her, someone is bound to. Croft is surprised this hasn't happened already. Once she knows, she will want to throw him out, though Croft has a feeling Angus McNiece won't let her, he won't want to lose the extra income.

"I could do with some tea bags," he says to Sandra. "If it's really no trouble."

◄◊►

"Were you really in prison?" the boy says. *Alexander*. He sits on the edge of Croft's bed, swinging his legs back and forth as if he were sitting on a tree branch, somewhere high up, in Oxleas Woods perhaps (do kids still go there?) where it is said you can hear the ghosts of hanged highwaymen, galloping along the side of the Dover Road in the autumnal dusk.

"Yes," Croft says. "I was. But I'm out now."

"What were you in for?"

"Does your mother know you're up here?" Croft replies. The idea that she might not know, that the boy is here in his room and that nobody has given their permission, makes Croft feel queasy. Or perhaps it is just the smell of the hardening gloss paint.

"Yes," the boy says, though Croft can tell at once that he is lying, that the child has *sneaked upstairs to see the prisoner*, that in the boy's mind this is the bravest and most daring feat he has ever performed. Croft wonders if Sandra realises she has given her son the same name as her own. Perhaps she does, perhaps the boy was named after her.

Alexander the Great.

Alexander Graham Bell.

Alexander Pushkin.

In Russian, the shortened form of Alexander (and Alexandra) is not Alex, but Sasha. Pushkin was shot in a duel. He died two days later in some agony from a ruptured spleen. He was thirty-eight years old.

"Shouldn't you be in bed?" Croft says. The boy looks at him with scorn. How old is he, exactly? Six, seven, eight?

"What did you do before you were in prison?"

"I took photographs," Croft says. "That was my job."

"Would you take one of me?"

"I might," Croft says. "But I don't have a camera."

The boy reminds him of someone, the lad who betrayed him perhaps. The boy is younger, of course, but he has the same bright knowingness, the same hopeful aura of trust as the lad who seemed to become his friend and then called him a murderer. Croft wonders what his Judas—Kip?—is doing now. Has he become a photographer himself, as he intended, or is he cooped up in some office, serving time?

-o-

Croft never dreamed in prison. The air of the place was sterile, an imagic vacuum. The outside air is different, teeming with live bacteria, primed to blossom into monstrosities as soon as he sleeps. In his dreams of Rebecca Riding, he begins to remember the way her hair felt, under his hand, the soft jersey fabric of her vest and underpants.

"Will you take me home now?" she says. Croft always says yes, though when he wakes, sweating with horror, he can't remember if this really happened or if it's just in his dream. There's cum on the bedsheet, still tacky. He steps out of bed and goes across to the window. Outside and below him, Lee Green lies hazy in the light of the streetlamps. In the hours between two and four, there is little traffic.

His legs are still shaking.

If he waits until five o'clock, a new day will begin.

Croft opens the window to let in the air, which is crisp, tinged with frost, the leading edge of autumn, easing itself inside him like a dagger. The orange, rakish light of Lee Green at night reflects itself back at him from the oval mirror on the front of the wardrobe.

Croft wishes he had a camera.

If he cannot have a camera, he wishes he could sleep.

—◦—

The bus to Forest Hill is the 122. They run every fifteen minutes, approximately. There's a stop more or less opposite the pub, at the bottom end of Lee High Road. It's the early part of the evening, after the main rush hour but still fairly busy. When Croft gets on, the bus is half empty, but after the stop at Lewisham Station, it's almost full again.

Croft moves upstairs, to the top deck. He does not mind the bus being packed, as Symes seemed to think he would. The crush of people, the sheer weight of them, makes him feel less observed. None of them know who he is, or where he is going. Friends of his from before, police officers and journalists living north of the river (Queen's Park and Kilburn, Ealing and Hammersmith, Camden Town) liked to joke about southeast London as a badlands, a no-man's-land of scabby takeaways and boarded-up squats. Croft looks out at the criss-crossing streets, the lit-up intersections and slow-moving traffic queues. Curry houses and fish-and-chip shops and eight-till-late supermarkets, people returning from work, plonking themselves down in front of a cop show, cooking supper. All the things that, once you are removed from them, take on an aspect of the marvellous. He feels southeast London enfold him in the darkness like a tatty anorak, like an old army blanket. Khaki-coloured, smelling of spilled beer and antifreeze, benzene and tar, ripped in several places but still warm enough to save your life on a freezing night.

The sky is mauve, shading to indigo, shading to black, and as they pass through Honor Oak Park, Croft thinks of Steven Jepsom, who once lived not far from here, in a grubby basement flat on the Brownhill Road. It was Jepsom they arrested first, but a lack of real evidence meant they had to let him go again.

Whereas in Croft's case, there were the photographs. It was the photographs, much more than Kip, that had testified against him.

Now, it seemed, Steven Jepsom had been Rebecca Riding's killer all along.

Croft remembered Symes's first visit to the prison, Symes telling him about Jepsom being re-arrested, almost a year before he, Croft, had been set free.

"It won't be long now," Symes had said. He gave Croft a look, and Croft thought it was almost as if he were trying to send him a signal of some kind, to claim the credit for Croft's good luck.

"Is there new evidence, then?" Croft asked.

"Plenty. A new witness has come forward, apparently. It's strange, how often that happens. There's no time limit on the truth, Dennis."

Croft dislikes Symes's insistence on using his first name. Using a first name implies familiarity, or liking, and for Symes he feels neither. He has always tried not to call Symes anything.

He tries not to think of Steven Jepsom, who is now in prison instead of him.

A guilty man for an innocent one. Straight swap.

Richard Symes lives on Sydenham Park Road, a residential street leading off Dartmouth Road, where the station is, ten minutes' walk from the bus stop at most. The house is unremarkable, a 1950s semi with an ancient Morris Minor parked in the drive. The porch lights are on. As he approaches the door, Croft thinks about turning around and heading back to the bus stop. There is no law that says he has to be here—the group is voluntary. But Symes won't like it if he doesn't attend. He will like it even less if he finds out that Croft turned up at his house and then went away again. He will see it as a mark against him, a sign of instability perhaps, an unwillingness to reintegrate himself into normal society. Could Symes report him for that? Perhaps.

That would mean more meetings, more reports, more conversations.

More time until he's off Symes's hook.

Croft decides it is better just to go through with it. It is an hour of his time, that is all, and he's here now, anyway. It's almost more trouble to leave than it is to stay.

He rings the bell. Someone comes to the door almost at once, a balding, fortyish man in a purple tank top and bottle-glass spectacles.

"You're exactly on time," he says. He steps aside to let Croft enter the hallway. Croft notices that, in spite of it being November and chilly, the man is wearing leather sandals, the kind Croft used to wear for school in the summer term and that used to be called Jesus sandals. Croft feels surprise that you can still buy them.

The Jesus man has a front tooth missing. The light of the hallway is sharp, bright orange. Croft follows the Jesus man along the corridor and through a door at the end. By contrast with the garish hallway, the room beyond is dim. The only illumination, such that it is, appears to be coming from a selection of low-wattage table lamps and alcove lights, making it difficult for Croft to find his bearings. He estimates that there are eight, perhaps ten people in the room, sitting in armchairs and on sofas. They fall silent as he enters. He looks around for Symes, but cannot see him.

"Our mentor is in the kitchen," says the man in the sandals. "He's making more drinks." He has an odd way of speaking, not a lisp exactly, but something like it. Perhaps it's his adenoids. Each time he opens his mouth, Croft finds himself focussing on the missing front tooth. Its absence makes the man look grotesquely young. *Our mentor?* Does he mean Symes? He guesses it's just the man's attempt at a joke.

A moment later, Symes himself appears. He is carrying a plastic tray, stacked with an assortment of mugs and glasses. Croft can smell blackcurrant juice, Ribena. For some reason this cloying scent, so reminiscent of children's birthday parties, disturbs him.

"Dennis, good to see you," Symes says. "Take this for me, would you please, Bryan?" He eases the tray into the hands of the Jesus man, who seems about to overbalance. "What are you drinking?"

"Do you have a beer?" Croft says. His eyes are on the Jesus man, who has recovered himself enough to place the laden tray on a low wooden bench. The thought of the Ribena or even coffee in this place fills him with an empty dread he cannot explain. A beer would at least be tolerable. It might even help.

"Coming right up," Symes says. The baggy cords are gone and he is wearing jeans, teamed with a hooded sweatshirt, which has some sort of band logo on the front. His wrists protrude awkwardly from the too-short arms.

He's dressed himself up as a kid, Croft thinks, and the idea, like the thought of the Ribena, is for some reason awful. Symes tells him to find himself a seat but all the sofas and armchairs appear to be taken. In the end he finds an upright dining chair close to the door. The chair's single cushion slides about uncomfortably on the hard wooden seat. Croft looks around. He sees there are more people in the room than he thought at first, fifteen or twenty of them at least, many of them now talking quietly amongst themselves. Immediately opposite him, an obese woman in a brightly coloured smock dress lolls in a chintz-covered armchair. She has shoulder-length, lank-looking hair. Her forehead is shiny with grease, or perhaps it is sweat.

Her small hands lie crossed in her lap. The hands, which are surprisingly pretty, are adorned with rings. The woman smiles at him nervously. Quite unexpectedly, Croft feels a rush of pity for her, a sensation more intense than any he has experienced since leaving the prison. He had not expected to see women here.

"Hi," Croft says. He wonders if the woman can understand him, even. There is a blankness in her eyes, and Croft wonders if she's on drugs, not street drugs but prescription medicine, Valium or Prozac or Ativan. There was a guy Croft knew in prison who was always on about how the prescription meds—the bennies, as he called them—were deadlier than heroin.

"They eat your fucking mind, man." Fourboys, his name was, Douglas Fourboys, eight years for arson. Croft had liked him better than anyone, mainly because of the books he read, which he didn't mind lending to Croft, once he had finished them. He had an enthusiasm for Russian literature, Dostoevsky especially. Douglas Fourboys was a lifelong Marxist, but at some point during the six months leading up to Croft's release, he had found God. He claimed he'd been sent the gift of prophecy, though Croft suspected this probably had more to do with the dope Fourboys's girlfriend occasionally managed to smuggle past the security than with any genuine aptitude for seeing the future.

"You've got to be careful, man," Fourboys had said to him, just a couple of days before his release. "They're waiting for you out there, I can see them, circling like sharks."

Fourboys had definitely been stoned when he said that. He'd reached out and clutched Croft's hand, then tilted to one side and fallen asleep.

Croft misses Fourboys; he is the only person from inside that he does miss. He supposes he should visit him.

"We know who you are," the woman says suddenly. "You're going to help us speak with the master. We've seen your pictures." She smiles, her thin lips slick with spittle. Her words send a chill through Croft, though there is no real meaning to them that he can fathom. The woman is obviously vulnerable, mentally challenged. Clearly she needs protection. Croft feels anger at Symes for allowing her to be here unsupervised.

Suddenly Symes is there, standing behind him. He pushes something cold into Croft's hand, and Croft sees that it's a bottle of Budweiser. The thought of the beer entering his mouth makes Croft start salivating. He raises the bottle to his lips. The liquid is icy, familiar, heavenly. Croft feels numbness settle over him, an almost-contentment. Whatever is happening here need not concern him. It is only an hour.

"I see you've met Ashley," Symes says. He squats down next to the armchair, leaning in towards the fat woman and taking her hand. He presses his fingers into the flesh of her wrist as if to restrain her, as if she is something dangerous that needs to be managed. The woman shifts slightly in her seat, and Croft sees that her eyes, which appeared so dull, are now bright and alive. He cannot decide if it is wariness he sees in them, or cunning.

She doesn't like Symes, though, this seems clear to him. Join the club.

"Ashley is my wife," Symes says. He grins into the face of the woman, a smile of such transparent artifice it is as if both he and she are playing a practical joke at Croft's expense.

Suddenly, in the overheated room, Croft feels chilled to the bone.

Is Symes serious? Snatches of words and images play themselves across his brain like a series of film stills: Symes's grin, the woman's slack features, the sticky word *wife*.

You're wondering if they fuck, Croft thinks. Is that all it is, though? He takes another swig of the beer and the thoughts recede.

"Would you excuse me, just for a moment?" Symes says. "There's a phone call I need to make. I'll be right back." He stands and walks away. The woman in the armchair looks after him for a second, then strains forward in her seat and puts her hand on Croft's knee. Croft can smell her breath, a sickening combination of peppermints and something else that might be tuna fish.

"You know him," the woman says, and for a moment Croft imagines she's talking about Symes, though the words that follow make his supposition seem impossible. "Even though you don't know it yet, you know him. He'll steep all his children in agony. Not just the agony of knowing him, but true pain." She tightens her grip on his knee, and Croft realises that she is strong, much stronger than she appears, or than he would have believed.

The mad are always strong, Croft thinks. He does not know how he knows this, but he knows it is true.

"Who are you talking about?" Croft says quietly. "Who is the master?"

The woman leans towards him. Her face is now so close to his that her features seem blurred, and Croft thinks for a confused moment that she is about to kiss him.

He sees himself straddling her. Her mounded flesh is pale as rice pudding.

"He is the tiger," she says. She grins, and her grin is like Symes's grin, only, just like the Jesus man, she has a tooth missing. The sight of the missing tooth fills him with horror.

"I need to get out of here," he says. "I mean, I need to use the bathroom." The room feels unbearably hot suddenly, stifling with the scent of unwashed bodies. He places his half-drunk beer on the coffee table, and as he makes his way back to the hallway, he finds himself wondering if the woman will take advantage of his absence to taste the alcohol. He imagines her thin lips, clamping themselves around the mouth of the bottle in a wet, round "o."

He can hear Symes's voice, talking softly off in another room somewhere, but Croft ignores it. The staircase leads upwards to a square landing, with four doors leading off it, all of them closed. Croft tries one at random, not through any logical process of deduction but because it is closest. By a stroke of luck, the room behind it turns out to be the bathroom after all. Croft steps hurriedly inside and locks the door. He sits down on the closed toilet seat, covering his face with both hands. The room feels like it's rocking, slowly, back and forth, like a ship in a swell, though Croft knows this is only the beer, which he is unused to. He has barely touched a drop of alcohol since leaving prison. He presses his fingertips against his eyelids, savouring the darkness. After a minute or so, he opens his eyes again and stands up. He lifts the toilet seat, pisses in an arcing gush into the avocado toilet bowl. He washes his hands at the sink. His face, in the mirror above, looks pale and slightly dazed but otherwise normal. It is only when he goes out on the landing again that he sees the photographs.

There are six of them in all. They are arranged in two groups of three, mounted on the blank area of wall at the far end of the landing and directly opposite the bathroom door. He had his back to them before, Croft realises, which is why he didn't see them when he first came upstairs. He recognises them at once. He thinks it would be impossible for an artist not to recognise his own work. One of the photos is of Murphy, or rather Murphy's hands, secured behind his back with a twist of barbed wire. The Kennington case. Four of the other photos are also work shots, all photos he took for the Met in the course of his twenty-year career as a forensic photographer.

Lilian Beckworth, a car crash victim.

The Hallam Crescent flat, gutted by fire.

The underpass near Nunhead Station where the Cobb kid was found.

The sixth photo, not a work one, is of Rebecca Riding. The police believed it had been taken less than thirty minutes before her death.

Croft told his lawyer and the police that the photos they found at his house were not taken by him. His camera had been stolen, he said, and then later returned, placed on his front doorstep, wrapped carefully in a Tesco bag. Whoever left it there had not rung the bell. When Croft later developed the film, he found pictures he remembered taking at various sites around Lewisham and Manor Park. He also found the photos of Rebecca Riding.

"The photos are good though, aren't they, Dennis?" the cop kept saying. "They're no amateur job. You're a professional. You remember taking these, surely?"

Croft said he didn't, and kept saying it. In the end, he could hardly remember, one way or the other.

It was true that they were very fine photographs. He'd spent some time working on them in his darkroom. The excellence of the results surprised even him.

Croft turns away from the photographs and goes back downstairs. In the stuffy living room, they are all waiting, and for a moment, as he returns to his place near the doorway, Croft gets the feeling that he has been lured there on false pretences. He brushes the thought away, sits down on the uncomfortable wooden chair. The hour passes, and at the end of it, Croft cannot remember a single thing that has been said. People are standing, going out into the hallway, pulling on coats. As Croft moves to join them, he feels a hand on his arm. It is Richard Symes.

"Some of us have clubbed together to buy you this," he says. "Your work means a great deal to us here. We're hoping this will help you find your feet again."

He hands Croft a package, a small but heavy something in a red-and-white bag. Croft knows without having to be told that it contains a camera. The gift is so unexpected that he cannot speak. Symes is smiling but it looks like a snarl, and finally it comes to Croft that he has been drugged, that this is what has been wrong all along, it would account for everything.

Drugs in the Bud.

Bennies in the beer.

It's the only thing that makes sense. Fourboys was right.

Outside, he feels better. The air is cold, bright as a knife. The sensations of nausea and unreality begin to recede. Croft walks smartly away, away from the house, along Sydenham Park Road and all the way to the junction with Dartmouth Road. He stands there, watching the traffic, wondering how much of the past hour was actually real.

◦

The camera is a Canon, a top-of-the-range digital. It is not a hobby camera. Whoever chose it knew exactly what they were getting.

He has given up asking himself why this has been done for him. Having the camera in his hands is like coming alive again. He remembers the dream he had before he was in prison, his idea of giving up the police stuff and going freelance.

He has been taking photographs of the boy, Alexander. They are in the old Leegate shopping precinct just over the road. The boy is in a t-shirt and clean jeans, it is all perfectly harmless. When Croft returns the boy to the pub afterwards, Sandra is behind the bar. There is a complicated bruise on her upper arm, three blotches in a line, like careless fingerprints.

Croft has a bank account now, with his dole money in. He has filled in a couple of application forms for jobs. One is for a cleaning job with Lewisham Council, the other is for a shelf-stacking job at Sainsbury's. He can afford to buy a drink at the bar.

"Why is the pub called The Old Tiger's Head?" he asks Sandra McNiece.

"It's from when it was a coaching inn," says Sandra. "Tiger used to be a slang word, for footman. Because of the bright costumes they wore."

"Is that right?" Croft says. Croft briefly imagines a life in which he asks Sandra McNiece to run away with him. They will travel to Scotland, to Ireland, wherever she wants. He will take photos and the boy will go to school. He does not dare to take the daydream any further, but it is sweet, all the same, it is overwhelming.

"That's boring," Alex says. "I think it's because they once found a tiger's head inside the wardrobe. A mad king killed him and brought him to London, all the way from India."

Sandra laughs and ruffles his hair. "What funny ideas boys have," she says. "What are you doing in here, anyway? You should be upstairs."

⤙⤚

Croft buys a small folding table from the junk shop at the end of Lee Road that sells used furniture. He places objects on the table—an empty milk carton, two apples, a Robinson's jam jar filled with old pennies he found at the back of the wardrobe—and photographs them, sometimes singly, sometimes in different combinations. He places the table in front of the wardrobe, so the objects are shown reflected in the oval mirror. Croft experiments with taking shots that omit the objects themselves and show only their reflections. At first glance, they look like any of the other photos Croft has taken of the objects on the table. They're not, though; they're pictures of nothing. Croft finds this idea compelling. He remembers how when Douglas Fourboys was stoned he became terrified of mirrors and refused to go near them. "There are demons on the other side, you know," he said. "They're looking for a way through."

"A way through what?"

"Into our world. Mirrors are weak spots in the fabric of reality. Borges knew it, so did Lovecraft. You have to be careful."

"You don't really believe this stuff, do you?" Croft knew he shouldn't encourage Fourboys, but he couldn't help it; his stories were so entertaining.

"I believe some of it," Fourboys said. "You would too, if you knew what I know. There are people who are trying to help the demons to break through. They believe in the rule of chaos, of enlightenment through pain, you know, like the stuff in *Hellraiser* and in that French film, *Martyrs*. They call themselves Satan's Tigers." Fourboys took a coin out of his pocket and began swivelling it back and forth between his fingers. "If you knew how many of those sickos were on the loose, it would freak you out."

The next time the boy comes to visit him in his room, Croft shows him how to set up a shot, then lets him take some photographs of the Robinson's jam jar. Afterwards, Croft takes some photos of Alex's reflection. He has him sit on the edge of the bed in front of the mirror.

"Try and make yourself small," Croft says. "Pretend you're sitting inside a cupboard, or in a very cramped space."

The boy lifts both his feet up on to the duvet and then hugs his knees. In the mirror shots, he looks pale, paler than he does in real life. It's as if the mirror has drained away some of his colour.

"What's in there?" Alex says. He's staring at the chimney alcove, at the built-in cupboard that Croft has been unable to open.

"I don't know," Croft says. "It's locked."

"Perhaps it's treasure," says the boy.

"If you can find out where the key is, we can have a look."

"I know what it'll be." Alex grins, and Croft sees he has a tooth missing. "It'll be the tiger's head." He throws himself backwards on the bed and makes a growling noise. "I bet that's where they've hidden it."

"Isn't it time for your tea yet?" Croft says.

"I'm scared of tigers," the boy says. "If they come on the TV, I have to switch off."

That night, Croft dreams of Richard Symes. There has been a break-in at Symes's house and there are cops everywhere. They're trying to work out if any valuables have been stolen.

Symes's throat has been cut.

There is no sign of Ashley Symes, or anyone else.

◂◦▸

At his next meeting with Symes, Croft is able to tell him he's been offered the shelf-stacking job. Symes seems pleased.

"When do you start?" he says.

"Next Monday." He wonders if Symes will say anything to him about a burglary at his home, but he doesn't. Instead, Symes asks him how he's getting on with his new camera.

"It's great to use," Croft says. "The best I've had."

"Why don't you bring some of your work with you to show us when you come on Tuesday? I know Ashley would love that. Bring the boy with you, too, if you like."

How does Symes know about Alex? For a moment, Croft feels panic begin to rise up inside him. Then he remembers Symes knows the Mc-Nieces, that it was Symes who found him his room. "I couldn't," Croft says. "He's only eight. His mother wouldn't allow it."

"What she doesn't know won't hurt her. It would be an adventure for him. All boys love adventures."

Croft says he'll think about it. He thinks about himself and Alex, walking down the road like father and son. On his way back to London Bridge station, Croft buys Alex a present from one of the gift shops jammed in under the railway arches near Borough Market, a brightly coloured clockwork tiger with a large, looped key in its side. It is made of tin plate, MADE IN CHINA.

The journey from London Bridge to Lee takes seventeen minutes. As he mounts the stairs to his room, he meets Sandra coming down.

"I've just been trying to find you," she says. "I found this. Alex said you were looking for it."

She holds something out to him, and Croft sees it is a key. "It's for that cupboard in the chimney alcove," she says. "We've not opened it since we've been here, so God knows what's in there. Just chuck out anything you don't need."

"That's very good of you," Croft says. He searches her face, for tiredness or bruises, anything he can hate McNiece with, but today he finds nothing. He thinks about asking her to come up for a coffee but is worried that his offer might be misconstrued. He closes his fingers around the key. Its hard, irregular shape forms a core of iron at the heart of his hand.

It is some time before he opens the cupboard. He tells himself this is because he has things to do, but in reality it is because he is afraid of what he might find inside. Late afternoon shadows pour out of the oval mirror and rush to hide themselves in the corners and beneath the bed. As the room begins to fill up with darkness, Croft finds he can already imagine the stuffed tiger's head, the mummified, shrunken body of a child, the jam jar full of flies or human teeth. When he finally opens the cupboard it is empty. The inside smells faintly sour, an aroma Croft quickly recognises as very old wallpaper paste. The wallpaper inside the cupboard is a faded green colour. It is peeling away from the walls, and in one place right at the back it has fallen down completely. The wooden panel behind is cracked, and when Croft puts his fingers over the gap he can feel a faint susurrus of air, a thin breeze, trapped between the wooden back of the cupboard and the interior brickwork.

Croft puts his whole head inside the cupboard and presses his opened mouth to the draughty hole. He tastes brick dust, cool air, the smell of damp earth and old pennies.

He closes his eyes and then breathes in. The cold, metallic air tastes delicious and somehow rare, like the air inside a cave. He exhales, pushing his own air back through the gap, and it is if he and the building are breathing together, slowly in and out. It is then that he feels the thing pass into him, something old that has been waiting in the building's foundations, in the ancient sewer tunnels beneath the street, or somewhere deeper down even than that. Its face is a hideous ruin, and as Croft takes it into himself, he is at last granted the knowledge he has been fumbling for, the truth of who he is and what he has done.

Strange lights flicker across the backs of his closed eyelids, yellow stripes, like the markings on the metal tiger he bought for the boy near Borough Market.

You are ready now, says a voice inside his head. Croft realises it is the voice of Ashley Symes.

◂◦▸

And in the end, it is easy. Both McNieces are downstairs, working the bar. Alex is alone in the living room of the first floor flat. The carpet is a battleground, strewn with Transformers toys and model soldiers. The tin-plate tiger is surrounded by aggressive forces. The TV is playing quietly in the background.

When Croft sticks his head around the door and asks if Alex would like to come on an assignment with him, the boy says yes at once. The boy knows the word *assignment* has to do with photography because Croft has told him so.

"Where are we going?" Alex says. It is getting on towards his bedtime, but the unexpectedness of what they are doing has filled him with energy.

Croft knows that unless he is very unlucky, the boy's absence will not be noticed for at least three hours.

"To visit some people I know," Croft says. "They keep a tiger in their back garden."

The boy's eyes grow large.

"You're joking me," he says.

"That's for me to know and you to find out."

The boy laughs delightedly, and Croft takes his hand. The journey passes uneventfully. The boy seems captivated by every small thing—the pale mist rising up from the streets, the lit-up shop fronts, the endlessly streaming car headlights, yellow as cats' eyes.

The only glances they encounter seem benign.

When they arrive at Symes's house, Alex rushes up the driveway to the front door and rings the bell.

"And who is this young man?" Symes says, bending down.

"Dennis says you've got a tiger, but I don't believe him," says the child. He is beginning to flag now, Croft senses, just a little. He is overexcited. The slightest thing could have him in tears.

"We'll have to have a look, then, won't we?" Symes says. He places a hand on the boy's head. Croft steps forward out of the shadows and towards the door.

Once he is inside, he knows, it will begin. He and Ashley Symes will kill the child. The rest will watch.

"You have done well," Symes says to Croft, quietly. "This won't take long."

"Will there be cookies?" Alex says.

Croft stands still. He can feel the thing moving inside him, twisting in his guts like a cancer.

He wants to vomit. Croft gasps for breath, sucking in the blunt, smoky air, the scent of macadam, of the hushed, damp trees at the roadsides and spreading along all the railway lines of southeast London. The fleet rails humming with life, an antidote to ruin.

He smells the timeswept, irredeemable city and it is like waking up. Above him, bright stars throw up their hands in surprise.

"Come here to me, Sasha," Croft says. He is amazed at how steady his voice sounds. "There's no time now. We have to go."

"But the tiger," the child whimpers. He looks relieved.

"There are no tigers here," Croft says. "Mr. Symes was joking. Come on."

The boy's hand is once again in his and he grips it tightly.

"Will we be home soon?" says the boy.

"I hope so," Croft replies. "We should be, if a bus comes quickly."

He does not look back.

THE HOUSE ON COBB STREET

LYNDA E. RUCKER

Concerning the affair of the house on Cobb Street, much ink has been spilled, most notably from the pens of Rupert Young in the busy offices of the *Athens Courier*; Maude Witcover at the alternative weekly *Chronictown*; and independent scholar, poet, and local roustabout Perry "Pear Tree" Parry Jr. on his blog *Under the Pear Tree*. Indeed, the ink (or in the case of Parry, the electrons)—and those from whose pens (or keyboards) it spilled—are all that remain today of the incidents that came to be known locally (and colloquially) as the Cobb Street Horror. The house itself was razed, its lot now surrounded by a high fence bearing a sign that announces the construction presumably in progress behind it as the future offices of Drs. Laura Gonzales and Didi Mueller, DDS. The principal witnesses in this case did not respond to repeated enquiries, and in one case, obtained a restraining order against this author. And the young woman in question is said by all to have disappeared, if indeed she ever existed in the first place.

—*Ghosts and Ghouls of the New American South*, by Roger St. Lindsay, Random House, 2010

—◇—

I wanted to embed the YouTube video here, but it looks like it's been removed. It was uploaded by someone bearing the handle "cravencrane" who has no other activity on the site. Shot in low quality, perhaps with someone's cell phone, it showed a red-haired woman in a gray wool coat—presumably Felicia Barrow—not quite running, but walking away from the lens rapidly and talking over her shoulder as she went. "Of course Vivian existed," she said. "Of course she did. She was my friend. That hack would print anything to make his story sound more mysterious than it was. Roger St. Lindsay, that's not even his real name." And then she was out of the frame entirely, and the clip ended.

The snippet purported to be part of a documentary in progress known as *The Disappearance of Vivian Crane*, but little else has been found about its origins, its current status, or the people behind it, and it is assumed that the project is currently dead. Felicia Barrow was located but had no comment about either the project or the fate of the Cranes.

–Perry "Pear Tree" Parry, blog post at *Under the Pear Tree*, June 26, 2010

◄o►

Vivian wakes.

It is a night like any other night and not like any night she has known at all.

The heart of the house is beating. She can hear it, vessels in the walls, the walls that exhale with that life's breath that is just as sweet to the house's groaning floorboards and arched doorways and soaring cupolas as her own breath is to her; she can hear it, heart beating and moaning and sighing and "settling." That was what her mother used to call it, in the other old house they lived in way back when, her a skinny wild girl; and maybe "settling" was the right word for what that old house did, that old house that was never alive, never had a pulse and a mind and—most of all—a desire, but "settling" was the least of what this old house did. Vivian knows that if she doesn't know anything else at all.

This old house is not settling for anything. This old house is maybe waiting, and possibly thinking, and could be sleeping, even, but never settling.

This house is getting ready for something.

She can feel that like she can feel the other things. She has watched cats before, how they crouch to pounce, their muscles taut, *rippling under the skin* it's said, and she thinks it now about the house—even though it's a cliché (phrases become clichés because they're true, she tells her students)—this house is doing it, tense and expectant, counting time, ticking off years and months and weeks and days and hours and minutes and seconds and fragments of seconds and fragments of fragments and soon time itself degrades, disintegrates, and dies.

And then the alarm is screaming, and Vivian wakes for real.

‑‑◦‑‑

Waking for real had become an important benchmark, and sometimes it took as many as several hours for her to be certain she had done so. She would be standing up in front of a class of freshmen who exuded boredom and eagerness in equal parts, talking about narrative point of view in "A Rose for Emily," and the knowledge would grip her: *I am here, this is real, I am awake.* And then she would drift, like one of the sunlight motes in the bright windows, and the class would wait—their professor was weird, a lot of professors were weird, *I'm still wasted from last night, can I borrow your ID, did you hear, did you, did you*—and the dull cacophony of their voices, familiar and banal, would bring her back, but past that point she could never bring *them* back, and often as not had to dismiss the class to save herself the humiliation of trying and failing to reengage them.

That the house was haunted was a given. To recite the reasons she had known this to be the case from the moment she crossed the threshold was almost an exercise in tedium: there were the cold spots, the doors that slammed when no breeze had pushed them, the footsteps that paced in the rooms upstairs when she knew she was at home alone. But Chris had been so pleased, so happy to be moving back home. He'd found the house for sale and fallen in love with it, shabby as it was, battered by decades of student renters and badly in need of much repair and renovation but a diamond in the rough, he was sure, and how was she to tell him otherwise? It wasn't just that neither of them believed in such things; that was the least of it. But to suggest that the house was less than perfect in any way was to reject it, and, by extension, him.

Chris, as it turned out, had noticed those things as well.

◄◦►

Authorities have ruled the death of thirty-eight-year-old Christopher Crane a suicide, resulting from a single gunshot wound to the head.

Crane shot himself at approximately two a.m. on Thursday, July 22, in the backyard of the house on Cobb Street in West Athens that he shared with his wife, Vivian Crane.

According to Chief Deputy Coroner Wayne Evans, investigators discovered a note of "mostly incomprehensible gibberish" that is believed to be Crane's suicide note.

Crane was born and raised in Athens and had recently returned to Georgia after seventeen years in the Seattle area. . . .

–"Crane Death Ruled Suicide," by Rupert Young, *Athens Courier*, July 29, 2008

◄◦►

When you watched those movies or read those books—*The Amityville Horror* had been her particular childhood go-to scarefest—what you always asked yourself, of course, was *why don't they leave?* Why would anyone stay in places where terrifying apparitions leapt out at you, where walls dripped blood, where no one slept any longer and the rational world slowly receded and the unthinkable became real?

Countless storytellers worked themselves into contortions and employed ludicrous plot contrivances to keep their protagonists captive, and yet the answer, Vivian learned, was so much simpler: You stayed because you gave up. You succumbed to a kind of learned helplessness that convinced you that the veil between worlds had been pulled back and you could not escape; wherever you went, you would always be haunted.

You entered into an abusive relationship with a haunted house.

And of course, there was also Chris to be considered. If the house did, in fact, capture the spirits of the souls who died there, shouldn't she stick around to keep him company, in case he wanted to contact her, in case he needed her for something?

But Chris had remained strangely silent on the subject; he either couldn't or wouldn't talk to her. She found herself growing angry at his reticence, angrier even than she'd been at him in life, when the house and its ghosts first began to come between them, as he was pronouncing her anxiety within its walls "neurotic" and "crazy," not yet knowing all the while those same ghosts had their ectoplasmic fingers deep inside him, in his brain and his heart, twisting them into something she no longer knew.

He was soundproofing one of the downstairs rooms so he could record music there, and then he wasn't; he stopped doing much of anything at all, she later realized, save for going to work, network administering something or other, but even there—well, nobody was going to tell a suicide's widow that her dead spouse would have been fired in short order, had he not offed himself before that eventuality could come to pass. But she wasn't a professor of literature for nothing; subtext was her specialty. In every interaction with his ex-coworkers and former supervisor, she read it: he'd been neither well-liked nor competent, she surmised, and yet that wasn't the Chris she'd known and loved and married and moved into the house with. That wasn't her Chris, the Chris with the still-boyish flop of brown hair in his eyes and penchant for quoting from obscure spaghetti westerns. Not her Chris with his left hand calloused from the fret of his bass and his skill at navigating not just computers but workplaces and the people therein. And not just work: he had a warmth and generosity toward his fellow musicians that never failed to stagger her (a tireless ability to offer constructive feedback on the most appalling demos and YouTube uploads, because, he said, assholes were rampant enough in the music world without his increasing the net total assholery out there). Nobody disliked Chris, or at least not until the final months of his life.

That was the Chris the house made.

◄०►

The first time for her, it was the little girls.

They were the worst of all; they had come to her when she slept in the guest room, coughing and feverish. She moved there so as not to disturb Chris with her tossings and turnings, her sweating and chills. That first time, she woke and heard them, an explosion of vicious whispers like a burst of static, and one word distinguishable above the rest, *her, her,*

her—and she never knew that three letters, a single breathed syllable, could be weighted with so much hatred. Next she became aware that she could not move, that her arms and legs and indeed her entire body seemed clamped in a vise; and finally, she knew that the vicious little girls floated somewhere above and just behind her head. She could see them in her mind's eye: four or five of them all with wide pale eyes, pert little noses, mouths half open to display rows of sharp, shiny teeth.

The morning after, she attributed it to fever (although she was really not *that* sick), or something else, googled phrases like *hypnagogic hallucination* and *sleep paralysis* and gazed on the Fuseli painting until she could no longer bear the image of the demon on the woman's breast and the mad-eyed horse thrusting its demented face through the curtains. She drank her coffee, cycled to campus (a bad idea; she had to pull over for three coughing fits in the two short miles she rode), and forgot about it.

She didn't forget about it; she'd had dreams stay with her before, mostly the unpleasant kind, and she hated those days, haunted by her own un conscious. She knew instinctively this was different. This was something from outside her. She could not have produced objective proof to show to someone that this was the case. She knew all about the games the mind could play to make oneself believe in its wild flights of fancy. And she knew in the depths of her soul (in which she did not believe, any more than she believed in ghosts or haunting) that the kind of words she'd googled and the daylight world with its prosaic explanations and even the most unwholesome depths of her own brain had nothing to do with the things that had stolen into her room that night and despised her with such vehemence.

She had always thought of hate as a human emotion, a uniquely human frailty, a condition from which we might have to evolve to survive. Never before had she considered the possibility that hate was the most essential thing there was; that the universe was an engine driven by hate, animals savaging one another, atoms smashing together, planets and worlds dying in explosions of rock and fire. And to have so much of that directed at her. *At her.* She sat stunned in her office at Park Hall, her eyes fixed on the fake wood grain of her desk, someone knocking and knocking at her door and she knew it was a student because he'd scheduled an appointment with her and yet she could not answer it, she could not move, she could only sit paralyzed by her newfound knowledge, and at last the knocking ceased and went away and she wished she could, too.

◄◦►

The existence of Christopher Crane has never been in question. The roots of the Crane family run deep in the soil of Clarke County, and though Crane himself was away for many years, he was fondly remembered as one of the founding members of the indie/alt-country group the Gaslight Hooligans, who went on to moderate mainstream success following his departure.

At least, this is how I remember Chris Crane, as do a number of people I know, but others insist on a different narrative. That Chris Crane never left town, that the Gaslight Hooligans broke up more than a decade ago after playing a few house parties and one or two dates in local clubs, to indifferent reception. Same as hundreds of other bands that spring up here each year and are soon forgotten.

Sources online and off are mixed in their reportage, but one thing is certain, that at least two and possibly more conflicting versions of the life of Chris Crane are out there. This introduces a disconcerting possibility: that we are all, now, existing in a dubiously real and unstable present, one in which Vivian Crane was and was not, and the house on Cobb Street at the heart of it all.

–Perry "Pear Tree" Parry, Google cache of a blog post made at *Under the Pear Tree*, July 9, 2010 (not available on the blog itself)

◄◦►

It is six months since she lost Chris. Her best friend, Felicity, has come from Seattle to visit her, has been staying in the house with her and urging her to get out. She doesn't need to do anything big, Felicity says, but she needs to do *something* besides go between home and campus. (This awful home, Felicity doesn't say, this terrible place that took Chris and is taking you. But Felicity knows.)

But she's hiding something from Felicity, and she's increasingly sure Chris was hiding the same thing from her in his last days. It's something that happened just before Felicity arrived, and afterward she tried to make Felicity postpone her visit (forever), but Felicity was having none of that. Felicity thinks Chris's suicide has opened the gulf between them, best friends from the age of five gone suddenly quiet and awkward in one another's presence. Felicity has no idea that the gulf is so much greater than that.

Vivian does not know whether to be overjoyed or horrified that she now bears physical proof that she isn't mad. A week before Felicity's visit, she is sleeping in the bed she and Chris shared. She has woken paralyzed once again, and something is screaming in the walls. This is not so bad; at least it's in the walls, and not in the room with her. She lies there and thinks about "The Yellow Wallpaper," a story she has taught to countless freshmen, and the poor insane narrator following the twisty patterns and the women creeping beneath them. Thinking of these creeping women serves, oddly, to calm her as the screamer eventually winds down, perhaps because she is able to make them into academic abstractions and symbols while the suffering of the screaming woman in the walls is so very real.

But it is not long before she senses a presence beside her, in the very bed next to her, and this is so terrible that she starts to shake all over in spite of the paralysis. If it were Chris, she would be sobbing with joy, but it is not Chris. It is something else. She cannot tell if it is male or female, or neither, or both. The something else takes her hand, weaves its awful fingers through hers in that intimate fashion, and she realizes that before now she has never known what *cold* truly means. From the palm of her hand, the cold blooms into her wrist, up her arm, and then throughout her body, and she thinks *this is my death* and knows they will find her some hours or days later and pronounce it "natural causes" without knowing there is nothing in the world so unnatural as the thing that has hold of her in the bed at that moment.

And then it's gone; she's heaving and sputtering and gasping and racing for the bathroom where she steps into a scalding hot shower, pajamas and all (for she is afraid to be naked), and she is scrubbing herself, shivering still, and her now ungripped hand is cold, so cold, and that's when she first uncurls her fingers from her palm and sees it there, a scorched circular shape, and then she looks closer and notices the head of the snake in the fleshy part at the base of her thumb and realizes what she is seeing: an Ouroboros, the serpent devouring its own tail. And she knows in that moment that she has been claimed by something terrible.

◄o►

The house on Cobb Street possessed several unique properties in regards to its purported haunting. There appeared to be no originating event, no horrific murders, no ghastly past prior to its possession of the Crane couple (and after reviewing the evidence, I believe this is indeed the best description of the effect the house had on Christopher and Vivian Crane). Locals remember no unsavory legends attached to the house. For roughly three decades prior to its purchase by the Cranes, it was simply another decaying student residence. The house was previously owned by two sisters, who spent their entire lives there. Its Wisconsin-based owner, a great-niece who died shortly after the Cranes purchased it, left its management to the local Banks Realty, who say no unusual problems were ever encountered beyond the usual wear and tear.

Yet few of its residents from the years immediately prior to the Crane purchase could be tracked down. Of those who reported any paranormal experiences at all, each attributed it to the ingestion of psilocybin mushrooms or LSD. All three were located as in-patients at separate mental health facilities. None had been roommates with or were aware of the others, nor had any of them discussed their experiences with anyone else, but all date the onset of their initial mental illness as subsequent to their residence at the house on Cobb Street. Each claimed to have once borne a circular tattoo on the palm of their left hand, visible now only in the faintest outline of one of the three: that of the snake Ouroboros, the symbol for infinity.

It appears to have been a symbol with which Vivian Crane was obsessed as well, since, following her disappearance, numerous versions of it were said to have been found scratched on the walls throughout her house. This evidence, combined with the temporal shifts reported by Ms. Crane and all three of the former residents interviewed, originally led this author to theorize that this particular "haunting" is an occurrence on the order of "freak" weather events such as rains of frogs, sudden tornadoes, and so on. In other words, not ghosts at all, but an anomaly in the very fabric of time and space, burst into existence at some stage in the last few years. And the Ouroboros symbols suggest some sort of intelligence lurking behind this anomaly, something perhaps even more fearsome than the ghosts that populate the rest of this volume.

–*Ghosts and Ghouls of the New American South*, by Roger St. Lindsay, Random House, 2010

◄◦►

I've been reading Roger St. Lindsay's account of our local haunting, and reckless and inaccurate as his speculations appear to me (not to mention entirely ignorant of the laws of physics, and this apparent even to myself who knows as little about the topic as anyone), his method is not entirely one of madness. His history of the house is more or less corroborated, although his theories do border on the ludicrous. By the way, an alert reader recently forwarded to me the details, available only with a "pro"-level subscription, of an IMDB page regarding the documentary *The Disappearance of Vivian Crane*. Currently Vincent Llewellyn, who made his name with the Poltergeist Rising series of fictional "found footage" horror movies, is attached to the project. Apparently, however, production on the Crane documentary was halted due to legal concerns.

–Perry "Pear Tree" Parry, blog post at *Under the Pear Tree*, August 12, 2010

◄◦►

Vivian wakes.

It is not a night like any other night. At first she cannot be certain why this is the case, and then she realizes: it's because of the silence.

This is a terrible thing. Like the silence of children up to no good, except this silence is sinister, not mischievous. She reaches to touch Chris and of course he is not beside her. She does this almost every night, but this time it reminds her of that other night. The last night. She had not been immediately concerned—why should she have been?—even though it wasn't like him to be up in the middle of the night, but then Chris had not seemed much like himself for some time. That night, she reached for the lamp and in the little pool of light she found her robe. She peeked into the guest room and at the sofa and Chris was nowhere. She went through the house looking for him, still not concerned, because none of it seemed real although she was certain it was not a dream.

Back up the stairs and down them again. It was here she began to call his name, here she started to get really worried. She wanted to be angry, because angry was better than worried, and she thought that she would be angry later, after finding him, angry at him for frightening her and happy for the chance to be angry because it would mean nothing was really wrong.

Later the questions would come, disbelieving: how could she have slept through the shotgun blast? Had she been drinking? Did she take drugs? Sleeping pills? Did she and Chris have a fight beforehand? They needn't have blamed her; she blamed herself. *How could you not have known, how could you not have done something, how could you, how could you?*

She had not been the one who found him propped against the back fence, his head ruined; a neighbor phoned the police shortly after it happened, reporting a gunshot, but this could not be possible, for she walked up and down the stairs and from room to room for hours, searching for him, long before she stumbled into a backyard awash in spinning lights and the sound of police radios and a cacophony of panic.

Some nights, the best nights, the police never arrived. On those nights, she searched until she, Vivian Crane née Collins—born Vancouver, Washington, June 10, 1971, raised in Seattle, the shy bookish only child of a single mother (father present only following occasional bursts of paternal guilt)—ceased to exist, or became a ghost, if that was indeed how one did become a ghost; she simply searched and searched the rooms, and the stairs, and the hallways again and again until she no longer remembered who she was or what she was looking for, and sometimes she woke and still could not remember for long moments where she belonged.

Driving Felicity to the airport in Atlanta at the end of her visit almost saved her. Almost. She remembered thinking that—remembered the hard and beautiful reality of Interstate 285 with its multiple lanes of frantic traffic, the billboards and the chain restaurants and the warehouses and the mundanity of it all. At Hartsfield, the busiest airport in the world, she stood in line at the check-in counter with Felicity and thought about sleek planes bearing her away to someplace, any other place, a place that was safe and faraway, and then she saw Felicity through the security gate. Afterward, she sat in the atrium in the main terminal for a while and chewed on a pesto chicken panini from the Atlanta Bread Company and thought about what to do next.

In the end, it was all too overwhelming: *where would I go how would I explain to people what would happen to me my job my life my belongings I don't know any other way.*

And she got in her car and she drove back home again.

Chris's death had branded her as much as the Ouroboros symbol ever would.

So now she wakes to the silence of infinity. She has a singular thought, to leave the house, and it is so strong she wonders that she has not thought it before. She has been sleeping in a T-shirt and a pair of yoga pants (she used to take yoga, long ago when she also used to be a real person); to change, to even find her shoes would delay her disastrously, and her feet hit the floor with a thump and she is running down the stairs; she half expects the corridor to stretch out forever before her like a horror movie or a dream but the corridor is normal and the door springs open to her touch and outside the stars are reeling and she gasps lungfuls of air that are not house-air and she is free; it is so easy, she need only not go back inside again. She doesn't have her keys (no time) so she cannot take the car, but she can run now, up the street, she can run forever if she has to, because even the simple act of breathing and running is an act of living and not one of extinction.

But here is nothing but silence. A dead, dark street, familiar houses blank and empty, no sound of traffic from the busy street a block away. No dogs barking, no sirens, nothing.

She will run back into the house and reset it; this time it will work.

Back inside the house. Deep breaths on the house side of the front door, and how has she not noticed the corrupted air, the choking rot and decay? Again she opens the door; again she steps outside; again and again and again and again and she never imagined eternity like this, isolated even from her fellow ghosts, an infinity of repeating the same futile action again and again until time itself does die.

→◇←

It is Athens's very own urban legend, one of short duration and dubious provenance, a tale of a woman who disappeared not only from her own life but from the lives of all of us. There is no record of her employment as an adjunct instructor at the university, though a few former students claim to recall taking her class. Chris Crane lived and died alone in the house on Cobb Street, although many insist this was not the case; some say his wife stayed there after his death, the wife in whom no one can quite believe or disbelieve in any longer. Some say it was she who was haunted, not the house, and she brought the haunting to all of us. Some say memory is forever shifting, never reliable; we take it on faith that we have lived all the days of our lives up to this moment.

But the handful of students who claim to remember Vivian Crane all produce the same account of the last day she turned up to class.

"She was going on and on about a snake eating itself, about time turning itself inside out and what would happen if you got caught in something like that, and where would something like that come from—God or another human being or just a natural force in the universe. And then she showed us this weird tattoo of the snake on the palm of her hand," says one young woman, who asked only to be identified by her first name, Kiersten. "And she said, 'What would it be like if reality had to constantly readjust itself in order to make things fit—what would it be like for the ones left behind?'"

This story is roughly the same as that told by two other individuals, both of whom asked not to be named or quoted at all. A fourth former student, who recounted a similar tale (with a few variations), has since recanted and asked not to be contacted again. When I attempted to follow up with the others, I was unable to find anything about them. I did contact the recanted student despite his request, but he would not speak with me and indeed purported not to know me.

And so it goes: the mystery appears to be solving itself by scrubbing out its own traces until there will be no mystery left at all.

But Chris Crane was a friend of mine; we grew up together, we went to college together, we did stupid things together, and had he gone away for seventeen years and come back with a wife, surely I would be one of the first to know about it?

–"The Crane Enigma," Maude Witcover, *Chronictown*, week of July 24–July 30, 2009

◄○►

She cycled home from campus that day as fast as she could, like she was outrunning something, even though she knew whatever it was could never be outpaced. She thought briefly of taking refuge in a church on the way; she had not believed in so very long that she was surprised at the tiny seed of comfort that began to unfurl deep in her chest when she thought it, but the only church she passed was the Southern Baptist one with the all-trespassers-will-be-towed sign in their parking lot and a dubious reputation with the progressive neighborhood in which it sat, and she imagined its doors would be locked literally, no need for the figurative.

She rode as fast as she could but it is not possible to ride fast enough when infinity itself is at your heels.

⟶⟨○⟩⟵

A small assortment of reporters and curiosity-seekers were on hand today for the planned demolition of the house at the center of what has come to be known as the Cobb Street Horror. The house had, in recent months, following the disappearance of Vivian Crane, become a major nuisance for law enforcement and neighbors, as several self-styled "urban explorers" broke in to photograph the bizarre signs and symbols—purportedly left on the walls by Ms. Crane—and a series of mounting disturbances were reported in the vicinity. Said disturbances included the sound of a woman screaming, day and night; the sight of several little girls running from the front of the house; and a figure whom no witness could adequately or consistently describe in terms of sex, age, or appearance crawling about the perimeter of the house.

Although the "urban explorers" spoke of signs and glyphs and drawings of the now-famous Ouroboros throughout the house, none of them ever produced any identifiable photograph from inside. A number of photography methods were experimented with, from top-of-the-line digital technology to old 35mm film and even a Polaroid at one stage, but neither the least nor the most sophisticated technologies produced any images. Save for one. One resourceful young woman went so far as to construct a "pinhole" camera out of a cardboard box, and with that captured a single image: in a low right-hand corner near the front door, written in very small letters with a ballpoint pen (as the woman described it), were the words "This house erases people."

Paranormal investigators assert that the existence of this photograph supports the idea that Vivian Crane herself was trying urgently to convey something important to those who read it; if so, however, it was that one time only, for while others who entered the house reported seeing the graffiti, no one else was able to reproduce the pinhole camera's photograph, not even the photographer herself.

The demolition of the house on Cobb Street commenced without incident; in fact, it was so routine that bystanders quickly lost interest and dispersed.

–Perry "Pear Tree" Parry, blog post at *Under the Pear Tree*, October 19, 2010

-◦-

The heart of the house is lost. The heart of the house is beating. The heart of the house is bleeding. The heart of the house is breaking. The heart of the house is longing, mourning, searching, willing itself back into being, circles within circles, time turned inside out. The heart of the house, like all of us, is mad and lonely and betrayed.

-◦-

No unusual activity has been detected along Cobb Street since the house was razed and the dental offices built. The dentists at the site report a thriving practice. Today, fewer and fewer locals appear willing or able to talk about the incident in the house on Cobb Street.

The symbol of snakes twining round a rod known as the caduceus is sometimes used on medical signs although in fact this represents a confusion with the single-serpented Rod of Asclepius, and thus this author feels it would be irresponsible to speculate about or attach any significance to the inclusion of the similar (if symbolically quite different) Ouroborous on the modest sign on the front lawn of the brick building. It ought, however, to be noted that on the day this author visited, several little girls were engaged in making similar chalk drawings on the sidewalk in front of the offices. On attempting to question them, this author was informed that they were not allowed to speak with strangers.

This author's sensitivity to the unsettling effects of their shrill voices and the flash of their fingers gripping the chalk and the sound of the chalk scratching at the sidewalk are all most likely attributable to the severe fever this author subsequently suffered through in his hotel room later that night.

For now, we can only say that the house on Cobb Street has gone, and has taken its mysteries with it.

–From the ebook edition of *Ghosts and Ghouls of the New American South*, by Roger St. Lindsay, published with added material in 2012

THE SOUL IN THE BELL JAR

KJ KABZA

Ten lonely miles from the shores of the Gneiss Sea, where the low town of Hume rots beneath the mist, runs a half-wild road without a name. Flanked by brambles and the black, it turns through wolf-thick hollows, watched by yellow eyes that glitter with hunger and the moon. The wolves, of course, are nothing, and no cutthroat highwayman ever waited beneath the shadows of those oaks. There are far worse things that shamble in the dark. This is the road that skirts Long Hill.

So the coachman declared, and so Lindsome Glass already knew. She also knew whose fault the shambling things were, and where their nursery lay: in the great, moaning house at Long Hill's apex.

She knew anxiety and sorrow, for having to approach it.

"Can't imagine what business a nice young miss like you has with the Stitchman," said the coachman.

Lindsome knew he was fishing for gossip. She did not reply.

"A pretty young miss like you?" pressed the coachman. Their vehicle was a simple horse trap, and there was nowhere to sit that was away from his dirty trousers and wine-stained smile. "You can't be, what, more than eleven? Twelve? Only them scienticians go up there. Unless you's a new Help, is that it? The ol' Stitchman could use a new pair of hands, says me. That big ol' house, rottin' up in the weeds with hardly nobody to tend to it none."

He laughed. "Course, it's no wonder. You couldn't get Help up there for all the gold in Yorken." He eyed her sideways. "So what's he have on *you*?"

The road wound upward, the branches overhead thinned, and the stones beneath the wheels took on the dreary glow of an overcast sky. November in Tattenlane meant sunshine, but Lindsome was not in Tattenlane anymore.

"Eh?" the coachman pressed.

Lindsome turned her pale face away. She fought against the quiver in her jaw. "Mama and Papa have gone on a trip around the world. They didn't say for how long, but I'm to stay here until they return. The Stitchman is my great-uncle."

Startled into silence, the coachman looked away.

The nameless road flattened, and the mad, untamed lawn of Apsis House sprawled into view. It clawed to the horizons, large as night, lonely as the world.

⋘

When Lindsome alighted with her single hat box and carpetbag, there was only one sour-mouthed, middle-aged man to meet her. He was tall and stooped, with shoulders too square and a neck too short, giving him an altogether looming air of menace. "Took your time, didn't you?"

Behind Lindsome, the coachman was already retreating down Long Hill. "I—I'm sorry. The roads were—"

"Where are your manners?" the sour-mouthed man demanded. "Introduce yourself."

Lindsome bit her lip. The quiver in her jaw threatened to return. *I must not cry*, she told herself. *I am a young lady.* Lindsome gripped the hem of her white dress and dropped into a graceful curtsey. "I . . . beg your pardon, sir. My name is Lindsome Glass. How do you do? Our meeting is well."

"S'well," the man replied shortly. "That's better. Now take your things and come inside. Ghost knows where that lack-about Thomlin is. Doctor Dandridge is on the cusp of a singular work, one of the greatest in his career, and he and I have far more valuable things to do with our time than coddle you in welcome."

Lindsome nearly had to run to keep up with the man's long, loping strides. "The house has three main floors, one attic, and two basements," he said, leading her past a half-collapsed carriage house. "Attic is dangerous and off-limits. Third floor is Help's quarters and off-limits. Basements are the laboratories, so they are *definitely* off limits, especially to careless little children."

The man pushed through a back door that cried on rust-thick hinges. Lindsome followed. The interior had a damp, close smell of things forgotten in the rain, and the air was clammy and chill. A small, useless fire guttered in a distant grate. Pots and pans, dingy with age and wear, hung from beams like gutted animals. Lindsome set down her hatbox and touched a bunch of drying sage. It crumbled like a desiccated spiderweb.

The man grabbed her wrist. "And don't. Touch. Anything."

Lindsome fearfully withdrew her hand. "Yes, sir."

A middle-aged woman, generous in girth but mousy in the face, hobbled out from a pantry, wiping her hands on her flour-smeared apron. "Good afternoon, Mister Chaswick, sir." She turned to Lindsome. Her smile was kind. "Is this the young miss? Oh, so pale, with such lovely dark hair. You'll be a heartbreaker someday, won't you? What's your name?"

"This is Lindsome Glass," said Chaswick. "Mind you watch her."

"Yes, Mister Chaswick."

"Don't trouble to see her up. I'll do it."

"Thank you, Mister Chaswick."

"Don't thank me. With your knees it takes you a century to get up the bloody staircase."

Chaswick led Lindsome deeper into the house, under moldering lintels, through crooked doorways, past water-damaged wainscoting and rooms hung with peeling wallpaper. The carcasses of upturned insects lay in corners, legs folded neatly in rictus. Paintings lined the soot-blackened walls, and Lindsome thought that perhaps they had portrayed beautiful scenes, once, but now most were so caked with filth that it was hard to divine their subjects. Here, a lake? There, a table of hunting bounty? Many were portraits with tarnished nameplates. Any names still legible meant nothing. Who was Marilda Dandridge, anyway?

"Are you paying attention?" Chaswick demanded. "Breakfast's at seven, supper's at noon, and dinner's at seven. We don't have tea or any of that Tatterlane nonsense here. Bath day is Sunday, wash day is Monday, and if you'd like to occupy yourself, I suggest the library on the second floor, as it contains a number of volumes that will ensure the moral betterment of a young person such as yourself."

"Do you have any picture books?" Lindsome asked.

Chaswick frowned. "I suppose you could borrow one of your great-uncle's illustrated medical atlases. Perhaps Porphyry's *Intestinal Arrangements of the Dispeptic* or Gharison's *Common Melancholia in the Spleen of the Breeding Female*."

Lindsome looked down at her shoes. "Never mind."

"You may also explore the grounds," Chaswick continued. "But don't cross paths with the gardener. Understand? If you ever hear the gardener working, turn around and go back at once.

"And mind the vivifieds. Doctor Dandridge is a brilliant, highly prolific man, and you'll see a great many examples of his work roaming throughout the area, many of which do not have souls consanguineous to their bodies. However, none of the vivifieds that Doctor Dandridge and I have created for practical purposes is chimeric, so you may safely pat the house cats and the horses in the stables. If you'd like to go for a ride . . .."

Something colorful moved at the edge of Lindsome's vision. Surprised at something so bright in so dreary a place, she stopped and backtracked. She peered around a corner, down a short hall sandwiched between a pair of much grander rooms.

The door at the end of the hall stood ajar. A handsbreadth of room beckoned, sunny yellow and smelling of lavender. A bookcase stood partially in view, crammed with spinning tops, painted wooden blocks, tin soldiers, stuffed animals, rattles, little blankets, papers cleverly folded into birds . . .

Lindsome stepped forward.

A woman exited the room. Her movements were quick, though she was old and excessively thin, with dark circles about her despairing eyes. She grasped the doorknob with bloodless talons, pulling it shut and locking it with a tiny iron key.

She turned and saw Lindsome.

Her transformation into rage was instantaneous. "What are you doing?" the woman bellowed, baring her long, gray teeth. "Get out of this hall! Get away from here!"

Lindsome fled to Chaswick.

"What's this?" said Chaswick, turning. "What! Have you not been following me?"

"There was a woman!" Lindsome said, dropping her things. "A thin woman!"

Chaswick grabbed Lindsome's wrist again. He bent over and pulled her close—lifted her, even, until she was nearly on her tiptoes and squirming with discomfort and alarm.

"That's Emlee, the housekeeper. Mind her too." Chaswick narrowed his eyes. "And that little hallway between the study and the card room? Definitely, *absolutely* off limits."

◄◦►

Chaswick deposited Lindsome in front of a room on the second floor. As soon as he had withdrawn down the grand staircase, Lindsome set her things inside and made a survey of the rest of the level. The afore-mentioned library was spacious and well stocked but poorly kept, with uneven layers of dust and book bindings faded by sun. Many volumes had been reshelved unevenly, incorrectly, or even upside-down, if at all.

Most of the other rooms were unused, their furniture wholly absent or in deep slumber beneath moth-eaten sheets. Two of the rooms were locked, or perhaps even rusted shut, including one next to what she assumed were her great-uncle's personal quarters, since they were the largest and, she could only surmise, at one time, the grandest. Now, like all else in Apsis House, their colors and details had darkened with soot and neglect, and Lindsome wondered how, if Dr. Dandridge were so brilliant, he could fail to control such misery and decay.

While exploring the first floor more thoroughly, she came across a squat, surly man in overalls who was pasting paper over a broken window in the Piano Room. He introduced himself as Thomlin, the Housemaster. Lindsome politely asked how did he do. Thomlin said he did fine, as long as he took his medicine and, as an illustration produced a silver flask, from which he took a hearty pull.

"May I ask you something, Mister Thomlin? What's at the end of the little hallway? In the yellow room?"

The house'm scowled as he lifted his paste brush from the bucket and slapped it desultorily over the glass. "Nothin'," he said. "Nothin' that a good girl should stick'er nose in. How a man wants to grieve, that's his business. No, no, I've said too much already." Juggling flask and brush, he took another medicinal dose. "I know everything that happens and ever did happen in these walls, you understand, inside and out. Wish I didn't, but I do. Housemaster, that's me. All these poor bastards—oops, pardon my language, young miss—I mean all these poor folks walk around in a fog a' their own problems, but a Housemaster sees everything as The Ghost sees it: absolute and clear as finest crystal, as not a soul else can ever understand. But good men tell no tales anyway. An' a gooder man you won't find either side of this whole blasphemous Long Hill heap. Why don't you go play outside? But don't never interrupt the gardener. Hear?"

Lindsome did not want to explore the grounds, but she told herself, *I must be brave, because I am a young lady*, and went outside with her head held high. Nonetheless, she did not get far. The weeds and brambles of the neglected lawn had long since matured into an impenetrable thicket, and Lindsome could barely see the rooftops of the nearby outbuildings above the wild creepers, dying leaves, needle-thin thorns, and drab, stenchful flowers. The late autumnal blossoms stank of carrion and sulfur, mingled with the ghastly sickly sweetness of mothballs. Lindsome pulled one sleeve over her hand and held it to her wrinkled nose as she picked her way along a downward-sloping animal trail that ran near the main house, the closest navigational relief in this unrelenting jungle, but she could get no corresponding relief from the smell.

She rounded a barberry bush. A little scream squeezed from behind her hand.

The stench wasn't the flowers. It was vivifieds.

In her path, blocking it completely, stood a white billy goat. He did not breathe or move. His peculiar, tipped-over eyes were motionless, his sideways pupils like twin cracks to the Abyss.

His belly had burst, and flies looped around his gaping bowels in humming droves.

Heart pounding, Lindsome backed away. The goat did nothing. Its gaze remained fixed at some point beyond her shoulder. As she watched, bits of its flesh grew misty, then resolidified. *It's all right*, Lindsome told herself. *It's just an old vivified, rotten enough for the soul to start coming loose. It's so old it doesn't know what it is or how to act. See? It's staying right there.*

Push past it. It will never notice.

Lindsome shuddered. But she was a young lady, and young ladies were always calm and regal and never afraid.

So Lindsome lifted the hem of her dress, as if preparing to step through a mud puddle, and inched her way toward and around the burst-open creature.

Its foul-smelling fur, tacky with ichor, brushed the whiteness of her garment. Lindsome closed her eyes and bit her lip, enough to bring pain, and a fly buzzed greedily in her ear. *I am not afraid. I am not afraid.*

She passed the goat.

At the first possible moment, she dropped her hem and sprinted down the path. The thicket thinned out into a place where the trail wasn't as clear, but she kept going, crashing through brittle twigs and dead undergrowth, prompting vivified birds to take wing. The corpses were poor fliers, dropping as swiftly as they'd risen. One splatted onto a boulder at the edge of the path, hard enough for the stitched-on soul to be shaken loose entirely in a shimmer of mist; the physical shell, without anything to vivify it, shrank in volume like a dried-up fruit.

The faint trail turned abruptly into a long, empty clearing that stretched back toward the house. The vista had been created with brisk violence: every stubborn plant, whether still verdant or dormant for the season, had been uprooted and lay in careless, half-dried piles, revealing tough, rocky soil. A second path connecting to this space had been widened and its vegetation thoroughly trampled. Lindsome silently blessed the unseen gardener's vigorous but futile work ethic and, slowing to a breathless, nervous walk, crossed the clearing. Despite the portending stink, there were no vivifieds in sight.

But as the path resumed, the stench grew stronger yet. Rot and cloying sweetness clogged Lindsome's nose so badly that her eyes watered and she breathed through her mouth. Young ladies remained calm and regal, Lindsome supposed, but they were also not stupid. Perhaps it was time to turn back.

The path ended at a set of heavy double doors.

To be truthful, a number of paths ended at these doors, with at least four distinct trails converging at the edges of the small, filth-caked patio. Lindsome imagined that her great-uncle, along with the unpleasant

Chaswick, exited from these doors when making expeditions into the haunted thicket for the few live specimens that must remain. *Do they only catch the old and injured,* she wondered, *or do they murder creatures in their prime, only to sew their souls right back on again?*

Lindsome tried the doors. They opened with ease.

The revealed space was not some dingy mudroom or rear hall, as Lindsome had expected, but a room so wide, it could have served as a stable were it not for its low ceiling and unfinished back. Instead of meeting a rear wall, the flagstone floor disintegrated into irregular fragments and piled up onto a slope of earth.

Three long tables ran down the center of the room to Lindsome's right, the final one disappearing into the total blackness of the room's far end. The tables were stone, their surfaces carved with deep grooves that terminated at the edges, above stained and waiting buckets.

Melted candles spattered the tables' surfaces. There were no windows.

The stench of the place flowed outward like an icy draft. Lindsome left a door open behind her, held her nose, and took a step inside. Even when breathing through her mouth, the vivified odor was a soup of putrification that clotted at the back of her throat, thick enough to drip into her belly. The sensation was unendurable. Surely that was a stone staircase leading up over the unfinished back wall, into less offensive parts of the house?

Three steps toward the staircase, Lindsome made the mistake of glancing behind her.

The entire front wall, lined floor to ceiling with cages and bars, bore an unliving library of vivifieds, every creature too large for its pen. Stoats stood shoulder-to-shoulder with badgers and owls, and serpents had no room to uncurl in their tiny cubes. Rabbit fur comingled with hawk feathers. Paws tapped and noses twitched and bodies lurched gently from side to side, but that great wall of shifting corpses, scales and hide and stripes, made no sound. Each rotting throat was silent.

Three hundred pairs of eyes watched Lindsome, flashing yellow and green, white and red. She fell into a table, hitting her shoulder against the stone.

Get up. Run away. She daren't breathe. *You silly fool. The ground was sloping outside. Remember? This is a basement.*

You cannot be here.

A door squealed open. A trickle of light dribbled down the steps.

Lindsome dove away from the table and behind the staircase's concealing bulk.

The door at the top opened fully. Candlelight flowed down the steps now, making hundreds of vivified eyes sparkle. "The sea lion, I think," said a voice. It was papery and thin, like a flake of ash that would crumble at the barest touch. "At the far end."

"Really, Albion," said Chaswick, stepping down onto the flagstones. He held high a five-branched candelabrum, his shadow stretching behind him. "We're overpreparing, don't you think?"

"Oh no, not hardly." An old, old man shuffled in Chaswick's wake. His head, wreathed in a wispy halo of white and framed by sizeable ears, seemed bowed under the weight of constant thought across many decades. His knobby fingers would not stop undulating, like twin spiders in a restless sleep. "One last test, before Thursday. I'm certain that a Kell Stitch at the brain stem, instead of a Raymund, will surprise us."

Chaswick's back heaved in a sigh. "I maintain that the original protocol would have sufficed. The first time around—"

"I was lucky," interrupted the man. "Very, very lucky. That ghastly knot was nothing but shaking hands and fortunate bungling. And besides—" He sighed, too, but instead of deflating, the exhalation appeared to lift him up. "Think of the advances, Chaswick. The discoveries I've made since then. How all these newer elements might work in concert—well. We cannot be too careful. I don't have to tell you what's at stake."

The two men moved into the blackness of the room's far end. The candelabrum revealed that the distant third of the wall was hidden behind a heavy black curtain.

"Of course, Doctor Dandridge," said Chaswick.

"The sea lion," Dr. Dandridge repeated.

Chaswick passed the candelabrum to his superior. When he turned to grip the curtain, Lindsome noticed what he was wearing.

Waders?

The curtain hissed partway aside upon its track. The candlelight fell upon tanks, tanks and tanks and tanks, each filled with an evil, yellowing liquid. Each held a shrunken animal corpse, embalmed and barely recognizable. The lowest third of the wall was but a single tank, stretching back behind the half-closed curtain.

A great, bloated shadow rolled within.

Lindsome shivered. She had never seen the dead creature's likeness. It must have been a specimen from the continent to the east, but whatever it was, it was not what they wanted, because Chaswick knelt by a tank on the second shelf, obscuring the monstrosity. He fitted a length of rubber hose to a stopcock at the bottom of his chosen tank, then ran the hose along the floor and out the open door. "Door's blown loose again. That useless Thomlin—I've asked him to fix the latch thrice this week. I swear to Ghost, I'd stick him in one of the tanks myself if he weren't a man and would leave behind anything more useful than ghostgrease."

Chaswick returned and opened the stopcock. The end of the hose, limp over the edge of the patio, dribbled its foul load into the weeds. The large corpse within the tank settled to the bottom as it drained, a limp, matted mess. Chaswick did something to the glass to make it open outward, like the door to an oven.

He gathered the dead thing to his chest and stood. Ichor ran in rivulets down his waders. "I don't mean to rush you, but—"

"Of course." Candelabrum in tow, Dr. Dandridge shuffled back to the stairs. "I'll do my best to hurry."

They ascended the steps, pulling the light with them and the squealing door shut.

Lindsome fled outside. After that chamber of horrors, the sticking burdock, Raven's Kiss, and cruel thorns of the sunlit world were the hallmarks of Paradise.

⤙⊶

At seven o'clock, some unseen, stentorian timepiece tolled the hour. Lindsome, who had elected to spend the rest of the afternoon in the library in a fort constructed from the oldest, fattest, dullest (and surely therefore safest) books she could find, reluctantly emerged to search for the dining room.

The murmur of voices and clink of silverware guided her steps into a room on the first floor nearly large enough to be a proper banquet hall.

Only the far end of the long table, near the wall abutting the kitchen, was occupied. A fire on the wall's hearth cast the head of the table in shadow while illuminating Chaswick's disdain.

"You are late," Chaswick said. "Don't you know what they say about first impressions?"

Lindsome slunk across the floor. "I'm sorry, Mister Chaswick."

From the shadows of a wingback chair, the master of the house leaned forward. "No matter," said Dr. Dandridge. "Good evening. I am Professor Albion Edgarton Dandridge. Our meeting is well. Please pardon me for not arising; I'm an old man, and my bones grow reluctant, even at the welcome sight of a face so fresh and kind as yours."

Lindsome had not expected this. "I . . . thank you, sir."

"Uncle Albion will do. Come, sit, sit."

Opposite Chaswick, Lindsome pulled out her own massive chair with some difficulty, working it over the threadbare carpet in small scoots. "Thank you, sir. Our meeting is well."

Chaswick snorted. "Mind her, Doctor. She's got a streak in her."

"Oh, I don't doubt it. Comes from my side." The old man smiled at her. His teeth were surprisingly intact. "Are you making yourself at home, my dear?"

Lindsome served herself a ladle full of shapeless brown stew. "Yes, sir."

"Don't mumble," said Chaswick, picking debris from his teeth with his fingernails. "It's uncouth."

"I am delighted that you're staying with us," continued Dr. Dandridge. Outside of the nightmarish basement, he looked ordinary and gentle. His halo of hair, Lindsome now saw, wandered off his head into a pair of bedraggled dundrearies, and the fine wrinkles around his eyes made him look kind. His clothes were dusty and ill-fitting, tailored for a more robust man at least thirty years his junior. She could not imagine a less threatening person.

"Thank you, sir."

"Uncle. I am dear old Uncle—" Dr. Dandridge coughed, a dry, wheezing sound and put an embroidered handkerchief to his mouth. Chaswick nudged the old man's water glass closer. "Albion," he managed, taking a sip from the glass. "Thank you, Chaswick."

"Yes, Uncle."

"And how is your papa?"

Lindsome did not want to think of him, arm in arm with Mama, strolling up the pier to the great boat and laughing, his long legs wavering under a film of tears. "He is very well, thank you."

"Excellent, excellent. And your mama?"

"Also well."

"Good, good." The doctor nibbled at his stew, apparently unfazed by its utter lack of flavor. "I trust that the staff have been kind, and have answered all of your questions."

"Well . . ." Lindsome started, but Chaswick shot her a dangerous look. Lindsome fell silent.

"Yes?" asked Dr. Dandridge, focused on teasing apart a gravy-smothered nodule.

"I was wondering . . ." dared Lindsome, but Chaswick's face sharpened into a scowl. ". . . about your work."

"Oh!" said Dr. Dandridge. His efforts on the nodule of stew redoubled. "My work. My great work! You are right to ask, young lady. It is always pleasing to hear that the youth of today have an interest in science. Young people are our future, you know."

"I—"

"The work, of course, builds on the fundamentals of Wittard and Blacke from the '30s, going beyond the Skin Stitch and into the essential vital nodes. But unlike Havarttgartt and his school (and here's the key, now), we don't hold that the heart, brain, and genitals, aka the Life Triad, are the necessary fulcrums. We hold—that is, I hold—that is, Chaswick agrees, and he's a very smart lad—*we* hold that a diversified architecture of fulcrums is key to extending the ambulatory period of a vivified, and we have extensive data to back this hypothesis, to the extent where we've produced a curve—a Dandridge curve, I call it, if I may be so modest, ha-ha—that illustrates the correlation between the number of fulcrums and hours of ambulatory function, and clearly demonstrates that while *quality* of fulcrums does indeed play a role, it is not nearly so prominent as the role of *quantity*. Or, in layman's terms, if you stitch a soul silly to a corpse at every major mechanical joint—ankles, knees, hips, shoulders, elbows, wrists—you'll still get a far better outcome than you would had you used a Butterfly Stitch to the heart itself! Can you imagine?"

Lost, Lindsome stared at her plate. She could feel Chaswick's smug gaze upon her, the awful look that grown-ups use when they want to say, *Not so smart now, are you?*

"And furthermore," Dr. Dandridge went on gaily, setting down his fork and withdrawing a different utensil from his pocket with which to attack his clump of stew, "we have discovered a hitherto unknown role of the Life Triad in host plasticity, which also beautifully solves the mystery of how a very small soul, like that of a mouse, can successfully be stitched to a very large flesh mass, like that of a cow, and vice-versa. Did Chaswick explain to you about our chimeras? The dogs with souls of finches, and the blackbirds with the souls of chipmunks, and in one exceptional case, the little red fox with the soul of a prize-winning hog? Goodness, was I proud of that one!" The old man laughed.

Lindsome smiled weakly.

"It is upon the brain, you see, not the heart," Dr. Dandrige went on, "that the configuration, amount, and type of stitches are key, because— and this is already well known in the higher animals—a great deal of soul is enfleshed in the brain. You may think of the brain as a tiny little seed that floats in the center of every skull, but not so! When an animal is alive, the brain takes up the *entire* skull cavity. Can you imagine? Of course, the higher the animal, the more the overall corpse shrinks at the moment of death, aka soul separation, due to the soul composing a greater percentage of the creature. This is why Humankind (with its large and complex souls) leaves no deathhusk, or corpse, at all—nothing but a film of ghostgrease. Which, incidentally, popular doggerel will tell you is absent from the deathbeds of holy people, being that they are so *very* above their animal natures and are 100 percent ethereal, but goodness, don't get me started about all *that* ugsome rot."

Dr. Dandridge stopped. He frowned at his plate. "Good grief. What am I doing?"

"A Clatham Stitch, looks like," said Chaswick gently. "On your beef stew."

"Heavens!" Dr. Dandridge put down his utensil, which Lindsome could now see was an aetherhook. He removed what looked like a monocle made of cobalt glass from a breast pocket, then peered through it at his plate. "There weren't any souls passing by just now, were there? The leycurrents are strong here in the early winter, dear Lindsome, and sometimes the departed souls of lesser creatures will blow into the house if we have the windows open. And when *that* happens—"

The lump of beef quivered. Lindsome dropped her fork and clapped a hand to her mouth.

From beneath the stew crawled a beetle, looking very put out.

Dr. Dandridge and Chaswick burst into guffaws. "A beetle!" cried the old man. "A beetle in the stew! Oh, that is precious, too precious for words! Oh, how funny!"

Chaswick, laughing, looked to Lindsome, her eyes saucer-wide. "Oh, come now," he said. "Surely you see the humor."

Dr. Dandridge wiped his eyes. The beetle, tracking tiny spots of stew, crawled off across the tablecloth at speed. "A beetle! Oh, mercy. Mercy me. Excuse us—that's not a joke for a young lady at all. Forgive me, child—we've grown uncivilized out here, isolated as we are. A Clatham Stitch upon my stew, as if to vivify it! And then came a beetle—"

Lindsome couldn't take it anymore. She stood. "May I be excused?"

"Already?" said Chaswick, still chuckling. "No more questions for your great-uncle, demonstrating your *very* thorough interest in and understanding of his work?"

Lindsome colored beneath the increasing heat of her discomfort. This remark, on top of all else, was too much. "Oh, I understand a great deal. I understand that you can stitch a soul to an embalmed deathhusk instead of an unpreserved one—"

Chaswick stopped laughing immediately.

"—even though *everybody knows* that's impossible," said Lindsome.

Chaswick's eyes tightened in suspicion. Dr. Dandridge, unaware of the ferocity between their interlocked stares, sat as erect as his ancient bones would permit. "Why, that's right! That's absolutely right! You must have understood the implications of Bainbridge's supplemental index in her report last spring!"

"Yes," said Chaswick coldly. "She must have."

Lindsome colored further and looked away. She focused on her great-uncle, who, in his excitement, had picked up the aetherhook once again and was attempting to cut a bit of potato with it. "Your mama was right to send you here. I never imagined—a blossoming, fine young scientific mind in the family! Why, the conversations we can have, you and I! Great Apocrypha, I'm doing it again, aren't I?" The old man put the aetherhook, with no further comment or explanation, tip-down in his water glass. "We shall have a chat in my study after dinner. Truth be told, you arrived at the perfect time. Chaswick and I are at the cusp of an astounding attempt, a true milestone in—"

Chaswick arose sharply from his chair. "A moment, Doctor! I need a word with your niece first." He rounded the table and grabbed Lindsome's arm before anyone could protest. "She'll await you in your study. Excuse us."

Chaswick dragged her toward the small, forbidden hallway, but rather than entering the door at the end into the mysterious yellow room, he dragged Lindsome into one of the rooms that flanked the corridor. Lindsome did not have an opportunity to observe the interior, for Chaswick slammed the door behind them.

"What have you seen?"

A match flared to life with a pop and Lindsome shielded her eyes. Chaswick lit a single candle, tossed the match aside, and lifted the candle to chest level. Its flicker turned his expression eerie and demonic. "I said, what have you seen?"

"Nothing!" Lindsome kept her free hand over her eyes, pretending the shock of the light hurt worse than it did, so that Chaswick could not see the lie upon her face.

"Listen to me, you little brat," Chaswick hissed. "You might think you can breeze in here and destroy everything I've built with a bit of flattery and deception, but I have news for you. You and the rest of your shallow, showy, flighty, backstabbing kindred? You abandoned this brilliant man long ago, thinking his work would come to nothing, and that these beautiful grounds and marvels of creation weren't worth the rocks the building crew dug from the soil, but with The Ghost as my witness, I swear that I am not allowing your pampered, money-grubbing hands to trick me out of my inheritance. Do you understand me? I love this man. I love his work. I love what he stands for. Apsis House will remain willed to *me*. And if I so much as see you bat your wicked little eyes in the doctor's direction, I will *ensure* that you are not in my way.

"Do I make myself clear?"

Lindsome lowered her hand. It was trembling. Every part of her was. "You think I'm—are you saying—?"

The vise of Chaswick's hand, honed over long hours of tension around a Stitchman's instruments, crushed her wrist in its grip. "Do I make myself clear?"

Lindsome squirmed, now in genuine pain. "Let me go! I don't even want your ruined old house!"

"What did you see?"

"Stop it!"

"Tell me what you've seen!"

"Yes," announced Dr. Dandridge, and in half a second, Chaswick had released Lindsome and stepped back, and the old man entered the room, a blazing candelabrum in hand. "Yes, stitching a soul to an embalmed, or even mummified, deathhusk would be a tremendous feat. Just imagine how long something like that could last. Ages, maybe. And ages more. . . ." His expression turned distant and calculating. "Just imagine. A soul you never wanted to lose? Why, you could keep it here forever. . . ."

Chaswick straightened. He smiled at Lindsome, a poisonous thing that Dr. Dandridge, lost in daydreams, did not see. "Good night, Doctor. And goodnight, Lindsome. Mind whose house you're in."

◂◦▸

Surviving the fervid conversation of her great-uncle was one thing, but after just five days, Lindsome wasn't sure how long she could survive the mysteries of his house. Chimeric with secrets, every joint and blackened picture was near bursting with the souls of untold stories. Lindsome was amazed that the whole great edifice did not lurch into motion, pulling up its deep roots and walls to run somewhere that wasn't bathed in madness and the footsteps of the dead. She searched the place over for answers, but the chambers yielded no clues, and any living thing who might supply them remained stitched to secrets of their own.

The only person she hadn't spoken with yet was the gardener.

Lindsome finally set off one evening to find him, under a gash of orange-red that hung over the bare trees to the west. She left the loop trail around the house. Bowers of bramble, vines of Heart-Be-Still, and immature Honeylocusts rife with spines surrounded her. A chorus of splintering twigs whispered beyond as unseen vivifieds moved on ill-fitted instinct.

"Hello? Mister Gardener?"

Only the twigs, whispering.

Lindsome slipped her right hand into her pocket, grasping what lay within. A grade-2 aetherblade, capped tight. She'd found it on the desk in Uncle Albion's study one afternoon. Lindsome couldn't say why she'd taken it. An aetherblade was only useful, after all, if one wanted to cut spirit-stitches and knew where those stitches lay, and Lindsome had neither expertise nor aetherglass to make solid the invisible threads. It would have done her just as much good to pocket one of Cook's paring knives, which is to say, not much good at all.

"Hello?"

Beneath the constant stink of corpses came something sweet. At first, Lindsome thought it was a freshly vivified, exuding the cloyingly sweet fragrance of the finishing chemicals. But it was too gentle and mild.

A dark thing, soft as a moth, fluttered onto her cheek.

A rose petal.

"Mister Gardener? Are you growing—"

A savagely cleared vista opened before her, twisting back toward the house, now a looming shadow against the dimming sky. The murdered plants waited in neat piles, rootballs wet and dark. Lindsome squeezed her stolen aetherblade tighter in relief. The things were newly pulled. He'd be resting at the end of this trail, close to the house, preparing to come in for the evening.

But he wasn't.

At the end of the vista, Lindsome halted in surprise. It was as if the gardener had known that Lindsome would come this way and had wanted to present her with a beautiful view, for in front of her lay another clearing, but this one was old and well maintained. Its floor held a fine carpet of grass, dormant and littered with leaves. The grass stretched up to the house itself and terminated at the edge of a patio. The double doors leading out were twin mosaics of diamond-shaped panes. Through them, Lindsome could see sheer curtains drawn back on the other side. Within the room, a gaslamp burned.

Its light flickered over yellow walls.

Lindsome's breath stuck in her throat like a lump of ice. She could see the shelves now, the stacks of toys, the painted blocks and tops and bright pictures of animals hung above the chair-rail molding. A tiny, overlooked chair at the patio's edge. An overlooked iron crib within.

Nobody had said the room was forbidden to approach from the outside.

Lindsome drifted across the grass. As she drew closer, she noticed something new. In the center of the room, between her and the iron crib, stood a three-legged table. Upon the table sat a bell jar. Perfectly clean, its translucence had rendered it invisible, until Lindsome saw the gaslight glance from its surface at the proper angle.

Within the bell jar, something moved.

Lindsome drew even closer. The bell jar was large, the size of a birdcage, but not so large as to dwarf the blur within. The blur's presence, too, had been obscured from behind by the stark pattern of the crib's bars, but it was not so translucent as the bell jar itself. The thing inside the glass was wispy. Shimmering.

Lindsome stepped onto the patio. The icy lump in her throat froze it shut.

Within the bell jar, a tiny, tiny fist solidified and pressed its ghostly knuckles against the glass.

Lindsome's scream woke Long Hill's last surviving raven, which took wing into the night, cawing.

◄○►

Thorns tore Lindsome's dress to tatters as she ran. "Chaswick!"

She fled toward the squares of gaslight, jumping over a fallen tree and flying up the main steps into the house. She called again, running from room to empty room, scattering dust and mice, the lamplight painting black ghosts behind crooked settees and broken chairs. "Someone help! Chaswick!"

Lindsome reached the kitchen. Cook was kneeling by the hearth, roasting a pan of cabbage-wrapped beef rolls atop the glowing coals. "Cook! Help! The yellow room! There's a baby!"

Cook maintained her watchful crouch, not even turning. "Sst!" She put a plump finger to her lips. "Hush, child!"

"The yellow room," cried Lindsome, gripping Cook's elbow. "I saw it. I was outside and followed a path the gardener made. There's a bell jar inside. It's got a soul in it. A captured human soul. He's keeping a—"

Cook planted her sooty hand over Lindsome's mouth. She leaned toward her, beady eyes pinching. "I said hush, child," Cook whispered. "Hush.

That was nothing you saw. That fancy gaslight the doctor likes, it plays tricks on your eyes."

Lindsome shook her head, but Cook pressed harder. "It plays tricks." Her expression pleaded. "Be a good girl, now. Stop telling tales. Lock your door at night. And don't you bring the gardener into this—don't you dare. That's a good girl?" Her eyes pinched further. "Yes?"

Lindsome wrenched herself away and ran.

"Chaswick!" She ran to the second floor, so upset that she grew disoriented. Had she already searched this corridor? This cloister of rooms? She could smell it. Fresh vivified. No—something milder. Right behind this locked door . . .

A hand touched Lindsome's shoulder. She squealed.

"Saint Ransome's Blood, child!" Chaswick said, spinning her about. A pair of spectacles perched on his nose, gleaming in the hall's gaslight. His other, dangling hand held a half-open book, as though it were a carcass to be trussed. "What's all this howling?"

Lindsome threw her arms about him. "Chaswick!"

He stiffened. "Goodness. Control yourself. Come now, stop that. Did you see a mouse?"

"No," said Lindsome, pressing her face into Chaswick's chest. "It was—"

"How many times must I tell you not to mumble?" Chaswick asked. "Now listen. I was in the midst of a very important—"

"A BABY!" Lindsome shouted.

Chaswick grew very still.

"It was—"

Chaswick drew back, gripped Lindsome's shoulder, and without another word marched her down the hall and through a door that had always been locked.

Lindsome glanced about. The place appeared to be Chaswick's quarters. The room was in surprisingly good repair, clean and recently painted, but all carpets, tapestries, cushions, and wallpaper had been removed. The only furniture was a desk, chair, and narrow bed, the only thing of any comfort a mean, straw mattress. The fire in the grate helped soften the room's hard lines, and Lindsome's fear of this stern and jealous man melted further under her larger one. "I'm sorry, Mister Chaswick, but I was walking outside, and there was a path that took me past the yellow room, and inside I saw a bell jar. And in it was an infant's soul. It solidified a fist and put it against the glass. I swear I'm not fibbing, Mister Chaswick. I swear by Mama's virtue, I'm not."

Chaswick sighed. He placed his book upon his desk. "I know you're not."

"You *know*?"

Chaswick shook his head, the flames highlighting the firm lines around his mouth. "I have said. The doctor is a brilliant man."

"But he—but you *can't* just—" Lindsome sputtered. "You can't stop a soul from going to Heaven! It's wrong! You'll—The Ghost will—you'll freeze in the Abyss! Forever and ever! The Second Ghostscroll says—"

"Don't quote scripture at me, girl, it's tiresome." Chaswick withdrew a small leather case from a pocket in his trousers, removed his spectacles, and slid them inside. "The Ghost is nothing but a fairy tale for adults who never grow up. Humankind is alone in the universe, and there are no rules save for those which we agree upon ourselves. If Doctor Dandridge has the knowledge, the means, the willingness, and the bravery to experiment upon a human soul—well, then, what of it?"

Lindsome shrank back. "He's going to—what?"

Chaswick set his mouth, the firelight carving his sternness deeper. "It's not my place to stop him."

Lindsome took a full step backward, barely able to speak. "You can't mean that. He can't. He wouldn't."

"In fact, I rather encourage it," said Chaswick. "Fortune favors the bold."

"But it's illegal," Lindsome stammered. "It's sick! They'd think he's gone mad! They'd put him away, and then they'd—"

She stopped. She stared at Chaswick.

They'd take away all of Uncle's property.

And they'd look in Uncle's will and give it to . . .

"You," Lindsome whispered. "It's you. You put this idea into his head."

Chaswick sneered. "His wife, Marilda, died in childbirth, and the doctor chose his unorthodox method of grieving, well before I ever set foot on Long Hill. Not that you'd know, considering how very little your ilk cared to associate with him, after the tragedy. Ask your precious mama. She doesn't approve of the yellow room, either." Chaswick's laugh was nasty. "Not that she thinks it's anything more than an empty shrine."

Lindsome backed toward the door. Chaswick advanced, matching her step for step. *You monster. You brute. What has my poor uncle done? What awful things has he already done?*

And what else is he going to do?

The door was nearly at her back. Chaswick loomed above her. "Go to bed, little girl," he warned. "Nobody is going to listen to your foolish histrionics. Not in this house."

Lindsome turned and fled.

She ran down the hall and into her own bedroom, where the bed sagged, the mold billowed across the ceiling like thunderheads, and the vivified mice ran back and forth, back and forth against the baseboards, without thinking, all night long.

Lindsome locked the door. *Cook would be proud.*

Then she lay on her bed and wept.

-o-

The night stretched like a cat, smothering future and past alike with its inky paws. Lindsome tossed in broken sleep. She dreamed of light glinting off curved glass, and something lancing through her heart. Chaswick above her, flames of gaslight for eyes, probing her beating flesh with an aetherhook. "What's all this howling?"

Under everything, roses.

-o-

An hour before dawn, Lindsome dressed and left the house. The sky was too dark and the clouds too swollen, but she couldn't stand this wretched place another moment. Even the stables, which held nothing but vivifieds, would be an improvement. The matted fur of dead horses is just as well for sponging away tears.

In the stables, Lindsome buried her face against the cold nose of a gelding. Did he have the same soul he'd had in life, she wondered, or did some other horse now command this body? What did it feel like, to be stitched imperfectly to a body that was not yours? She remembered the grade-2 aetherblade in the pocket of her coat. She recalled the few comprehensible bits of her great-uncle's post-dinner lectures. Lindsome drew away from the horse, wiped her face on her sleeve, and produced the aetherblade.

The horse watched her, exhibiting no sign of feeling.

Lindsome plunged the tool behind the horse's knee, between the physical stitches of a deep, telltale cut that could never heal. She circled the creature, straining to see in the poor light, plunging the aetherblade into every such cut she could find.

The horse's legs buckled. It collapsed to the floor.

Its neck still functioned. The horse looked up at her, expressionless. Lindsome searched through its mane, shuddering, trying to find the final knot of stitching that would—

Set it free.

Lindsome stopped.

The horse did not react.

"Wait for me," Lindsome said, setting down the aetherblade on the floor. "There's something I have to do. I'll be right back."

The horse, unable to do anything else, waited.

But she didn't come back.

⊸⊙⊱

Something was wrong with the sky, Lindsome thought, as she trotted toward the house. It was too gray and too warm after last night's chill. There shouldn't be thunderheads gathering now. Not so late in autumn.

And something was wrong with the vivifieds. Instead of rustling in the depths of the thicket, they lurched up and down the irregular paths in a sluggish remembrance of flight. A snake with a crushed spine lolled in a hollow. A pack of coyotes, moving in rolling prowls like house cats, moved single file in a line from the stables to the well, not even swiveling an ear as Lindsome squeezed past.

Near the main steps of the house, the burst-open billy goat had gotten ensnared in a tangle of creepers, its blackened entrails commingling with blackened vines.

Lindsome resolutely ran past it.

A dead sparrow fell from the sky and pelted her shoulder, and a frog corpse crunched beneath her foot. A hundred awful things could smear her with their putrescence—but oh, let them, because she was a lady. And ladies always did what needed doing.

There.

The gardener's careful path to the yellow room.

She was at the final vista, now. Then the private patio. The sheer curtains were closed, but one of the patio doors was open, swinging to and fro on the fretful breeze.

In the center of the room, the three-legged table waited, but the bell jar was gone.

Lindsome slumped in gratitude. Uncle Albion had finally come to his senses. Or Chaswick had felt guilty about their talk last night, or careless Thomlin had knocked it over and broken it, even.

But then Lindsome remembered.

Today is Thursday.

Her throat made an awful squeak. She turned back and ran, up the vista and through wilderness to the ring path.

To the basement. Where ranks of monsters rotted as they stood, and the flesh of nightmares yet to be born floated in tanks, dreaming inscrutable dreams.

One of the doors to the basement stood open, too, swinging in the mounting wind. Lindsome ran inside. By now, she was panting, her back moist with sweat, her heart fighting to escape the hot prison of her chest. The foul air choked her. She bent double and gagged, falling to her knees on the icy stones.

Scores of waiting eyes watched her.

The wall of bodies began to moan, hundreds of bastard vocalizations from bastardized throats that had long ago forgotten how to speak. Pulpy flesh surged forward against bars and railings, jaws unhinging, the sound rising like the discordant sirens of an army from the Abyss.

Beneath them, Lindsome began a keening of her own, tiny and devoid of reason.

She did not know how she stepped to that far corner, where the future nightmares waited, but step she did, into a forest of burning candles. Some had toppled over onto the floor, frozen in sprays of wax. Some had melted into puddles, now aflame. The plentiful light showed all the tanks and that long, black curtain pulled fully back.

The giant tank on the bottom, as long as two men laid end to end, was drained, empty, and open.

The moaning grew. Lindsome's keening grew into a wail, though she could not hear it, only watch as her feet pointed her around and sent her across the basement and up the stone steps.

The door at the top was already open.

Lindsome's wail squeezed down into words, screamed loud enough to tear her throat as thorns will tear a dress. "Uncle Albion!"

Someone emitted a distant, ringing scream.

Lindsome couldn't breathe. She stumbled through the first floor, gasping, her uncle's name a mere whisper on her wide-open lips.

She found a door that Chaswick had forbidden, the door to the other basement-cum-laboratory. Or rather, she found the space where the door should have been. Both door and molding had been torn away.

As if the unseen gardener had entered the house, signature violence in tow.

"Uncle," Lindsome gasped. Outside, lightning flickered, and Lindsome saw four steps down. Dark smears daubed the floorboards. Further within, the glitter of metal and broken glass.

A bloody handprint on the wall.

The scream came again, an animalistic screech of distilled and mortal terror. Lindsome backed away from the stairs. Her legs quaked too much to run now.

She walked to the grand staircase. A painful flash of lightning illuminated the entire house—the puddles of ichor through which Lindsome trod, the monstrous gouges in the wood and wallpaper on either side of her, the gaslamps torn from their mounts.

The mental image of a tiny fist, its knuckles bumping the inside of a tank as long as two men laid end to end.

Lindsome found Chaswick on the staircase. He had ended up like the billy goat outside, his stomach torn open, his entrails tangled in the shattered spindles of the banister.

"Linds . . ." One of his hands, slimy and bright, pawed at the banister. She stared at him.

"Up . . ." Chaswick whispered. "Up . . ." His head twitched in the direction of the second floor. "If you . . . love . . . then up . . ."

Lindsome's head nodded. "Yes, Mister Chaswick," her mouth said.

His gaze clouded. The room flickered, as if under a second touch of lightning, and the pools of blood below him flashed into a sizzle.

Lindsome blinked, and Chaswick was gone. In his place, a pile of clothing lay tossed against the spindles, commingled with heavy black ghostgrease.

Somehow, Lindsome was running.

Sprinting, even. Up the stairs. "Uncle Albion!" she cried, and realized that she could speak again, too. Yet again, Lindsome heard that scream, that inhuman terror.

"Albion!" someone else called. Emlee, the gaunt old housekeeper. Third floor. The devastation continued up the staircase.

"Get out!" Her uncle. Alive. "Go!"

"No—not when she's—" A crash.

"Run, damn your miserable old hide! If ever you loved me as I loved you, Albion, then *run*!"

And that scream. That Ghost-forsaken scream.

Lindsome ran, up and up and out, tripping over shredded carpet, torn-down paintings, shattered vases and urns. From around a corner came a ghastly crunch, then booms and bangs, the sound of something mighty hurtling down a staircase.

"No, Marilda! Stop!"

Lindsome rounded the corner. The servants' staircase lay before her, walls half-ripped asunder, ichor on the steps.

Lindsome took them one flight down. At the bottom lay the house-keeper's clothes, black with ghostgrease.

"Uncle!" Lindsome wailed. "Uncle, where are you? We have to hide!"

His bedroom. Outside in the hall. Uncle Albion's door was open.

So was the door next to his, the one that had looked rusted shut.

The stench inside was unspeakable. Lindsome fell to the carpet and vomited, despite her empty stomach, hard enough for bile to dribble over her lips. Vivified. An ark of freshly vivified. They had to be stacked to the ceiling, packed like earth in a grave.

But when she looked up, all she saw were briars.

Roses. Thousands upon thousands of roses. Fresh, dried, rotting, trampled, entire bushes of them, as though a giant had uprooted them and brought them in here.

They were woven into a gigantic nest.

In the center sat Thomlin. His eyes were rolled up, showing nothing but white. He grasped his knees to his chest and rocked, like all those windblown, yawning doors, moaning like that wall of rotting flesh. A frothy river of drool dribbled down his chin.

Lindsome did not speak to him. It was clear that Thomlin would never speak again.

The siren song of that inhuman scream rang out, and Lindsome ran out into the hall. She called her uncle's name, shouted it, even, but received no answer.

She ran into his room, searching. The knobs of a rope ladder lay bolted into his windowsill.

"Uncle!" Lindsome peered over the sill. The ladder still wobbled from a recent descent, trailing down into a tight copse of saplings. Lindsome scrambled down. "Uncle Albion! Wait!"

Lightning cut her shadow from the air. The boom that answered split the sky, a rolling bang that made Lindsome squeal and cover her ears. In seconds, its echoes vanished under static, the sound of a million gallons pouring down. Lindsome was immediately soaked. The tatters of her dress slapped at her legs as she ran, and so heavy was the downpour, Lindsome couldn't see.

The path became slick. Lindsome slipped and went sprawling, face-first, and a fallen branch tore a gash in her arm. Lindsome screamed and rolled aside, curling around her wound, blinded by rain and tears.

Get up.

The thing will get you. Get up!

Weeping, squeezing her arm, Lindsome struggled to her feet. She stumbled along a trough of mud. She ripped off a strip of her soaked dress and tried to tie it around her wound to protect it.

A vivified hunting dog lumbered past, Cook's sodden apron hanging from its jaws.

The sky lit up again, illuminating a great gash in the thicket. Uprooted plants, unearthed rocks, and crushed branches paved the way. How dare anyone keep working in the shadow of such horrors? Lindsome yelled for her uncle, for the gardener, for someone and anyone as she stumbled down that fresh avenue, arm throbbing and poorly tied scrap of dress soaking through with red.

No creature hindered her. The fleeing vivifieds had disappeared.

Instead came roses. Thicker and thicker still, the tangled walls burst with roses, like puddles of gore on a battlefield. She moved in a forest of them, boughs bending to enclose the path overhead, their stink so strong not even the downpour could erase it. It was black beneath the boughs, black and dripping. Torn-off petals dribbled down between the branches, sticking to her hair, her hands, her face.

The tunnel turned and opened.

Not even the looming branches of this deadly forest could cover a space so large. The clearing was a pit of trampled thorns and bowed-in walls, canes of briars thrashing in the gusts, petals smeared everywhere like a violent snowfall. It stank of roses and death, water and undeath, and though naked sky arced above this grove of wreckage, the light was not strong enough for Lindsome to understand the pair of shapes that waited at the far end.

But then the lightning came.

Its brilliance bore down, and Lindsome understood even less, though what she saw burned itself into her vision with the force of a dying sun. One was large, impossibly large. An alien mountain of fur and rot, waiting on trunk-thick limbs, bearing eyes that knew—even if the throat could not speak, even if those ghastly hands could not move with the mastery and grace that memory still begged for.

And one was small. A baby of that species. The size of two men, laid end to end.

Lindsome did not know that she kept screaming. There was only feeling, a single feeling of eclipsing terror so hot she felt her own soul struggling to tear free. The pain in her arm disappeared. She felt neither cold nor wet. Only this searing moment, as the small one rolled in its nest of thorns and flailed, as though its soul had never learned to walk.

The mountain of rot took a step forward, until it towered protectively over the wriggling thing below.

It reached out a hand toward Lindsome.

The eclipse reached totality. Lindsome went down, her heartbeat a ringing roar.

⊸⊙⊷

"Miss?"

Something struck the front of her thighs with brisk force. Lindsome grunted.

"Miss?"

"Leave her. She's a woodcutter's child, innit? Girl a' the woods?"

"In woods like these? Not on yer hat. An' look at her bleedin' arm, ye piece-wit. That's no small hurt. Miss?"

Lindsome opened her eyes. She was lying on her side in the sodden leaves, at the edge of a nameless road. The earth smelled good, of dirt and wind and water, and the branches of the bare trees overhead swayed and knocked in the bleak sunshine.

Two men stood over her, one holding the reins of a pair of horses. The other held a staff, with which he rapped Lindsome's thighs again.

Lindsome's eyes went to the horses. They were the horses of poor men, witless, subpar animals bought for cheap with zero cost of upkeep: vivifieds.

Lindsome began to cry.

One of the men mounted, and the other placed Lindsome at his comrade's back. She clung to his coat and sobbed as they rode out of the deserted wood.

They asked her questions, but Lindsome did not answer. They rode to the low town of Hume and deposited her on the steps of the orphanage, where kinder, cleaner, better-dressed men and women asked her the same things, but Lindsome only wept. She did not protest when they steered her inside, bathed her, tended her arm, dressed her in worn but clean things, and gave her a bowl of oatmeal and honey. She hardly ate half before falling dead asleep at the table and barely noticed when a pair of strong, gentle arms lifted her up and placed her upon a cot.

The streets of Hume were buried in the snow of the new year before Lindsome spoke a single word.

◀◦▶

She had to tell them something. So Lindsome, in the course of explaining who she was and that she did in fact have living parents who might someday appear to fetch her, decided to say that the household of her Great-Uncle Albion had succumbed to a foolish but gruesome accident. He had planned to perform a stitching experiment on a pack of wolves that were not yet dead, Lindsome claimed, and the rest of the household, making heated bets on whether this holy grail of vivology was in fact possible to obtain, had gathered in the laboratory to watch. Lindsome had been spared from the ensuing tragedy because she did not care about the bet and had been playing outside, alone. The constable's men, who went to Apsis House to investigate as soon as the spring thaw came, found evidence to corroborate her story. The interior of Apsis House was torn apart, as if indeed by a pack of infuriated wolves, and not a trace of anyone living—including the great Professor Albion Edgarton Dandridge himself—could be found.

The spring after that, Lindsome's parents returned, refreshed from travel but baffled and scornful of the personal and legal complications that had evolved in their absence. At the conclusion of the affair, the judge gave them the property deed to Apsis House. They wanted to know what on Earth they were supposed do with such a terribly located, wolf-infested wreck, and told Lindsome that she would have it, when she came of age.

The day she did, Lindsome attempted to sell it, but nobody could be persuaded to buy. She couldn't even give it away. The deed finally sat unused in a drawer in her dressing table, in a far-away city in her far-away grown-up life, next to the tin of cosmetic power she used to cover up a long, ugly scar upon her arm. Her husband, to whom she never told the entire truth, agreed that the property was probably worth-less, and never suggested that they visit Long Hill or take any action regarding Apsis House's restoration. Nor did their three daughters, once they were grown enough to be told the family legends about mad Uncle Albion, and old enough to understand that some things are best left where they fall.

And besides—now that Lindsome knew what it was to have and love a child, she couldn't bear to interrupt what might still move up there, within that blooming forest of thorns. If they were both intact, still, the least Lindsome could do was give them their peace; and if they were not, Lindsome could not bear the thought of finding one of them alone, endlessly screaming that desperate, lonely scream, until however long it took for Albion's sturdy handiwork to unravel.

As Chaswick had said, Uncle Albion was a brilliant man.

It could take a very long time.

CALL OUT

STEVE TOASE

Opening the field gate, Malcolm sensed something born wrong sheltered in the old cattle shed. The sickly sweet smell of decay spread across the hillside. Round his feet, half-blind, featherless jackdaws cawed. Malcolm hesitated, not wanting to cross the grass, to make those final steps on this late-night call out. Bill Hoden had already started over the field. He lifted up his left hand and beckoned Malcolm on, holding a damp cigarette between two remaining fingers.

"Never seen owt like it, Veterinary. Not in fifty years of farming. Knew something wasn't right when it hit the cobbles. Birth waters scorched the floor stone-white clean." He coughed and spat a mouthful of phlegm into the mud.

"How was the mother?"

"Cooked from the inside out. Like she'd been in one of those microwave ovens."

Malcolm pulled his coat tighter.

Bill undid the padlock on the double doors. The broken boards scraped on the floor. Malcolm waited for Bill to go first, but the old hill farmer just stood there.

"Aren't you going to show me the animal, Bill?"

Shaking his head, Bill stayed exactly where he was.

"Seen it once. Don't need to see that again."

Malcolm noticed an old leather-bound book under Bill's arm, *King James* in faded gold on the cover.

Reaching into a pocket for his torch, Malcolm stepped into the shed. The smell was worse now. As a country vet, he was used to rot. Hoof infections, orf, or abscesses, his work year was filled with the scent of decaying flesh. This was something else. Like bathing in abattoir waste.

Inside, the temperature rose, first to a pleasant glow, then more furnace-intense as he walked deeper inside. His eyes stung and his throat gagged.

◄o►

Hilary had taken the phone call, scribbling the details on the Welcome To Yorkshire writing pad and shouting up the stairs. Malcolm had come down, wrapped in a towel, roughly drying his hair. Squinting to decipher her writing, he read the note, making out Bill's name and the farm, Crop Hill, underlined three times.

"You haven't written down what the problem is," he said, walking to the living room door.

Turning the sound down on the TV, Hilary turned round on the sofa.

"Bill never told me. Before you say anything, I did ask. He just said for me to get Veterinary up to the farm fast."

Malcolm sighed, already getting cold, and went upstairs to find some warm clothes.

◄o►

Using an old cloth handkerchief, Malcolm covered his face and walked deeper into the barn. The remains of the mother slumped in the corner, steaming in the cold, limbs half-gnawed.

None of his training had prepared him for this. None of his training had prepared him for being a rural vet full stop. He'd learnt how to recognize ringworm and deliver a calf. Learnt about anatomy. But his studies never covered how to translate Swaledale dialect and how it differed from Wharfedale, or how to keep your fingers working at three in the morning in a fierce moor wind. No, you picked that up as you went along. He wiped his forehead and turned the torch on. The light caught on the air. The bulb faded until the flimsy filament glow was the only thing visible and he remembered not picking up the newly charged batteries before he'd left the house.

He could hear the creature breathing, creaking out each broken lungful of air.

Malcolm creased his ammonia-burnt eyes. The beast's hide was sticky with amniotic fluid, membrane caught between yellow teeth. Fur tarblack, apart from the ears, stained clot-red.

Malcolm started breathing again—shallow, though. He knew what waited in the corner. Not from Stickland's book on anatomy or Cunningham's Veterinary Physiology, but tales told over pints of sour beer, in polished wood taprooms.

Only a handful of days had passed from arriving in the Dales for him to hear the first tales of bargests, the red-eared, shape-changing hell hounds that skulked the stones of Troller's Gill and the streets of Thirsk. There were stories of them hunting travellers across High Moss and carrying trusting cattle herds into tannin-stained water. Of course, they were just one of a cast of thousands, alongside boggarts, giants, cursed chairs, all used to scare children to bed and incomers from the fields. He'd paid these folk stories little attention. His countryside was one of dirt tracks and distemper, not hell hounds and hauntings.

Malcolm could do nothing here apart from become food. He kept the creature in line of sight and backed up to the door, reached behind him and pushed. The thick planks gave, then held.

"The door seems to be stuck, Bill," he said.

"Not stuck, Veterinary. Locked."

"Well, unlock it, then."

"Can't do that, Veterinary."

"What do you mean, you can't do that? Open the door, Bill," Malcolm said, trying to keep his voice even.

"Got family to think of. Yon beast needs feeding," the farmer said, pausing. Through the boards, Malcolm could smell tobacco burn as Bill sucked on a hand-rolled cigarette.

"Stop messing about, Bill. I've got family, too. Open this door," Malcolm said. The creature's eyes started to open.

"Not my problem," Bill said.

Malcolm undid his jacket and reached into his pocket for his mobile phone from under old receipts. Tissues fluttered to the floor like anemic, torn butterflies. With his right hand steadying the left, he turned the phone on, the small screen pulsing faint light. The stack of lines in the top corner refused to appear. No signal. He waited, staring, not wanting to look round, giving the phone screen all of his attention. It stayed blank, no service provider name or EMERGENCY CALLS ONLY appearing like a hidden portal to transport him out of this place. His fingers went numb. The phone clattered, back popping off, spitting the battery across the dirt.

He collected the phone up and dropped the shattered plastic into his pocket, then banged on the door.

"Bill? Are you still there?" he asked.

"I am, veterinary. I'm not going anywhere," the old farmer said. Malcolm could picture him leaning against the wall, cap pulled down low against the ice that laced the air up here, no matter what the time of year.

"I know you're not going to let me out, but can you do me a favor? Can you get my vet's bag out of my car? The door's open," he said, trying to keep his voice steady.

"Don't think I can. I know what you carry in that black bag. Surgical tools, syringes, tranquilizers. Get that for you, and you'll try and stop the beast. You're too good a bloke. I don't want you suffering, thinking you can get out. Just go over there. Let the creature do its thing. All nice and quick-like."

Malcolm checked his pockets for bubble packs of ketamine, finding two, both empty.

Crouching low, he looked around the shed. The walls looked ramshackle, but the planks were thick and soaked with a hundred years of creosote. There was no way he was going to break out by hand. Squinting, he scanned the walls for tools. A muck crome or a silage knife, anything he could use to prize his way out.

"You still there, Veterinary?" Bill said.

For a moment Malcolm thought about not answering.

"Yes," he said, still scanning round for tool racks.

Slipping on the cobbles, Malcolm walked to a side wall and got his fingers behind one of the planks. The wood stayed where it was, pushing a splinter the length of a scalpel into his palm, blood pooling. He wiped his hand on his jacket and sat down, back against the wall. The bargest was in no rush to move, its eyes not leaving him once. Damp from the floor seeped through Malcolm's trousers, turning his skin to ice.

Try as he might, he couldn't rationalize this. Here was just another creature. Shaped by story and drunken bragging but a creature of flesh and bone, nonetheless. Even so, the cunning burning in the newborn, thousand-year-old creature's eyes charred his marrow with fear.

It was hopeless. He was stuck in here with this animal. Animals were his work. His life. He'd spent the last ten years tending them, keeping them alive, even when he knew most of them were destined for the slaughter-house. He pulled out his wallet, hand shaking as he undid the clasp. His hand spasmed, tipping coins and credit cards around him in a fan. Reaching down, he picked up a photo, now coated with half-rotten straw. He tried to clean the dirt off, so he could see Hilary and Tamsin properly, but they just became more obscured under a fine brown film of decay.

The photo was of Tamsin's graduation. The proudest day of his life, watching his daughter follow in his footsteps. He stared at their faces. Every few moments, he closed his eyes to try and recall them, but they stayed out of sight, reluctant shadows of a past cut off by these wooden walls. After a while, he kept his eyes shut and sobbed his throat raw.

Outside, he could hear Bill mumbling to himself. He sounded as scared as Malcolm felt.

The beast acted like it had all the time in the world, sitting on its haunches. There was no need to rush. Malcolm was going nowhere.

A drunken memory surfaced through the panic and, under his breath, Malcolm thanked Old Marley. Cut hand cradled in his lap, he pushed himself up from the floor, cramp bringing him tumbling down more than once. Crouching, he let his fingers drift across the floor like dangled puppets. Straw stuck to the cobbles in patches, layered and thick. It came away in strips, each laminate clouding the air with the stench of animal waste. Using small movements, Malcolm worked his way across the barn, pulling up decades of trampled bedding and dung, piling the fragments in stacks behind him. All the time, the creature watched, steam condensing against Malcolm's skin.

Not many listened to Marley. Not many understood the creased shepherd, anyway, much less when he was on the outside of half a bottle of scotch, but Malcolm took the time and paid for the drinks. Marley cared for his animals more than anyone Malcolm had met. Get past the slurring and he could tell a good story, for the price of a single malt, of course.

Marley was the first to mention the bargest to Malcolm, first to describe the red ears and the culling stare. He didn't know if Marley's story of being pursued over the moors was true. He didn't know if the whispered story of keeping one side of Moor Gill, the beast the other, was an embellishment. At the moment, he had little to lose and little left to try.

Outside, he could hear Bill stumble his way through the Lord's Prayer. If it weren't so serious, it would be funny. Dale gossip whispered the only time Bill saw the inside of church was to dip the collection plate.

Shifting along the ground, Malcolm carried on pulling fragments of dirt from the floor, slowly revealing the channel. Only shallow, the drain carried water along the barn to a stone slab trough at the other end. Now out of sight of the creature, Malcolm reached under the wall and pulled away fifty years of mud, the dirt pushing nails away from his fingers.

Only a trickle came at first, water the color of port. He wiped his face, leaving a stain across his forehead, scrabbled back and banged against the door. The creature looked up at the noise, spit dripping onto the floor.

"Don't be struggling, Veterinary. If it were me, I'd be scooting across that barn. Get it over and done with," Bill said, his voice close as if he were trying to peer through the gaps.

"Well, I'm not you, Bill," Malcolm said, his teeth grinding as he tried to keep from shivering.

"Ay, you're right at that, Veterinary. I'm outside; you're stuck in there."

"Might get out, yet."

"Might be pigs fly. I'd rather bet on that than you making through the night," Bill said.

Malcolm listened to him pause as he took another drag of his cigarette.

"Don't drag it out. I know it's not fair on you, but I don't want you to suffer more than you have to, Veterinary. I'm not a cruel man."

Malcolm ignored him.

He knew time was running low. His movements had been slow, trying to disturb the fetid air as little as possible. The creature might be less than twelve hours old, but the thing that clung inside was older than the hills themselves. The bargest blistered with cunning.

Cold mud coated Malcolm's hands up to the knuckles, all feeling gone. He pressed on, scooping up handfuls of muck, throwing them over his shoulder, getting careless. Outside, Bill stopped stumbling his way through scripture and listened to the dirt slip down the walls.

The folk tales never came with specifics, or volume tables. Never said how much liquid needed to flow. Whether a river or a stutter. Malcolm kept digging the channel free.

The water was sticky, more sludge or soup, but it flowed, nonetheless. He watched it creep across the floor, rivulets spilling between the cobbles until the stone submerged below the neonatal stream.

An expression passed across the creature's face, one Malcolm had never seen on an animal: confusion. Not the dislocated confusion of pain. Genuine wonderment at the lack of its own comprehension of the situation. Then anger.

Malcolm watched the creature's skin dragged in through its mouth, now turned to a raw wound. Ribs and muscles glistened on the outside of its torso, like offal on a butcher's slab. Malcolm's brain protested, breaking down in the face of this. In that moment, he knew that if it couldn't kill him to feast, the bargest would kill him with fear.

Somewhere deep inside, in the place that cocooned stories, he realized he must turn his back. If he didn't, and soon, his heart would turn itself inside out of his chest in sympathy.

With effort, he pivoted each footstep. Outside, Bill started on the Psalms, sung in a discordant tenor to no tune a congregation would recognize.

Eyes closed, Malcolm faced the wall, whispering childhood stories to himself. The bargest's breath scorched his jacket, wax running from charred cotton and dripping on the floor. Every nerve was telling him to turn. He stayed the other way, elective blind.

The whispers started. Fears and memories dragged from childhood. Voices of dead people Malcolm had buried deep squirmed their way out. His back was soaked with sweat, now. Then the promises of wealth and debauchery started. The offers of gold and power, if only he would turn. If only he would look just once. He didn't even need to open his eyes, just peek. Just peek enough to step over the little, tiny stream bisecting the barn.

His throat was full of sand. He couldn't speak, even though every inch of skin wanted to let the air burn his lungs and turn it against the walls, like Joshua against the walls of Jericho. He wanted to scream till his teeth powdered and tongue rotted at the root. He wanted to open his eyes and see the sun stream through the oak tree, outside his childhood bedroom, to sacrifice every minute of his adult life just to wake up from this stained and bitter nightmare in the cocoon of his childhood.

Malcolm stayed silent because he knew, deep down, even when the lies delivered in Hilary's voice were at their most persuasive, that to survive the next few moments, he must not turn around.

Even when something brushed his cheek or took his hand. Even when he could no longer feel the cobbles beneath his feet or know if he were asleep or awake, he still did not turn round.

Malcolm never knew how long he stood facing that wall before his legs gave out, crumpling to the floor, head catching the straw and bringing a dreamless sleep.

Daytime had arrived when he came to, a dull, gray light visible through his sore eyes. He looked over the trickle of stream. The back wall of the shed had gone, broken planks littering the hill beyond, tufts of thick, black hair caught on the rusted nails. Still, he didn't cross the water, instead smashing his shoulder again and again into the padlocked door until the wood gave, spreading a bruise across the top of his arm.

He half-expected to find Bill slumped on the grass outside, or mauled beyond recognition, but the field was empty apart from a pile of half-smoked cigarettes, a ripped-up copy of the *King James Bible*, and a flock of half-blind, featherless jackdaws cawing in the mist.

THAT TINY FLUTTER OF THE HEART I USED TO CALL LOVE

ROBERT SHEARMAN

Karen thought of them as her daughters, and tried to love them with all her heart. Because, really, wasn't that the point? They came to her, all frilly dresses, and fine hair, and plastic limbs, and eyes so large and blue and innocent. And she would name them, and tell them she was their mother now; she took them to her bed, and would give them tea parties, and spank them when they were naughty; she promised she would never leave them, or, at least, not until the end.

Her father would bring them home. Her father travelled a lot, and she never knew where he'd been, if she asked he'd just laugh and tap his nose and say it was all hush-hush—but she could sometimes guess from how exotic the daughters were, sometimes the faces were strange and foreign, one or two were nearly mulatto. Karen didn't care, she loved them all anyway, although she wouldn't let the mulatto ones have quite the same nursery privileges. "Here you are, my sweetheart, my angel cake, my baby doll," and from somewhere within Father's great jacket he'd produce a box, and it was usually gift-wrapped, and it usually had a ribbon on it—"This is all for you, my baby doll." She liked him calling her that, although she suspected she was too old for it now, she was very nearly eight years old.

She knew what the daughters were. They were tributes. That was what Nicholas called them. They were tributes paid to her, to make up for the fact that Father was so often away, just like in the very olden days when the Greek heroes would pay tributes to their gods with sacrifices. Nicholas was very keen on Greek heroes, and would tell his sister stories of great battles and wooden horses and heels. She didn't need tributes from Father; she would much rather he didn't have to leave home in the first place. Nicholas would tell her of the tributes Father had once paid Mother—he'd bring her jewellery, and fur coats, and tickets to the opera. Karen couldn't remember Mother very well, but there was that large portrait of her over the staircase. In a way, Karen saw Mother more often than she did Father. Mother was wearing a black ball gown, and such a lot of jewels, and there was a small studied smile on her face. Sometimes when Father paid tribute to Karen, she would try and give that same studied smile, but she wasn't sure she'd ever got it right.

-‹o›-

Father didn't call Nicholas "angel cake" or "baby doll," he called him "Nicholas," and Nicholas called him "sir." And Father didn't bring Nicholas tributes. Karen felt vaguely guilty about that—that she'd get showered with gifts and her brother would get nothing. Nicholas told her not to be so silly. He wasn't a little girl, he was a man. He was ten years older than Karen, and lean, and strong, and he was attempting to grow a moustache; the hair was a bit too fine for it to be seen in bright light, but it would darken as he got older. Karen knew her brother was a man, and that he wouldn't want toys. But she'd give him a hug sometimes, almost impulsively, when Father came home and seemed to ignore him—and Nicholas never objected when she did.

Eventually Nicholas would say to Karen, "It's time," and she knew what that meant. And she'd feel so sad, but again, wasn't that the point? She'd go and give her daughter a special tea party then, and she'd play with her all day; she'd brush her hair, and let her see the big wide world from out of the top window; she wouldn't get cross even if her daughter got naughty. And she wouldn't try to explain. That would all come after. Karen would go to bed at the usual time, Nanny never suspected a thing. But once Nanny had left the room and turned out the light,

Karen would get up and put on her clothes again, nice thick woollen ones, sometimes it was cold out there in the dark. And she'd bundle her daughter up warm as well. And once the house was properly still she'd hear a tap at the door, and there Nicholas would be, looking stern and serious and just a little bit excited. She'd follow him down the stairs and out of the house; they'd usually leave by the tradesmen's entrance, the door was quieter. They wouldn't talk until they were far away, and very nearly into the woods themselves.

He'd always give Karen a few days to get to know her daughters before he came for them. He wanted her to love them as hard as she could. He always seemed to know when it was the right time. With one doll, her very favourite, he had given her only until the weekend—it had been love at first sight, the eyelashes were real hair, and she'd blink when picked up, and if she were cuddled tight she'd say "Mama." Sometimes Nicholas gave them as long as a couple of months; some of the dolls were a fright, and cold to the touch, and it took Karen a while to find any affection for them at all. But Karen was a girl with a big heart. She could love anything, given time and patience. Nicholas must have been carefully watching his sister, just to see when her heart reached its fullest—and she never saw him do it; he usually seemed to ignore her altogether, as if she were still too young and too silly to be worth his attention. But then, "It's time," he would say, and sometimes it wasn't until that very moment that Karen would realise she'd fallen in love at all, and of course he was right, he was always right.

Karen liked playing in the woods by day. By night they seemed strange and unrecognisable, the branches jutted out at peculiar angles as if trying to bar her entrance. But Nicholas wasn't afraid, and he always knew his way. She kept close to him for fear he would rush on ahead and she would be lost. And she knew somehow that if she got lost, she'd be lost forever—and it may turn daylight eventually, but that wouldn't matter, she'd have been trapped by the woods of the night, and the woods of the night would get to keep her.

And at length they came to the clearing. Karen always supposed that the clearing was at the very heart of the woods, she didn't know why. The tight press of trees suddenly lifted, and here there was space—no flowers, nothing, some grass, but even the grass was brown, as if the sunlight couldn't reach it here. And it was as if everything had been cut away to make a perfect circle that was neat and tidy and so empty, and it was as if it had been done especially for them. Karen could never find the clearing in the daytime. But then, she had never tried very hard.

Nicholas would take her daughter, and set her down upon that browning grass. He would ask Karen for her name, and Karen would tell him. Then Nicholas would tell Karen to explain to the daughter what was going to happen here. "Betsy, you have been sentenced to death." And Nicholas would ask Karen upon what charge. "Because I love you too much, and I love my brother more." And Nicholas would ask if the daughter had any final words to offer before sentence was carried out; they never had.

He would salute the condemned then, nice and honourably. And Karen would by now be nearly in tears; she would pull herself together. "You mustn't cry," said Nicholas, "you can't cry, if you cry the death won't be a clean one." She would salute her daughter too.

What happened next would always be different.

When he'd been younger, Nicholas had merely hanged them. He'd put rope around their little necks and take them to the closest tree and let them drop down from the branches, and there they'd swing for a while, their faces still frozen with trusting smiles. As he'd become a man he'd found more inventive ways to despatch them. He'd twist off their arms, he'd drown them in buckets of water he'd already prepared, he'd stab them with a fork. He'd say to Karen, "And how much do you love this one?" And if Karen told him she loved her very much, so much the worse for her daughter—he'd torture her a little first, blinding her, cutting off her skin, ripping off her clothes and then toasting with matches the naked stuff beneath. It was always harder to watch these executions because Karen really *had* loved them, and it was agony to see them suffer so. But she couldn't lie to her brother. He would have seen through her like glass.

⊸◦⊶

That last time had been the most savage, though Karen hadn't known it would be the last time, of course—but Nicholas, Nicholas might have had an inkling.

When they'd reached the clearing, he had tied Mary-Lou to the tree with string. Tightly, but not *too* tight—Karen had said she hadn't loved Mary-Lou especially, and Nicholas didn't want to be cruel. He had even wrapped his own handkerchief around her eyes as a blindfold.

Then he'd produced from his knapsack Father's gun.

"You can't use that!" Karen said. "Father will find out! Father will be angry!"

"Phooey to that," said Nicholas. "I'll be going to war soon, and I'll have a gun all of my own. Had you heard that, Carrie? That I'm going to war?" She hadn't heard. Nanny had kept it from her, and Nicholas had wanted it to be a surprise. He looked at the gun. "It's a Webley Mark IV service revolver," he said. "Crude and old-fashioned, just like Father. What I'll be getting will be much better."

He narrowed his eyes, and aimed the gun, fired. There was an explosion, louder than Karen could ever have dreamed—and she thought Nicholas was shocked too, not only by the noise, but by the recoil. Birds scattered. Nicholas laughed. The bullet had gone wild. "That was just a warm up," he said.

It was on his fourth try that he hit Mary-Lou. Her leg was blown off.

"Do you want a go?"

"No," said Karen.

"It's just like at a fairground," he said. "Come on."

She took the gun from him, and it burned in her hand, it smelled like burning. He showed her how to hold it, and she liked the way his hand locked around hers as he corrected her aim. "It's all right," he said to his little sister gently, "we'll do it together. There's nothing to be scared of." And really he was the one who pulled the trigger, but she'd been holding on too, so she was a *bit* responsible, and Nicholas gave a whoop of delight and Karen had never heard him so happy before, she wasn't sure she'd *ever* heard him happy. And when they looked back at the tree, Mary-Lou had disappeared.

"I'm going across the seas," he said. "I'm going to fight. And every man I kill, listen, I'm killing him for you. Do you understand me? I'll kill them all because of you."

He kissed her then on the lips. It felt warm and wet and the moustache tickled, and it was hard too, as if he were trying to leave an imprint there, as if when he pulled away he wanted to leave a part of him behind.

"I love you," he said.

"I love you too."

"Don't forget me," he said. Which seemed such an odd thing to say—how was she going to forget her own brother?

They'd normally bury the tribute then, but they couldn't find any trace of Mary-Lou's body. Nicholas put the gun back in the knapsack, he offered Karen his hand. She took it. They went home.

—◦—

They had never found Nicholas' body either; at the funeral, his coffin was empty, and Father told Karen it didn't matter, that good form was the thing. Nicholas had been killed in the Dardanelles, and Karen looked for it upon the map, and it seemed such a long way to go to die. There were lots of funerals in the town that season, and Father made sure that Nicholas' was the most lavish, no expense was spared.

The family was so small now, and they watched together as the coffin was lowered into the grave. Father looking proud, not sad. And Karen refusing to cry—"Don't cry," she said to the daughter she'd brought with her, "you mustn't cry, or it won't be clean"—and yet she dug her fingernails deep into her daughter's body to try to force some tears from it.

—◦—

Julian hadn't gone to war. He'd been born just too late. And of course he said he was disappointed, felt cheated even, he loved his country and whatever his country might stand for, and he had wanted to demonstrate that love in the very noblest of ways. He said it with proper earnestness, and some days he almost meant it. His two older brothers had gone to fight, and both had returned home, and the younger had brought back some sort of medal with him. The brothers had changed. They had less time for Julian, and Julian felt that was no bad thing. He was no longer worth the effort of bullying. One day he'd asked his eldest brother what it had been like out there on the Front. And the brother turned to him in surprise, and Julian was surprised too, what had he been thinking of?—and he braced himself for the pinch or Chinese burn that was sure to follow. But instead the brother had just turned away; he'd sucked his cigarette down to the very stub, and sighed, and said it was just as well

Julian hadn't been called up, the trenches were a place for real men. The whole war really wouldn't have been his bag at all.

When Julian Morris first met Karen Davison, neither was much impressed. Certainly, Julian was well used to girls finding him unimpressive: he was short, his face was too round and homely, his thighs quickly thinned into legs that looked too spindly to support him. There was an effeminacy about his features that his father had thought might have been cured by a spell fighting against Germans, but Julian didn't know whether it would have helped; he tried to take after his brothers, tried to lower his voice and speak more gruffly, he drank beer, he took up smoking. But even there he'd got it all wrong somehow. The voice, however gruff, always rose in inflection no matter how much he tried to stop it. He sipped at his beer. He held his cigarette too languidly, apparently, and when he puffed out smoke it was always from the side of his mouth and never with a good, bold, manly blast.

But for Julian to be unimpressed by a girl was a new sensation for him. Girls flummoxed Julian. With their lips and their breasts and their flowing contours. With their bright colours, all that perfume. Even now, if some aged friend of his mother's spoke to him, he'd be reduced to a stammering mess. But Karen Davison did something else to Julian entirely. He looked at her across the ballroom and realised that he rather despised her. It wasn't that she was unattractive, at first glance her figure was pretty enough. But she was so much older than the other girls, in three years of attending dances no man had yet snatched her up—and there was already something middle-aged about that face, something jaded. She looked bored. That was it, she looked bored. And didn't care to hide it.

Once in a while a man would approach her, take pity on her, ask her to dance. She would reject him, and off the suitor would scarper, with barely disguised relief.

Julian had promised his parents that he would at least invite one girl on to the dance floor. It would hardly be his fault if that one girl he chose said no. He could return home, he'd be asked how he had got on, and if he were clever he might even be able to phrase a reply that concealed the fact he'd been rejected. Julian was no good at lying outright, his voice would squeak, and he would turn bright red. But not telling the truth? He'd had to find a way of mastering it.

He approached the old maid. Now that she was close, he felt the usual panic rise within him, and he fought it down—look at her, he told himself, look at how *hard* she looks, like stone; she should be *grateful* you ask her to dance. He'd reached her. He opened his mouth to speak, realised his first word would be a stutter, put the word aside, found some new word to replace it, cleared his throat. Only then did the girl bother to look up at him. There was nothing welcoming in that expression, but nothing challenging either—she looked at him with utter indifference.

"A dance?" he said. "Like? Would you?"

And, stupidly, opened out his arms, as if to remind her what a dance was, as if without her he'd simply manage on his own in dumb show.

She looked him up and down. Judging him, blatantly judging him. Not a smile upon her face. He waited for the refusal.

"Very well," she said then, though without any enthusiasm.

He offered her his hand, and she took it by the fingertips, and rose to her feet. She was an inch or two taller than him. He smelled her perfume and didn't like it.

He put one hand on her waist, the other was left gently brushing against her glove. They danced. She stared at his face, still quite incuriously, but it was enough to make him blush.

"You dance well," she said.

"Thank you."

"I don't enjoy dancing."

"Then let us, by all means, stop."

He led her back to her chair. He nodded at her stiffly and prepared to leave. But she gestured towards the chair beside her, and he found himself bending down to sit in it.

"Are you enjoying the ball?" he asked her.

"I don't enjoy talking either."

"I see." And they sat in silence for a few minutes. At one point, he felt he should get up and walk away, and he shuffled in his chair to do so—and at that she turned to look at him, and managed a smile, and for that alone he decided to stay a little while longer.

"Can I at least get you a drink?"

She agreed. So he went to fetch her a glass of fizz. Across the room, he watched as another man approached and asked her to dance, and he suddenly felt a stab of jealousy that astonished him. She waved the man away, in irritation, and Julian pretended it was for his sake.

He brought her back the fizz.

"There you are," he said.

She sipped at it. He sipped at his the same way.

"If you don't like dancing," he said to her, "and you don't like talking, why do you come?" He already knew the answer, of course, it was the same reason he came, and she didn't bother dignifying him with a reply. He laughed and hated how girlish it sounded.

At length she said, "Thank you for coming," as if this were *her* ball, as if he were *her* guest, and he realised he was being dismissed. He got to his feet.

"Do you have a card?" she asked.

Julian did. She took it, put it away without reading it. And Julian waited beside her for any further farewell, and when nothing came, he nodded at her once more and left her.

⊷

The very next day, Julian received a telephone call from a Mr. Davison, who invited him to have dinner with his daughter at his house that evening. Julian accepted. And because the girl had never bothered to give him her name, it took Julian a fair little time to work out who this Davison fellow might be.

Julian wondered whether the evening would be formal, and so overdressed, just for safety's sake. He took some flowers. He rang the bell, and some hatchet-faced old woman opened the front door. She showed him in. She told him that Mr. Davison had been called away on business and would be unable to dine with him that evening. Mistress Karen would receive him in the drawing room. She disappeared with his flowers, and Julian never saw them again and had no evidence indeed that Mistress Karen would ever see them either.

At the top of the staircase, Julian saw there were two portraits. One was a giantess, a bejewelled matriarch sneering down at him, and Julian could recognise in her features the girl he had danced with the night before, and he was terrified of her, and he fervently hoped that Karen would never grow up to be like her mother. The other portrait, much smaller, was of some boy in army uniform.

Karen was waiting for him. She was wearing the same dress she had worn the previous night. "I'm so glad you could come," she intoned.

"I'm glad you invited me."

"Let us eat."

So they went into the dining room and sat either end of a long table. The hatchet-face served them soup. "Thank you, Nanny," Karen said. Julian tasted the soup. The soup was good.

"It's a very grand house," said Julian.

"Please, there's no need to make conversation."

"All right."

The soup bowls were cleared away. Chicken was served. And, after that, a trifle.

"I like trifle," said Karen, and Julian didn't know whether he was supposed to respond to that, and so he smiled at her, and she smiled back, and that all seemed to work well enough.

Afterwards Julian asked whether he could smoke. Karen said he might. He offered Karen a cigarette, and she hesitated, and then said she would like that. So Julian got up, and went around the table, and lit one for her. Julian tried very hard to smoke in the correct way, but it still kept coming out girlishly. But Karen didn't seem to mind; indeed, she positively imitated him, she puffed smoke from the corner of her mouth and made it all look very pretty.

And even now they didn't talk, and Julian realised he didn't mind. There was no awkwardness to it. It was companionable. It was a shared understanding.

◄○►

Julian was invited to three more dinners. After the fourth, Mr. Davison called Mr. Morris, and told him that a proposal of marriage to his daughter would not be unacceptable. Mr. Morris was very pleased, and Mrs. Morris took Julian to her bedroom and had him go through her jewellery box to pick out a ring he could give his fiancée, and Julian marvelled, he had never seen such beautiful things.

Julian didn't meet Mr. Davison until the wedding day, whereupon the man clapped him on the back as if they were old friends, and told him he was proud to call him his son. Mr. Morris clapped Julian on the back too; even Julian's brothers were at it. And Julian marvelled at how he had been transformed into a man by dint of a simple service and signed certificate. Neither of his brothers had married yet, he had beaten them to the punch, and was there jealousy in that back clapping? They called Julian a lucky dog, that his bride was quite the catch. And so, Julian felt, she was; on her day of glory she did nothing but beam with smiles, and there was no trace of her customary truculence. She was charming, even witty, and Julian wondered why she had chosen to hide these qualities from him—had she recognised that it would have made him scared of her? Had she been shy and hard just to win his heart? Julian thought this might be so, and in that belief discovered that he did love her, he loved her after all—and maybe, in spite of everything, the marriage might just work out.

For a wedding present, the families had bought them a house in Chelsea. It was small, but perfectly situated, and they could always upgrade when they had children. As an extra present, Mr. Davison had bought his daughter a doll—a bit of a monstrosity, really, about the size of a fat infant, with blonde curly hair and red lips as thick as a darkie's, and wearing its own imitation wedding dress. Karen seemed pleased with it. Julian thought little about it at the time.

❧

They honeymooned in Venice for two weeks, in a comfortable hotel near the Rialto.

Karen didn't show much interest in Venice. No, that wasn't true; she said she was fascinated by Venice. But she preferred to read about it in her guidebook. Outside there was noise, and people, and stink; she could better experience the city indoors. Julian offered to stay with her, but she told him he was free to do as he liked. So in the daytime he'd leave her, and he'd go and visit St. Mark's Square, climb the basilica, take a gondola ride. In the evening he'd return, and over dinner he'd try to tell her all about it. She'd frown, and say there was no need to explain, she'd already read it all in her Baedeker. Then they would eat in silence.

On the first night, he'd been tired from travel. On the second, from sightseeing. On the third night, Karen told her husband that there were certain manly duties he was expected to perform. Her father was wanting a grandson; for her part, she wanted lots of daughters. Julian said he would do his very best, and drank half a bottle of claret to give him courage. She stripped off, and he found her body interesting, and even attractive, but not in the least arousing. He stripped off too.

"Oh!" she said. "But you have hardly any hair! I've got more hair than you!" And it was true, there was a faint buzz of fur over her skin, and over his next to nothing—just the odd clump where Nature had started work, rethought the matter, given up. Karen laughed, but it was not unkind. She ran her fingers over his body. "It's so *smooth*, how did you get it so smooth?

"Wait a moment," she then said, and hurried to the bathroom. She was excited. Julian had never seen his wife excited. She returned with a razor. "Let's make you perfect," she said.

She soaped him down, and shaved his body bald. She only cut him twice, and that wasn't her fault, that was because he'd moved. She left him only the hairs on his head. And even there, she plucked the eyebrows, and trimmed his fine wavy hair into a neat bob.

"There," she said, and looked over her handiwork proudly, and ran her hands all over him, and this time there was nothing that got in their way.

And at that, he tried to kiss her, and she laughed again, and pushed him away.

"No, no," she said. "Your duties can wait until we're in England. We're on holiday."

So he started going out at night as well, with her blessing. He saw how romantic Venice could be by moonlight. He didn't know Italian well, and so could barely understand what the *ragazzi* said to him, but it didn't matter, they were very accommodating. And by the time he returned to his wife's side, she was always asleep.

◄o►

The house in Chelsea had been done up for them, ready for their return. He asked her whether she'd like him to carry her over the threshold. She looked surprised at that, and said he could try. She lay back in his arms, and he was expecting her to be quite heavy, but it went all right really, and he got her through the doorway without doing anything to disgrace himself.

As far as he'd been aware, Karen had never been to the house before.

But she knew exactly where to go, walking straight to the study, and to the wooden desk inside, and to the third drawer down. "I have a present for you," she said, and from the drawer she took a gun.

"It was my brother's," she said.

"Oh. Really?"

"It may not have been his. But it's what they gave us anyway."

She handed it to Julian. Julian weighed it in his hands. Like his wife, it was lighter than he'd expected.

"You're the man of the house now," Karen said.

There was no nanny to fetch them dinner. Julian said he didn't mind cooking. He fixed them some eggs. He liked eggs.

After they'd eaten, and Julian had rinsed the plates and left them to dry, Karen said that they should inspect the bedroom. And Julian agreed. They'd inspected the rest of the house; that room, quite deliberately, both had left as yet unexplored.

The first impression that Julian got as he pushed open the door was pink, that everything was pink; the bedroom was unapologetically feminine, that blazed out from the soft pink carpet and the wallpaper of pink rose on pink background, And there was a perfume to it too, the perfume of Karen herself, and he still didn't much care for it.

That was before he saw the bed.

He was startled, and gasped, and then laughed at himself for gasping. The bed was covered with dolls. There were at least a dozen of them, all pale plastic skin and curls and lips that were ruby red, and some were wearing pretty little hats, and some carrying pretty little nosegays, all of them in pretty dresses. In the centre of them, in pride of place, was the doll Karen's father had given as a wedding present—resplendent in her wedding dress, still fat, her facial features smoothed away beneath that fat, sitting amongst the others like a queen. And all of them were smiling. And all of them were looking at him, expectantly, as if they'd been waiting to see who it was they'd heard climb the stairs, as if they'd been waiting for him all this time.

Julian said, "Well! Well. Well, we won't be able to get much sleep with that lot crowding about us!" He chuckled. "I mean, I won't know which is which! Which one is just a doll, and which one my pretty wife!" He chuckled. "Well."

Karen said, "Gifts from my father. I've had some since I was a little girl. Some of them have been hanging about for years."

Julian nodded.

Karen said, "But I'm yours now."

Julian nodded again. He wondered whether he should put his arms around her. He didn't quite like to, not with all the dolls staring.

"I love you," said Karen. "Or rather, I'm trying. I need you to know, I'm trying very hard." And for a moment Julian thought she was going to cry, but then he saw her blink back the tears, her face was hard again. "But I can't love you fully, not whilst I'm loving them. You have to get rid of them for me."

"Well, yes," said Julian. "I mean. If you're sure that's what you want."

Karen nodded grimly. "It's time. And long overdue."

·↞·↠·

She put on her woollen coat then, she said it would be cold out there in the dark. And she bundled up the dolls too, each and every one of them, and began putting them into Julian's arms. "There's too many," he said, "I'll drop them," but Karen didn't stop, and soon there were arms and legs poking into his chest, he felt the hair of his wife's daughters scratching under his chin. Karen carried just one doll herself, her new doll. She also carried the gun.

It had been a warm summer's evening, not quite yet dark. When they stepped outside, it was pitch, only the moonlight providing some small relief, and that grudging. The wind bit. And Chelsea, the city bustle, the pavements, the pedestrians, the traffic—Chelsea had gone, and all that was left was the house. Just the house, and the woods ahead of them.

Julian wanted to run then, but there was nowhere to run to. He tried to drop the dolls. But the dolls refused to let go, they clung on to him, he could feel their little plastic fingers tightening around his coat, his shirt buttons, his skin, his own skin.

"Follow me," said Karen.

The branches stuck out at weird angles, impossible angles, Julian couldn't see any way to climb through them. But Karen knew where to tread and where to duck, and she didn't hesitate, she moved at speed—and Julian followed her every step, he struggled to catch up, he lost sight of her once or twice and thought he was lost for good, but the dolls, the dolls showed him the way.

The clearing was a perfect circle, and the moon shone down upon it like a spotlight on a stage.

"Put them down," said Karen.

He did so.

She arranged the dolls on the browning grass, set them in one long neat line. Julian tried to help; he put the new doll in her wedding dress beside them, and Karen rescued her. "It's not her time yet," she said. "But she needs to see what will one day happen to her."

"And what is going to happen?"

Her reply came as if the daughters themselves had asked. Her voice rang loud, with a confidence Julian had never heard from her before. "Chloe. Barbara. Mary-Sue. Mary-Jo. Suki. Delilah. Wendy. Prue. Annabelle. Mary-Ann. Natasha. Jill. You have been sentenced to death."

"But why?" said Julian. He wanted to grab her, shake her by the shoulders. He wanted to. She was his wife, that's what he was supposed to do. He couldn't even touch her. He couldn't even go near. "Why? What have they done?"

"Love," said Karen. She turned to him. "Oh, yes, *they* know what they've done."

She saluted them. "And you," she said to Julian, "you must salute them too. No. Not like that. That's not a salute. Hand steady. Like me. Yes. Yes."

She gave him the gun. The dolls all had their backs to him, at least he didn't have to see their faces.

He thought of his father. He thought of his brothers. Then, he didn't think of anything.

He fired into the crowd. He'd never fired a gun before, but it was easy, there was nothing to it. He ran out of bullets, so Karen reloaded the gun. He fired into the crowd again. He thought there might be screams. There were no screams. He thought there might be blood . . . and the brown of the grass seemed fresher and wetter and seemed to pool out lazily towards him.

And Karen reloaded his gun. And he fired into the crowd, just once more, please, God, just one last time. Let them be still. Let them stop twitching. The twitching stopped.

"It's over," said Karen.

"Yes," he said. He tried to hand her back the gun, but she wouldn't take it—it's yours now, you're the man of the house. "Yes," he said again.

He began to cry. He didn't make a sound.

"Don't," said Karen. "If you cry, the deaths won't be clean."

And he tried to stop, but now the tears found a voice, he bawled like a little girl.

She said, "I will not have you dishonour them."

She left him then. She picked up her one surviving doll, and went, and left him all alone in the woods. He didn't try to follow her. He stared at the bodies in the clearing, wondered if he should clear them up, make things tidier. He didn't. He clutched the gun, waited it for to cool, and eventually it did. And when he thought to turn about, he didn't know where to go, he didn't know he'd be able to find his way back. But the branches parted for him easily, as if ushering him fast on his way, as if they didn't want him either.

⟶o⟶

"I'm sorry," he said.

He hadn't taken a key. He'd had to ring his own doorbell. When his wife answered, he felt an absurd urge to explain who he was. He'd stopped crying, but his face was still red and puffy. He held out his gun to her, and she hesitated, then at last took it from him.

"Sorry," he said again.

"You did your best," she said. "I'm sorry too. But next time it'll be different."

"Yes," he said. "Next time."

"Won't you come in?" she said politely, and he thanked her, and did.

She took him upstairs. The doll was sitting on the bed, watching. She moved it to the dressing table. She stripped her husband. She ran her fingers over his soft smooth body, she'd kept it neat and shaved.

"I'm sorry," he said one more time; and then, as if it were the same thing, "I love you."

And she said nothing to that, but smiled kindly. And she took him then, and before he knew what he was about, he was inside her, and he knew he ought to feel something, and he knew he ought to be doing something to help. He tried to gyrate a little. "No, no," she said, "I'll do it," and so he let her be. He let her do all the work, and he looked up at her face and searched for any sign of passion there, or tenderness, but it was so *hard*—and he turned to the side, and there was the fat doll, and it was smiling, and its eyes were twinkling, and there, there, on that greasy plastic face, there was all the tenderness he could ask for.

Eventually she rolled off. He thought he should hug her. He put his arms around her, felt how strong she was. He felt like crying again. He supposed that would be a bad idea.

"I love you," she said. "I am very patient. I have learned to love you."

She fetched a hairbrush. She played at his hair. "My sweetheart," she said, "my angel cake." She turned him over, spanked his bottom hard with the brush until the cheeks were red as rouge. "My big baby doll."

And this time he *did* cry, it was as if she'd given him permission. And it felt so good.

He looked across at the doll, still smiling at him, and he hated her, and he wanted to hurt her, he wanted to take his gun and shove the barrel right inside her mouth and blast a hole through the back of her head. He wanted to take his gun and bludgeon with it, blow after blow, and he knew how good that would feel, the skull smashing, the wetness. And this time he wouldn't cry. He would be a real man.

"I love you," she said again. "With all my heart."

She pulled back from him, and looked him in the face, sizing him up, as she had that first time they'd met. She gave him a salute.

He giggled at that, he tried to raise his own arm to salute back, but it wouldn't do it, he was so very silly.

There was a blur of something brown at the foot of the bed; something just out of the corner of his eye, and the blur seemed to still, and the brown looked like a jacket maybe, trousers, a uniform. He tried to cry out—in fear, or at least in surprise?—but there was no air left in him. There was the smell of mud, so much mud. Who'd known mud could smell? And a voice to the blur, a voice in spite of all. "Is it time?"

He didn't see his wife's reaction, nor hear her reply. His head jerked, and he was looking at the doll again, and she was the queen doll, the best doll, so pretty in her wedding dress. She was his queen. And he thought she was smiling even wider, and that she was pleased he was offering her such sweet tribute.

BONES OF CROW

RAY CLULEY

Maggie tapped her cigarette twice on the pack before putting the filter to her mouth, an affectation she'd picked up years ago when she first started smoking. She'd seen it in a movie; it packed the tobacco tighter or something. Whatever the reason, it was as much a part of her habit now as sneaking up to the roof to enjoy it. Her lighter was a cheap throwaway but it did the job. She cupped the flame, brought it to her cigarette, and sucked in the day's first glorious breath of nicotine. Pocketing the lighter, she took the cigarette from her lips and exhaled the smoke with a sigh.

The block of flats she lived in was fifteen floors high with a view of urban sprawl and a sky that was early morning grey. Not that she came up for the view. She did like the air, though, away from the traffic and the fast food smells. Up here, the only pollution was of her own making, clinging to her clothes and making her father tut and grumble. "Your health," he'd say, meaning his. He'd say it the same way he said, "There's no need, I'll do it" and "You should get out and find a husband." He didn't mean it.

The roof had a low wall running around it. It wasn't the greatest safety precaution, coming up only as far as Maggie's thighs, but she supposed it stopped someone simply stepping off the edge. If you wanted to do that you at least had to make some effort. In her younger years she'd considered it, but only in the absent way she supposed most teenagers did. Now her suicide of choice came one drag at a time. With every breath, she died a little.

There were two small buildings on the roof. One housed the stairwell. The other was some kind of storage facility, its door chained shut. Maybe there was a generator in there or tools or something. Otherwise the roof was nothing but scattered puddles and low walls.

Maggie went to the wall and glanced down at the people on their way to work. Or, more likely, on their way to look for work. Once upon a time she'd wanted that too, hoping to make something of herself like her sisters, but with her father's pension and disability benefit, and the benefits they were claiming for her, there was little need. It used to bother her how rarely she went out, but the television showed her all that she was missing and it wasn't much. And as for marriage, children . . . well, there was still time. In theory. Until then there was always plenty to do around the flat. Cleaning. Cooking. Plus she had her smoking.

Maggie turned from the street and leant back against the wall in a sort of half sit, half lean, posture. She braced herself with her hands on either side, smoke curling up from the cigarette between her fingers, and looked out across the roof. The opposite wall blocked her view of the city so all she saw was grey sky, but she knew that beyond it was the park, a grand term for what was little more than a pathetic triangle of grass with a solitary climbing frame and a circle of asphalt where the roundabout used to be. It had been taken away because kids were using the wheels of their mopeds to turn it faster than it was designed for. A girl had been flung from it, flying briefly before cracking her head open. Maggie remembered seeing it on the local news. The family petitioned the council to get rid of what they called a death trap, though their daughter hadn't died and it had been her own fault anyway.

She smoked her cigarette down then checked her watch, knowing the time she'd see. Time to wake father. Time for his breakfast and time for his pills. Time for hers. A final drag and she twisted out what was left on the bricks behind her, dropping the butt into a pile gathered in the corner between roof and wall.

"Okay."

She pushed herself away from the wall and hoped the momentum would help carry her to the door, to the stairs, and back down to the flat.

⤙⚬⤏

Maggie's father had developed chronic obstructive pulmonary disease almost immediately after Maggie's mother left him. In his more romantic moments, he claimed it was because he couldn't breathe without her, but of course it was because he'd smoked most of his life. Now his puffs came from an oxygen canister. His lungs were weak and his natural defence mechanisms were so reduced that he required various medications to fight infections. Maggie looked after him though. She'd effectively raised her two sisters as well but they'd flown the nest as soon as they were able. She didn't hate them for that. She tried not to hate them for that. Just as she didn't hate her father for needing her so much.

Maggie lit one cigarette from another, stubbing one out and drawing breath from the next. The view from the roof hadn't changed much since morning. It was still overcast, low cloud giving the late afternoon a premature evening light. Instead of time flying, though, it seemed to barely pass at all.

Day in, day out, her routine was the same. Her father couldn't perform even the simplest of tasks without suffering a shortness of breath, but really all he needed was her company. Someone to watch television with. It was as much her duty as checking his oxygen and feeding him his pills. He had a plastic organiser for his medication, which Maggie sorted for him because he couldn't get the lids off the bottles. All he had to do was tip the day's cocktail into his palm and then into his mouth and drink a glass of water, but when the time came, he either spilled the pills onto the floor or made such a pathetic attempt to hook them from the container that inevitably Maggie would end up feeding them to him one by one. Pop one in his mouth, raise the water, tip it to swallow, and repeat, wiping away what spilled between repetitions.

Maggie sighed, glanced at her watch, and took another pull on her cigarette. Today he'd coughed one of the pills back up. It had slipped down his chin on a thin line of saliva. He'd wiped his mouth but the pill fell into the fibres of his dressing gown.

"I've got it, Dad." She plucked it from his sleeve, pressed it between his lips, and helped him with the water.

"You're a good girl. Why haven't you been snapped up yet?"

Maggie stared across the roof as if she might find the answer in the grey sky, the bricks and stone. She thought of all she could do to improve her life. It didn't take long. She took in a lungful of smoke and examined the burning end of her cigarette, tapping away its ash. There was less of it left than she'd thought.

She flicked the butt away across the roof, a tiny flare for no one to see. It sparked as it bounced and skittered out of sight behind the small storage building. Whatever was in there she didn't much care, but she did worry there might be litter behind it. Newspapers or magazines, somehow dry, or a puddle of something flammable.

She pushed herself away from the wall to check, surprised at her own recklessness; she always crushed them out, the wall black-spotted with proof. She must've been more frustrated with her father today than she thought. Or with herself. She was due on soon. Maybe that was it.

The cigarette smouldered where it lay. She squashed it out beneath her shoe and saw she'd been right to check. There *was* litter, a whole load of it, gathered in the narrow channel between storage building and the outer wall. Except litter seemed too accidental a term for it.

"What the hell?"

A lot of it was newspaper and magazine pages, polystyrene food cartons, plastic carrier bags, but there were other kinds of street debris too. An old traffic cone, a FOR SALE sign, even a scaffold pole leaning at an angle across it all, resting on the wall. The rubbish had been shaped into something like bedding and Maggie's first thought was of a homeless person, but then a homeless person who could get into the building would probably tuck up under the stairs somewhere, or in the foyer by the post boxes. There were clothes, though. Mismatched items, some with pegs on them, all of it grubby with bird shit and roof filth. A torn duvet cover was draped over something bulky in the middle of it all. Maggie dragged it aside.

There were eggs underneath.

"What the *hell*?"

There were four of them, four of the biggest eggs Maggie had ever seen. They had to be fake. *Had* to be. Each was knee high, about the same size as a barrel for a water cooler. Each was the colour of cement and speckled with dark freckles. She squatted beside them, pressing the back of her hand to her nose and holding her breath against the moist sour odour, the musky wet straw smell of a pet shop. She reached for one of the eggs but withdrew suddenly because she'd read somewhere that touching an unhatched egg meant it would be abandoned. The bird would—

Bird?

Maggie laughed and reached out again. Touched it. And again she snatched her hand back.

It was warm. And something inside had . . . moved. A vibration of life beneath her skin.

Maggie stood and dug the cigarettes from her pocket, double-tapped one, and popped it in her mouth. She sparked a flame, lit it, puffed a hurried breath, and said for a third time, "What the hell?"

Darker clouds were gathering, and the small light fixed to the outside of the storage building blinked to life prematurely, tricked into thinking it was night. A storm was coming. Maggie could feel it in the sky.

She smoked her third cigarette, staring at the eggs. They shone like small speckled moons beneath the light. If it hadn't started raining, she probably would have smoked her packet empty watching them, wondering what on earth could have put them there.

◄○►

Maggie was awake at first light, despite having stayed up late. She smoked the day's first cigarette out of her bedroom window, enjoying the cool air, and thought about going to the roof earlier than usual. She'd Googled different types of eggs, and she'd browsed various images, but found nothing useful. The largest eggs nowadays came from the ostrich, but they were only a pathetic six inches high. Not even close. The great elephant bird of Madagascar had laid eggs that were a foot or so high but they were extinct now.

Maggie smiled. Egg-stinct. Eggs-stinked. She blew smoke into the morning air.

Anyway, the eggs on the roof were twice the size of the Madagascan ones. Even the largest dinosaur egg she could find online wasn't much bigger than the elephant bird's.

Outside, the city was slowly coming to life. An Asian man was pulling at the metal blind of a newsagents, rattling it up, and a street sweeper was doing his or her best to tidy the city. Someone was walking a dog that kept trying to squat, yanking the lead before it could foul the pavement. A jogger, favouring the empty streets over the tiny nearby park, was running a course that would end in the same place it began.

In the park, someone was standing on the climbing frame. The climbing frame was two upright ladders with another leaning at an angle, and connecting all three was a horizontal section of bars to swing across. The figure was balancing in the middle of this, standing on the bars rather than hanging below them. Too big to be a child. Maggie was several storeys up, and a good distance away, but she still had the distinct impression that whoever was down there was staring straight at her.

"Hello," she said quietly, bringing her cigarette up for another breath, giving a little wave.

The figure shuffled sideways a few steps. Maggie supposed they had to go sideways because of the climbing frame, but wouldn't they want to see where they were stepping? Once it had shuffled to its new position, the figure opened up a long coat, black with black beneath, and Maggie wondered if she was looking at a flasher down there, or some other kind of pervert.

"Goodbye."

She scraped her cigarette out on the bricks of her window sill and brought the stub inside, pulling the window closed. She levered it shut and went to make a coffee. Maybe the person down there knew about the eggs. Maybe they'd put them there, and was waiting to see how Maggie would react. Maybe it was some sort of elaborate joke.

She readied a cup for her father, though he wouldn't be up for some time yet, and she put his morning pills on a saucer. She spooned coffee granules into her own cup and took her own pills waiting for the kettle to boil. Tiny ovoids in her mouth, sitting on her tongue. She thought about the eggs on the roof. She thought about keeping one, bringing it down to the flat stuffed under her jacket, "Oh, I'm pregnant, Dad, didn't you know?" Like he'd ever believe her. Like she could ever compete with Julie or Jess. Like she would ever had kids. She spat the pills into the sink and washed them away. It didn't matter. Looking after Dad was more than enough.

She took her coffee up to the roof.

In the early hours of the morning, the air on the roof smelled different. There was a coolness to it, a fresh promise that today was new and anything could happen. She liked the quiet, too. Few cars, no TVs in the flats below, workmen yet to arrive at the site opposite, filling the world with their radio and banter. She didn't pause to enjoy the air or the peace, though. She went straight to the space behind the storage building, half expecting to find only a clutter of litter, but the nest was still there. The eggs were still there. She raised her cup to them, "Good morning," and took a sip. It was very hot but good, and the smell of it did something to dispel the rotten odour of the nest. "Sleep well?"

She wondered how long they'd been there before she'd found them. Some eggs, she knew from her research, were actually fossils never to hatch. What were these? One had been warm yesterday, hadn't it? She crouched to touch it, the same one as before, and yes, there it was. An internal heat. Or maybe a residual warmth. She gave it an experimental tap and though it didn't yield beneath her knuckles, she could tell that it might, with enough pressure.

There were no feathers in the nest. That was unusual, wasn't it?

Because four giant eggs was completely normal.

She took another sip of coffee and put the cup on the wall before pressing both hands to the egg. She caressed it, marvelled at how smooth it was, just like a real egg. With one hand on either side, she attempted to lift it. It was heavy, and something inside fidgeted, a confined squirm that made Maggie snatch her hands back. She wiped them on her jeans as she stood then took up her cup again, glancing out to the park.

That same figure was still on the climbing frame. It hunched suddenly as she watched, and with the action came a shrill scream that broke into a sequence of aborted noises. Then it dropped from its perch and its coat opened, opened, opened far too wide on either side and flapped, flapped, because it wasn't a coat at all; with two hard beats of its wings, the thing was aloft.

Maggie fumbled the cup she'd hardly taken hold of and it spilled, dropped, smashed, "Shit!" She glanced down as she stepped away from it and when she looked up again, the sky was clear. She peered over the wall and saw nothing coming. Still, she left the broken pieces of her cup where they lay. She headed for the stairs, not running but certainly hurrying. Dad would be wanting his morning cuppa and she had to take her pills.

She didn't look up and she didn't look back.

—◦—

She was supposed to be watching an old movie with her father but her mind wasn't on the plot. At least she didn't have to follow any conversation though; he was wearing the full breathing mask today rather than the nostril tubes. It fitted around his nose and mouth and it prevented him from talking. He had to look his question at her when she got up during the adverts.

"Toilet," Maggie said. She checked his oxygen, adjusting it on her way out. "Cuppa tea, Dad?"

He nodded, returning to the black-and-white world of the TV.

Maggie had a packet of cigarettes hidden in a box of tampons in the bathroom. She grabbed them and flicked the kettle on in the kitchen before letting herself out into the corridor. She closed the door quietly and lit the cigarette early; she needed the nicotine *before* getting to the roof this time. She was confident there wouldn't be enough smoke to set off the alarms. Confident, too, that they probably didn't work anyway.

It had been a few days since her last visit to the roof. Since then, she'd enjoyed her cigarettes in the bathroom, extractor fan on, her hand and face at the tiny open window because she was too worried about what she might see from her own. The one in the bathroom had glass that was opaque even though they were so high up, and more importantly it didn't face the park. She'd had nightmares about the park, dreams in which the thing she'd seen there had flown right at her, crashing into her bedroom in an explosion of glass and brick only to drag her out screaming, both of them screaming, and then she was falling until she was suddenly awake. One night she'd woken from this to find her father shuffling in the hallway. He'd opened his dressing gown and released a flock of dark birds at her and she'd woke a second time, smothered beneath her blankets. She was ready to check the roof again now if only because it might put an end to the dreams.

At the door to outside, cigarette somehow half gone already, Maggie paused. She listened. Nothing. She opened the door.

As soon as it was open, she heard shrieking, an endless series of short, sharp, stuttered cries, *shrie-shrie-shrie-shrie-shrie*, and she knew what had happened.

The eggs had hatched.

Cigarette in her mouth, Maggie put both hands to her ears as she nudged the door wider. The things weren't loud, exactly, but shrill and constant, overlapping. *Me! Me! Me! Me! Me!*

She stepped out onto the roof with her eyes to the sky. She checked the park. A woman with a pram was walking through, that was all.

Eventually Maggie was able to look away and lower her hands, wincing at the din but knowing she'd get used to it. She could get used to anything. She dropped her cigarette, stepped it out, and approached the nest, careful to keep her distance. She only wanted to see them.

They were ugly little things. A shuffling mass of black, puffy with erratic plumage, they held their beaks up to *shriek-shriek-shriek!* at the sky. Pale grey eyelids clenched closed against what little sun there was; they beat at each other blindly with stubby wings as they fidgeted into new positions.

When a dark shape blurred into her peripheral vision, Maggie screamed and crouched and covered her head with her arms. The thing dropped from a high position behind her, landing at the nest. It settled on the scaffold pole as Maggie scurried backwards towards the stairs in a crab position, hands and shoes slipping on the wet roof.

The bird was huge, even hunched over. As tall as her but more broad. Wings the size of ironing boards folded against its body. It was entirely black, so black that it gleamed, and the one glassy eye Maggie could see was so dark it absorbed all other colours. A hole's shadow, dark as ink not written. In its beak, in its terrible split black beak, it held a giant snail.

The young in the nest jumped, jumped, knocked against each other, and beat their stumpy wings. They snapped at the air and set up a discordant chorus of shrill calling so intense it forced Maggie to stop fleeing just so she could cover her ears again. She still heard the crack, though, when the mother slammed its catch down against the roof wall. *Crack! Crack-crack!* A couple of those, then the bird held its catch on the wall, talons spread to grip it steady. The beak came down. Hard, quick, darting stabs. *Crack! Crack-crack-crack!* And Maggie realised at last that what she saw was not a snail. Of *course* it wasn't a snail.

"Oh, Christ."

Its beak withdrew from the motorcycle helmet with a string of something red and meaty. It tossed this to its nest. As the young fought over the flesh, it pecked again at the hole it had made in the visor, scooping more from inside, nodding to throw more strips to its children. Maggie saw blood spill from the opening, a single thick line of it running down the helmet to drip into the nest where the three snapped at thrown morsels until the helmet was dropped for them to peck at. They rammed their beaks into whatever gap they could find, nudging and shrieking at each other in between.

Beyond them, visible now as they fed themselves, was the last egg. The one she'd touched had not hatched.

The young were quickly done. They craned their necks upwards, tipped their heads back, and held their beaks open for short pauses between squawks. The mother dipped to each in turn, opening its beak in theirs to regurgitate a previous meal. Perhaps the rest of the motorcyclist. Perhaps something else. Maggie tried not to think of the woman she'd seen in the park. The one with the pram.

"Oh fucking *Christ*."

The bird looked up. It turned its head one way then the other, locking one dark eye at a time on Maggie. It shuffled sideways on its perch, as she'd seen it do on the climbing frame, then arched its body forwards with its beak open wide. A long bloody tongue uncurled from inside with a scream of vowels, accompanied by the spreading of wings. They unfolded like vast blankets.

Maggie scrambled in retreat until she felt the closed door press against her back. She slapped around for the handle.

The bird's long call became a sharp sequence of noises like nails being wrenched from wood. It flapped its wings, leapt, and swooped at her.

Maggie yanked herself to her feet and the door open at the same time. She rolled around the frame, slammed the door shut behind her. Holding it closed, she braced herself for an impact that never came. When the automatic light in the stairwell finally registered her existence, it blinked and flickered a rhythm as quick as her breathing.

Another cry resounded off the walls, deafening in the confined space of the stairwell.

Maggie shoved herself away from the door and took the stairs down two at a time, chased by a long dark echo.

⟶⟶

Maggie's father had died while she was on the roof. All those years she'd spent with him and she hadn't been there when it happened. It didn't seem fair.

At the cremation, people gave Maggie their condolences and platitudes, spoke of a tough man she didn't recognise, spoke of mods and rockers but never explained how her father fit in. The man they knew had died long ago. The man in the photographs her sisters provided for the wake—Dad on his motorbike, Dad with his wife and girls—was a stranger to Maggie. The man she knew wore a faded grey dressing gown and had died with his eyes bulging and his hands twisted into claws that couldn't get the mask from his face, couldn't turn the oxygen dial. He'd wet himself, too. The small living room had been ripe with his odour.

Maggie spent the funeral thinking about a group of crows. Everyone in black. She thought of her father's bulging eyes, his clawed hands, his stink, and found it hard to say she loved him. She let her sisters say it for her and thought of crows.

There had been few things to do afterwards. He only had a small selection of mismatched clothes to sort through. He'd left her with little more than his ashes. She had seen her sisters through their grief, but they didn't stay long. They invited her to stay with them for a while, but they said it the same way Dad said a lot of things he didn't mean. Within a fortnight of his passing, the house was finally empty and Maggie could do whatever she wanted. Hell, she could even smoke.

She went to the roof.

She tried to light a cigarette but her hands were shaking too much. She had to hold one with the other to keep the flame steady enough, puffing out quick breaths of relief before releasing a slower drag that calmed her. It would be her last one.

A chill breeze carried her smoke away and swept her hair into tangles. She zipped up her jacket to the sounds of them all screeching, hacking out their staccatos, calling her to their nest.

They were even uglier close up. The beaks seemed too wide for their feather-fluffed faces, and the eyes bulged beneath closed grey lids. Their squat heads were ruffled with a scruff of down that extended to the wattle of their throats. They were all elbows and claws, it seemed, feathers dark like tar, wafting their stench around as they *shrie-shrie-shrie-shrie-shrieked!*

Maggie dropped what was left of her cigarette and twisted her heel on it. "Stop it," she said.

At the sound of her voice they became louder, scrabbling at the debris of their nest as they shoved each other, straining their heads and necks for their next meal.

"*Stop* it," Maggie said, "Stop it, stop it, *stop it!*"

She grabbed the nearest one under the foreshortened stubs of its arms or wings or whatever the hell they were and barely registered the weight of it. She scooped it up and cast it skyward, over the edge of the roof. It hung there for a moment, turning with the force of the throw, and faced her. It rawked and beat at the air, caught in the pause between up and down, flailing with limbs barely feathered. It had never seen another fly, not yet, but that didn't matter. Seeing it done didn't mean you could do it yourself.

Gravity snatched it away.

Maggie grabbed the next—it was warm in her hands, wriggling—and she turned on the spot to throw it harder, farther. "Fly!" she said, and watched it drop.

The crash of the first one landing was followed by the wailing repetition of a car alarm. She didn't hear the second one.

Maggie put her hands on the third sibling, pinning its wings, and raised it to chest height. It snapped at her breasts and her head so she held it straight-armed and turned her face away from its beak. She walked it to the wall and let it go.

"There," she said, facing the remaining egg. "Just us." She stepped into the nest with all its filth. She crouched, put her palms on the egg, and caressed the smooth coolness of its shell. Nothing pulsed inside. Nothing moved. It was cold. It may as well have been stone for all the life it had. She tapped at it with her knuckles—"Hey!"—then knocked her fist against it, "Wake up!" She held it by the top and rocked it to and fro, pulling the base free from a caked mound of bird shit. The broken pieces of her coffee mug lay nearby. She retrieved a section that was mostly handle, dirtied with smears of black and white, and tossed it aside. Another fragment, cleaner, was a sharp triangle of ceramic. It fit snug in her hand.

She drove it down hard against the egg.

The egg cracked. Another hit, and a network of fissures flattened the crown. The cup shard broke its way inside. She pulled it out and threw it away, hooked her fingers into the egg, and pulled at the shell. It came away easily, a viscous fluid spilling over her hands and into her lap, releasing a stench as thick as the albumen or yolk or whatever it was that coated her, a bloody sepia slime that stank like snotty menses.

There was a dead bird inside.

It lay against a concave wall of shell as if sleeping, head burrowed into its partially feathered chest. Maggie cupped the beak under one hand and gently raised the face. It was mostly pink puckered skin, slick with fluid, a patch of feathers wet against its head. Its eyes were wide black domes without lids, sightless pupils dark as blindness. Dark like oil. Dark like tar. Maggie saw herself reflected there, distorted.

"Poor thing."

She unzipped her jacket, took it off, and lay it on the ground. She slipped both hands into the remains of the egg and gently withdrew the bird from inside. It was much lighter than the others, all loose bone, sagging skin, and limp feathers. Its talons had been tucked beneath its body but now they dangled, flaccid grey-ringed toes curled with the weight of hard claws. Maggie lay the creature on her jacket and folded both halves over it, tucked in the top and bottom, made a neat parcel of what she'd found.

"You'll be okay now."

She took the cigarettes from the pocket of her jeans, withdrew the lighter, and lay them on top of the jacketed bird before settling herself into the nest. She fidgeted, clearing a space amongst the papers and food boxes. Flies buzzed at the motorcycle helmet but she kicked it away and the dark cloud dispersed after it, reforming once it had stopped rolling. Her backside slid on a cushion of thick droppings, and she put her hand down into something bloody, but she no longer cared about things like that.

She waited.

She didn't have to wait long. The car alarm was still repeating, but over that came the *whump!* . . . *whump*! . . . *whump*! of beating wings. Maggie looked up and, yes, there it was, swooping down at her, bigger than before, diving with urgent speed and the scream of an eagle in descent, talons outstretched.

Maggie tipped her head back. She closed her eyes.

The claws did not come. She was buffeted by a wing-made wind, but not struck. She felt the nest-litter stir as the dark bird hovered, smelled the damp feathers beating near her face. She heard the scrape of metal on bricks and knew that it had settled upon its scaffold roost.

Maggie opened her mouth.

The bird screamed for her and thrust its beak in hard. The suddenness of it surprised her but her cry was strangled before it could become sound. She squeezed her eyes closed tighter and grabbed at the scruff of its feathers, all spiny and coarse and thick as starless night, impossible to wrench free no matter how hard she pulled in pain. And still the beak came, filling her throat, stretching her lips around it so that the corners of her mouth split. A mass of feathers smothered her as the point of its beak rooted deeper until finally it found what it wanted. Maggie opened her eyes then. Something inside was wrenched free and her eyes were suddenly wide, hands falling limp to her sides as she gagged around whatever it was that came up her throat, thick and moist and ravelling out of her. She convulsed, gasped, retched. With a flick of its head the bird tossed it aside and Maggie saw twin black sacks fold open like tiny wings before they fell away. When the bird's beak entered her a second time, rummaging, she barely felt it. The third time she felt even less, saw all that was black and bloody coming out of her—black heart, black feathers—and was only dimly aware that the jacket beside her stirred. With her arms by her side, fists clenched, she leaned back as the dark bird emptied her, twitching like the jacket as the big bird broke her bones and scooped her hollow, scattering her insides like ashes to be borne on the wind.

When all that remained of her was a vacant sack of skin and clothes, Maggie collapsed in upon herself, mouth open as if hungry for all she had lost.

Her jacket burst open with a sudden flurry of fledgling energy, and a long shrill cry that might have been pain, might have been joy.

INTRODUCTION TO THE BODY IN FAIRY TALES

JEANNINE HALL GAILEY

The body is a place of violence. Wolf teeth, amputated hands.
Cover yourself with a cloak of leaves, a coat of a thousand furs,
a paper dress. The dark forest has a code. The witch
sometimes dispenses advice, sometimes eats you for dinner,
sometimes turns your brother to stone.

You will become a canary in a castle, but you'll learn plenty
of songs. Little girl, watch out for old women and young men.
If you don't stay in your tower you're bound for trouble.
This too is code. Your body is the tower you long to escape,

and all the rotted fruit your babies. The bones in the forest
your memories. The little birds bring you berries.
The pebbles on the trail glow ghostly white.

THE TIN HOUSE

SIMON CLARK

The young detective looked out of the window. The killing happened right there in front of him. He watched the stoat chase the rabbit across the meadow—the gold-coloured predator appeared tiny in comparison to what seemed almost a behemoth of a rabbit. The stoat ran alongside its fleeing prey before burying its teeth into the rabbit's neck. From here, in the Chief's office, the young detective heard the agonised scream of the rabbit as it fell to the ground, kicking and dying.

The Chief studied a computer screen so Mark Newton had ample time to consider this undeniable fact: life and death battles are constantly being fought just a few yards away from us: whether it's the stoat slaying the rabbit, or a neighbour struggling with terminal illness, or entire armies of bacteria waging war beneath a single fingernail. *Life vs. Death. Forever and ever, amen.*

After closing the computer file, the Chief took a swallow of coffee, and said, "The Tin House. Heard of it?"

"It's before my time with this squad, but I remember it from the news. The owner of the Tin House went missing." *Too light on detail,* Newton warned himself; he still wanted to impress his new boss, so he dug deeper into his memory. "A man in his seventies by the name of Lord Alfred Kirkwood lived alone at the house. His neighbour found the lights out, a rear door open, and a bowl of tomato soup on the kitchen table. It was still warm."

"You'll go far," grunted the Chief, "or you'll go insane. There's only so many details of a case that a policeman should memorise, you know? Particularly if it's not their case."

"It's an old habit from when I was a boy. I loved mysteries. Probably even quite a bit obsessed by them."

"Well, you better not admit to your colleagues that you have obsessions; they'll get the wrong idea entirely."

"Yes, sir."

"Anyway, back to business. The Tin House case is unsolved. Lord Kirkwood never turned up, either dead or alive. Seeing as six months have gone by since he vanished, I'm putting the case into deepfreeze. When there's a legal presumption of death, Kirkwood's nephew will inherit everything. What I want you to do is take these keys—one will open up the Tin House—I want you to photograph every room. And I mean every room, no matter how small."

Newton frowned. "Surely we've a detailed photographic record of the house already?"

"We have—from six months ago, but it's a requirement of the police authority's insurance company that we photograph houses, cars, livestock, every blessed thing that we hand back to owners, just in case the owner decides we've damaged their property in some way and hits us with a compensation claim: believe me, it happens. Once you've done that, give the keys to Kirkwood's nephew. Jeremy Kirkwood is meeting you at the house."

Newton had a suggestion. "I could show the nephew that the house is in good order. After all, don't we trust him?"

"*No. We do not.*" The Chief spoke with feeling. "The Kirkwood family is famous for suing people." He shot Newton a telling look. "I also learned that the first Lord Kirkwood, back in the eighteenth century, made a fortune from the slave trade."

"Really?"

"Kirkwood shipped thousands of Africans to the Caribbean where he sold them to plantation owners. With the proceeds, he bought twenty thousand acres of land near the coast and built a mansion."

As a new detective, Newton was conscious that he should question his own superior, to prove he was listening—that and thinking analytically. "The Kirkwood trade in slaves must have been over two hundred years ago. That can't be relevant to a man going missing six months ago, surely?"

"Can you immediately assess what is relevant to a case?"

"It's ancient history."

"Ancient history or not, the Kirkwood family are, at this present time, still living on proceeds earned from selling slaves. All that capital generated from kidnapping African men, women, and babies was invested here in Britain. The man you will meet . . ." He glanced at his watch. ". . . forty minutes from now enjoys a luxurious life style as a result of one of the most barbaric commercial enterprises in the history of the human race. Okay, detective . . . time you went to the Tin House."

⟨o⟩

The drive from town to the coast took thirty minutes. Newton went alone. He remembered the route from childhood when his family spent two weeks here every August. The only thing markedly different from back then was the weather. Today, fine snowflakes tumbled from a November sky, and even though it was only mid-afternoon, he drove with the headlights burning into a gloomy landscape.

As a child, Newton had loved his time at the coast; in his imagination, the vast sandy beaches became transformed into mysterious deserts that contained secret castles and hidden treasure. The real mystery occurred there when he was ten years old; his mother asked him to bring her glasses from a drawer. That's where he discovered a letter from his mother's sister. The letter clearly revealed that they'd had a major falling out, and the letter closed with a stark PS in capital letters: SO YOU'RE FINALLY GOING TO LEAVE YOUR MARK ON THE WORLD. He interpreted YOUR MARK as referring to him. The comment was clearly designed to hurt his mother. Though he loved solving mysteries, the ten-year-old Mark Newton decided not to delve into this particular one. He had a lurking sense of dread that some family disaster would happen if he ever discovered the truth behind that letter's bitter postscript.

Satnav efficiently directed him to the Tin House. The building stood on a narrow coastal road with its back to the beach and the sea. There were no other houses within half a mile—so the neighbour who discovered that Lord Kirkwood had vanished, leaving a still warm bowl of soup, must have happened by due to sheer good chance. With no sign of the Lord's nephew, Newton decided to start work immediately and photograph the building's interior as his superior had ordered. Photographs would prove that while under the protection of the police, the property hadn't been burgled or vandalised, so no claims could be lodged by the next of kin.

After parking at the side of the road, which seemed to be one of those quiet, backwater ones, he headed up the drive. A plaque above the front door announced: THE TIN HOUSE.

"And, yes," he murmured, "the house is actually made of tin."

The two-story house had been clad in corrugated tin sheets, which were green in colour. They even covered the roof. At some point after Kirkwood's disappearance, the windows had been covered with mesh security screens. From the outside, anyway, the house looked in a perfectly good state.

As he tapped his knuckles on a tin wall, he imagined what the din would be like inside during a fierce hailstorm. Meanwhile, he breathed deeply, enjoying the tang of salt air. From the distance came the forceful hiss of surf. He pictured himself on that very beach twenty years ago: an adventurous child with senses tuned for the next mystery that came his way.

"Hey you . . . get out of there; it's private property."

Newton saw a man striding through the drive gates. Aged about forty, he wore a bulky jacket in brown leather; he also wore an expression several degrees nearer anger than irritation.

"Mr. Kirkwood?" he asked pleasantly.

"Who are you?"

"I'm Detective Newton. You are Mr. Jeremy Kirkwood?"

"Of course I am. Who else would be hanging around this Godforsaken hole?"

"I'm here to photograph the house; then I'll give you back the keys."

"Photograph the house? Whatever for?"

Newton explained that taking photographs before handing over keys to next-of-kin was standard procedure.

"Police rules and regulations, eh?" snorted Kirkwood. "You'd think taxpayers' cash would be better spent on catching murderers."

Newton's professionalism dictated that he would neither like nor dislike the man, although he suspected Kirkwood's face probably always wore an expression of bad temper. This gentleman had been born with angry bones. For some reason, Kirkwood didn't approach Newton, and he remained near the driveway gates, hunching his shoulders against the cold.

The man shot him a sour look. "So this it, you're closing the case on my uncle?"

"Lord Kirkwood is still listed as missing."

"But scaling things back, eh? Taking things easy on the investigation?"

The Chief had told Newton that the case would be going in the deepfreeze, seeing as investigations had reached a dead end; however, the case wouldn't be officially closed. After Newton politely stated that the investigation would continue, he pulled the keys from his pocket and nodded in the direction of the front door.

"I'll take the photographs," Newton told him. "You might want to check inside for yourself."

"No, thank you." Jeremy Kirkwood spoke primly. "I'm staying out here."

"It's starting to snow again."

"If I go in there, I'll be sneezing all night." He scratched his throat as if he'd started to itch. "My family used that shack as a beach house. Whenever I stayed here, I'd have a violent allergic reaction to the place: spores, or dust, or something. Wild horses wouldn't drag me in there."

"It'll probably take me about ten minutes."

"Go and take your ten minutes, then." The man visibly shuddered as he gazed up at the bedroom windows. "What a God-awful box it is. Being in there's like being in a tin coffin. The place scared me half to death when I was a boy. I'd lie in bed at night and hear the entire house squealing, tapping, clicking, moaning. That God-awful racket kept me awake for hours." He permitted his stone-hard features to soften into something near a smile. "I didn't realise back then that the sounds were caused by all those tin sheets contracting as they cooled after the heat of the day. Ergo: contraction of metal, not noisy ghosts." He briskly cleared his throat. "My sisters tried to convince me it was haunted. Nothing like siblings to tease one, eh? Especially at the witching hour."

"What made your uncle choose to live out here?"

"Pardon?"

"After all, he'd have been an extremely wealthy man, so what made him want to spend his time in a small beach house made from tin?"

"Well, detective, that's none of your business, is it?" Jeremy Kirkwood thrust his clenched fists into his jacket pockets. "Didn't you say ten minutes?"

◄o►

People often describe a haunted house as an Unquiet House. The Tin House wasn't the least bit quiet—though whether that suggested this quirky building was actually haunted wasn't, he decided, for him to judge one way or the other. As Newton walked along the hallway toward the kitchen, he heard a series of clicking sounds, together with squeaks, loud popping noises, and the creak of timbers under pressure. He recalled Jeremy Kirkwood talking about the racket the tin cladding made during the night as it cooled.

"This is November," he told himself. "It's been cold all day. This can't be the metal contracting."

He rested his palm on the kitchen doorframe. The woodwork trembled as it might do if the house was hit by a storm. But outside was relatively still. Just a few snowflakes drifted by. This is a mystery. He loved mysteries—he'd love to spend time investigating the popping noises and the sharp tapping coming from upstairs, but he'd been ordered to take the photographs then hand the keys to Jeremy Kirkwood. Perhaps there were rats in the walls—however, rodent infestation wouldn't be a police matter.

Newton switched on the kitchen light. The place had been left tidy by the forensic team. Of course, the bowl of soup that the missing man had abandoned had gone—no doubt for fingerprint and DNA testing. He photographed the old fashioned stove, the Belfast sink, then moved onto the lounge. Again—tidied, vacuumed, and untouched by man or rat . . . at least, untouched in the last six months anyway. After taking photographs of the 1950s era armchairs, he worked his way through the ground floor rooms. Meanwhile, the scratching, tip-tapping, and popping continued. Dear God. Who'd live in a house made of tin?

Upstairs, he photographed tidy bedrooms and a trim bathroom. He'd been ready to head back downstairs when he recalled the Chief's order: *I want you to photograph every room. And I mean every room, no matter how small.*

He checked the master bedroom. Straightaway, he realised he'd missed a narrow door in the corner. As he walked toward it, he glanced out through a window that was covered by steel mesh. From up here, he could see the dark expanse of ocean. While on the driveway stood Lord Kirkwood's nephew, and heir to his fortune. A man with a motive. Though no doubt the Chief's team would have scrutinised that angle already: *greedy, impatient nephew murdering rich uncle* would top the list of suspects. Jeremy Kirkwood had retreated to the driveway gates where he stood, glaring at the house. The man's expression was strange. He looked as if he expected the building to lunge forward and bite him. Kirkwood appeared decidedly scared of the Tin House.

Newton took a moment to scrutinise details of the master bedroom. Several framed photographs of Lord Alfred Kirkwood hung from the wall. The missing man clearly preferred to see photographs of himself when he woke in the morning. On a table beside the window was a hairbrush. He noticed long, white hairs sticking to the bristles. When he glanced back at photographs of the elderly Lord he saw the same white, shoulder-length hair. In his youth, the man must have been an aristocratic dandy.

He opened the narrow door in the bedroom to discover a small ante-chamber. Perhaps four feet by eight feet, the vestibule might have been used for storage, although now it was completely empty.

After taking the single photograph, he'd have walked away if it wasn't for a sudden, frantic clatter from the far end of the room, which formed part of an outside wall. There was a rapid, metallic popping, as if tiny, bone-hard fists rapped on the tin sheet at the far side. For some reason, he felt compelled to rest his palm against that part of the wall. This was the only section to be covered in wallpaper; the paper itself had a furiously busy pattern of tiny red roses peeping out from green leaves.

The wall vibrated powerfully against his hand. A mystery all right; however, a mystery he wasn't ordered or paid to solve, and one hardly relevant to the case of the missing lord.

As he walked away, the metallic popping changed. The sound morphed from pell-mell clattering to a unified rhythm: whatever objects or vermin that attacked the metal cladding had now begun to strike it at the same time; pretty much in the same way a dozen different drummers in a percussion band would strike the same beat.

The door swung shut behind; immediately the room crashed to darkness. He could see nothing. The pounding on the wall intensified—growing louder as it did so. Maybe it was Kirkwood's claim that he was allergic to the house that caused the effect. But suddenly Newton's skin began to itch. His chest tightened and breathing in that dark, little chamber became difficult. Quickly, he tugged open the door. The light from the bedroom spilled in. He quickly strode back along the narrow room to where the sound seemed to emanate from the rose-covered wallpaper. He balled his fist and slammed it against the wall. The drumming sound irritated him. For a moment, he even told himself that the metallic popping coming from the other side made his skin itch. His fingernails scratched at his face, making the looser parts of the skin slide over the jawbone.

The clatter from the other side grew louder.

"Shut up."

He pounded the side of his fist against the wall again. If there were rats in there, they'd get a nasty shock. But the rodents or whatever made the noise didn't scarper; instead the rapping grew louder. The sound goaded him. It demanded to know if Mark Newton HAD LEFT *HIS MARK* ON THE WORLD.

Remembering that line in his aunt's letter twisted a nerve to the point he felt a blaze of fury. As the metallic drumbeat reached a crescendo, he stood back then delivered such a hell of a kick to the wall. His police training had taken over. He used that particular kick he'd practiced so often to kick down some drug peddler's front door. The loud drumming against the metalwork had stopped at least. Now he could hear nothing but his own heartbeat.

When he looked down he saw, to his surprise, that he'd managed to slam the toe of his shoe through not only the wallpaper with its blood red roses, but the plywood panel. Damn it. Now he'd have to photograph the damage he'd inflicted on the house. Cop turns vandal. He imagined the Chief's anger when Jeremy Kirkwood submitted the repair bill.

He crouched down before the hole he'd made . . . a gaping one at that, almost a foot wide. Outside, Jeremy Kirkwood must have clearly heard the crash, so no use in pretending this injury to the house had happened a long time ago. Duty and honesty dictated that he would report truthfully that he'd inflicted the damage.

The hole, large though it was, revealed nothing but shadow. No rats, no vermin of any kind. He raised the camera, centred the yawning black void on the screen, then took the picture. The brilliant flash dazzled him; however, a moment later his vision had returned to normal, and he could check that he'd accurately recorded the effects of his violence against the Tin House.

He studied the photograph on the camera's screen. A second later, he scrambled to his feet and was running for the door. The image of what had been revealed behind the wall had fixed itself as firmly in his mind as it had been fixed into the camera's memory card. He had not only photographed broken plywood, he'd also taken a photograph of a face. A human face.

-◦-

Snow was falling again. November gloom crept in from the ocean so that the house resembled a block of shadow.

Newton hurtled outside through the front door. He raced past Jeremy Kirkwood at the driveway gates.

"Hey! What's wrong?" bellowed Kirkwood. "Hey! Answer me!"

Newton threw himself into the driver's seat, started the engine, and slammed the car into reverse. Jeremy pounded on the car's roof as he hit the accelerator pedal.

The man yelled, "What are you running away from? What's in there?"

He glanced up at Kirkwood's stark, white face. There wasn't just anger in his eyes, there was dread, too. Newton felt a huge lightning bolt of fear, because he remembered seeing the photograph of the face he'd just taken—the face in the wall.

He punched the vehicle forwards across the road, through the driveway gates, and across the lawn. When the headlamps blazed fully on that forlorn building, he braked, leaped out, and a moment later he pulled a crowbar from the back of the car. Before Kirkwood had time to react, Newton attacked the front of the house. He jammed the sharp end of the crowbar between where two sheets of tin cladding overlapped; once he'd done that, he began to lever them apart with a furious strength.

"Hey you!" Kirkwood actually screamed the words. "Hey! Leave that alone! Stop that!"

Newton put his foot against the wall to brace himself and heaved. Nails that fixed the tin cladding to the wooden frame began to snap with brittle-sounding bangs.

"Stop that!" Kirkwood bellowed from the end of the driveway, but he didn't come any closer. "What the hell do you think you're doing, you little bastard! Stop it, or I'll report you!"

"Who to? The police?"

A section of corrugated tin flapped loose. He gripped one side of it before ripping away an entire six by four sheet. That's when the car's powerful headlamps revealed the secret of the grim house.

"You're insane!" screamed Kirkwood.

"I'm not the one who's insane." He stared at what had been stretched tightly over the building's timber skeleton. "It's one of your damned ancestors that was insane. See! He went and covered the framework in skin . . . human skin . . . the skin of men, women, and children."

"What!" Kirkwood gaped; his eyes bulged. "What did you say?"

"I kicked a hole in the wall upstairs. There's a face on the other side . . . at least, the skin from a face."

"You *are* insane."

"See for yourself."

This time the man did gingerly approach the house. He gazed at what had been illuminated by the car's lights.

Newton gazed, too, with emotions that flashed from astonishment to absolute revulsion. There, nailed across the timbers, were the skins of human beings. They'd been scraped clean of meat, blood, hair, and subcutaneous matter. Clearly, they'd been treated too; some form of hide tanning process had been applied.

The tightly stretched-out skins were dark red in colour. Originally, the skins must have been black but the tanner's chemicals had reddened the flesh. He found himself thinking that the skins resembled sheets of red plastic. They were glossy—even wet looking. The headlights shone through them, casting a blood-red glow on the vertical plywood boards behind.

Both men stared in silence. The spectacle was horrific—it was distressing, too. The skins had been cut away from each body in a single piece. Each skin, or "hide," contained a face—a stretched-out face, like a leather mask. Eye sockets formed gaping holes. Lips had dried into hard circles. Nostrils, too.

One of the most noticeable and unsettling features were the fingernails; these were at the ends of strips of skin that had once covered fingers. Each fingernail was white—a gleaming, pearl white, as if it had somehow been carved from an oyster shell. He knew that was hardly a rational comparison—right now, however, he found it hard to stay rational, or calm.

Jeremy Kirkwood repeatedly swallowed; he was close to vomiting. "Who are they?"

"Your ancestors traded in slaves. Your family still lives on slave money today."

"These are the skins of slaves? But . . . why do this?"

"In the past, books were sometimes bound in human skin. So why not a house bound in human skin?"

"No, you're lying!"

Newton spoke with cold certainty. "Picture this: Two hundred years ago, your ancestors kidnapped thousands of men, women, and children from their homes in Africa. They were chained together, and they were transported in ships without adequate ventilation, food, or clean water. Hundreds would have died on the way. Those that survived faced a harrowing life of forced labour until they died."

Kirkwood stared at the dried-out face of a young child. A split in the skin ran from the corner of its mouth to the distorted opening of an eye. "But why on earth would anyone cover a house in human skin?"

"Undoubtedly, your ancestors were superstitious. They were terrified that the ghosts of slaves would come looking for revenge. Superstitious people have been doing something like this to protect themselves from vengeful spirits for thousands of years. In some cultures, they make shrunken heads from their victims, or even eat part of their bodies. In the case of your ancestors, they decided to adopt elements from voodoo cults and incorporate the skin from a number of slaves into the fabric of the house."

Despite his fear, Jeremy Kirkwood moved closer. "If they're stretched over the entire frame of the building, there must be dozens and dozens."

"And dozens of your ancestors must have been involved with this barbaric ritual."

"What do you mean?"

"Even after the abolition of slavery, your ancestors continued to be wealthy because of the money they made from selling human beings. They also continued to believe that the slaves could somehow come back from the dead and hurt them, so they made sure they still kept these talismans for protection."

"This house . . . I knew this house wasn't right . . . even as a child, I knew something was wrong . . ."

"Your uncle knew, too. That's why he rarely left what he believed to be the magic protection of this building. But he left in the end . . ."

At that moment, the wind started to blow from the sea. Newton thought he could hear those grim diaphragms made from tightly-stretched human skin softly hum as they began to vibrate. When the breeze quickened, the strips of finger skin fluttered. The white fingernails attached to the ends struck the tin sheets, making a popping and clicking sound. This is must have been what he'd heard earlier. Like tiny bone-hard fists hammering at the metal.

Jeremy Kirkwood gave a shriek. "Cover them up! Cover them!"

He seized the corrugated section of metal that Newton had pried off, and tried to push it back over those tremulous skins.

The fingernails tapped against that piece of tin as Kirkwood tried to shove it back into place. Instantly, the tapping became a furious clatter. In the glare of the headlights, Newton noticed filaments attached to one of those dead fingernails.

"Wait." He pushed Kirkwood away.

"I'll sue you! I'll sue the entire police force! You'll pay for this!"

After silencing the man with an angry glare, Newton turned his attention to the pearlescent fingernail. Between finger and thumb, he carefully removed the filament from the nail then held it in front of the headlamp. A single long, white hair. Straightaway, he remembered photographs in the master bedroom of Lord Alfred Kirkwood, the white-haired man who'd lived on the wealth generated by the slave trade. And he pictured the fine white hair still adhering to the hairbrush.

He fixed his eyes on the lord's nephew, who stood there panting, with the tin sheet in his hands. He held up the hair for him to see. "I'm certain a DNA test will prove this belonged to your uncle."

"How did it get stuck to one of those disgusting things?" He threw a frightened glance at the red material stretched tight over the woodwork. The distorted faces pulsated as the breeze played upon them. The lips tightened and slackened as if mouthing words. "And why did my uncle disappear?"

"Perhaps the magic doesn't work anymore. Occult protection doesn't last forever."

The skins billowed as the winds blew harder. Fingernails rapped louder on the walls of the Tin House.

Jeremy Kirkwood appeared to freeze, his muscles locked tight. "My God . . . I'm the next of kin. I inherit everything. All the slave money. They'll try and kill me, too!" His eyes blazed with terror. "You're a policeman . . . you've got to protect me. It's your job, you bastard!"

The man that Newton had judged to have been born with angry bones swung the six-foot by four-foot tin panel. It struck the side of the detective's face. That heavy piece of metal cut him down as if it were an axe. Its sharp edge sliced open his jaw, blood sprayed—an aerosol of crimson in the car's light.

He must have passed out for a moment, because when he opened his eyes, he realised he lay on the lawn, looking up at both Jeremy Kirkwood and the front of the house.

The human skins were melting. That's what it looked like. Those skins that were almost the size of bed sheets slipped downward from the building's timber skeleton. Jeremy stared at what was happening. He appeared fixed there. Hypnotised.

The skins continued to slide downward. Newton saw something dripping down through the narrow gap between the tin cladding and the frame at the bottom of the wall. The dripping effect resembled dark treacle being poured from a jar. Thick and continuous. These were yet more leathery remains sliding down from behind the intact panels. He realised he should try and stop his wound from bleeding, only he found he couldn't move, either. He lay there on the grass propped up on one elbow. He watched the skins, and he realised they weren't melting after all—they were sloughing from the woodwork. Detaching themselves from the house. Breaking free.

The car's headlamps not only illuminated the dark red hides, but shone through them.

He could only compare those relics as something that resembled outstretched sheets on a washing line, except they moved into the wind. The mask-like faces at the top of the hides contained distorted holes where the eyes and mouths had once been. He caught sight of the whorl of navels in the centre of the hides. He saw the black discs that were the nipples.

When the detached skins reached the inheritor of the Kirkwood's bloody fortune, they enclosed him. Sheets of human wrapping paper. They formed a parcel of Jeremy Kirkwood. His silhouette struggled inside for a while . . . but as time passed the struggles stopped . . . then even the silhouette was gone. Dissolved away. Dissipated. Broken down into slime and hair.

Newton managed to follow the paper-thin human remains that billowed and flapped across the dunes to the sea. He glimpsed peeled faces that formed part of those rippling sheets of skin. Although his senses still reeled after being struck by a section of the Tin House, he knew deep down that those skins that had once housed the bones of men, women, and children were truly free. Now they were heading for the ocean. Newton wondered if, given the right tides, favourable currents and enough time, the waters from which all life once emerged would finally carry its precious cargo back home.

THE FOX

CONRAD WILLIAMS

The wind came for us as soon as we laid our heads on the pillows, as if it had been waiting for that moment. It spanked against the canvas, testing the guy ropes that were meant to keep the tent grounded. I kept thinking it would tear free at any moment and sail off into the sky. Kit was sleeping. Perhaps the weather didn't affect her as much as it did me, or maybe she was able to shut it out; she was often talking to me about the powers of meditation. I concentrated on sleep but succeeded only in detecting another sound scampering around beneath the howl of the wind. It overcame the squeak of the tyre on the rope hanging from the oak branch, and the lowing of the cows in the next field, aggrieved at being out in such violent weather. It was something stealthier than that. Something that I almost dismissed as nothing, but for the way it kept coming back, like a heartbeat; trotting, slick. It might have been my wife's breathing, and I might have believed that had I been tired enough.

I got out of bed and stumbled in the dark for the torch that I realised was still in the car down by the farmhouse. I checked on the children, Megan and Lucy, but they were softly snoring. You could always tell Lucy was deep because she would be murmuring, babbling, sometimes even laughing in her sleep. Her eyes were wide open. I was exactly the same when I was a baby. I bent over her and kissed her but she did not respond. There was a moment of panic when I thought that there would be something wrong, but she was breathing; she blinked when I brushed a fingertip against her eyelashes. It was as if she were doing what I had been doing, minutes before, listening intently to the scream of the weather, studying it almost, maybe identifying something that shifted beneath the patterns that were laid over the countryside. And I heard it again now. A beat against the flow; an anti-rhythm.

I went to the entrance that I had assiduously tied down not two hours previously, and started unpicking the knots. The tent smelled of old smoke from the stove that had been forced back down the flue by the wind. I paused as the last loop slipped free of the toggles. It was weird, feeling on the threshold between comfort and open miles of thrashing wild. Quickly, I ducked outside and loosely tethered the tent flaps. I could see nothing: cloud cover prevented any moonlight from picking out the shape of the farmhouse or the trees, though I could hear them hissing their shock over the ferocity in the sky. I felt afraid in that moment, at the glib way in which we had pitched ourselves against nature; thrown ourselves into the pit of the dark, separated from all it contained by one thin, trembling wall of canvas. It taught me, in a second, how dependent I was on light, and how the absence of it, rather than call to any base instincts in me, showed me how far removed I was from the wild. We'd come out here to connect, or reconnect, with nature. But that wasn't quite it. We were finding the version of nature we expected: the field of sunflowers or rapeseed; scores of sullen, jawing cows; clean, clear lakes. Real nature, though, wasn't about some plot of land set out of sight of the main road and an axe for you to chop your supplied share of logs to size. It was this anti-rhythm and the movement of things best suited to darkness.

I heard, as I was fussing with the tent ties, the slide of grass against something more substantial than wind. I got myself back inside, feeling under scrutiny, feeling the skin on my back tighten. I picked my way to the bedroom where the walls were heaving like bellows, and Kit was a pale shape on the bed, uncertain, ill-defined, something being dissolved. I lay next to her and, risking her anger at being woken up by my cold body, held on to her. She moaned, and shifted away slightly, but did not stir. I listened to the snuffling and scuffling around the fringes of the tent and I wished I had tied down the knots in the flap more tightly.

◄o►

I dream of russet flames flickering over white, and black slashes through amber. Do you keep secrets from your wife? I do . . . Christ, I do . . .

◄o►

When I woke up, the bed next to me was empty. The wind had died down and there was a familiarity to the silence; it seemed settled, steeled somehow. There was a note on the dining table: *Gone to see if there are any eggs for breakfast. Can you get a fire going? Need coffee!* I swept open the tent flap and was shocked by what I saw. Snow everywhere; a good couple of inches of it. I was struck by the bizarre notion that the blustery weather had been pinned down by it, like something nasty swept under a rug. It was so expansive, so unbroken, I had to shield my eyes to be able to see anything within it. I stood and rubbed my arms, wishing I'd brought an extra sweater and trying to understand what exactly was "glamorous" about "glamping."

My wife was on maternity leave from her job as a primary school teacher, but I work in academic publishing (lots of dry articles, punctuated by occasionally fascinating pieces on art or literature or history) and a slew of deadlines over the summer meant we'd been unable to get away for any kind of family break until the autumn half term. A "staycation" in a tent—albeit a very upmarket one—near the New Forest had not been my idea of a holiday. I was angling more for a week in a bustling city that also had some nice beaches—Barcelona, say, or Tunis—but Kit had demanded something flight-free. I was trying to understand how it was that we'd ended up on a posh camping trip to Siberia when I spotted the girls, a couple of hundred yards away, hunched over the chicken coop. Something wasn't right about their shape. I saw Kit trying to move Megan away from the chicken-wire fence; Lucy lolling around in the carrier strapped to Mum's shoulders. I saw Kit's face as she turned back towards the tent, a white oval, but at this distance I could see the concern stitched into it. I knew my wife, and her postures of defence. I hurriedly pulled on my jogging bottoms and ran barefoot down the hill, wondering how far it was to the nearest hospital. But Kit would have started to move, wouldn't she? She'd be calling out to me, or hurrying the girls down to the house, where we had parked the car.

Megan was trying to push past her mother and now I was able to breathe more easily. Kit was just trying to shield Lucy from what was inside the coop. Or rather, what wasn't. The chicken-wire had been torn open. All four chickens were gone. No feathers, no signs of a fight whatsoever. Just one spot of blood on the ramp leading into what Megan had been referring to as the "chook-chook's bunga-oh."

"Kit?" I called out.

"Can you take Megan back up to the tent?" Kit's voice was taut, flustered.

I took Megan by the hand and gently drew her away. I was thinking about foxes, but they didn't kill and eat things on the spot, did they? Didn't they take them away to eat? And didn't they just take one? Four chickens, there had been. I'd counted them with the girls on our arrival. Foxes didn't hunt in packs.

"I'm going down to the house," Kit said. "To let them know." She moved away with Lucy when she was sure Megan was no longer able to see the blood. Megan didn't understand what the big deal was and, to be honest, neither did I.

"I know the chickens is being deaded," she said. "I could see the blood comed out."

"We don't know what happened," I said. "There was only a little bit of blood. Maybe one of the chickens had a nosebleed. Or a beakbleed."

"Or maybe it was hurted by something that wanted to eat it all up."

"You could be right," I said. "Sometimes, in the countryside, there are animals that want to eat other animals."

"Then why did it eat all of the chickens?"

"Maybe it was hungry. Really starving hungry. Or maybe the chickens escaped. Maybe whatever it was got scared away. The farmer might find them later."

We walked back to the tent and I persuaded Megan to stop talking about the chickens and do something else until Kit and Lucy returned. "Look," I said, "you brought a big pile of books. Read something. Or draw a picture."

◄◦►

I cajoled a small fire out of the kindling and newspaper and was waiting for the right time to add one of the halved logs when Kit and Lucy pushed through the tent flap, dragging the cold with them. The baby's smell was in it; sharpened, cleaned. I went over and kissed her velvet head as she goggled at me from the carrier. She was gumming at one of Kit's knuckles—she was probably cutting a tooth—and Kit used her free hand to flick at the strands of brown hair that fell across her vision, something she often did, even when it was too short to hinder her sight, when she was annoyed or nervous.

"The farmer's utterly perplexed. He said they've not had a fox problem here for years. He's out of his head with worry. Says it's not good for business."

"Us, he means. Paying guests."

"I suppose so. At least it shows he's concerned."

"Will he do anything about it though?"

Kit sat down and started unclipping Lucy, her fingers spooling with drool. "What can he do? It's nature. We don't get free eggs in the morning, that's all."

"But it just gives *carte blanche* to any meat-eating animal out there to come and attack our holiday site. Bears. Tigers. Velociraptors."

"Oh, you're making light of the situation. That's good, I suppose. Is Daddy being silly? Is he?"

I had to turn away because I didn't want her to see the sweat building up on my face. I had done it with my own hands and I had smiled while doing it. Fourteen then, just. Old enough to know better, I suppose. And now, over forty, I couldn't think about it without feeling horribly nauseous. *The child is father to the man.* Well, yeah, maybe. The child is also a hideous, bastard stranger.

I concentrated on the fire while Kit changed Lucy and Megan showed us the picture she'd drawn of the chicken coop, which was little more than a mass of red felt tip. We had breakfast and while Megan cleaned up the dishes, I eyed the edge of the field, wondering what we were supposed to do now. The planned cycle ride looked unlikely; I doubted these secluded roads had ever encountered anything as exotic as a council gritter. Similarly, the fields, which had appeared so inviting on the day of our arrival, were now forlorn and desolate. I knew from bitter experience that there was nothing so dispiriting as a forced march across wintry countryside. It was to the blanket box that I turned; inside, on top of the extra bedclothes, were a number of stacked, worn cardboard boxes. Board games and jigsaw puzzles. The puzzles were serious affairs; I couldn't see Megan sustaining her interest in completing a picture of the Swiss Alps from ten thousand pieces. The board games were hardly better. Players' tokens and dice were missing; the lack of instruction manuals meant some games were impenetrable. But we bumbled through it all until lunch. Megan seemed happy enough just playing with some of the plastic tokens.

I put together a table of salad and cold meats and we ate the food without the same fervour as we might if it had been warm outside. Soup or something hot on toast seemed the more suitable meal. Bolstered by fuel, however ill-fitting, I felt freshly determined to make something of the day, especially as the leaden sky was breaking up and patches of blue were appearing. I chased the girls into their boots and wrapped Lucy warm before getting her into the sling that I'd positioned around my shoulders. Every time I secured her there, and then stood up, I was shocked by how heavy she was getting. It would be hard work—my back would be damp, my shoulders sore by the time we finished our walk—but I would be rewarded by being able to nuzzle her head and feel the strong grip of her tiny fingers upon my own.

I loaded the stove with a couple more logs in the hope that the fire would keep going until we got back and then we were out in the fresh air, shocked by the cutting attack of it. It was like jumping into icy water. Lucy giggled as she snatched at gasps the wind was trying to steal back from her mouth. Megan went on ahead as we made our way down to where the narrow path that ran alongside a stark, weather-blackened fence (now concealed by a good foot of snow) led to a pond and a play area. You could just make out the shapes through the trees, maybe half a mile away. I'd brought along a few plastic bags and a towel to clear away the snow and dry off the seating areas, knowing that Megan would want to have a go on the swings and the slide. Kit fell into step by my side and clutched at me. Already the deep cold had stiffened her hands. She suffers from Raynaud's phenomenon, which causes her fingers and toes to become discoloured and inflexible in cold weather. In serious cases it can bring about gangrene, but luckily, Kit's symptoms ran only to a paling of the skin and a little numbness.

She lifted her head to smile at Lucy and a fan of her brown hair fell from the hem of her woollen hat, sweeping across her sight to isolate her eye so that it seemed strangely dislocated from her. There was a lack of colour to her eye, shaded as she was both from the growing light, and that small, protective curtain of hair. It was more like a black hole, unresponsive, lifeless. For a brief second, I was looking into the face of a person I did not know at all, despite ten years of marriage. The jolt that I got from that was disguised by our unsure tramping over uneven ground, and when she shifted her gaze and her smile to favour me, she was Kit again—filled with vim and the combative teasing I found so alluring—and the moment was gone.

The smell of woodsmoke drifted down from the tent.

"How are your fingers?" I asked.

"Like a bundle of sticks," she said. "If we get low on kindling later, just ask me and I'll snap a couple off for you."

I winced, but she was smiling. "I'll be fine," she said. "It's not as if we're on our way to have a crack at the north face of the Eiger, is it?"

We watched Megan enter the circular paddock that contained all the playground rides. Emptiness was developing a theme with me; with her hood up, and for as long as she didn't turn around (her legs and feet, in white stockings and Wellington boots were lost to the background), you might almost believe her coat was being animated by the wind and nothing else. It was an observation I'd normally have shared with Kit, but coming so soon after the illusion of her eye, I wasn't confident I could keep the edge from my voice. Anyway, Lucy had spotted the rides too by now and she was reaching out to them, making little cooing noises in her throat.

I called out to Megan to wait while I dusted off the snow with the towels—Lucy jiggling around and yelling in the carrier as I did so—and then suggested using the bin bags as makeshift sacks to sit in once she'd climbed to the top of the slide. Holding on to Lucy as I pushed her on the swing, I could see Kit huddled into her coat as she watched Megan repeat the journey from the bottom to the top to the bottom again, each trip accompanied by her laughter, which was distorted within the rustling of the bin bag.

And then, as Lucy was beginning to get upset by the cold her motion was creating, Megan's clockwork descent failed to occur. I could just see the tips of her boots sticking out from the metal guard flanking the slide's top deck. "What's up, Meg?" I called, as I lifted Lucy from the swing and began the arduous task of strapping her back into her pouch. "Have you frozen up there?"

Kit strode to the slide and reached out her arms. "What is it, chick?"

Megan was crying. Now that we'd spotted something wrong, the tears came harder, her upset suddenly more audible. "Thuh-thuh-puh, poor chu-chicken," she was saying, over and over. I went up the ladder and coaxed her down the slide to her mum. Kit held her while she stuttered and hitched. She was worried the fox, or whatever it had been, would come back for the rest of them, once the farmer had rounded them up.

I stood up and banged my head on the slide roof. Biting down hard on the stream of swear words queuing to be aired, I turned around and saw a red stain in the snow, about six feet shy of the water's edge. *Jesus*, I thought. *What now?*

"Wait here," I called to Kit, jumping to the ground. Entwined with Megan, she gave me a look as if to say, *Where do you think I'm going to go?* I tramped out of the paddock and south, my eyes fixed on that patch of red. I found myself thinking: *please let it just be blood.*

It was a fox, lying on its flank, nose pointing towards the pond, legs arranged as if in mid-trot. It had recently died, I guessed, although with the drop in temperature and the lack of flies, it was difficult to tell. Its eye stared in accusation but whatever had killed it was no longer in evidence. *Poison*, I thought, *but would that be likely on a farm where children were given free rein?* I thought it might have been shot, but there was no blood, no sign of ballistics. Which didn't mean it hadn't happened, of course. The cold had got inside me, despite the fleece-lined jacket; despite the insane baby-heat of Lucy.

I was going to leave it but a voice in my head told me to wait. Turn it over. *Make sure.*

It was preposterous. Twenty-five years had gone by. It was time to walk away; I didn't need Lucy spending any more time with a dead animal. What if it was diseased, for Christ's sake? But in spite of myself I pressed my boot into the stiff curve of its gut and toed it over. The bright green of the grass it revealed was as much a shock as finding its other eye absent. I stalked back to Kit and Megan. Megan had rallied somewhat, perhaps persuaded that there were going to be no more chicken murders, but truth be told, I was feeling a little ragged and emotional. A dead body is a dead body, no matter what species. Never nice to see. At least, that's what I was choosing to blame my quickening breath and sweaty palms upon. It was an excuse, at least, to call time on our little expedition and we hurried back to the tent where the wood in the stove was burning ferociously. I warmed up some milk from the cool chest and made hot chocolate.

I finished mine first and started pulling my boots back on.

"What now?" Kit said.

"It's my turn to break the news to the farmer. He needs to know his charming little couple of acres is turning into a slaughterhouse."

"It's just a dead fox," she whispered.

"It could have been poisoned," I said. "I don't like the idea of our kids skipping gaily through the daisies and kicking up lethal pellets in their wake. Or it could have died from some nasty ailment. What if it's contagious?"

I took Kit's silence for agreement and got myself outside before she could throw up any more barriers.

If you're a parent, especially of young children, you'll appreciate how rare it is to find yourself on your own. There's always some task involved, whether it be the school run, playtimes, bath-times, or meals and all those bits in between, which usually involve nappies from hell and the kind of weird conversations you imagine could only ever happen elsewhere if you were behind the walls of a prison for the mentally deficient.

Being back outside in that crystallised air felt suddenly different because of the solitude, even though it had only been a matter of half an hour since our visit to the playground. It was strange. I understood, a little, what it must be like to be a wild animal mooching around in open countryside. I felt hunted, exposed. Guarded. I walked by the tyre swing, kicking off its cap of snow, and enjoyed the dissonance between the creak of the rope and the crunch of my boots in the white. I glanced over at the slide, and to the right, the pond. I stopped. The green patch was there: a weird, bucolic fox-ghost, but the fox itself was gone. I thought about that for some time. A good thing, obviously. You don't want corpses lying around a child-friendly campsite. Obviously the farmer was up and about, perhaps alarmed into action by that morning's incident at the coop. But it all seemed very . . . swift. And it bothered me slightly that the farmer, if he had retrieved the fox, hadn't come to let us know. I couldn't believe that he'd just want to sweep it under the carpet; he surely would have seen my footprints and we were the only people staying on his land. A hired hand, then. Someone who didn't know that we knew the chickens had been attacked. Well, I'd soon find out.

The main living quarters of the farmhouse was a long building with a low roof. Part of it had been turned into an honesty shop; you went along and stocked up on whatever you needed—bread, bacon, pasta and the like—writing down what you'd taken in a large ledger, and at the end of the week it was totted up and added to your bill. Further along were some centrally-heated showers for those guests who didn't want to trust themselves to the tepid showers running off the heat from the stoves in the tents. Across the way was a large barn filled with bales of hay wrapped in black polythene to feed livestock over the winter months. I drove Kit nuts whenever we saw them in the fields because I would always be compelled to say: "Big rabbits around here."

The farmer lived at the end of the row; his car, a BMW, was parked next to ours. It hadn't been anywhere for a while. Snow still covered the bonnet. I took the opportunity to rescue our torch from the glove compartment just as a pink oval slid across the inside of a kitchen window hung with pretty, blue curtains. There was the chunk of a heavy lock sliding back and the farmer appeared at the door, wiping his mouth with a black napkin. "All okay?" he asked. "Do you need more wood?"

"No thanks," I said. "We're okay for wood. I was going to tell you, in light of what happened this morning with the chickens . . . we found a fox up by the pond. It was dead. But it's gone now. I just looked. I guess you must have found it."

His face had changed from polite curiosity to alarm, his skin colouring all the while.

"I didn't move anything," he said, with a force to suggest he would otherwise have left it there to rot. It was beginning to snow again: big, serious flakes. If it carried on for much longer, getting home would become a problem.

"Then you have some pretty efficient scavengers knocking about," I said.

"Show me," he said, and held up his finger to indicate I should wait. A minute later he reappeared wearing a dark green windcheater and a woolen hat.

I took him back the way I'd come and pointed beyond the fence at the pond. Immediately, he climbed over and started striding through the thigh-high grass, snow shivering and tumbling in his wake. He cast glances back over his shoulder as we came around the lower edge of the pond. It was only as we were nearing the fence on the other side that I realised he was asking me silent questions: we'd bypassed the body's location. Snow had erased the green patch. No amount of kicking through the ground layer would reveal the fox's final resting place now.

"Do you have an assistant?" I asked. "A lad?"

"I do. But he's not in today. It's just me."

"What could have taken it?"

The farmer shrugged and eyed the clouds. "Hawk?"

"Another fox?" I said.

"I bloody well hope not," he said. "I spent an age on that coop today, reinforcing it. Two chickens in there now. Anyway, foxes aren't social. They're lone wolves, if you see what I mean."

"I hope you're right. I'll keep an eye out, anyway."

The farmer nodded. "You're staying on then?"

"Of course. The weather's a bit grim, and we've got an upset daughter, but this is our holiday. We'll make the best of it."

"Well, thank you. And I'd appreciate it if you didn't mention this in any online reviews you might write. Quite up to you, of course, but . . . well, people come from the towns and the cities to the countryside and it can . . . surprise them now and again. Nature. You can't control it, can you?"

◄◦►

What a day. Little had happened, really, but what had was intense, memorable, life-changing perhaps. There was plenty to talk about but Kit and I did everything we could to steer the obvious discussions towards safer waters. We got Megan into her pyjamas and stroked her hair and reassured her. We promised her that no matter what the weather was like in the morning we'd go for a trip out somewhere special. Horse riding maybe.

Once Megan was in bed, I asked her what story she wanted me to read to her.

"The Hungry Ghosts," she said.

"What?"

"The Hungry Goats."

I flipped through the pile of books, unnerved and not fully understanding why. Here it was: *The Hungry Goats*. The cover showed a picture of a goat happily munching on clothes hanging from a washing line. I read her the story, delivering the lines with more gusto than usual, and tucked her in.

Kit accepted a small glass of red wine from me and settled into the rocking chair with Lucy for her evening feed. Kit seemed swollen and in pain, the milk dripping from her nipple even as Lucy's mouth sought it. I watched my daughter suckle at that heavy breast, never failing to be fascinated by her appetite, and the way she stared, wide-eyed and curious, up at Kit's face as she guzzled her meal. Despite myself, I was getting aroused. My wife had embodied the blossoming cliché in pregnancy. Her skin glowed. Her hair was so soft.

Nature. The hungry ghosts.

"I'm going to check the ties," I said. Kit was smiling at me, one eyebrow arched. She knew me so well. I slipped from the tent, trying to hide my erection and served only to draw attention to myself.

You can't control it, can you? I had tried. Many years before.

I went out into a cold that was fierce enough to draw tears from my eyes; it was being stirred by a restless wind. At least the snow had stopped. I went around the perimeter of the tent, checking knots and listening for sounds beneath the howl of the wind. I thought I could hear the chickens sounding rattled in their coop, perhaps because of the repairs the farmer had made, or a memory of the traumatic event that morning, if poultry even had memories. Well, here was one chicken who could remember. In detail so vivid it was like flicking through a catalogue of photographs.

◄○►

That day. I was fourteen years old. I'd gone out feeling torn up inside as if someone had injected a million pieces of hot glass into my lower abdomen. I'd been seeing a girl. Alice, her name was. We used to kiss and fondle each other through our clothing for hours, and then she'd go home, leaving me feeling congested and annoyed. Masturbating was a poor substitute. Although I was a virgin, I knew I wanted to go all the way with Alice, who was a year older. She'd already done it with a previous boyfriend, but she said I was too young and she didn't want to take the risk. If I made her pregnant, that would be both our lives ruined, and if anybody found out she was sleeping with a fourteen-year-old, she'd be arrested. Not to mention the social stigma. She'd be torn apart.

So we got flustered and sticky in her room one afternoon when her parents were at work and we should have been in school. It was winter; it was cold. We clung to each other as much to try to get warm as for any hope of progressing from fingers under jumpers and French kisses which left our mouths sore. Then she pushed me away; I think I'd put my hand down the back of her knickers.

"You can't do that," she said, as if it was a game of Scrabble and I'd submitted a proper noun. By that time I was resigned to another evening of blue balls so I allowed my temper to come through and I told her to fuck off and I left. She didn't come after me, which I'd secretly been hoping for, and I walked all the way home expecting the truancy officer to jump me at any minute. Only I didn't make it back. I would have done, had I taken the route I followed ninety-nine times out of a hundred; right at the Horse & Jockey, over the railway bridge by the scrap-iron yard, along Folly Lane and right into the street where I lived. But this time I went down Hawley's Lane, past the gasworks and under the railway, turning left towards the road that ran parallel to Folly Lane, but on the south side of the school rather than the north; the better to avoid any staff.

I was dawdling, trying to time it so I'd get home at the time I usually arrived after school finished. The edge of the school fields came down to the corner of that road; later it would all be sold for the inevitable march of cheap housing. We were spoilt, back then, for green spaces.

I saw Beaky and Hardman, two lads from my year. The teachers probably didn't even know their given names. They might as well have been christened Ne'er-do-well Beak and Trouble-maker Hardman, rather than Anthony and Charlie. They weren't solid mates of mine, but we were on nodding terms and back then that was good enough to merit passing half an hour in someone's company. Sometimes I let them see my homework book, in return for chocolate or cans of pop.

Charlie was carrying something.

"What have you got there?" I asked him.

"It's our kid's," he said, as if I'd accused him of thieving it. It was an air rifle. A handsome one.

"Give us a go."

"Knob off," Charlie said. "We're going down the woods, see if we can bag us a jay. Ant's granddad wants a blue feather for his hat. Said he'd give him a tenner if he got him one."

I fell into step with them though I hadn't been invited along. I asked them if I'd been missed at school and neither of them said they'd heard anything. Beaky asked me where I'd been and I curried favour by giving them some juicy details of my time with Alice, much of it fabricated.

By the time we got to the clearing in the woods, the sky had become close and metallic; it was March and the weather would not improve for at least another month. Beaky set up some targets on the old collapsed tree trunk: a discarded Barratt's Shandy can, a bottle filled with earth, a polystyrene cup. Charlie went first, pumping the action to load the gun with compressed air and loading the breech with a tiny metal pellet from a tin in his pocket. He missed every time.

"We're only twenty feet away," I said.

"Do you want a go, or not?"

Beaky went next. I could tell he was pissed off that I was there, and that they'd have to share the pellets. At least he hit something; the glass bottle. But because it was full of soil it didn't shatter in the satisfying way we'd expected. It just made a kind of dull noise and split in two. He was happy enough, though. I accepted the rifle from him, along with his cocky rejoinder that he'd like to see me beat his so-called "high score."

"Just imagine Alice's fanny instead of the target and you'll nail all of 'em," Charlie said. And though I didn't want her to be there, Alice slipped into my thoughts in her tight T-shirt and short-shorts, her hair tied back, her lips shiny with gloss. I felt heat for her in the centre of my belly and busied myself getting a decent stance and shutting out all the chatter from the boys.

I pumped the action and raised the sight to my eye. I blinked, and there was fire.

I daren't breathe. The fox came out from behind the tree like something made from the space it occupied; it didn't seem real. This wood was too dull and lustreless for it. I actually thought that, once it saw us and scampered away, its flicking tail would paint glorious colour into every dark grey or dark green niche it passed in front of.

"Shoot it," Beaky said.

I didn't hesitate.

I don't know why I did it. I was blinded by its sinuous beauty, smiling at the everyday miracle of it—we'd often heard urban foxes, these known and yet utterly alien creatures, loosing their banshee screams in the winter streets, on the prowl for something tasty hanging from an overloaded dustbin—even as I pulled the trigger. The noise of the air gun, an ugly spit of violence, did not cause the fox to flinch and scamper away; I doubt it even heard the retort. It went down as though it had been instantaneously filleted of every bone in its body.

"Bastardo!" Charlie laughed. "Clint Eastwood or what? You cold-blooded killer."

We went to inspect the body. The pellet had taken its eye out. I felt queasy. I had a hard-on for the vestiges of Alice in my memory, and now this. It didn't feel right.

"What are you going to do?" Charlie asked. "You should skin the fucker. Take its head off. Have it as a trophy."

"It's a fox," I said. "It's not a rhino."

"Bury it, then," Beaky said. He was reaching for the rifle.

"You bury it."

"Not my mess."

I placed a hand against the fox's flank. It was warm and soft. I felt something moving through it. The last pulse of blood, maybe. Muscle memory. Something. I half expected the colour of it to come away on my skin when I lifted my hand clear.

Boredom was setting in. Beaky and Charlie ended up taking pot shots at the sky. They asked if I was coming and I said no. They wandered off. Charlie said something hilarious about fox AIDS and wearing a condom, and then it was just me and the fox and the closing of the day. I stayed for another hour, until it started to rain. I'd left my coat at Alice's. I felt myself shiver and I could no longer look at the fox because with every tremor of cold it felt as though it was the fox, and not me, that was moving.

I wanted to bury it, but the ground was too hard. In the end I toed a stack of leaf mould over the body. I said I was sorry. And I left.

That night I came down with the shittiest cold I'd ever had. I remember Mum sitting with me for some of it, though I can't remember what she said at the time. She was holding my hand. Sweat was lashing off me. With the coming of dawn, it seemed to just vanish, as if it was something that could only exist at night-time. Since then we always referred to it as my vampire flu. Mum said she was worried I might have contracted pneumonia and she was dithering over a call to the emergency services on a couple of occasions when my breath turned shallow, but Dad stayed her hand and told her to wait.

I ate an enormous breakfast and slept all day. My dreams were filled with red. I was well enough to go out that evening, a Saturday, and Alice had called, but I put her off. I took Dad's raincoat and went back to the woods on my own. The fox was gone from the mound of leaves. I'd kind of expected that. I was getting a sore on my palm from where I kept rubbing it against my jeans. I felt the same movement I'd felt within the dwindling fox echoed in my own chest.

I went a bit nuts then, thrashing around in the rain and mould, kicking over the targets from the day before, to the point where I was exhausted with panic, little yelps rising from my throat. And when I'd stopped having my self-indulgent fit, the yelps continued. I went behind the huge banks of rhododendron bushes that surrounded the clearing and was hit by the cold, damp smell of musk just before I saw a litter of fox pups; I counted six of them. Somehow they'd climbed out of their earth, but they were tiny and blind, still. They were cold and starving. I was too wiped out by my outburst, and the aftershock of the flu, to feel anything but dismay. I moved as though someone else was controlling me. I took off the raincoat and tied its sleeves together to form a handle. I picked up the fox cubs and placed them inside, trying to ignore the little nips and licks they gave to my knuckles. I knelt down close to the entrance to the earth and listened but it was quiet in there now. I zipped up the coat and pulled the toggles shut at the bottom, creating a loop with the ends, then drew the hood down over the coat and tucked it through the loop, tying it off tightly. In the rain, I hurried home, pausing on the way to dump the fox cubs in the canal. I never went back to the wood again.

◄○►

In the dark, a bleating.

I had stayed up late, reading. I spend so much of my waking day poring over dry texts that it's something of a blessed relief to have some time to wallow in a bestseller so purple you have to check your fingers afterwards in case they've been dyed beetroot. The girls had gone to bed a couple of hours previously. I'd worked my way through half a bottle of merlot and I was approaching a state of relaxation where I thought I might be able to sleep. No gales tonight.

I found myself reading the same line over and over. Tiredness. But there was something wrong. Something I'd read. Tonight? A feature I'd worked on in the past? Something nagged at me like a child prodding a worm with a stick. Something to do with foxes. Or maybe it was just that I'd seen only chickens and cows at the farm. No sheep. Which didn't mean there weren't any, of course. It was a big farm, and we hadn't explored as fully as we might.

Again, bleating, in the distance. It sounded all wrong. It sounded horrible. Was it a sheep trapped or injured? A sheep giving birth? Wasn't it a bit early in the year for lambing season?

I thought about heading down to the farmer but what if he didn't have any sheep? I could imagine the disdain, like something tangible, pouring off him. *Not you again.* And another fruitless quest to find an animal that wasn't anything to do with him. No. But it was under my skin now and I had to check it out. I'd be listening out for that bleat all night otherwise.

I pulled on my boots and coat and reached for the torch. A quick check on the tribe—Kit out for the count, Megan and Lucy safe and warm, curled up with each other in their secret den—and I let myself out. Clear sky, big moon. The snow had developed a thin crust, and my boots made a satisfying crunch through it as I headed down past the chicken coop and the two unoccupied glamping tents to the far edge of the field. The bleating came again. It sounded desperate; reconciled, even, to its fate. At least it seemed as though I was heading in the right direction.

I came to the edge of the field and negotiated a collapsed portion of wooden fencing mired with rusty barbed wire. Moonlight picked out a set of tracks in snow that had otherwise remained untouched since it settled. They weren't sheep tracks, though. These were shallow, made by something small and fleet. I breathed deeply and felt the cold scour away all the torpor that had draped over my limbs earlier. I felt fresh and alive, alert. Wildness awaking in the lizard part of the brain. I felt I could sense sap shifting through the smallest netted veins of a leaf; trace the course of a money spider's journey through the air on gossamer strands. Or it might just have been the merlot.

Another bleat. A low, end-of-tether sound, just ahead. But I couldn't see anything. Just the ongoing reach of snow. I kept walking, listening for more signals of distress, but they did not come. Confounded, I turned to go back and saw more tracks, criss-crossing those that had gone before. Some busy creature, making mischief while my back was turned. There was nature in a nutshell, I supposed: small things tip-toeing around behind the big things. Again I was haunted by some detail I had missed, a warning in text form, but I read millions of words each year, and anyway, what link could there be between my job and a tent holiday in the middle of nowhere?

Suddenly, fatigue slipped back through the cracks. My feet were aching and the cold was turning my face stiff. I wanted bed. I wanted to spoon with Kit and feel the curve of her belly under my fingers. I headed back to the fence and edged through the riot of wood and wire. A length of it snagged in my jeans, another on the hood of my coat. Great. I tried to extricate myself without pricking my legs/body on those sharp knots; *how long it had been since my last tetanus injection?*

Trapped, flailing, I nevertheless snapped bolt upright at the sudden scream. I couldn't tell if it was human or animal; it had some weird glassy quality, as if the temperature in the air had shaped it into something brittle and fine. But then words began to form out of that mindless howling: my name.

Kit, calling my name.

I thrashed at the wire, no longer caring if I sliced myself open on it, and stumbled into the snow as I sprang clear. I ran as fast as I could and there was heat in my chest and I was crying, I could barely see where I was going, and all I could see through the tears was a sheep's head with fox's eyes, and I remembered what I'd read, in this piece about legend and lore in the animal kingdom, about the way that a fox will sometimes lure its prey to a position of vulnerability by disguising its voice, pretending to be an injured lamb.

I got to the tent and all the gas lamps were on. Kit was pacing back and forth, her fists clenched by her sides. She was screaming unintelligibly now, just animal noises of distress, her mouth wide, spit hanging off her teeth. She looked as if she'd gone mad. My own voice underneath hers—*What is it? What is it?*—sounded panic-weak, far away, unattached to me at all. But maybe I wasn't saying anything, and I was only thinking it, because I knew the answer to my own question. I pushed by Kit and threw myself at the children's bed to find the girls gone and nothing remaining but a single spot of blood.

STEMMING THE TIDE

SIMON STRANTZAS

Marie and I sit on the wooden bench overlooking the Hopewell Rocks. In front of us, a hundred feet below, the zombies walk on broken, rocky ground. Clad in their sunhats and plastic sunglasses, carrying cameras around their necks and tripping over open-toed sandals, they gibber and gabber amongst themselves in a language I don't understand. Or, more accurately, a language I don't *want* to understand. It's the language of mindlessness. I detest it so.

Marie begged me for weeks to take her to the Rocks. It's a natural wonder, she said. The tide comes in every six hours and thirteen minutes and covers everything. All the rock formations, all the little arches and passages. It's supposed to be amazing. Amazing, I repeat, curious if she'll hear the slight scoff in my voice, detect how much I loathe the idea. There is only one reason I might want to go to such a needlessly crowded place, and I'm not sure if I'm ready to face it. If she senses my mood, she feigns obliviousness. She pleads with me again to take her. Tries to convince me it can only help her after her loss. Eventually, the crying gets to be too much, and I agree.

But I regret it as soon as I pick her up. She's dressed in a pair of shorts that do nothing to flatter her pale lumpy body. Her hair is parted down the middle and tied to the side in pigtails, as though she believes somehow appropriating the trappings of a child will make her young again. All it does is reveal the greying roots of her dyed black hair. Her blouse . . . I cannot even begin to explain her blouse. This is going to be great! she assures me as soon as she's seated in the car, and I nod and try not to look at her. Instead, I look at the sun-bleached road ahead of us. It's going to take an hour to drive from Moncton to the Bay of Fundy. An hour where I have to listen to her awkwardly try and fill the air with words because she cannot bear silence for anything longer than a minute. I, on the other hand, want nothing more than for the world to keep quiet and keep out.

The hour trip lengthens to over two in traffic, and when we arrive the sun is already bearing down as though it has focused all its attention on the vast asphalt parking lot. We pass though the admission gate and, after having our hands stamped, onto the park grounds. Immediately, I see the entire area is lousy with people moving in a daze—children eating dripping ice cream or soggy hot dogs, adults wiping balding brows and adjusting colourful shorts that are already tucked under rolls of fat. I can smell these people. I can smell their sweat and their stink in the humid air. It's suffocating, and I want to retch. My face must betray me; Marie asks me if I'm okay. Of course, I say. Why wouldn't I be? Why wouldn't I be okay in this pig pen of heaving bodies and grunting animals? Why wouldn't I enjoy spending every waking moment in the proximity of people that barely deserve to live, who can barely see more than a few minutes into the future? Why wouldn't I enjoy it? It's like I'm walking through an abattoir, and none of the fattened sows know what's to come. Instead they keep moving forward in their piggy queues, one by one meeting their end. This is what the line of people descending into the dried cove looks like to me. Animals on the way to slaughter. Who wouldn't be okay surrounded by that, Marie? Only I don't say any of that. I want to with all my being, but instead I say I'm fine, dear. Just a little tired is all. Speaking the words only makes me sicker.

The water remains receded throughout the day, keeping a safe distance from the Hopewell Rocks, yet Marie wants to sit and watch the entire six-hour span, as though she worries what will happen if we are not there to witness the tide rush in. Nothing will happen, I want to tell her. The waters will still rise. There is nothing we do that helps or hinders inevitability. That is why it is inevitable. There is nothing we can do to stem the tides that come. All we can do is wait and watch and hope that things will be different. But the tides of the future never bring anything to shore we haven't already seen. Nothing washes in but rot. No matter where you sit, you can smell its clamminess in the air.

The sun has moved over us and still the rocky bottom of the cove and the tall weirdly sculpted mushroom rocks are dry. Some of the tourists will not climb back up the metal-grated steps, eager to spend as much of the dying light wandering along the ocean's floor. A few walk out as far as they can, sinking to their knees in the silt, yet none seem to wonder what might be buried beneath the sand. The teenager who acts as the lifeguard maintains his practiced, affected look of disinterest, hair covering the left half of his brow, watching the daughters and mothers walking past. He ignores everyone until the laughter of those in the silt grows too loud, the giggles of sand fleas nibbling their flesh unmistakable. He yells at them to get to the stairs. Warns them of how quickly the tide will rush in, the immediate undertow that has sucked even the heaviest of men out into the Atlantic, but even he doesn't seem to believe it. Nevertheless, the pigs climb out one at a time, still laughing. I look around to see if anyone else notices the blood that trickles down their legs.

The sun has moved so close to the horizon that the blue sky has shifted to orange. Many of the tourists have left, and those few that straggle seemed tired to the point of incoherence. They stagger around the edge of the Hopewell Rocks, eating the vestiges of the fried food they smuggled in earlier or laying on benches while children sit on the ground in front of them. The tide is imminent, but only Marie and I remain alert. Only Marie and I watch for what we know is coming.

When it arrives, it does so swiftly. Where once rocks covered the ground, a moment later there is only water. And it rises. Water fills the basin, foot after foot, deeper and deeper. The tide rushes in from the ocean. It's the highest tide in the world over. It beckons people from everywhere to witness its power. The inevitable coming in.

Marie has kicked off her black sandals, the simple act shaving inches from her height. She has both her arms wrapped around one of mine and is staring out at the steadily rising water. She's like an anchor pulling me down. Do you see anything yet? she asks me, and I shake my head, afraid if I open my mouth what might come out. How much longer do you think we'll have to wait? Not long, I assure her, though I don't know. How would I? I've refused to come to this spot all my life, this spot on the edge of a great darkness. That shadowy water continues to lap, the teenage lifeguard finally concerned less with the girls who walk by to stare at his athletic body, and more with checking the gates and fences to make sure the passages to the bottom are locked. The last thing anyone wants is for one to be open accidentally. The last thing anyone but me wants, that is.

The sun is almost set, and the visitors to the Hopewell Rocks have completely gone. It's a park full only with ghosts, the area surrounding the risen tide. Mushroom rocks look like small islands, floating in the ink just off the shore. The young lifeguard had gone, hurrying as the darkness crept in as fast as the water rose. Before he left he shot us a look that I couldn't quite make out under his flopping denim hat, but one which I'm certain was fear. He wanted to come over to us, wanted to warn us that the park had closed and that we should leave. But he didn't. I like to think it was my expression that kept him away. My expression, and my glare. I suppose I'll never know which.

Marie is lying on the bench by now, her elbow planted on the wooden slats, her wrist bent to support the weight of her head. She hasn't worn her shoes for hours, and even in the long shadows I can see sand and pebbles stuck to her soles. She looks up at me. It's almost time, she whispers, not out of secrecy—because no one is there to hear her—but of glee. It's almost time. It is, I tell her, and try as I might I can't muster up even a false smile. I'm too nervous. The thought of what's to come jitters inside of me, shakes my bones and flesh, leaves me quivering. If Marie notices, she doesn't mention it, but I'm already prepared with a lie about the chill of day's end. I know it's not true, and that even Marie is smart enough to know how warm it still is, but nevertheless I know she wants nothing more than to believe every word I say. It's not one of her most becoming qualities.

The tide rushes in after six hours and thirteen minutes, and though I'm not wearing a watch I know exactly when the Bay is at its fullest. I know this not by the light or the dark oily colour the water has turned. I know this not because I can see the tide lapping against the nearly submerged mushroom rocks. I know this because, from the rippling ocean water, I can see the first of the heads emerge.

Flesh so pale it is translucent, the bone beneath yellow and cracked. Marie is sitting up, her chin resting on her folded hands. I dare a moment to look at her wide open face and wonder if the remaining light that surrounds us is coming from her beaming. The smile I make is unexpected. Genuine. They're here! she squeals, and my smile falters. I can't believe they're here! I nod matter-of-factly.

There are two more heads rising from the water when I look back at the full basin, the first already sprouting an odd number of limbs attached to a decayed body. The thing staggers towards us, the only two living souls for miles around, though how it can see us with its head cocked so far back is a mystery. I can smell it from where we sit. It smells like tomorrow. More of the dead emerge from the water, refugees from the dark ocean, each one a promise of what's to come. They're us, I think. The rich, the poor, the strong, the weak. They are our heroes and our villains. They are our loved ones and hated enemies. They are me, they are Marie, they are the skinny lifeguard in his idiotic hat. They are our destiny, and they have come to us from the future, from beyond the passage with a message. It's one no one but us will ever hear. It is why Marie and I are there, though each for a different reason—her to finally help her understand the death of her mother, me so I can finally put to rest the haunting terrors of my childhood. Neither of us speak about why, but we both know the truth. The dead walk to tell us what's to come, their broken mouths moving without sound. The only noise they make is the rap of bone on gravel. It only intensifies as they get closer.

For the first time, I see a thin line of fear crack Marie's reverie. There are nearly fifty corpses shambling toward us, swaying as they try to keep rotted limbs moving. If they lose momentum, I wonder if they'll fall over. If they do, I doubt they'd ever right themselves. Between where we sit and the increasing mass is the metal gate the young lifeguard chained shut. More and more of the waterlogged dead are crowding it, pushing themselves against it. I can hear the metal screaming from the stress, but its holding for now. Fingerless arms reach through the bars, their soundless hungry screams echoing through my psyche. Marie is no longer sitting. She's standing. Pacing. Looking at me, waiting for me to speak. Purposely, I say nothing. I'll let her say what I know she's been thinking.

There's something wrong, she says. This isn't—

It isn't what?

This isn't what I thought. This, these people. They aren't *right* . . .

I snigger. How is it possible to be so naive?

They are exactly who they are supposed to be, I tell her with enough sternness I hope it's the last she has to say on the subject. I don't know why I continue to make the same mistakes. By now, I'd have thought I would have started listening. But that's the trouble with talking to your past self. Nothing, no matter how hard you try, can be stopped. Especially not the inevitable.

Dead flesh is packed so tight against the iron gates that it's only a matter of time. It's clear from the way the metal buckles, the hinges scream. Those of the dead that first emerged are the first punished, as their putrefying corpses are pressed by the thong of emerging dead against the fence that pens them in. I can see upturned faces buckling against the metal bars, hear softened bones pop out of place as their lifeless bodies are pushed through the narrow gaps. Marie turns and buries her face in my chest while gripping my shirt tight in her hands. I can't help but watch, mesmerised.

Hands grab the gate and start shaking, back and forth, harder and harder. So many hands, pulling and pushing. The accelerating sound ringing like a church bell across the lonely Hopewell grounds. I can't take it anymore, Marie pleads, her face slick with so many tears. It was a mistake. I didn't know. I never wanted to know. She's heaving as she begs me, but I pull myself free from her terrified grip and stand up. It doesn't matter, I tell her. It's too late.

I start walking toward the locked fence.

I can't hear Marie's sobs any longer, not over the ruckus the dead are making. I wonder if she's left, taken the keys and driven off into the night, leaving me without any means of transportation. Then I wonder if instead she's watching me, waiting to see what I'll do without her there. I worry about both these things long enough to realize I don't really care. Let her watch. Let her watch as I lift the latches of the fence the dead are unable to work on their own. Let me unleash the waves that come from that dark Atlantic ocean onto the tourist attraction of the Hopewell Rocks. Let man's future roll in to greet him, let man's future become his present. Make him his own past. Who we will be will soon replace who we are, and who we might once have been.

The dead, they don't look at me as they stumble into the unchained night. And I smile. In six hours and thirteen minutes, the water will recede as quickly as it came, back out to the dark dead ocean. It will leave nothing behind but wet and desolate rocks the colour of sun-bleached bone.

THE ANATOMIST'S MNEMONIC

PRIYA SHARMA

Samuel Wilson's life wasn't a search for love at every turn. There'd been girls he'd liked, with whom he'd managed fragile love affairs, but something was always lacking no matter how hard he tried. Something that failed to ignite.

Sam knew what it was. He knew that love and objectification weren't the same but he had a passion for hands. His arousal in every organ, the mind, the skin, the parts he'd once been told were made for sin, depended on the wrists, the palms, the fingertips.

Why don't we ask Sam to the party? I've invited Judith. We should introduce them.

Women were keen to intervene on his behalf.

Your Mother wants you to bring your friend Sam to Sunday lunch. She says he looks like he needs feeding up. Yes, your sister's also coming.

Colleagues, friends, friends' girlfriends, wives, and mothers were all eager to help him along on a romantic quest.

What's Sam like? No, I don't fancy him. I only have eyes for you. I'm just curious. He's such a nice, unassuming guy. I don't get why he's single.

They were taken with his unconscious charm. He was a millpond of a man. They wanted to see what sort of woman would make him ripple.

None guessed the secret so incongruous with the rest of him. The thing he'd denied himself.

Sam couldn't tell them for fear they'd make a tawdry fetish of the fundamentals of his happiness.

He couldn't tell them about the hands.

⟶

Sam, aged nineteen, had seen a fortune teller. There was a painted caravan on the outskirts of a funfair. He was close enough to childhood to find the fair childish, not old enough to enjoy its novelty with a pang of nostalgia. He wasn't having fun. His friends were raucous. Boorish. The whirling neon and cheap hotdogs made him feel sick. The quiet caravan seemed like a retreat. He was at the age and stage where he had queries about his life. Later the classmates he'd arrived with questioned his disappearance but he deflected them with vagaries and shrugs.

It was a formulative experience. The palm reader, twenty years his senior, took him in with a glance that measured his vitality. His every possibility. His diffidence hid his differences from his peers. The ardour and sensitivity overlooked by girls his own age.

Imogen (the palmist's real name) didn't go in for hoop earrings or headscarves. Her uniform was black and flattering, fit for funerals and seductions. Although her youth was behind her, Imogen was still young enough to want to feel it.

They sat on opposite sides of the table. Imogen was fleshy where expected of an older woman but with slender limbs. She used her hands and wrists to express everything.

Sam felt an unexpected thrill, the exact location of which was uncertain, when she leant across the table and seized his waiting hands in hers. He liked how she took charge despite her diminutive size. The way she examined him for clues. She dropped his left hand, having exhausted its information. It lay between them on the table, aching to be held again. Sam watched her pink tongue dart out between plum painted lips to wet the tip for her forefinger. She traced a damp circle around his palm, her face close so that she could peer into his future. Close enough to feel her breath on his skin. Close enough to see a single silver strand in the darkness of her parting.

She announced his hands were the instruments of fate and their message was explicit.

"Your heart line's unusual. It springs from Saturn. It's a chain pattern. Unforked. You're a sensual man. You'll have unique needs. Your line of affection shows a strong attachment, the sort that only happens once in a lifetime. You'll find true love because of her hands."

Most initiations involve fumbling and misunderstandings but this wasn't Imogen's first time with a first timer. As they lay together in the half light of her caravan, Imogen explained her trade to Sam using their own hands as primers.

"Life," she explained, "is laid out in lines: life, heart, and head. The lines of destiny, affection, and the sun." She traced each one out, stimulated every nerve.

"The whole universe is right here." She kissed his palms, his mounts of Venus, Mars, Mercury, and the moon.

The next lesson was in the significance of fingers, after which she sucked each one in turn. She praised the nails that pinned down his nature, well formed, crescents rising at the base.

Sam didn't care about his own hands. They were whole and functional, fit for purpose. He was more concerned with hers. Imogen had the hands of Aphrodite. Her wrists were fine. Refined. He could encircle them with ease. Her hands touched him everywhere. They moved him. Not love but distilled desire. Eroticism crystallised.

Nineteen. A late age for imprinting but it was testament to Imogen's hands. The image of them roaming over him. She couldn't foresee the Pavlovian associations that would occur.

Whoever Sam loved would need hands as beautiful as hers.

❧

Samuel had met with other hand worshippers. They were the reason for his reticence. He was puzzled by their games. The act of washing up became burlesque as hands were engulfed in suds. A game of Rock, Paper, Scissors was frank porn. They didn't care about hands the way he did. Hands were mystical, magical, not to be leered at as they went about their daily chores. Hands were delicate and complex. The ultimate Darwinian organ. The sign of a higher being. Opposable thumb above paw and claw.

Why shouldn't they be the localisation of desire?

Sam decided, at thirty-two, he couldn't ignore his needs anymore. He copied the number he'd found onto a pad. It sat by the phone for weeks before he called.

"Hello."

"I'm sorry." He winced at this inauspicious beginning, unsure why he'd apologised. "Are you Beth Hurt? I found your website."

"I am."

She sounded younger than he'd expected. He tried to imagine her face. Her hands.

"My name's Sam Wilson. I wonder if you can help me." He stalled. In the silence that followed, he was afraid she'd hang up.

"Let me tell you a bit about what I do. I'm a medical illustrator. I have an anatomy degree as well as fine arts training. I do medical textbooks, teaching aids, exhibition posters, and company brochures."

He was thankful that Beth Hurt was gracious, trying to put him at ease.

"I need a drawing."

"What of?"

"A pair of hands. I work in advertising." This part was true. "I'm applying for a job with a rival agency so I can't go to my art department."

The last part was a lie. It was for a very different advert. A more personal one.

M, 32, single, solvent, sincere, seeks F to share music, books, food, film and the other fine things in life. Beautiful hands essential.

All he needed was an illustration.

"Tell me a bit more about what you want."

Sam discussed hand anthropometry. He specified dimensions. Palm to wrist ratio. Finger length. Shape of the nails. The glorious proportions of the flawless hand. "Most of all, they must be beautiful."

"All hands are beautiful," she mused. "They all tell a story."

Sam didn't know how to disabuse Beth Hurt of this. The subtleties of the mind, the sense of humour, the face and body were subjective. He had a non-judgemental approach to those and found their variations spectacular. Hands were different. Hands were absolutes.

"Beautiful to me then."

◄o►

Sam normally coped with the monotony of motorways by seizing on their differences. The ballet of the cars. The flowers that flourished on the verges. The flash of the central barrier. Graffiti that decorated the bridges overhead. Who blew, who sucked, and other such stuff.

He didn't need to scrutinise the minutiae of the journey now. He had other things on his mind.

He turned off at Beth's junction onto a series of dual carriageways and roundabouts. Then a town. Trees. A school. A row of shops. People queued at a bus stop. Life went on around him unencumbered while he was overcome with hope.

Sam couldn't tell if Beth's street was on its way up or down. A handsome Georgian terrace past its prime. It exhibited signs of aspiration and neglect. Some of the basement flats paraded rows of geranium in pots while others had old sheets hung at the windows and peeling door paint.

He found the right house and examined the bells by the door. Beside Beth's was a brass plaque that bore her name and nothing else.

The voice that answered via the intercom wasn't hers. It was more melodic, lower in its range.

"Come up. Second floor. I'll leave the door open. Beth's on the phone."

The communal hall's flower prints and beige carpet gave no clue as to what waited upstairs. He took the stairs two at a time.

The door was ajar. Beth Hurt's hall was painted matt charcoal. A set of daguerreotypes hung upon one wall, formal portraits that were trapped beneath a silver skin. He liked these antique pictures from the past. Their eyes were alive in a way that eluded modern printing techniques. There were shelves loaded with curios. A set of opera glasses and a peacock fan. Metal syringes shining in their case. A porcelain phrenology head. A nautilus shell.

A navy surgeon's brass bound chest lay open against one wall. Sam read the label by each viscous instrument, designed for hasty amputations. The line drawing in the lid was a pictorial guide to removing a limb. There were clamp-like contraptions, a pair of petit tourniquets, to stem blood loss. An amputation knife, its curved blade designed to sweep around the limb's flesh and cut right down to bone. The zigzag teeth of the tendon and D-shaped saws looked like something from a joiner's bag.

A door at the end of the corridor opened. It was Beth Hurt.

"Sorry to keep you waiting, come through. Did Kate offer you a drink?"

"No, but don't worry. I'm Sam."

He held out a hand. She took it. Firm grip. Warm, soft skin. Her hair was short enough to allow its rightful curl around her face. It was a shade between brown and red.

"It's nice to finally meet you."

Sam felt a tug of something akin to recognition. He suppressed the urge to giggle. He knew from the wide spread of her smile that she did too. There was a softening around her eyes that drew him in.

"You've come a long way. Let me get you a drink. What would you like?"

"Go on then. A coffee would be great."

Beth opened the door and called out.

"Kate, kettle's on. Do you want one?"

"Love one," came the distant reply.

Kate. Friend, lover, or just flatmate? It occurred to Sam that Beth had grown suspicious. Did she regret inviting him here instead of somewhere neutral? Had she rung around until she found a chaperone?

Sam waited in Beth's professional space, free to look around. It was a patchwork of diagrams and charts. Line drawings and sketches. Plastic models. Some of the words and pictures made him blush. A painting of a dissected heart hung over her desk. Bloodied meat and gaping valves. A fist of an organ, much misunderstood and mythologized. It was just a pump after all.

Sam was examining a set of photos of a dissected brain when Beth retuned carrying a tray. He caught the top note of her scent as she handed him a mug. A citrus smell that energised him. His eyes dropped to her hands.

They were too square, too fleshy to reveal a pleasing amount of the sinews beneath. Bitten nails. Ink stained flesh. Palms seamed and furrowed. Creases like bracelets at her wrists.

"Would you be more comfortable in another room?"

He took a final look at the brain photographs and grinned.

"No, it's only the sight of my own blood that makes me faint but if I feel funny I'll let you know."

"Do you think it's ghoulish?"

Sam sipped his coffee as he looked at a watercolour of a dissected leg. "No. Your work's stunning."

"Would you believe that I wanted to be a children's illustrator? I used to make up stories and draw pictures to go with them for my sister after our mum died."

It was such a personal disclosure that made him embarrassed that he'd lied to her about his reasons for the commission. Her unguardedness disarmed him. She'd let him into her home. He felt he could tell her anything now that he was here.

"So what happened?"

"I took a job with a medical publisher because I was strapped for cash. The editor had loved my work on a book he read to his daughter at bedtime. He said it was just the right look."

"What sort of kid's book was that?"

They both laughed.

"Once I finished the job I knew I didn't want to do anything else. Isn't it strange how you know that you like something, right away?" She laid out the final drawing before him. "Is this what you had in mind?"

"It's brilliant." He meant it. One hand was partially folded against the other. They were elegant and tapered. Beth had made technical perfection seem informal. "You have real talent."

"Oh no, it's just about knowing the anatomy. It changes the structure of the work. May I?"

The way she took his hands made him dizzy.

"The finger bones are called the phalanges. Three to each finger. Two in the thumb."

She touched each one in his little finger and his thumb by way of demonstration. Sam felt the start of gnawing elation.

"Fascinating." He'd been preoccupied with aesthetics, not construction or mechanics, but her words thrilled him.

"And these are the metacarpal bones." Sam swallowed when she ran her finger across his palm. "At one end they form the knuckles and at the other they articulate with the wrist bones, which are my favourites."

"Why?" He relished her pleasure.

"They're interesting. Each one has a different shape and name but they fit together like a jigsaw."

She made him arch his thumb to reveal two taut lines along his wrist.

"This gap is called the anatomical snuffbox." She pointed to the space between the pair of tendons. "The bone which forms the floor is the scaphoid."

"Scaphoid," he repeated.

"The rest of the wrist bones are the lunate, triquetral, pisiform, trapezium, trapezoid, capitate, and hamate." She worked her way over the wrist to show him where each bone was. "I like the hamate. It has a hook."

He felt like he was party to the arcane.

"How do you remember all that?" Sam wanted her to know he was impressed.

"Hard work. And mnemonics. Lots of mnemonics."

"The only mnemonic I know is Richard of York gave battle in vain, for the rainbow."

A spot of colour had appeared high on Beth's cheeks. It conjured up Beth Hurt in bed, postcoital, flushed and loose limbed. Intuition told him the reason for her flush.

"What's the mnemonic?"

"What?"

"For the wrist."

"Scared lovers try positions that they can't handle." Beth tried to sound unabashed.

The physiology of their attraction couldn't be faked. The symptoms of their chemistry. They were close. Sam's pupils dilated. It was hard to breathe. His heart no longer functioned as just a pump. His blood was hot. His throat was dry. Beth was a loadstone and he'd been magnetised. Their heads were tilted in sympathy. Lips parted in empathy.

He couldn't. Beth's hands were lacking.

"The picture . . ." He moved away. "It's perfect."

"I hope you find what you want."

"Pardon?"

"Get what you want. The job." She sounded magnanimous in rejection. Courageous. "I wish you the best of luck."

"I'll treasure this, no matter what. Not because of its anatomy but because you've pictured exactly what I described."

"I've a confession. It was easier than you think."

"What do you mean?"

"I had a model."

"A model?"

He'd imagined such hands could only be imagined.

"Yes, Kate, my sister. Do you want to meet her?"

◄◦►

Sam could see the shades of sisterhood on their faces. Kate was at ease amid the depictions of flayed flesh and dismembered limbs. She was an elongated, elegant version of her sibling. Undeniably the better looking of the two, but with paler hair and skin. A less vivid version of Beth.

"I thought introductions were in order. Sam, Kate. Kate, Sam."

"Hi."

"Nice to meet you."

Sam searched her smile, this Madonna of the Hands, but all that it revealed was her teeth.

"Sam loves the picture. I thought you two should meet."

Kate's hands were partially covered by the cuffs of her jumper. The fine rib clung to her wrists. Her tapered fingers ended in short nails, painted with a dark polish. It should have tantalised him.

Sam thrust out a hand, desperate to connect. As she took it, Sam waited for the jolt of hormones. Instead of a spark, there was just a seeping disappointment as her perfect hand lay in his.

"It's a good job you liked it." Kate thrust her hands back into her pockets. "Beth's promised me a modelling fee."

The trio laughed in unison.

"I'm going to get another drink." Beth glanced at him. "Coffee all round?"

She went, closing the door behind her with a careful click.

"Beth says the drawing's for a job interview. What's it for?"

"A hand cream campaign. I'm in advertising. What do you do?"

"I've just finished my degree. I'm a dietitian."

"Your place is great."

"I wish it were mine. I'm just staying here until I can get somewhere."

Sam nodded. Of course it was Beth's.

"Beth's a diamond. She's always looked out for me."

It was Beth that Sam was thinking of. There wasn't enough of Kate, pleasant as she was, to fill the room. Her hands, though fabulous, couldn't compensate for Beth's absence.

Hands though, they were absolutes.

⤙⚬⤚

Sam and Beth were bare beneath the sheets. It was her turn to be taught.

"Life," Sam explained, "is laid out in lines: life, heart, and head. The lines of destiny, affection, and the sun." Each one was traced out. Then there was the significance of fingers. The predictions of nails.

Imogen had been exorcised.

Scaphoid, lunate, triquetral, pisiform, trapezium, trapezoid, capitate, hamate.

The words Beth had taught him lingered in his mouth. He tried to pass them back to her, tongue to tongue. She was too weak to twist away.

Desire drove Sam. He didn't stop to consider the outrageousness of his demands. The flat was upended by his passions. The kitchen had become an impromptu theatre. The surgical instruments lay on the floor. Kate had been easily overcome. She lay where she'd fallen, in Beth's studio. Beth, though he'd surprised her, put up a greater fight. Sam kissed the bruise on her face, from the blow that had finally subdued her.

It was dirty work. Sam was glad that he'd been right that it was only his own blood that made him feel faint. The cuts he'd made with the amputation knife were ragged. The petit tourniquets were sound and stemmed Beth's bleeding. He'd not used them on Kate, not from unkindness but because there wasn't time.

Cautery was a more tricky matter. He'd improvised with a knife, heated on the hob until the blade glowed. He touched it to the places on Beth's bloody stumps that leaked.

Sam covered his clumsy suture work with wrappings of scarves. Kate's hands cooled quickly, despite their new attachment to Beth. It was a fleeting few hours that Sam couldn't hold onto for long enough. It left him hungry.

He put his lips to the perfect palms, to Beth's mouth. Her lips were pale. She shivered as he covered her body with his.

Beth whimpered, limp in the hands of fate.

THE MONSTER MAKERS

STEVE RASNIC TEM

This is all I can bear of love.

Robert is calling the children in, practically screaming it, how we all need to go, *now*. But I'm too busy gazing at the couple as they talk to the park ranger, the way their ears melt, noses droop, elongating into something else as their hair warps and shifts color, their spines bend and expand, arms and legs crooked impossibly, and their eye sockets migrating across their faces so rapidly they threaten to evict the eye balls.

"Grandpa! Please!" little Evie cries out, but now I look at the park ranger, who has fallen to his knees, his face pale and limbs trembling, mouth struggling to form a word that does not yet exist. Because it isn't the way it is in the movies; human beings cannot accept such change so easily—at some point the mind must shut down and the body lose itself with no one left to tell it what to do. "Please, Grandpa, *now*," Evie wails, and the intensity of her distress finally gets to me, so that I hobble over to the battered old station wagon as fast as I can, which isn't very fast. Because Evie is that special grandchild, you see. Evie has my heart.

The car bucks once as Robert gives it gas too quickly. It rattles, then corrects itself. Alicia is safely in the backseat beside me, but I'm not sure if she ever left. She doesn't move as much as she used to. But it's amazing how young she looks—her long hair is still mostly blonde, even though she's about my age, whatever that might be. We agreed long ago not to keep track anymore. I've loved her as long as I've known her. The trouble is, these days I can't remember how long.

The grandkids are both on the other side of Alicia. They're small, so I can't see all of them, just four skinny legs which barely reach beyond the front edge of the seat, and the occasional equally skinny arm. They kick and wave, thrilled. Despite their fear—they have no understanding of what they've caused, or why—they're quite excited about what's happening to them. I suspect this is the way some addicts or athletes feel—something takes over you, as if it were a spirit or a god, seizing your blood and bones, your muscles—and it makes you run around or die. From this angle, there's no discernible difference between Evie and Tom, but they are not twins, except in spirit. They sing softly as they often do, so softly I can't make out the words, but I've come to believe that their singing is the background music to all my thoughts.

As we leave the park, I can hear the long howls behind me, the humanity disintegrating from those poor people's voices. My grandchildren laugh out loud, giddy from the experience. These changes always seem to happen around certain members of my family, although none of us have precisely understood the relationship or the mechanism. Why did the couple change but not the ranger? I have no idea. Perhaps it is some tendency in the mind, some proclivity of the imagination, or some random, genetic bullet. My grandchildren possess a prodigious talent, but it's not a talent anyone would want to see in action.

Up in the front passenger seat, Jackie pats Robert's shoulder. I don't know if this is meant as encouragement, or if he even needs it. My son has always been sane to a fault. His wife's face looks worried, the skin so tight across her cheeks and chin it's as if she wears a latex mask. But then Jackie always was the nervous sort. She's not of this family; she simply married into it.

"Dad, I thought I asked you not to tell them any more stories." Robert's voice is barely under control.

They're both angry with me, furious. They blame me for all of this. But they try not to show it. I don't think it's because they're careful with my feelings. I think it's because they're somewhat frightened of me. "Telling stories, that's what grandfathers do," I say. "It's how I can communicate with them. The stories of our lives and deaths are secrets even from ourselves. All we are able to share are these substandard approximations. But we still have to try, unless we want to arm ourselves with loneliness. I just tell the children *fairy tales*, Robert. That's all. Stories about monsters. Something they already know about. Monster stories won't turn you into a monster, son. Fairy tales simply tell you something you already knew in a somewhat clever way."

Once upon a time, perhaps gods and monsters walked the earth and a human might choose to be either one. But not anymore. Now people grow and age and die and then are forgotten about. It's the "great circle," or whatever you want to call it. It's sobering information but it can't be helped. I don't tell Robert this—he isn't ready to hear it. He loves his poor, pathetic flesh too much.

"Why couldn't you stop? What will it take to make you stop!" Robert is howling from behind the steering wheel. For just a moment, I think he's about to change, expand, become some sort of wolf thing, but he is simply upset with me. Robert is our only child, and I love him very much, but he has always been vulnerable, frightened by the most mundane of dangers, as if he were unhappy to have been born a mortal human (I'm afraid the only kind there is).

Robert always refused to listen to my bedtime stories, so he's really in no place to evaluate whether they are dangerous or not. The members of our family have been shunned for ages, thought to be witches, demons, and worse. No one wants to hear what we have to say. "Your children simply understand the precariousness of it all. And this is how they express it."

"No more, Dad, okay? No more today."

Whatever my son decides to do, he's likely to keep us all locked up at home from now on. The only reason we went out today was because he knows the children need to get out now and then, and he didn't think we'd run into anybody in that big state park. Besides, it doesn't happen every time, not even every other time. There's no way to predict such things. I've witnessed these transformations again and again, but even I do not understand the agency involved.

I can't blame him, I guess. Sometimes human life makes no sense. We really shouldn't exist at all.

Back at the old farmhouse, I'm suddenly so exhausted I can barely get out of the car. It's as if I've had a huge meal and now all I can manage is sleep. The adrenalin of the previous few hours has come with a cost. I suspect my food must eat me rather than the other way around.

Alicia is even worse than before, and Robert and Jackie each have to pull on an arm to get her to stand. The grandkids push on her butt, giggling, and aren't really helping.

Once inside, they take us up to our room. "I get so exhausted," I tell them.

"I know," Jackie replies. "You should just make it stop. We'd all be happier if you just made it stop."

She's like all the others. She doesn't understand. It happens, but I've never been sure we can make it happen. Perhaps we simply show what has always been. Her children are learning about death. It's a lesson not everyone wants to learn.

She must think that, because I'm an older man, I'm likely to do foolish things. But we have such a limited time on this planet, I want to tell her, why should we avoid the foolish? I feel like that deliverer of bad news whom everyone blames.

Robert is less courteous as he guides us up the stairs, his movements abrupt and careless. He's obviously lost all patience with this—this caring for elderly parents, this endless drama whenever the family goes out. He'll make us all stay home now, planted in front of the television, transfixed by god-knows-what mindless comedy, locked away so that we can't cause any more trouble. But the children have to go out now and then. An active child trapped inside is like a bomb waiting to go off.

Periodically he loses his balance and crashes me into a railing, a wall, the doorframe. Each time he apologizes but I suspect it is intentional. I don't mind especially—each small jolt of pain wakes me up a bit more. You have to stay awake, I think, in order to know which world you're in.

By the time they lay both of us down in the bed, I'm practically blind with fatigue. Almost everything is a dirty yellow smear. It's like a glimpse of an old photograph whose colors have receded into a waxy sheen. Perhaps this is the start of sleep, or the beginning of something else.

Several times during the middle of the night, Alicia crawls beneath the bed. Is this what a nightmare is like? Sometimes I crawl under the bed with her. The floor is gritty, dirty, and uncomfortable to lie on. It's like a taste of the grave. It's what I have to look forward to.

I pat Alicia's arm when she cries. "At least you still have your yellow hair," I tell her. She looks at me so fiercely I back away, far far back under the bed into the shadows where I can hear the winds howl and the insects' mad mutter. I can stay there only a brief while before it sickens me but it still seems safer than lying close to her.

I wake up the next morning with my hand completely numb, sleeping quietly beside my face. I scrape the unfeeling flesh against the rough floorboards until it appears to come back to life. Alicia isn't here; she's wandered off. Although much of the time she is practically immobile, she has these occasional adrenaline-driven spurts in which she moves until she falls down or someone catches her. She is so arthritic, these bouts of intense activity must be agony for her. I can hear the grandchildren laughing outside and there is this note in their tone that drives me to the window to see.

The two darlings have the mail carrier cornered by the garage. We never get mail here and I think how sad it is that this poor man will doubtless lose his life over an erroneous delivery. They chatter away with their monkey-like talk at such a high pitch and speed I cannot follow what they say, but the occasional discrete image floats to the top—screaming heads and bodies in flame. None of these images appears in any of the stories I have told them, although of course Robert will never believe this. What he does not fully appreciate is that out in the real world all heads have the potential for screaming, and all bodies are in fact burning all the time.

On the edge of the yard, I spy Alicia. She has taken off all her clothes again and now scratches about on all fours like some different kind of animal. The Roberts of the world do not wish to admit that humans are animals. We may fancy ourselves better than the beasts because of our language skills, because we possess words in abundance. But all that does is empower us with excuses and equivocations.

The mail carrier has begun to change. He struggles valiantly but to no avail. Already his jaw has lengthened until it disconnects from the rest of his face, wagging back and forth with no muscle to support it. Already his hair drifts away and his fleshier bits have begun to dissolve. These are changes typical, I think, of a body left in the ground for months.

At first Evie laughs as if watching a clown running through his repertoire of shenanigans but now she has begun to cry. Such is the madness of children, but I must do what I can to minimize the damage. I make my way stiffly downstairs with a desperate grip on the banister, my joints like so much broken glass inside my flesh, and as I head for the door I see Robert come up out of the cellar, the axe in his hands. "This has to stop . . . this has to stop," he screams at me. And I very much agree. And if he were coming for *me* with that axe all would be fine—I somehow always understood things might come to this juncture—but he sweeps past me and heads for the front door and my grandchildren outside.

I take a few quick steps, practically falling, and shove him away from the door. I see his hands fumble the axe, but I do not realize the danger until he hits the wall and screams, tumbles backwards, the blade buried in his chest. "Robert!"

It's all I have time to say before Jackie comes out of the kitchen screeching. But it's all I know to say, really, and what good would it do to lose myself now? He would have hated to die from clumsiness, and that's what I take away from this house when I leave.

Out on the lawn, the children are jumping up and down laughing and crying. There is a moment in which time slows down, and I'm heartsick to see their tiny perfect features shift, coarsen, the flesh losing its elasticity and acquiring a dry, plastic filler look, as if they might become puppets, inanimate figures controlled by distant and rapidly-vanishing souls. I see my little Evie's eyes dull into dark marbles, her slackened face and collapsing mouth spilling the dregs of her laughter. I think of Robert dead in the farmhouse—and what a mad and reprehensible thing it is to survive one's child.

But of course I can't tell these children their father has died. Maybe later, but not now, when they are like this. If I told them now they might savage the little that remains of our pitiful world. In fact, I can't tell them anything I feel or know or see.

"Help me find your grandmother!" I shout. "She's gotten away from us, but I'm sure one of you clever children will find her!" And I am relieved when they follow me out of the yard and into the edge of the woods.

I have even more difficulty as I maneuver through the snarled tangle of undergrowth and fallen branches than I thought I would. I'm out of practice, and with every too-wide step to avoid an obstacle, I'm sure I'm going to fall. But the children don't seem to mind our lack of progress;

in fact, they already appear to have forgotten why we're out here. They range back and forth, their paths cross as they pretend to be bees or birds or low-flying aircraft. Periodically they deliberately crash into each other, fall back against trees and bushes in dozens of feigned deaths. Sometimes they just break off to babble at each other, point at me, and giggle, sharing secrets in their high-pitched alien language.

Now and then I snatch glimpses of Alicia moving through the trees ahead of us. Her blonde hair, her long legs, and once or twice just a bit of her face, and what might be a smile or a grimace; I can't really tell from this distance. Seeing her in fragments like this, I can almost imagine her as the young athletic woman I met fifty years ago, so quick-witted, who enthralled me and frightened me and ran rings around me in more ways than one. But I know better. I know that that young woman exists more in my mind, now, than in hers. That other Alicia is now like some shattered carcass by the roadside, and what lives, what dances and races and gibbers mindlessly among trees is a broken spirit that once inhabited that same beautiful body. Sometimes the death of who we've loved is but the final act in a grief that has lingered for years.

I think that if Alicia were to embrace me now, she'd have half my face between her teeth before I had time even to speak her name.

As mad as she, the children now shriek on either side of me, slap me on the side of the face, the belly, before they howl and run away. I wonder if they even remember who she is or was to them. How only a few years ago, she made them things and cuddled them and sang them soft songs. But we were never meant to remember everything, I think, and that is a blessing. It seems they have already forgotten about their parents, except as a story they used to know. The young are always more interested in science fiction, those fantasies of days to come, especially if they can be the heroes.

I watch them, or I avoid them, for much of the afternoon. Like a baby sitter who really doesn't want the job. At one point, they begin to fight over a huge burl on a tree about three feet off the ground. It is only the second such tree deformity I've ever seen, and by far the larger of the two. I understand that they come about when the younger tree is damaged and the tree continues to grow around the damage to create these remarkable patterns in the grain.

Their argument is a strange one, although not that different from other arguments they've had. Evie says it'll make a perfect "princess throne" for her after they cut it down. The fact that they have no means to cut it down does not factor into the argument. Tom claims he "saw it first," and although he has no idea what to do with it, the right to decide should be his.

Eventually they come to blows, both of them crying as they continue to pummel each other about the head and face. When they begin to bleed, I decide I have to do something. I have handled this badly, although I can't imagine that anyone else would know better how to handle such a crisis. I stare at them—their flesh is running. Their flesh runs! Their grandmother is gone, and they don't even know that their father is dead. And they dream wide awake and the flesh flows around them.

What do I tell them? Do I reassure them with tales of heaven—that their father is now safe in heaven? Do I tell them that no matter what happens to their poor fragile flesh there is a safe place for them in heaven?

What I want to tell them is that their final destination is not heaven, but memory. And you can make of yourself a memory so profound that it transforms everything it touches.

My Evie screams, her face a mask of blood, and Tom looks even worse—all I can see through the red confusion of his face is a single fixed eye. I try to run, then, to separate them, but I am so awkward and pathetic I fall into the brush and tangle below them, where I sprawl and cry out in sorrow and agony.

Only then do they stop, and they come to me, my grandchildren, to stare down at me silently, their faces solemn. Tom has wiped much of the blood from his face to reveal the scratches there, the long lines and rough shapes like a child's awkward sketch.

This is my legacy, I think. These are the ones who will keep me alive, if only as a memory poorly understood, or perhaps as a ghost too troublesome to fully comprehend.

We try and we try but we cannot sculpt a shape out of what we've done in the world. Our hands cannot touch enough. Our words do not travel far enough. For all our constant waving we still cannot be picked out of a crowd.

My grandchildren approach for the end of my story. I can feel the terrible swiftness of my journey through their short lives. I become a voice clicking because it has run out of sound. I become a tongue silently flapping as it runs out of words. I become motionless as I can think of nowhere else to go.

I become the stone and the plank and the empty field. I am really quite something, the monster made in their image, until I am scattered, and forgotten.

THE ONLY ENDING WE HAVE

KIM NEWMAN

The windshield wipers squeaked . . . like shrilling fiddles, scraped nerves, the ring of an unanswered phone. Another reason to trade in her '57 Ford Custom. For 1960, she'd like something with fins. Not that she could afford next year's showroom model.

Unless Hitch coughed up the ransom.

For the thing it was all about. The *mcguffin*.

The thing the audience doesn't care about, but the characters do.

"Good eeeev-ning," Hitch said, every goddamn morning . . . like in his TV show with that nursery/graveyard tune burbling in the background. "Funeral March of the Marionettes." *Dump-da-dumpity-dump-da-dump* . . .

"Good eeeev-ning, Jay-y-ne . . ."

His gargling-with-marbles accent was British. Not like David Niven or Peter Lawford, but British crawled out from under a rock. Hitch was a wattled toad in a grey-flannel suit, with inflating cheeks and jowls. His lower teeth stuck out like the Wolf Man's. His loose, babyish lips got moist when she came on set. Even before she took off the bathrobe. When she unwrapped the goods, he was spellbound. After a half hour, he'd have to gulp down drool with a little death-rattle.

"Jayne Swallow? Do you *swallow*, Jayne . . . do you?"

Every morning the same routine. Even before the robe came off.

"Take a bird name, chickie," her agent, Walter, had said . . . "bird names are good."

So, goodbye Jana Wróbel . . . hello, Jayne Swallow.

She should have gone with Joan Sparrow or Junie Peacock. By the time she signed on for Hitch, it was too late. She'd heard all the lines.

The set was festooned with dead birds. They stank under the hot lights. Chemicals. The glass eyes of the mountain eagle perched above a doorway reminded her of Hitch's watery ogling.

Hitchcock. That was a bird name, too. And a dirty meaning, which no one threw in the director's face every morning.

"Good morning, Mr. Softcock . . . Good afternoon, Mr. Halfcock . . . Good eeev-ning, Mr. Cocksucker . . . how do you like it?"

He'd screech like a bird at that . . . *Scree! Scree! Scree!*

There was a bird name in his damn movie. Janet Leigh's character. Jayne's character. Crane. Marion Crane.

. . . which made Jayne and Janet Hitch's Marion-ettes. The whole shoot was their funeral, scored with the slow, solemn, ridiculous tune. Jayne danced and strings cut into her wrists and neck.

In the end, the wires were snipped and she fell all in a heap, unstrung. Over and over. Like a sack of potatoes. Like a side of beef with arms and legs. Chocolate oozed from her wounds. Then she got up and died all over again.

Dump-da-dumpity-dump-da-dump . . . *Scree! Scree! Scree!*

She drove North on the Pacific Coast Highway.

To disguise herself, in case anyone from the studio should be crossing the road in front of the car, she'd worn sunglasses and a headscarf. Marilyn's famous I-don't-want-to-be-recognized look. She'd taken off the disguise when she was safely out of Los Angeles and the rain got heavy.

Even without the shades, it was hard to see the road ahead. Short-lived, clear triangles were wiped in thick water on the windshield. A deluge. Mudslide weather. After months of California sun, you found out where the ceiling leaked. There wasn't much traffic, which was a mercy. The car weaved from side to side as the wheel fought her grip. Her tires weren't the newest. She struggled, as if she'd been force-fed booze by a spy ring and set loose on a twisty cliff road to meet an unsuspicious accident.

The squeak of the wipers. The beat of her heart.

The voices in her head. Hitch's. Her agent's. Hers.

"Do you swallow, *Jayne* . . . do you?"

Tony Perkins's. "I like stuffing . . . birds."

Scree! Scree! Scree!

The window-seals were blown. Water seeped into the car, pouring in rivulets over the dash and inside the doors. Droplets formed this side of the glass, too many to wipe away with her cuff. Her seat was damp. She shivered. She'd been fighting the flu since her first day in the shower. With all the water, no one noticed her nose was streaming . . . except Becca, the make up woman, and she kept secrets like a priest in a confessional.

She could still feel water on her body. For days, she'd been pounded by studio hoses. The temperature varied from lukewarm to icy. The pressure kept up. Extra steam was pumped in, to show on film. She'd been scalded and she'd been frozen, but most of all she'd been soaked. She thought she'd never be dry again.

Before Jayne got into the fake bathtub each morning, Becca had to apply three moleskin patches that transformed her into a sexless thing, like that new blonde doll her niece had, Barbie . . . or a dressmaker's dummy with a head.

She might as well not have a head . . . her face would not be in the film. Janet Leigh's would be. The most Jayne would show was a tangle of wet blonde hair, seen from behind, as the knife scored down her unrecognizable back.

. . . in the book, the girl in the shower had her head cut off with an axe. One chop. Too swift for Hitch. He preferred the death of a thousand cuts. A thousand stabs. A thousand edits.

She was the only person on the crew who'd read the novel—not especially, but just by coincidence, a few months ago. Something to read while a photographer got his lights set *just so*. The first rule of show business was always take a book to read. There was so much waiting while men fiddled before they could start proper work. On the average Western, you could read *From Here to Eternity* while the bar room mirror was being replaced between fights.

Hitch disapproved of Jayne's book-learning. He intended to make a play of keeping the twist secret . . . not letting audiences into theaters after the movie started, appearing in jokey public service messages saying "Please don't tell the ending, it's the only one we have." But the picture's last reel wasn't an atomic plan guarded by the FBI. The paperback was in every book-rack in America. If it were down to Hitch, he'd confiscate the whole run and have the books pulped. It wasn't even *his* ending, really. It was Robert Bloch's. The writer was seldom mentioned. Hitch pretended he'd made it all up. Jayne sympathised . . . . Bloch was the only participant getting a worse deal out of the movie than her.

A clot of liquid earth splattered against the windshield, dislodged from the hillside above. The wipers smeared it into a blotch. She saw obscene shapes in the mud pattern, setting off bells at the Catholic Legion of Decency. Soon, the dirt was gone. Eventually, water got rid of all the disgusting messes in the world.

After a few hours in the movie shower, those patches would wash off Jayne's censorable areas. It didn't matter what spirit-gum Becca tried. Water would always win.

Then, spittle would rattle in Hitch's mouth. He would observe, lugubriously, "I spy . . . with my little eye . . . something beginning wi-i-i-ith . . . N! Nipple!"

Always, the director would insist on pretending to help Becca re-apply the recalcitrant triangles . . . risking the wrath of the unions. The film's credited make up men were already complaining about being gypped out of the chance to work with naked broads and stuck with be-wigging skeletons or filling John Gavin's chin-dimple. There was an issue about whether the patches were make up or costume.

Jayne had posed for smut pictures. Walter said no one would ever know, the pay was better than extra work, and the skin game had been good enough for Marilyn. For *Swank* and *Gent*—she'd never made it into *Playboy*—they shot her as was and smoothed her to plasticity with an airbrush. For the movies, the transformation was managed on set.

"Have you shaved today, Jayne Swallow? Shaved *down there*?"

Unless she did, the crotch-patch was agony to get off. No matter how many times it washed free during the day, it was always stuck fast at the end of the shoot. She was raw from the ripping.

"I thought of becoming a barber," Hitch said. "If you need a hand, I have my cut throat . . ."

At that, at the thought of a straight-razor on her pubes, he would flush with unconcealable excitement . . . and her guts would twist into knots.

"You'll love Hitch," Walter said. "And he'll love you. He loves blondes. And bird names. Birds are in all his films."

Sure, she was blonde. With a little help from a bottle. Another reason to shave *down there*.

We can't all be Marilyn. We can't all be Janet Leigh.

Being Janet Leigh was Jayne's job on this film.

Body double. Stand-in. Stunt double. Torso dummy.

Oh, Janet did her time in the shower. From the neck up.

The rest of it, though . . . weeks of close-ups of tummy, hands, feet, ass, thighs, throat . . . that was Jayne.

"It's a shower scene," Walter said.

She'd thought she knew what that meant. She'd done shower scenes. Indoors, for sophisticated comedies. Outdoors, for Westerns. Show a shape behind a curtain or a waterfall, and then let Debra Paget or Dorothy Provine step out wrapped in a towel and smile.

They always joked about shooting a version "for France." Without the curtain.

In France, Brigitte Bardot showed everything. Hitch would have loved to have BB in his sights. But Hollywood wasn't ready yet . . .

So, a shower scene . . .

A *Hitchcock* shower scene.

Not a tease, not titillation—except for very specialized tastes (ie: his). Not a barber's scene, but a butcher's. Not for France, but for . . . well, for Transylvania or the Cannibal Islands or wherever women were meat to be carved . . .

There were caresses . . . the water, and the tip of the blade.

Not a single clean shocking chop but a frenzy of *pizzicato* stabs.

"This boy," Hitch said, embarrassing Tony Perkins, "he has an eye for the ladies . . . no, a *knife* for the ladies."

She'd been prodded, over and over. She'd been sliced, if only in illusion—the dull edge of the prop drawn over the soft skin of her stomach, again and again. After the fourth or fifth pass, it felt like a real knife . . . after the fourth or fifth day, she thought she was bleeding out, though it was only chocolate syrup, swirling around her dirty feet . . .

Some shower scene.

Her skin still burned with the rashes raised by the knife . . . with the little blisters made when the lights boiled the water on her shoulders. The sores scraped open and leaked as she was wrapped in a torn curtain, packaged like carved meat, suitable for dumping in a swamp.

She was uncomfortable in her clothes. She might never be comfortable in her clothes again.

If she kept driving North (*by North-West?*), she'd hit San Francisco . . . city of ups and downs . . . But before then, she'd need to sleep.

Not in a motel. Not after this week's work.

Her blouse was soaked through. No amount of towelling would ever get her dry.

"Do you swallow, *Jayne* . . . do you?"

The soles of her feet were ridged, painful to stand on.

"I spy . . . with my little eye . . . something beginning wi-i-i-ith . . . P."

Pigeon? Psychopath? Perkins?

"Pudenda!"

Every time the crotch-skin came off, Hitch sprung another letter on her . . . another word for vagina. F. C. T. Q. P. M.

M for Mousehole? Whoever said that?

Sometimes Hitch took the knife himself and got in close. He said Perkins wasn't holding it right, was stabbing like a fairy . . .

Perkins's eyes narrowed at that. They didn't slide over Jayne's body like Hitch's, or any of the other guys on the crew.

. . . but it was an excuse.

The director just plain liked sticking it to a naked woman.

Any woman? Or just Jayne?

He'd have preferred doing it to Janet, because she was a Star. Really, he'd have wanted to stab Grace Kelly or Ingrid Bergman, who were more than Stars. But he'd make do with Jayne Swallow . . . or Jana Wróbel . . . or some blonde off the street.

Oh, he never touched her with anything that wasn't sharp. Never even shook hands.

"How do you shake hands with a naked lady?" he'd asked, when they were introduced—she'd been cast from cheesecake 8 x 10s, without an audition—on set. How indeed? Or was that his way of avoiding physical contact with her? Did he not trust himself?

Others *had* auditioned, she learned . . . but turned him down. They'd found out what he wanted and preferred not to be a part of it. Blondes who did naked pin-ups, strippers, *girls who did stag films* . . . they didn't want to be cut-up in a shower, even with Janet Leigh's head on top of their bodies.

So, Jayne Swallow.

Scree! Scree! Scree!

Now, she really had what Hitch wanted . . . and he'd have to pay more than scale to get it back. But it wasn't the money. That wasn't her mcguffin. She wanted something else. What? Revenge? Retribution? To be treated like a person rather than a broken doll?

It wasn't just Hitch. She stood in for Janet Leigh. He stood in for everyone who'd cut her.

Since driving off the Lot, she'd been seeing him everywhere. In the broken side-mirror, through the misted-over rear window. In every film, there he was, somewhere. If only in a photo on the wall. Unmistakable, of course. That fat, double bass-belly . . . that caricature silhouette . . . doleful, little boy eyes like raisins in uncooked dough . . . the loose cheeks, like Droopy in the cartoons . . . that comb-over wisp.

He was waiting for a bus. He was smoking a cigar. He was getting a shoe-shine. He was wearing a too-big cowboy hat. He was smirking in a billboard ad for an all-you-can-scoff restaurant. He was fussing with dogs. He was the odd, short, fat boy out in a police line-up of tall, thin, unshaven crooks. He was up on a bell-tower, with a high-powered rifle. He was in a closet, with a bag full of sharp, sharp knives. He was in the back seat with a rope. He wore white editors' gloves to handle his murder weapons.

She looked at the mirror, and saw no one there.

Nothing beginning with H.

But there was a shape in the road, flapping. She swerved to avoid it.

A huge gull, one wing snapped. The storm had driven it ashore.

It was behind her now. Not road kill, but a road casualty. Suitable for stuffing and mounting.

Hitch said that about Marion Crane, too, in a line he'd wanted in the script but not snuck past the censors. They were Jesuits, used to playing word games with clever naughty schoolboys.

Birds . . . Crane, Swallow . . . suitable for stuffing and mounting.

Another dark shape came out of the rain and gained on the car. A man

on a motorcycle. A wild one? Like Brando. No, a highway cop. He wore
a helmet and a rain-slicker. Water poured in runnels off the back of his
cape. It looked like a set of folded, see-through wings. His goggles were
like big glass eyes.

Her heartrate raced.

. . . stop, thief!

Had the studio called the cops yet? Had Hitch denounced her sabotage?

"I'll take it out of her fine sweet flesh," Hitch would say. "Every pound
of meat, every inch of skin!"

She was a thief. Not like Cary Grant, suave and calculating . . . but a purse-
snatcher, vindictive and desperate . . . taking something not because it was
valuable to her but because it was valuable to the person she'd stolen from.

The cop signaled her to pull over.

He had a gun. She didn't. She was terrified.

Cops weren't your friends.

She'd found that out the minute she got off the bus in Los Angeles. She'd
been young and innocent then, with a hometown photo studio portfolio
and a notion to get into the movies. She learned fast. Cops locked you
up when you hadn't done anything. Cops squeezed the merchandise and
extracted fines that didn't involve money. They let the big crooks walk
free and cracked down on the hustlers. They always busted the wrong
man. Beat patrolmen, vice dicks, harness bulls, traffic cops. The enemy.

Her brakes weren't good. It took maybe thirty yards to pull over. With
a sound like a scream in the rain.

The wipers still ticked as the motor idled. The screech slowed.

In the rear-view, she saw the cop unstraddle his ride. The rain poured
off his helmet, goggles, cape, boots. He strode through the storm towards
her. He wasn't like the city cops she'd met, bellies bulging over their belts,
flab-rolls easing around their holstered guns. He was Jimmy Stewart lean,
snake-hipped. A cowboy with an armored skullcap.

If she put on a burst of speed, would she leave him here?

No, he'd catch her. Or she'd go off the cliff into the Pacific.

The knuckle rap came at her window. The cop didn't bend down. She
saw the leather jacket through his transparent slicker. A wild one, after all.

She tried to roll the window down and the handle came off. It did
sometimes, but there was a trick to fixing it back. She didn't bother with

the trick. She opened the door, first a crack, then halfway, using it to shield against the rain, and ducked her head out to look up at the cop.

His goggles gave him the eyes of Death.

Two little television sets strapped to his face, playing the opening of that show. *Dump-da-dumpity-dump-da-dump* . . . there Hitch was, in a fright-wig, being funny, holding a noose or a big bottle with POISON stamped on it. A non-speaking woman boiling in a pot or strapped to a saw-horse.

"Good eeev-ning," he said.

Not Hitch, the cop. And not with a British accent.

She waited for it. The come-on. Tonight's *stawww-ry*.

"Going mighty fast?" "Where's the fire, lady?" "The way you look, the things you do to a man . . . that ought to be against the law . . ." "See what you've done to my night-stick, ma'am . . ." "Swallow, huh? Well . . .?"

"License and registration?"

He was unreadable. Not a movie cop.

She didn't ask what she'd done wrong. She knew enough not to open up that debate. She found her documents, sodden and fragile as used tissue, in the glove compartment.

Whenever she showed her papers, she was irrationally afraid they'd turn out to be false—or the cop would say they were. That blanket of guilt was impossible to shuck, even when she hadn't had things to feel guilty about. She *knew* these papers were legit, but they weren't in the name she was using. In the photo on her driver's license, Jana wasn't as blonde as Jayne.

Her papers got wetter as the cop looked them over.

"Wróbel," he said, pronouncing it properly.

Then he asked her something in Polish. Which she didn't speak.

She shrugged.

"Not from the Old Country, then?"

It might as well have been Transylvania.

"Santa Rosa, originally," she admitted.

"Hollywood, now," he said, clocking her address.

She was too cold to give him a pin-up smile. Usually, cops asked if she was in pictures . . . she must be too bedraggled for that now.

"You must be in pictures . . . dirty pictures," was the usual line. Said with a grin, and a hitch of the belt buckle into the gut.

"You must be in pictures . . . horror pictures," was the new take. "You must be in pictures . . . Alfred Hitchcock pictures."

"Watch your driving," the cop actually said. "This is accident weather. How far have you got to go?"

She had no definite idea, but said "San Francisco."

"You won't make it by nightfall. I'd stop. Check into a motel."

"That makes sense, sir."

"No need for 'sir.' 'Officer' will do."

The cop's skin, under the rain, was grayish. This weather grayed everything out, like a black-and-white movie. The hillside mud should have been red, like blood . . . but it washed over the road like coffee grounds. Dark.

"Makes sense, officer."

"Good girl," he said, returning her license and registration.

A motel. Not likely. When Hitch's film came out, people wouldn't check into motels without thinking twice. People wouldn't take showers. Or climb stairs. Or go into fruit cellars. Or trust young men with twitchy smiles who liked to stuff (and mount) birds.

If the film came out now. She might have scratched that.

The cop turned and walked back to his motorcycle. Rain on his back, pouring down his neck.

Why had he stopped her? Suspicion, of course. But of what?

The theft can't have been reported yet. Might not be until Monday morning. Word couldn't be out. This cop wasn't rousting a woman motorist for kicks, like they usually did. Maybe he was just concerned? There had to be some cops like that . . .

While she had the door open, water rained in. Her shoes were soaked.

She pulled the door shut and tried to start the car. The motor seized up and died. Then choked, then drew out a death scene like Charles Laughton, then caught again . . . and she drove on.

Damn, December night fell quick.

Now, she was driving through dark and rain. The road ahead was as murky as a poverty-row back-projection plate. Her right headlight was on the fritz, winking like a lecher at a co-ed.

The cop was right. She had to pull over. If she slept in this leaky car, she'd drown. If she drove on, she'd end up in the sea. The Ford Custom did not come with an optional lifeboat. She wasn't sure hers even had a usable spare tire.

Through blobby cascades on the windshield, she saw a flashing light.

VACANCY.

A motel. She remembered her vow. No motels, never again . . . she knew, really, there was little chance of being butchered by a homicidal maniac. That was just the movies. Still, there was every chance of running into a travelling salesman or an off-duty cop or an overage wild one, and being cajoled or strong-armed or blackmailed into a room with cheap liquor and "Que Sera Sera" on the radio. The ending to that story would surprise to no one.

She'd been photographed in motel rooms. She'd been interviewed in motel rooms. She'd auditioned for movie projects that didn't really exist. If some dentist wanted to call himself a producer and play casting couch games, he hooked onto a script about giant leeches or dragstrip dolls just to set up his own private orgy. She'd checked into a motel with a young actor—not Tony Perkins, but someone a few steps behind him—and posed for bedroom candids leaked to the scandal sheets to squelch whispers that the rising stud preferred beach boys to bikini babes. In print, they put a black bar across her eyes.

She'd been abandoned in motels, too . . . left with bills for booze and damages. Some guys couldn't have a party without breaking a lamp or knocking a picture off the wall. Or hurting someone, just to hear the squeal and see blood on their knuckles.

VACANCY.

The light flashed like a cliff-top lantern on a cliff in a three-cornered hat picture, luring storm-tossed ships onto the rocks to be looted.

She was more likely to die on the road than in this place.

So, she pulled off the highway and bumped downhill into a parking lot. There were other cars there. The lights were on in a single-storey building.

HACIENDA HAYSLIP.

Like every other place in California, this motel impersonated an Old Spanish Mission—protruding beams, fake adobe, concrete cactus, a neon sombrero over the name.

Once, the Pacific was the far edge of the world. The Jesuits got here first, even before the bandits. Jayne had been to Catholic school. She was

more afraid of priests than outlaws. Priests were worse than cops. Beyond
the shadow of a doubt. Cops just played the game by rules that favored
them. Priests took the same liberties, but told you it was God's will that
you got robbed or rousted or raped.

She parked as near the office as possible and made a dash from her car
to the lit-up shelter. By now, she couldn't get much wetter.

Pushing through the front door, she was enveloped by heat. The office
was built around an iron stove that radiated oppressive warmth. Windows
were steamed up. Viennese waltz music came from an old-fashioned
record player.

In a rocking chair by the stove sat a small thin woman, knitting. On
a stool behind the front desk perched a fat young man, reading a comic
book. They both turned to look at her. She must be a fright. Something
the cat would drag in.

"Arthur," said the woman, "see to the customer . . ."

Her voice was like a parrot's, chirruping words it couldn't understand. The
thin woman had a grating, shrill tone and another British accent . . . a comedy
fishwife or a slum harridan. *Cockney*. Jayne had heard other Englishmen say
Hitch was a cockney. He went tight around the collar if it was said to his
loose-jowelled face. It was a put-down, she guessed—like "polack" or "hunkie."
David Niven and Peter Lawford weren't cockneys. Cary Grant *for sure* wasn't
a cockney. Hitch was, and so was this woman who had somehow fetched up
on the far side of the world, in the country of Jesuits and outlaws and Indians
and gold-diggers.

"In the fullness of time, Mahmah," said the fat young man.

He didn't sound cockney. He had a James Mason or George Sanders
voice. A suave secret agent, a bit of a rogue . . . but coming out of a bloated,
cherubic face, that accent was all wrong. Jayne wondered if Arthur was
another fairy. Was that why mother and son—"Mahmah" must mean
"Mother"—had said goodbye Piccadilly and farewell Leicester Square?

She stood there, dripping and steaming.

Arthur finished reading to the end of the page, lips moving as he
mouthed the balloons. Then he neatly folded over the top corner and
shut the comic. *Journey Into Mystery*. He tidied it away with a stack of
similar publications, shuffling so the edges were straight as if he had just
finished an exam and wanted his desk neat.

"What might the Hacienda Hayslip do for you, madame?"

"A room, for the night."

"Nocturnal refuge? Most fortuitous. We do indeed rent rooms, nightly. Have you a reservation?"

Before she could answer, his mother piped up . . . "A reservation! What does she look like, a squaw? Who ever has a reservation, Arthur?"

"Formalities must be observed, Mahmah. Did you, madame, have the foresight to contact us by telephone or telegram . . . or is this more in the manner of an impromptu stopover?"

"The second thing," she said.

"Spur of the moment? Fortunate for you, then, that one or two of our luxury cabins are unoccupied at present and can therefore be put at your disposal . . . are you of a superstitious or numerological bent?"

She shook her head.

"Don't give her Thirteen," said the old woman.

Arthur sucked his cupid's bow lips between his teeth, making his mouth into a puckered slit. He was thoughtful or annoyed.

"I don't mind," she said.

So far as she could recall, none of the rooms she'd been groped or duped or roughed up in had had the unlucky number. Ordinary numbers were bad enough.

"It's too close to the edge, Arthur," said the old woman. "Be the next to go."

"How would you like a cabin on the beach?" Arthur asked Jayne.

"Normally, that would sound nice. Just now, dry and warm is all I want."

"It's not nice," shrilled Arthur's mother. "Not nice at all. My son is trying to be funny. We sit on the cliff here and it's crumbling away. The dirt's no good. The rain gets in, loosens it up. The far cabins have gone over the edge. They tumble onto the beach. In pieces. You should hear the fearful racket that makes."

Arthur blew out his lips and smiled.

"Indeed, madame. We are in a somewhat precarious position. Some might opine that my mother made a poor investment. Others might rule this our just lot. For we have incurred the ire of the Almighty, by our many, many sins. My mother, though you'd not think it of her now, was once a very great harlot. A woman of easy virtue, baptized in champagne.

Powdered and painted and primped and pimped and porked and poked and prodded and paid. Showered with gifts of opal and topaz and red, red rubies. She dragged fine men to ruin. Duels were fought. Balconies jumped from. Revolvers discharged into despairing brains. Foolish, feckless, and fickle were her many, many admirers. All dead now, though their sins remain."

At this speech, the old woman cackled and grinned.

Jayne looked again at Arthur's mother. Her skin had shriveled onto her bones. Her face was a pattern of wrinkles and her hands were vulture claws. She smiled and showed yellow teeth. She wore a black, feathery wig that matched her dress.

"Did you think, madame, to find the notorious Birdie Hayslip sat by the stove at this stop on your journey through life? Knitting her own shroud?"

"Shut up, Arthur, you're making her blush!"

Birdie! There was a bird name and no mistake. Walter would have loved it.

"Just sign her in, boy. Sign her in. Don't let her get away. We can't afford to lose customers. Not in these trying times. Income tax and the Bomb."

Arthur took the registration book from beneath the desk. It was bound in fleshy red leather.

She hesitated before signing. She was a thief in flight, she remembered. She wouldn't want to be tracked and traced. Her situation couldn't be unusual. Couples who stayed in joints like this mostly passed themselves off as Mr. and Mrs. Smith. She wrote *Jana Wróbel*, but with a scribble—so it couldn't be read, let alone pronounced—and gave her address as Century City, California.

"Madame Wobble," said Arthur, without irony, "you shall have Cabin Number Seventeen. . . . Come this way . . ."

Reaching behind him, he took a key from a board. It was attached to a fist-sized plaster cactus.

He slipped off his high stool and came out from behind the desk.

Arthur Hayslip was not a dwarf but was well under five feet in height and balloon-bellied. His hair was thinning, though she thought him not much more than twenty. He wore a velvet Little Lord Fauntleroy jacket and child's slacks. He was a plump, aging baby—but precise and delicate, as if performing all his gestures for television cameras.

"Galoshes, Arthur," Birdie reminded her son.

He slipped on his waterproof overshoes, and took down a big yellow fisherman's slicker with attached hood. The protective clothing was made for a hardy six-footer and he disappeared into it. He looked like a fairy tale character, but she wished she had a more rainproof topcoat too.

"Shall we venture out, Madame Wobble? Into the storm?"

"It's Miss Wobble," she corrected.

"You hear that, Arthur! *Miss*. I saw straight away. No wedding band. She's *available*!"

Birdie cackled again and the laughter turned into a coughing fit. She did not sound like a well person.

"I have to fetch some things from the trunk of my car."

"The boot, Arthur," said Birdie. "She means the boot."

"You always misremember, Mahmah . . . you took steps in 1939, dragged me from our native shores. When I was but a babe, the Jerries started dropping whizz-bangs. There was something in the newspapers about a War. There was a term for British subjects who fled to safer climes for the duration. Gone With the Wind Up. I am a naturalized American, a real-life nephew of my Uncle Sam . . ."

He didn't sound it.

"Or was it Uncle Irving, Uncle Montmorency, Uncle Yasujiro, Uncle Fedor, Uncle Harry, or Auntie Margaret. Mahmah has never confided which, if any, of my many uncles might also have been my . . ."

"Arthur, don't be vulgar. She's not interested. Can't you tell?"

He took an umbrella from a rack by the desk and pushed open the door with it. The storm roared, and the waltz record stuttered after the music stopped. He opened the umbrella to shield them as they stepped outside. He had to stretch his arm like the Statue of Liberty's to get above her head. They still got soaked.

They trudged across muddy asphalt to her car and she popped the trunk.

In the dark, in the cold, in the wet, her face still burned.

There it was. In a sack, tied like a post-bag.

Arthur reached into the trunk with his free hand and took . . . not the sack, but her overnight bag. He ignored the mcguffin.

"I'll just bring this along," she said, picking it up casually.

"That is your right and privilege, my dear."

The trunk wouldn't catch the first time she slammed it down, nor the second. Arthur had both hands full, so he couldn't help. Finally, she wrestled it and locked it. The sack started to get wet. What was inside might be dangerous when wet.

A covered walkway kept some of the rain off. They went past the main building.

Lights were strung up, but several of the bulbs were dead. Darkness encroached. The cabins were originally in a square around a swimming pool, but—as Birdie had said—the cabins at the far edge were gone, leaving only stumps. Beyond, unseen, was the cliff. A crack ran through the concrete bottom of the pool. It could no longer hold water, though temporary puddles collected, swirling and eddying into the fissure. This was an empty pool you could drown in.

The hacienda would eventually wind up on the beach.

Her cabin was well away from the crumbling edge of the property. No immediate danger.

Arthur put her overnight bag down and unlocked Cabin Seventeen. He reached in and turned on the lights, holding the door open for her. She took her bag and walked across a squelching WELCOME mat. Arthur let his umbrella down and followed.

There were twin beds. No, *two* beds. One a single for a giant, the other a cot for a circus midget. Between them was a low table with a two-headed bedside lamp, a crystal ashtray that fit the definition of blunt instrument and a Gideon Bible open to the Flood.

Above the table was a picture in a heavy gilt frame. A chubby naked woman was being bothered from behind by a giant swan with human eyes.

"A classical subject," Arthur commented. "Leda and Zeus. So *earthy*, the Gods of Greece."

Other pictures hung around the room, less ornately framed, less immediately eye-catching. Slim, big-eyed women dressed in the style of the Roaring Twenties. Fringes and feathers.

"Do you recognize Mahmah? She was always photographed, at the height of her infamy."

Jayne wasn't even sure the pictures were all of the same woman. She couldn't fit them over the Birdie who sat by the stove.

"The cabin has the full amenities, Miss Wobble. Through there . . ."

He indicated a closed door.

"Modern plumbing, a flush toilet, washbasins, a bathtub . . ."

"Shower?"

Arthur shrugged, non-committally.

"I could do with a long soak in a hot tub, after the rain and the drive . . ."

"I regret to inform you that . . . temporarily, there is no hot water. It seems one can have light but no hot water or hot water but no light, and after dark the need for illumination takes primacy . . . tomorrow morning, perhaps, after sun-up, something warm can be arranged."

Jayne tried to live with the disappointment.

She wanted at least to get out of her wet clothes and towel off.

Arthur showed no sign of leaving. Did he expect a tip? His waterproof dripped on the rug. He strolled about, looking at the pictures.

"Once, Mahmah was a nymph, a naiad . . . now, she is a gorgon, a harpie . . . time can be so cruel, don't you think, Miss Wobble? Though it is no more than she deserves, for was Mahmah not cruel when she had the chance . . . is she not still cruel, when she gets the opportunity?"

"I wouldn't know."

"Of course not. You are an innocent party in this situation . . . my m-m-mother deserves to die, don't you think? And not naturally. No, that would not be just. She is a most exquisitely *m-m-m-murderable* personage."

He had worked hard to overcome a stutter, but it slipped back.

"Shootable? Poisonable? Throttlable? Bludgeonable?"

Arthur's fat-wreathed eyes came alive. He reminded Jayne of . . .

"Stabbable? Slashable? Beheadable? Deadable?"

His recitative was almost a tune. *Dump-da-dumpity-dump-da-dump . . .* He broke off.

"Happy thoughts, Miss Wobble."

"But morbid," she ventured.

"Practical. What do you do for a living, Miss Wobble? Presuming that you do live . . . ?"

Normally, she would say she was an actress—which was partially true. But that always prompted the same response. "Have I seen you in any-thing?" And that lead, if the enquirer was at all interesting, to "If you've watched most of my pictures, you've seen me in not much of anything at all . . ." Then, smiles, drinks, and a happy ending.

Now, she was a thief, a saboteur. She had to be careful. Arthur was *not* interesting, not in that way.

"I'm in motion pictures. Makeup girl."

"An interesting expression. Makeup girl? What do you make up for?"

"Hard nights, mostly. Filling in the cracks so the camera doesn't see."

Arthur unbuttoned his slicker. He took it off and hung it on a coat-tree, as if it belonged there. She hadn't invited him to stay.

"The camera sees all, though," he said, pointing at one of the portrait pictures. A dramatic, Satanic pose—a big-eyed vamp resting her chin on her crossed wrists, under a stuffed goat head on a pentacle. Jayne thought she *could* see Birdie in this jazz-age sinner. The eyes were the same.

"The laughter is frozen and the rot shows through," said Arthur. "The pleasure garden in spring is a family plot in autumn. Photography makes corpses of us all. Snatches little dead moments and pins them down for all eternity. You apply makeup to the dead, too."

"Not me. I work with actresses."

"Actresses *should be* dead, don't you think? Mahmah once called herself an 'actress,' though she never set her dainty foot on a the boards. Stage fright, would you believe? Who would you wish dead, Miss Wobble?"

Men. Hitch.

"Me? Oh, no one. I say live and let live, you know. I like love stories. Not stories with murders."

"All great love stories end in murder, though. Or *could* end in murder . . ."

He sat down in a cane armchair, crossing his stubby legs and settling his stomach into his lap.

His torso was like a big egg, with another big egg—his head—set on top of it. Soft-boiled, unshelled. If she had a knife, like the movie prop knife, could she cut into those eggs? Find the yolks still molten and trickling.

Arthur's murder talk was getting to her.

"How would *you* like to murder my mother, Miss Scribble?"

That was like a stab to the chest.

"You couldn't be traced. Not with your signature, your *phony* address . . ."

Phony. That stood out. A wrong word. American, not consistent with Arthur's British manner of speaking.

"I can be counted on to give a most misleading description. You wouldn't even be a woman. You'd be a man . . . a swarthy, horny-handed man . . . the type my mother is attracted to, but who are no good for her, no good for anyone . . . a man's man, a man from the Isle of Man . . . a man with big hands, workman's hands, neck-snapping, larynx-crushing hands. Afterwards, we would both be free . . ."

"Free?"

"Yes. I would be free of Mahmah, of this place. You would be freer, free of . . . of the constraints of petty Protestant morality."

"I'm Catholic."

"Well, easy to do it then! You sin on Saturday night and are washed clean Sunday morning . . . just take care not to die unshriven between the two sacraments. The sacraments of murder and confessional."

"I don't really like this, Mr. Hayslip. I'm not comfortable."

"We're just talking, Miss Alias . . . shooting the breeze, yarning away the night hours while the storm rages without . . . without what, I always think, without what?"

"I'm not going to kill anyone," she said.

"A bold, sweeping statement. Would you kill to protect yourself from, say, a vile ravisher?"

Too late for that.

"Or to secure an inheritance, a fortune that you could use on good works if it were liberated from a miser who makes no use of it?"

"Is your mother rich?"

"No, she's *strange*. She hasn't a bean, Miss Alibi. Just this place. Half on the cliff. Half on the beach. She has only her memories. Her *disgusting* memories."

"I'm sure she's not as bad as that. She's just a woman."

Arthur leaned forwards, eyes shining. "*Just* a woman? *Just*? Maybe . . . maybe, at that . . . but it's no excuse, is it? It's no reason she should be spared from God's judgment. Quite the opposite. It was Eve, was it not, who lead mankind into Sin? Eve, the *femme fatale* and the farmer's wife. Eve who brought about the Fall. Should not Eve be punished, *over and over and over . . .* ?"

A thin line of spit, like spider-silk, descended from Arthur's wet mouth. He repeatedly slammed a pudgy, soft, tiny fist into the palm of his other hand.

It struck Jayne that Arthur Hayslip was hateful, but harmless.

If she killed this stranger's mother, what would he do for her? What wouldn't he do for her? Rain rattled the windows. The cabin shook, like a train compartment on an express.

"You don't know how to do it to a woman, do you?" she said. "You blame her, your mother, but it's your weakness."

He drew back. "I am a man of the world, my dear," he said. "Your sex holds no mystery for me. I know too much for that."

She tittered. He flushed, red.

"You couldn't hurt a fly, if you wanted to. You don't want to murder your mother, you want *someone else* to murder your mother. But that would be the end for you, the ending you didn't guess was coming. The twist in the last reel. There would be nothing. Without her, you'd be a dummy without a ventriloquist . . ."

"Mummy," he murmured, "mummy's dummy . . ."

All at once, she didn't want to press on. There was no point in it, in making an unhappy wretch more wretched. That wasn't heroic, that was bullying. She'd been bullied enough herself to hate that.

How many times had she been stripped and stabbed this week? In play, in fun, for *entertainment*? She had been murdered, over and over . . .

"Has he asked you to top me?" shrilled a voice from the door. "He asks all the lodgers to top me. All the ones he fancies, at least. Girlies and boysies, he's not too particular . . ."

Birdie flapped into the room, trailing a soaked shawl. Her wig shone with rainwater.

She pinched her son's pendulous earlobe and yanked.

"Naughty Arthur, bothering the girlies . . ."

Arthur's face screwed up with pain.

"Lord knows I've tried, ducks . . . but my boy's just a nasty little shit. No other words for it. I'll get him out of your hair and you can turn in. He tell you about the hot water?"

"There isn't any?"

"That's right. Pity, but there it is. Come on, Arthur . . . time to say nighty-night."

Birdie pulled Arthur out of the chair. She was taller than him.

"Be polite," she insisted, twisting the earlobe.

"Nighty-night, Miss," he said, through tears. "Nighty-night, Aphrodite in a nightie . . ."

Birdie took the umbrella and dragged her son back through the cabin door. They disappeared into the rain and darkness.

Jayne shut the door.

Her heart was pounding and her face burned. She was more embarrassed than afraid. She would leave early tomorrow.

For where? They'd be after her, by then. Hitch's agents. Paramount *and* Universal. Walter.

Think of that later. After sleep.

The door blew open again and Arthur was there, breathing heavily. He had broken free of his mother.

"What's in the sack?" he asked.

The question knifed into her heart.

Birdie came up behind Arthur, fingers hooked into talons, screeching . . . *Scree! Scree! Scree!*

Jayne backed away and clutched the sack.

"What would you *do* for what's in the sack?"

"Nothing. There's nothing. Nothing. A negative."

Arthur smiled wickedly as Birdie dragged him away again, kicking the door shut.

Jayne sat down on the big bed and hugged the sack. It was heavy, lumpy, hard. Useless, yet beyond value. A measure of her suffering, but just deadweight. She threw it away and it lay like an extra pillow.

She would sleep on the other bed, the small one.

If she could sleep . . .

She went into the bathroom and turned on the light. It was tile-floored. The mirror had a scrollwork border etched into the glass. The claw-foot bathtub bled rust into the cracks between the tiles. There was no shower attachment.

She ran the tap, just to make sure. Icy cold bit her fingers.

At least there were towels.

She breathed mist on the mirror and wrote *JANA* in it, then watched her name vanish as the exhalation evaporated.

She undressed, not like she did for pictures. Not for show, but to get out of her heavy, sodden clothes. She unpeeled damp, sticky layers—cardigan, skirt, blouse, slip, brassiere, shoes, stockings, panties. She would have to wear most of these again tomorrow, since she'd not thought to bring more than a change of underthings. They wouldn't dry completely by then.

What was she doing?

The towels weren't wet but they weren't warm. The rough nap rubbed her skin the wrong way. She saw herself naked in the mirror. Without moleskin patches. She didn't look the way she did on film. She looked already dead. Her next makeup artist would be a mortician.

There was a bathrobe. She pulled it on, wrapping it tight over her stabbable breasts, her slashable back, her sliceable limbs.

She turbaned her dried, scraggly hair with another towel.

Turning out the bathroom light, she stepped back into the bedroom.

Arthur was sitting on the big bed, the sack open. He had scratches down one side of his face. His velvet jacket was soaked. His slicker still hung in the cabin.

"What is this?" he asked.

The pie-shaped can lay on the bed, sealed with tape.

"Negative."

"Answer me," he insisted, angry. "No word games."

"Negative," she said. "*Film* negative."

Arthur smiled, the penny dropping.

"Motion pictures," he said. "*Dirty* pictures?"

"I'm naked in them," she admitted. "And dead, like you said. Snatched dead moments. Useless moments."

He ran his fat fingers over the can. She knew he wanted to *see* . . . but it was hopeless: he'd need to make a positive print, run it on a projector . . .

"It's the thing you're chasing after, Arthur. A woman, me, being cut up. It's the only evidence it happened. The only evidence it happened to *me* . . ."

She had stolen *weeks* from Hitch. Weeks it would take to stage again, with Janet or some other stand-in . . . if he could ever get it just so, just the way he wanted, which she doubted was possible, or hoped wasn't possible.

The studio would pay, if Hitch wouldn't.

Arthur scratched at the tape seal with his fingernails.

Jayne heard Hitch in her skull, ranting at her, raving at his loss . . . swearing vengeance and retribution and blood . . . impotent fury. "I shall make sure the chit will never work in this town again!" She'd heard that before . . . so had everyone. Sure, she could be blacklisted, but blacklists were broken all the time. Being dead to one producer just bumped you up on another's books. Plenty would hire her *because* she'd pissed off High and Mighty Cocky Mr. Hitch. Directors without TV shows, who no one would recognize in the street . . . David Selznick, William Castle, William Wyler . . . the giant leech and dragstrip doll guys. She'd do all right.

The tape tore away in Arthur's fingers and the can popped open. A coil of 35mm negative came loose, like guts spilling from a wound. Arthur tried to grasp it, but the edges scored his palms.

He saw the reverse image of her naked in the shower—a thin black body bleeding white—repeated over and over.

He smiled and she saw Hitch's slobbering leer imposed briefly over the fat boy's face.

M-m-m-murder!

She grabbed the film and looped it around and around his fat neck.

Arthur yelped.

She wound it tighter. The edges bit into his soft throat. There was blood, which made the film slick, tough to hold.

Jayne didn't say anything. She just tried to kill a man. Any Hitch with a cock would have done.

The murder weapon was a murder. A negative murder.

"Good eeeev-ning, Jay-y-ne . . . do you *swallow*? Do you, do you?"

Shootable? Poisonable? Throttlable? Bludgeonable?

Dump-da-dumpity-dump-da-dump . . .

Stabbable? Slashable? Beheadable? Deadable?

She made a noise in the back of her throat. More a croak than a screech.

Scree! Scree! Scree!

His fat hands flapped against the sleeves of her bathrobe. His sausage fingers couldn't get a grip on the flannel.

Dump-da-dumpity-dump-da-dump . . .

It was like wrestling a marionette, strangling it with its own strings.

Doo-doo-doo . . . Doo-doo-doo . . .

The door opened again and Birdie came in—wig gone, showing a mummy-like scalp, scaled with the last wisps of white hair—an umbrella raised like a dagger.

"Get your hands off my boy," she screamed. "My precious, precious boy . . ."

"Mummy," Arthur gargled, tears flowing freely, "*mummy*! She's hurting me."

The umbrella blows were feeble, hurt less than a prop knife, but the words—the panic, the love, the desperation!—cut through Jayne's hot fury, dashed cold water over her homicidal impulse.

She let go of the film. She let go of her rage.

The old woman hugged her son and stroked his wounds. The fat young man shoved his face against his mother's shrunken breast. They held each other, locked together in an embrace tighter than death. They rocked together, crone and baby, crying away the pain, all the pain . . .

"I didn't mean any harm," Jayne said.

. . . she wouldn't kill, after all . . . she wouldn't hurt a fly.

This was it, she realized, looking at mother and son, monsters both, bound by a ferocious love that seemed so much like murderous hate it was hard to recognize until the last moment.

This was it. The only ending they had.

THE DOG'S PAW

DEREK KÜNSKEN

Francis Perry shifted in the chair in front of Mr. Lewis's antique desk. Lewis scanned the proposal, motionless pen poised between tan fingers. Lewis's office was almost as big as the ambassador's. The equatorial sun burned slanting lines through the curtains, bleaching the hardwood floor. Rows of diplomatic commissions from Lewis's postings hung on one wall: Harare, Sanaa, Dongola, Lagos, Dhaka, Freetown, Kinshasa, and now Sayhad. The Democratic Republic of Hadhramaut was Perry's first posting.

Another wall displayed framed magazine articles about development projects Lewis had led. It didn't include articles about Lewis himself. The absent six-page *National Geographic* feature on Lewis's career had inspired Perry to join the Development Service and to seek out the most difficult posting on the planet to learn directly from him.

On the last wall was a black-and-white photograph of a Bedouin man sitting in the gravel beside a road, looking up at the camera in surprise. One foot emerging from his robes wore a black dress shoe. The other leg ended in a goat's foot. His expression was haunted. In the background, farther down the road, a woman in a niqab looked back.

Lewis grimaced. Perry shifted.

"Perry, honour killings are down 7 percent and prosecutions are up 4. We've got to think bigger. I would have expected a young development officer to be ready to handle this." Lewis set down his pen. "This afternoon, I'll bring you along again to show you what a strategic intervention looks like."

"Thank you, Mr. Lewis."

"Not everyone can handle the suffering we see in the Service, Perry. In the beginning, I didn't know if I could. You have a lot of potential, Perry."

Lewis handed him the stillborn proposal.

-◦-

An armoured Bronco four-by-four took Lewis and Perry from the capital at Sayhad to Parim, a farming town. The driver rattled them over corrugated roads. Lewis reviewed the newspaper like he was still in his office waiting for tea. Perry gripped the worn door handle, scanning the cracked countryside through the fishbowl of the bulletproof glass. Hard yellow grass defied the sun. Low cinderblock houses punctuated the road. Everything was so exotic. It was exciting to be in the middle of nowhere, riding to the rescue like knights. Perry had a digital camera in his pocket, but didn't want Lewis or the driver to see him taking pictures.

Lewis laid the newspaper between them. Perry wondered what might go through the mind of a genius like Lewis. Perry had read the newspaper three times. Had he seen what Lewis had seen?

The front page of the Hadhramaut People's Voice chronicled Akram Abdullah, a farmer and father to fifteen-year-old Amirra. About a month ago, Abdullah had woken to find his right arm, from the elbow down, turned into a dog's paw. He'd hidden the paw. Weeks later, he'd gotten his son to chop it off, so that he could claim he'd lost it in an accident. He'd barely survived the amateur amputation. The next day, he'd woken in the hospital. His left arm, from the elbow down, had become a dog's paw.

They slowed. Rude houses of cement and dirty stucco squatted over broken pavement, wind-scoured cars and quick, flinching dogs with dangling teats. Perry affected Lewis' calm. At the end of a dirt laneway, they settled in front of a one-storey cinderblock house with a cement roof. Perry sprung into the hot air. The driver hopped out to open the door for Lewis. He smoothed his shirt, walked to the door, and rapped sharply on the metal. It cracked open, revealing a sad, middle-aged face nestled in a slate-grey hijab. Lewis held up his embassy identification. It dangled between them, rotating. Lewis spoke in Arabic.

"I've come from the embassy in Sayhad to speak with your husband, ma'am. May we come in?"

A stricken look darkened her expression. She'd likely spent the last days turning away journalists and had probably never expected her husband's shame to attract diplomats. Lewis' stance and expression softened. His posture curved, descending from authority and status to empathy. Brilliant.

"I'm here to help, ma'am," Lewis said. "This has been a hard time for you. I'm a friend."

Tears ran suddenly down her rough, rounded cheeks. She wiped them in embarrassment. Her retreat left the doorway free. Lewis stepped in gently. Perry followed. The darkened home smelled of cumin. The door creaked shut, sealing out the day.

Ochre cushions were set on the floor. An unvarnished table bent under a black television. A newscaster spoke silently while Arabic script ran across a bright red line at the bottom of the screen. Closed red curtains soaked the sunlight with a bloody tinge. Mr. Abdullah sat on one of the cushions, staring at the television. His bandaged stump rested on a blanket that covered his knees. His other arm hid beneath the cover. A brass ashtray sat beside him.

Lewis sat on the cushion beside Mr. Abdullah. Mr. Adbullah turned away. His lips trembled. His shoulders shook. Lewis pulled a metal cigarette case from his pocket and lit an unfiltered Brazilian cigarette before holding it out to Mr. Abdullah. After long seconds, Mr. Abdullah took it in his lips. Lewis lit one for himself. Perry stood beside Mr.Abdullah's wife. She made nervous little fists with her hands. Perry held his breath, learning.

A cloud of grey smoke grew around them. Tears leaked from Mr. Abdullah's eyes. Lewis put his arm around him and took his cigarette to dash off the ash. He left the cigarettes in the ashtray.

"You are a great man," Lewis said in Arabic.

Abdullah shook his head.

"You have a big heart," Lewis insisted, "and I've come to help you." Choking sobs burst from Mr. Abdullah. His shoulders trembled.

"Tell me why you cut off your arm," Lewis whispered.

Abdullah's browned lips pressed into a damp line.

Lewis sighed. "Show me your arm."

Abdullah turned his head sharply away.

"These marks are a sign," Lewis said, "nothing more. Show me."

Abdullah shook his head, but Lewis held him and lowered the blanket slowly. Mr. Abdullah's wife squeaked and turned away. The edge of the blanket revealed a dog's paw, furred in brown, with black pads under the foot, hugged close to Mr. Abdullah's chest. Lewis gently pulled at the paw. He stroked the fur.

"We can fix all this," Lewis said.

Abdullah's plump lip trembled.

"I love her," he finally said. His voice cracked.

"This isn't your fault," Lewis said, "but it's your responsibility to fix this."

Abdullah sobbed. "She's my little girl."

Lewis shook his head. "She's a woman now. No father should pay for the sins of his child. Any more than a child should pay for yours."

Lewis held the paw higher, between them. "This is not a price you can pay like a dowry," Lewis said gently. "This is a reminder of what has to be done."

Abdullah wiped at his tears with the bandaged stump of his right arm. "I can't do it," Abdullah said. "Not my little Amirra."

"Look here," Lewis whispered, stroking the fur of the paw again, in front of Abdullah's eyes. "This shame is not just yours. It is not just your daughter, your son, and your wife who have to bear this with you." Lewis swung his arm expansively. "All of Parim bears this shame with you. All your neighbours feel this shame. Each one of them waits for you to make this right. You do not have to face this alone."

"Amirra is my little girl," Abdullah moaned.

Lewis pulled the paw in front on Abdullah's face. Adbullah turned away.

"What shame will your daughter bring on Parim next? Will your wife wake up with a goat's hoof for a foot? What will you say to your neighbour when his son has a sheep's head? What restitution could you possibly offer to make that better? Would you offer to shake his hand with this?" Lewis shook the paw.

"Once the stain spreads, it is harder to clean. It has stricken you twice.

The behaviour of your daughter has brought you to hiding in your house, unable to light your own cigarettes."

Abdullah cried. His shoulders hunched.

Lewis released the offending paw, but Abdullah would not bring it close, even to hide it. It trembled before him. Lewis put his arm over the man's shoulders and pulled the blanket back up over the paw.

"Let us work with your neighbours to fix this. No man should have to bear this alone."

They breathed together. Perry held his breath. Abdullah's wife sobbed beside him.

Mr. Abdullah's tears dripped onto the blanket in fat drops. Finally, he nodded.

Perry's heart thumped. A bitter happiness rose in him. He despaired of ever being able to manage people the way Lewis could.

Lewis held the man until he stopped crying and the cigarettes burned themselves out in the ashtray. Then, he rose, said a quiet word to Abdullah's wife and opened the door. The stark, baking sunlight fell at his feet. Perry followed him out.

The driver opened the door for Lewis. Perry went to the other side and opened the door.

Lewis turned his blue eyes on Perry. "Organize a rectification ceremony for a week from today," Lewis said. "Make sure the press is here. Talk with the town elders in case Abdullah changes his mind. We'll come back next week. Write me speaking notes and sound bites."

"Yes, Mr. Lewis," Perry said. Lewis turned back to the scenery. Perry pulled out a small notepad and jotted all he'd need to do. He'd never written any speaking notes.

◄○►

The laws, judges, and police were usually a thicket of obstacles to progress in any country. The Democratic Republic of Hadhramaut was fourth from the bottom of the United Nation's Corruption Index and the fifth poorest country in the world. Neither ranking made work easier. As part of Perry's training as a development officer, Lewis had sent him to intervene with the authorities on a case.

The Hadhramaut Public Security Forces, Capital District, Barracks Four, squatted between a Western Union office and a station that received a weekly train from Yemen. Steel bars over the windows bulged like insect eyes.

Perry's diplomatic ID got him through the reception and into the detention office. Major Ibn Ghassan, the Barracks Commander, met him there. Ibn Ghassan had caramel skin, sleek black hair, and a grey camouflage uniform. He shook Perry's hand assertively.

"I thought you or your Lewis might come," Ibn Ghassan said in Arabic. Perry opened his hands disingenuously.

"Well, I don't think either of you are going to work your magic on this one," Ibn Ghassan said. "This is murder pure and simple. I'm going to give it to the public prosecutor this week."

"Major, let's not be hasty about anything," Perry said.

"Don't be hasty?" Ibn Ghassan said. "Come see the evidence."

He pivoted in his polished boots and Perry had to stretch his steps to keep up with him. The Major unlocked a door and stepped through. The sweet, greying smell of death hit Perry. His eyes watered and he gagged.

The corpse of a teenage girl curled on a blocky wooden table. Dirt crusted her cheeks. She'd lost her hijab and a sandal. Her long abaya bunched at her waist, showing dirt-dusted pants. Conical piles of dirt rested on the table under the corner of her mouth and under her nose. Her ears were packed into shapelessness with dirt.

Ibn Ghassan regarded him from the other side of the table. Fighting not to retch, Perry stepped forward. He breathed through his mouth to avoid the smell. It soaked in through his pores.

"This is sixteen-year-old Jasmine Malik," Ibn Ghassan said. "She disappeared nine days ago. Her teachers reported it. We found the body under a new cement deck in front of her house." He crisply pulled a pen from his chest pocket, pointing first at the girl's hands, which were behind her back, and then her feet. "She'd been bound and buried alive. Her stomach and lungs are filled with dirt."

"I heard that you aren't even considering bail for her family," Perry said.

"Murder is murder," Ibn Ghassan said.

"Major," Perry said, "I think we can agree that extenuating circumstances are at play here."

"I have no evidence of that."

"Fourteen witnesses from three families saw Ms. Malik talking with boys on a number of occasions." Perry didn't feel diplomatic. Lewis would have known how hard to push.

"Are you saying that this was an honour crime?" Ibn Ghassan asked innocently.

"I'm saying that there is more evidence than just a body."

Ibn Ghassan shook his head. "What you have here is a family that decided to murder a girl. I don't know what things are like in your country, but justice in Hadhramaut works."

"Hadhramaut signed the UN Convention on Family Honour," Perry said.

"The UN can fuck itself," Ibn Ghassan said. "Who the hell are they to come into our country and tell us what to do? I know the law. Until the legislature of Hadhramaut passes a new one, murder is murder."

Ibn Ghassan's vehemence disconcerted him. He imagined the ambassador being chastised in the Foreign Ministry because Perry had pissed off a well-connected police commander.

"Your laws may not have changed yet, Major, but they're drafting the legislation. I'm one of the technical advisors. Until the bill passes, the Convention obliges officers of the state to take issues of family honour into account when considering prosecution. Your president signed the Convention."

"Do you want me to show you what the law says right now?" Ibn Ghassan asked.

"Among other things," Perry said evenly, "we monitor compliance with the Convention. Our observations feed into decisions about bilateral aid funding."

Ibn Ghassan's face reddened. A quarter of Hadhramaut's budget came from foreign aid. Perry stood his ground and breathed deeply, unintentionally filling his nose with the stink of decay.

"Wait here," the Major said.

He stormed out and slammed the door behind him, leaving Perry with the corpse of the Malik girl. His stomach clenched. A yellow light bulb hung from the ceiling. He took a cell phone picture of her for his report and then looked away, breathing through his mouth. He examined the mortar between the bricks and ran his finger along the dusty roughness to grind the image of Jasmine Malik out of his mind.

Ten minutes later, Ibn Ghassan opened the door. "Get out of my barracks," he said.

Perry followed him slowly out of the room.

"Send me the witness statements if you want," Ibn Ghassan said. "I'm not wasting my men's time to get them."

"That shouldn't be a problem at all." Perry walked to the door. "I appreciate your help, Major, and we'll make a note of it when we speak with the Prime Minister."

"Just get out," Ibn Ghassan said.

Perry stepped outside. The white embassy jeep was parked in front of the barracks. Two security police with automatic rifles stood to either side of it while two others, stripped to their t-shirts, kicked the driver on the pavement. Ibn Ghassan held out a paper. Perry took it as the security police backed away. The driver moaned, bleeding.

"Your employee had an overdue traffic infraction," the Major said. "The embassy should take more care in its background checks on its employees. If you ever need help in checking your staff, please let me know."

The door to the barracks slammed at Perry's back. The security police lounged on the steps and snickered at him.

⊸⊶

Perry printed Lewis's speaking notes for the rectification ceremony. His office was much smaller than Lewis's, with a view of the embassy carpool and a clutch of palm trees through two spotless windows. Other than a picture of his mother, the art on the walls was watery and pale. Lewis appeared at the door.

"I've been summoned to meet the Minister of the Interior right now with the ambassador," Lewis said.

"Will you be back for the Parim event?" Perry asked.

"You go. Make sure everything goes off perfectly." Lewis smiled. "You're ready for this. Use the speech you prepared." Then Lewis was gone.

Perry flustered with papers and then hurried to the carpool. The driver stood by the Bronco. The flesh around one eye was swollen. Dried blood crusted the neat stitches on his jaw. The driver opened the door. Perry sat in the air-conditioned shade. The driver closed the door.

He didn't deserve to be treated like Lewis. Or maybe he did. A diplomat needed to focus to represent his country. There would be a speech. Local and national press. Photos.

The driver pulled out of the parking lot. Perry practiced Lewis's speech, but anticipation kept the words on the paper. He glanced at the driver and then pulled out his camera to freeze the moving scenery distorted through the fish bowl window.

After two hours, they turned into the driveway of Mr. Abdullah's house. Wind-scoured Ladas and a few shiny Toyota trucks clogged the way and filled the holes. The driver veered off the lane and bounced over the field, stopping in front of a crowd. The Bronco rocked as the driver closed his heavy door, leaving Perry in his cool shell. Then, his door opened, pulling in hot air.

Perry squinted. Fifty or sixty faces watched him. Some serious and wrinkled. Others smooth and festive. A camera with a telephoto lens clicked. Many hands clutched stones.

He watched them. They watched him. The noise died. He didn't see Mr. Abdullah. The silence dragged and the speaking notes he'd written seemed suddenly trite. Brown, self-sufficient faces waited to measure the words of a white man barely out of university, here to change their country. A shrivelled man in a traditional keffyeh emerged from the crowd and smiled. He shook Perry's hand and faced the crowd.

"Mr. John Lewis wishes to say a few words," the old man said in Arabic. Perry's stomach dropped. He hesitated.

"Mr. Lewis wanted to be here. He asked me to say a few words. I am Francis Perry." The faces were stony. The cameras lowered. Perry swallowed around a dry mouth and delivered his speech without using his notes. He stumbled over his vision of a world without shame. People looked away and started kicking at the dust when he spoke about his commitment to helping the world. One man lit a cigarette and talked with his neighbour while Perry faltered over responsibility. More conversation sprang up in the middle of the crowd. Perry ended with a call to action and a thank-you. No one clapped.

The old man nodded. "Very nice," he said. He cupped Perry's elbow and steered him through the crowd. They had formed a circle about twenty feet wide, centered in front of Mr. Abdullah's house. They turned to Perry. An oppressive silence bloomed.

A surprised shriek broke it. The door opened. A man in his twenties, wearing a yellow button-down dress shirt, dragged a struggling girl out by her wrist. Amirra tugged with her whole body and clutched the doorframe with her other hand. Mr. Abdullah's wife hesitated behind them before clawing Amirra's hand free. Amirra fell onto the dirt. The hem of her abaya rose, showing white socks, running shoes and jeans. Her mother slammed the door. Amirra turned towards her house, but the man in the yellow shirt was there. She retreated to the middle of the circle. Her hijab was askew, showing fine black hair.

The crowd looked at her. The old man held something out to Perry. He focused on it with difficulty. The picture of the girl in the middle of the circle disturbed him. She was pretty. The old man held a stone in his palm, the size of a fist. Perry accepted it. Heavy.

Perry looked up, to see what would happen next. Everyone had a stone hefted. They watched him. The old man leaned in, close enough to smell of cigarettes. He extended his hand towards Amirra. "We would be honoured, Mr. Perry," he said.

Perry's stomach lurched. Amirra's sobs warbled into low moans. "I'm sorry," she said over and over. Perry looked away. Faces looked back, losing their patience. Perry's hand shook. He lifted the stone.

Amirra stared back, pleading. Fear eroded her words. Amirra flinched as Perry threw.

The stone bounced off the ground, spinning into someone's shin on the other side of the circle.

Laughter burst out. Deep, howling laughter. Men, women, and children.

Amirra trembled, stony-faced, tears running down her cheeks.

The old man held Perry's arm, laughing and patting him on the back. Perry felt his face warm. Extended hands offered other stones. Perry took one. The crowd leaned to watch him like he was about to burst a piñata. He aimed carefully.

Amirra moaned. The sound touched the bottom of his stomach. The sight of white running shoes and jeans emerging from her long black dress unsettled him.

The stone made a sharp thud against her forehead. The sound throbbed in his hand, as if he still held the stone. A wet, surprised sob burst from Amirra's lips. She fell onto one elbow. Gulped for air.

The air filled with stones. The pitch of Amirra's cries changed sharply as stones thumped her head, her arms, her ribs. Perry's stomach turned. He'd never seen a stoning before.

Amirra shrieked, shielding her head. Her lips and nose shone slick with blood. Stones snapped and thudded until blood sucked her abaya to her body. Her face became unrecognizable.

Perry looked away. He swallowed viscous saliva. He couldn't throw up. The old man looked at him strangely. Perry breathed deeply.

"Mr. Abdullah," Perry said.

The old man shepherded Perry through the crowd. He banged on Mr. Abdullah's door, and yelled an order in thick Arabic. Mr. Abdullah's wife opened the door. Perry stepped into the gloom. Marched to Mr. Abdullah. He knelt gracelessly and yanked away the blanket.

The bandaged stump of Abdullah's left arm was still there, but the right arm was hairy and muscled, ending in five short, stubby fingers. Perry clutched the hot hand. Abdullah would not look at him. His tears dripped on his lap, mixing with Perry's.

The room darkened. The crowd pressed at the doorway, peering in. Perry put his arm around Abdullah as he'd seen Lewis do and wiped his cheeks in embarrassment.

◄○►

The next morning, Perry took down the picture of his mother. In the parking lot, the driver scrubbed the tires of the Bronco with a soapy brush. Lewis appeared at the door. His shoes glowed.

"So how did it go?" Lewis asked.

"We got some good press," Perry said, holding up a newspaper clipping. "I bought you a copy."

"I've already got a copy," Lewis smiled.

Perry nodded, unsure of what to say.

"Would you like to sit down, Mr. Lewis?" Perry asked into the silence.

Lewis shook his head. "I just came to say good job." He smiled. "How do you feel?"

Coiling feelings bit at one another in his stomach. He hadn't been able to eat that morning. "Fine, Mr. Lewis."

"Missing the first throw was genius," Lewis said. "Was it on purpose?"

Perry's cheeks warmed. He winced. "Nerves," he said.

"It's hard to fake that kind of honesty until later in your career. Your instincts were dead on with Mr. Abdullah. Bringing up tears at just the right time makes you look warm and sympathetic."

"Thank you."

Lewis vanished.

Perry put the newspaper clipping under glass and hung it on the wall where the picture of his mother had been.

FINE IN THE FIRE

LEE THOMAS

I didn't answer the phone when my brother, Toby, called. His name appeared on the screen of my cell like a bad biopsy result, and instead of answering, I threw back another slug of beer and returned my attention to the television set. The sitcom wasn't particularly interesting, nor was the company of my wife, who'd already decided our marriage was unsalvageable, though it would be another month before she let me in on the fact. She sat on the sofa, frowning. I didn't bother to ask what was wrong. By that point, *unhappy* had become a default setting her face hit whenever we shared space, so I barely acknowledged it. What are you going to do? Shit happens, and when enough shit happens, you go Pavlovian. Talking to my wife hurt, so I stopped talking to her. I treated my brother with a similar, perhaps greater, level of avoidance. His phone calls invariably included an ample portion of four-alarm crazy and a request for cash. Since I had the routing information for his bank account, I could send him money. Why not cut out the miserable attempts at conversation and the grief?

When the phone rang again three minutes later, my wife climbed off the sofa and left the room. I closed my eyes and waited for the ringing to stop. If it was important—and it was always important to Toby—he could leave a message. I figured God had created voice mail for just such occasions.

So many months later, as the anniversary of that day bears down, I know I should have answered the phone. I get that now. Sometimes when a boy cries wolf, there really are teeth at his neck, but how was I supposed to know? I'd come to think of Toby's head as a scalding pot, and I'd learned to keep my fingers away from it.

Once upon a time, Toby was the golden boy, the Prince of Barnard, Texas. I wish I could ask what happened to him and wonder on the question with genuine naiveté. But I know what happened. The cause. The effect. The whole of it was as clear as an image beaming through a polished projector lens.

-◦-

Sundays are for church and fried chicken. I sit at the dinner table with Daddy, and I'm thinking about the morning sermon. The story of Lot's wife remains vivid and horrible, and I try to imagine what it must feel like to have every speck of my body turned to grains of salt. I see the ceramic saltshaker in the middle of the table. It is in the shape of a white hen with a pink bow, the wife of the peppershaker rooster. And I wonder if I became a pillar of salt, would people—maybe my own parents—shave bits of me off to fill their shakers so I could flavor food?

My father smokes a cigarette before the meal and asks me if I've finished all of my weekend homework, and I lie and say, "Yes, sir," and then Toby, who is fifteen years old, opens the kitchen door and stands on the porch, wiping dust from the seat of his Lee jeans. His shirt is torn at the shoulder. Patches of dirt cover his knees and shins. Mussed hair juts away from his scalp in haphazard clumps. A bruise blossoms on his jaw, and his left eye is already good and swollen. Though his appearance could be attributed to any number of accidents, I believe he has been in a fight.

A yelp of distress flies from my mother's lips, and she rushes to the door. Slowly, my father rises from his chair and crosses the room to join her.

Frightened by Toby's face, shocked by the damage, I find myself more upset to think that someone would dare strike him. Besides being taller than most boys his age, Toby is an athlete, a star on the baseball diamond and the football field. Thick muscles cover his arms and legs; he has our daddy's build. And even without such physical attributes, Toby would have made an unlikely target, because people liked him. He didn't bully or shove or insult any of his classmates the way the other football players did. What kind of fool had the nerve to lay fists on him?

Then the phone rings, and Toby's eyes open wide, and fear simmers in those eyes. I've never seen my brother afraid before, except for the pretend fear he acted out when we were little kids, playing Cops and Robbers. Mama remains with Toby, fussing and tutting and asking him what happened. Daddy leaves the doorway and goes to answer the phone.

◄◦►

As children, Cops and Robbers was our favorite game, and Toby always played the hero. The games would begin with me mortally wounded, dying in my brother's arms and Toby vowing revenge against some "motherless cur"—a phrase he'd picked up from an old movie.

Then after a spluttering death, worthy of a Shakespearean royal, I would resurrect as said cur and we'd spend an hour running around the backyard jabbing our plastic guns at each other and saying, "pow," and "bang," and "eat lead." It was common. Normal. A cliché enacted by kids all over the world.

It made sense that Toby would play the hero. Not only was he two and half years older than me, he also embodied the term. He was just plain good at everything. Give him a baseball bat, or a math equation, or a guitar and he would figure out how to make them work. People called him "Brilliant," "Amazing," and "Genius." His best friend, Duke Manheim, used to call Toby, "Flat out impossible," with a tone that revealed the awestruck depths of his admiration. The last few times I visited Toby, he could no longer hold a cigarette between his fingers; they trembled too badly. Instead, he pinched the filter between his teeth and sucked them down in a few desperate puffs.

◄◦►

Daddy answers the phone and at first he smiles. "Hey there, Rick," he says, and I know it's Mr. Manheim, Duke's father and one of Daddy's best friends. The call does not interest me as much as my brother's condition, so I return my attention to Toby, who finishes wiping the dirt from himself and insists Mama leave him be as he steps into the house. Instead of remaining in the kitchen, Toby creeps out of the room without a word. No, "Hey, kid," or "Hey, squirt," for me.

I look to Mama for an explanation, but the concern and confusion on her face matches the gray swirl of chaos in my head. She wipes her hands on her apron and turns to Daddy. I follow her gaze and am surprised to see the expression on my father's suddenly red face. I can't tell if he's about to scream or vomit. He notices us gawking at him and pulls the phone away from his ear.

"Betty, take Peter on out of here." His voice is so quiet and dry it whispers like a desert breeze. Mama opens her mouth with a question, but the words die on her tongue. "Just go on now," he says. "Be sure to get that chicken off the burner. We don't want it scorched."

⊶⊙⊷

The phone rang again. I switched the device to vibrate and then stood and passed through the kitchen on the way to my workbench in the garage. Its gouged wooden top was bare—no toys or toasters or bikes needed my attention. The rows of tools on the pegboard were little more than decorative these days. I hadn't had a new project on my bench since my daughter, Jocelyn, had gone off to college.

Above the bench was a small board with a number of keys, each one hung on a hook beneath a neatly printed label. I lifted the set that opened the doors to my parents' house—Toby's house now—and slid them in my pocket. Then I leaned on the bench and tried to remember the last thing I'd fixed there. The lamp from Jocelyn's room? My old ten-speed? I couldn't be certain.

I'd picked up the tinkering bug from my father, and though a good deal of his talent had been lost in the genetic translation that was me, I managed to fix most of the household items that landed on my bench. My father, however, had been truly gifted in this regard. He could repair just about anything, spot the failure in a second flat, and once he identified the problem, he set to fixing it. His days were spent selling heavy equipment at the John Deere facility in Barnard, but on the nights he wasn't bowling at the Longhorn Lanes or swapping stories at the VFW hall, he mended, repaired, and even invented. He was the master of broken things. Everything could be fixed, could be improved.

⟶

Mama escorts me to the door of the bedroom I share with my older brother and tells me to wait inside while she goes to talk with my father. Toby lies on the bed, staring at the ceiling.

He doesn't look at me when I enter.

"You were in a fight?" I ask.

He doesn't answer. Instead he crosses his arms over his eyes, and I wonder if he's crying. On the shelves above his bed sit his shining trophies—for bowling and basketball, for baseball and football. Thirteen of them. I know because I've counted them a hundred times. My shelves hold books and a single award: a tiny third place trophy for peewee football that has sat without a companion for five years.

"Who'd ya' fight with?"

"Duke." Toby croaks the word but there are no signs my brother is crying, and that reassures me.

"Duke is your best pal," I say, confused.

"No he's not." Toby rolls onto his side, facing away from me.

I know the wounds on his jaw and eye are pressed into the pillow and they must ache, but he doesn't roll back toward me. He doesn't move. I continue to ask questions, but he won't reply, and I persist and I pester, because nothing makes sense to me. Folks admire Toby, they celebrate him, and the only people who weren't his friends were the ones too intimidated to get close, so why had Duke Manheim thrown fists at my brother? At the boy he himself had proclaimed, "Flat out impossible"?

The door opens and Daddy steps inside. He crosses his arms, gazing at me without so much as a glance for my brother.

"You go on down and eat your supper," he says. "I need a word with Toby."

"What did Mr. Manheim say?" I ask.

"Never you mind about that."

And I know it's bad. I can tell by the frown on my father's face. Whatever Duke's father told him was hateful and wrong, but it was more than that. "He lied," I say, though I have no idea what was actually said. My only instinct is to defend my brother from the motherless cur's accusations. "You know he did. Toby didn't do nothing wrong. Duke's a liar and Mr. Manheim's a liar and that's all there is to it."

"Go eat your supper, Peter," is my father's quiet response.

⎯⟨◦⟩⎯

I stretched out on the sofa and listened to my brother's messages. Each word stung like needles passing through my chest, and after listening to the last message—"The machine still works, Petey. It still works." —it felt as if a surgeon were yanking the sutures tight, pulling my ribs together so that my heart had no room to beat.

How could my father have built that thing? He wasn't a bad man, ask anyone. Nearly a hundred people had attended his funeral, and all of them spoke of his kindness, his humor, his helpfulness. He was a Christian, but quietly so, never waving his Bible, never wielding scripture like a weapon. As a father, he was evenhanded and warm. He believed in the belt; he used it infrequently but with great seriousness.

Lying on the sofa, looking at the ceiling and through it, imagining my wife in bed, turned to the wall the way Toby had been turned away, I remembered the sound of my father's belt cracking across my brother's backside as tears fell from my cheeks—more salt for the fried chicken on my plate. My mother said nothing. She ate nothing, merely pushed a fork through her potatoes, creating trenches as if preparing soil for planting.

⎯⟨◦⟩⎯

"Your brother is going to be staying in the workshop for a time," my father says.

I don't understand. "What did he do?"

"He'll be staying in the workshop for a time," my father says as if I hadn't heard him. "Go fetch my army cot from the attic and take it down to the kitchen. Then your mother will take you into town for a cone and a coke."

⎯⟨◦⟩⎯

I grew restless on the sofa. The past and present fell on me like blankets of fiberglass, scratchy and insulating, keeping things in that I'd rather expel. I stood. In the kitchen I took a beer from the fridge. With my tongue and throat soothed, I sat on a barstool at the kitchen island and traced the lines of grout that formed gutters in the tiled countertop. My finger pushed against a pile of mail, scooting the low stack toward the counter's edge.

No one said a word about what my brother had done. At the Dairy Queen, my mother revealed nothing about what she knew, if in fact she knew anything. It was very possible my father hadn't shared what Rick Manheim had said with her. You didn't talk about the bad things, and the worse a thing was, the quieter you kept it. It was a practice everyone in Barnard seemed to ascribe to. At school the next day and the day after that, I noticed no changes in the way my schoolmates behaved around me, no whispers of scandal, no sidelong glances of pity or disgust. If Duke Manheim had said anything to his buddies at Beall's High, it had yet to filter down to McNeil Middle School. Whatever had occurred between my brother and Duke was terrible enough that neither they nor their fathers would let the information escape.

As a kid, I wasn't equipped to think in broad terms, so my speculations were laughable. I imagined Toby had called Duke a bad name or maybe he'd stolen one of his friend's toys or record albums.

Again I nudged the stack of mail. A bill lay on top of the pile; it was from Willow House, where Toby lived, had lived for the past eight years. I found it comforting such institutions no longer called themselves asylums.

◂◦▸

The beefsteak is tough and the potatoes have been boiled too long and decompose into mush beneath my fork and nothing has flavor no matter how much salt I add. My father sits on my right and smokes a cigarette. His eyes are like Toby's—red and dull. He looks as if he's been awake since Sunday afternoon, since Mr. Manheim's phone call. My mother chats throughout the meal, talking about Mrs. Burlingson's crop of squash and raspberries, and Mrs. Turred's lousy washing machine flooding her basement again, and how Mr. Evans at the grocery told her that he'd caught the Perry boy trying to pilfer candies from the rack by the register. She babbles on and on. It seems she speaks about every family in Barnard except ours. As she clears the dishes, my father stubs out his cigarette and immediately lights another.

"I'm driving on up to Dallas," he says through a cloud of blue-gray smoke.

My mother halts as if someone has put a gun to her back. "The dealership sending you?" she asks.

"I'll be heading out here shortly," he says, not answering her question. "I'll try to be back by supper tomorrow, but no need to wait on me. I'll call if things take longer than expected."

Mama continues on to the sink and gently places the dinner plates in it.

"That's fine," she says. "We're having hot dogs and beans. They'll keep well enough."

⏤⟡⏤

I finished my beer, rinsed the bottle, and placed it in the recycling bin. With my ass propped against the counter, I listened to Toby's messages again with the same ache and constriction in my chest. Though very late, after two in the morning, I decided to call him back, but he didn't answer. I left a message so thick with false enthusiasm at hearing from him, I felt ashamed. The performance was as pitifully overblown as my childhood death scenes.

Granted, at that point my brother was no longer able to detect such variances in vocal patterns. He heard what he wanted to hear and inferred the emotions he expected. Oddly enough, in many other ways, his condition had improved. His paranoia and the violent outbursts it caused had lessened considerably, and I was grateful for that. Still, they shouldn't have let him out of the home, not without supervision. A guy like my brother couldn't care for himself, not for long, not for days and nights at a time.

⏤⟡⏤

After Daddy leaves for Dallas, I ask Mama why Toby has to stay outside, and she tells me that Daddy thinks it is best. I persist, because as always, I'm told nothing.

"Don't worry so much about this. Your brother is going to be fine, Petey, just fine. Your father is taking care of him."

I note the oddity of her comment. She speaks as if Toby is sick or injured, rather than being punished for whatever had caused his fight with Duke Manheim. My confusion grows and feeds my frustration, but my mother deflects my questions, tuts them away, smiles at me as if humoring a feeb. After a time, I become convinced she doesn't know what's wrong with Toby. I can tell by the confusion in her eyes and the way she smoothes her hair and the way she smiles, which isn't really a smile at all, and I know that asking her questions is pointless.

◄◦►

My mother accepted my father's silences with the same gravity she'd accepted every word he'd ever spoken. As a boy, I'd thought she had as many answers as my father, an equal on the plain of adulthood with her husband, but that wasn't the case at all. She wasn't a partner quite so much as an appendage, a utensil, an appliance with a good nature and a pleasant face. It wasn't until my father died that I understood the depth of her dependence on the man. Without my father, she turned to me for answers, looked to me to make her decisions. *Should I sell the house, Petey? Should I move in with your Aunt Ruby and Uncle Lou? Isn't it better if I don't go to the hospital? My visits always upset Toby so. If you think I should, I will but . . .*

◄◦►

I called Willow House's emergency number, but went directly to voice mail. Once the tone sounded, I let them know that Toby had slipped out again. I asked that they not involve the authorities, though I know they are bound by law to do so. Leaving my number, I hung up and dig in my pocket for the keys I'd taken from the hook in the garage.

Then I leave the house. In my car, I consider leaving Toby to the professionals at Willow House. All I had to do was call them back and give them the address. There was only one place he could be.

"The machine still works, Petey. It still works."

◄◦►

It's Friday, and I'm walking up the dirt drive to my house. The dust is thick and joins the pollen and both fill the air creating a golden filter for the afternoon sun, which hangs, glaring over the roof. The door to my father's workshop is open, and I see Toby inside. He is holding a small bucket and a brush, and he's covering the window in the door with black paint. He is concentrating on the task, lining up his brush carefully before touching it to the pane and sweeping it across the glass. He is so absorbed in the task that my arrival at the door surprises him.

He flinches and steps back and then his posture relaxes. "Hey, squirt," he says, and the familiarity, the normality of the greeting refreshes like a gulp of sweet tea.

"Hey," I reply. "Whatcha doing?"

"Painting," he says.

"Painting windows?"

"That's what it looks like," he says.

I notice something is missing from my brother's eyes. They are red and the lids are heavy and a dull cast covers them.

"Why?"

"It's a project I'm working on with Daddy," he says. He seems unsure of the words, and he gazes at the concrete floor of the workshop and then back at the black band he has painted on the glass. "It's a secret."

"Are you gonna come back inside?" I ask.

"Not for a while," Toby says. He dips the brush into the bucket and stirs the black paint gravely.

"Why not?" I'm desperate for information, and even though I see my brother pulling into his thoughts, moving away from me as surely as if he were being dragged behind a speeding truck, I persist. "What happened? What did you do?"

"You better go on inside, now," he says.

I look past him into my father's shop. The space was always off limits to us unless we had permission from our father to enter it for a tool or a can of oil. It is large, a converted two-car garage. The floor is clean and cleared except for the army cot, which Toby has made up neatly with sheets and a blanket. The workbenches form a large L in the far corner, and they are similarly devoid of clutter. Neatly organized shelves run floor to ceiling on the right just beyond the cot.

Switching tack I ask, "Can I help?"

Like my father, Toby responds as if I've said nothing at all. "You better go on inside."

Then he scrapes his brush along the side of the paint can and presses its bristles to the window. With his customary precision, he coats the glass from frame to frame without getting a speck of paint on the trim.

◄○►

It is the middle of the night and I can't sleep. I'm still not used to having the room to myself. Toby's absence is a hole I fear I'll be dragged into. I leave my bed and go to the window and stare down on Daddy's workshop, and the dark building with its black windows makes me think of a haunted house, and I think my brother is the phantom prowling it. Daddy's truck is parked only a few feet from the door. He's back from Dallas. I don't remember having heard him come home.

After I tire of looking at the workshop, I leave the window and then leave my room and wander down the hall to the stairs. Though I've made no conscious decision about where I'm going, I creep downstairs and detect a muffled clicking sound that draws me to the kitchen. Daddy sits at the table under the cone of light falling from the hanging brass fixture, bent over a box with a number of colored wires snaking from its side. A brown paper bag rests to his left. Next to this is the slide projector Mama bought at the flea market in Bastrop. She'd never used it so far as I knew, but she'd been very proud of "the deal" she'd found at the time, and I wonder why Daddy has scavenged the device from the hall closet.

He looks up and fixes grim eyes on me. The overhead light casts shadows down his face, and the dark patches beneath his eyes and chin, and the lines around his mouth look like blotches of rot. A stricken quality passes over his face, and he blinks, and I wonder if he recognizes me at all. He puts down his screwdriver and rubs his eyes and I again think he looks as if he hasn't slept since Mr. Mannheim's call all those days ago. His hair is greasy and flat and the skin on his face hangs as if the muscles beneath have relinquished their grasp.

"Peter," he says quietly. He reaches out and lifts the brown paper bag from the tabletop and lowers it to the floor beside his feet. "You shouldn't be up."

"Did you have a good trip to Dallas?"

"Fine," he says dryly.

I think to ask if he's found anything that will help Toby, but the expression on his face, empty of all but flickers of life, warns me away from the question. So I stand there silently, following the trajectory of the wires poking from the metal box before him, and I look back to the slide projector sitting like a turtle near the edge of the table, and I take in the spools of wire and the cutters and a box with the word *rheostat* stenciled across its oatmeal-colored cardboard box.

"You should be in bed," he says.

"Maybe I could help."

"Get your ass to bed, Peter!"

◄○►

The following day, I see neither Daddy nor Toby, but when I'm outside playing in the yard, kicking a ball across the scrub grass and dirt, I hear evidence of their presence in the workshop. Whispers. The clicking of tools. At one point, I kick my ball toward the back wall of the workshop and press my ear close to the blackened window. The glass muffles Daddy's voice, but I recognize his tone, and I realize he is doing all of the talking. I want to hear the words but they are garbled and incomprehensible like prayers spoken under water.

I imagine my father and brother hunched over the slide projector and various electrical wires and components. Daddy might be pointing at a device and a wire and explaining why the two must be joined in a specific way, and I think Toby is lucky to be spending so much time with Daddy. A tickle of jealousy joins my curiosity, and for a time I forget that Toby is being punished, or that he's not well. I still don't understand his condition, but I know I want to join them in the workshop, to be part of the project. Resting my foot on the red ball, I look around the yard, searching for an excuse to knock on the workshop door. But instead of finding a magic key that will justify my intrusion, I see Mama standing at the corner of the house. Her arms are crossed, and she frowns at me.

Later that night, I'm watching television. It is near my bedtime. Mama has given me a plate of two cookies and a small glass of milk to enjoy while Carol Burnett and her co-stars stumble and mug for the camera.

Just as a skit is about to end, the lights in my house dim and the television screen goes green-black in a hiccup of electric current. I think little of it. Such hiccups are common during storms or high winds. But it isn't storming, and I hear no gusts in the eaves. A roar of laughter, harsh and mocking, pours from the television when it comes back on, and I feel a chill. A minute later, the lights flicker off again.

◄○►

Vast stretches of darkness gave way to the occasional streetlamp. Driving toward my childhood home, I attempted to shake off the memories, hoping to loosen the tightness in my chest, but the program in my head was nearing an end, and I didn't have a switch to turn it off, not even a rheostat to adjust its power.

What I remembered clearly was that things in our house seemed to return to normal after the night of the flickering lights. The next morning, I found Toby at the breakfast table. He appeared exhausted and confused, but his fatigue didn't seem quite so dire. He wore a clean white t-shirt and a baseball cap, which he'd pulled low on his brow. Mama had fixed pancakes and bacon and Toby tore through them. My father joined us. Unlike Toby, he barely ate. His exhaustion remained, and he smoked cigarettes through the meal, blowing smoke onto his plate, as if in a trance.

Nothing was said about Toby or the workshop or what they had constructed within it, but apparently the experiment had done some good, because for the first time in a week, Toby slept in our room. He went to school on Monday, and when he came home he let himself into the workshop, where he would stay for an hour. And then supper. And then to bed. The spark in his eyes had not returned, and he wore his baseball cap everywhere, somehow eluding Mama's rule about hats at the dining table, which also distressed me because it wasn't usual, but he was back in the house and things had reached a level of normality. And I started to believe the darkness that had tarnished our golden boy was finally being wiped away.

A week before Christmas, my father had his first aneurism. It didn't kill him, that would take six more years and two more "cerebral events," but that night, he died some in my eyes, because I saw what he'd built. I discovered his answer to my brother's troubles.

◄○►

After my mother's tears and my father's expression of perplexed misery, and after the paramedics and the ambulance, and after the red lights vanish over the hill and the front door closes behind me, I trudge to the sofa and fall onto it. Toby is already there, staring at the television; both his face and the appliance screen are dark.

"Do you think Daddy's going to die, Toby?"

"No," he snaps. His gaze doesn't wander from the blank-glass nothing of the TV. "He can't."

"He looked real bad."

"He's a great man, Petey. He's strong. He'll be okay."

And I know Toby is not stating a fact; he is voicing a wish.

"But what if he's not?" I ask.

"Shut up, Petey," Toby says. His command scalds me into silence and I lower my head because I can't look at him anymore. We're silent for a time before he says, "Go on up to bed. I've got things to do."

-◦-

I do as I am told and I lay in bed, but my eyes are open, and I'm angry at Toby for dismissing me. Abandoning me. The house still stinks of the fish Mama fried for supper. My pillow is as hard as stone and the pillowcase feels scratchy and hot on my neck. My thoughts crackle and pop like damp kindling. I don't understand how my family could crumble, just fall apart like a dirt wall in a hard wind. I don't understand because no one has told me anything that sounds true. *Toby will be okay. Daddy will be okay.* But how can anyone know that? They can't is the answer, but I'm supposed to accept the meaningless phrases as gospel?

Daddy is in the shadows staining my ceiling, and Toby is there, too. They are strangers to me.

I leave the bed and cross to the window and look down on the workshop, and I know Toby is there, and I decide I deserve to know what is happening. So, I walk out of the room, down the stairs, and out the front door, and I cross the walk to the dirt drive and I stare at the workshop door. Toby has done an excellent job and the windows are impenetrably black, but there is a narrow crack beneath the door and I see it is filled with gray light. The light remains for twenty seconds and then goes out, only to reignite after a single beat of my heart. I reach out for the doorknob and pause. The light goes out again; it returns.

Holding my breath, I turn the knob and push the door open. Initially a glaring disc beaming from across the room blinds me. The odors of the place—oil, sawdust, and sour sweat—burrow into my nostrils. A dull hum fills my ears. I lift my hand to shield my eyes from the light and it goes out, but a fog of green covers my vision the way it does after a camera's flash. I close my eyes and the swirling murk remains. The lamp ignites again and before I open my eyes, I turn away.

I am aware of the shelves on the right side of the workshop and that something—One of Mama's sheets?—hangs against the nearest wall. But my gaze lands on my brother and fills with the sight of him.

Toby lies on his cot. He has pushed his hands through leather straps affixed to the metal frame, and they are knotted into fists. His eyes are wide and he's shaking his head frantically. There is something on his head. It is a small cap with metal arms that reach out to press against his temples. Rubber tubing hangs from these shiny appendages and drape the sides of his face where they connect to a wooden dowel wrapped in gauze. Toby clamps the dowel between his teeth like a horse bit. He struggles to get his hands free of the leather straps when the light goes out again.

It comes back on with a click, and the dull hum returns. Toby's back arches and his body goes rigid. His eyes are rolled back and white, and lines of tendon and vein appear on his neck as if he's swallowed a vine plant that is trying to push its way through his skin.

I scream. It does nothing to lessen my dread. I shout my brother's name but he is paralyzed. I step forward and then back up and then forward again. The light dies, and the humming stops, and I turn toward the bench at the back of the room. When the light comes back on, the apparatus atop the wooden surface comes clear. A plug juts from the wall socket; a white cord runs to a junction box, topped by the black knob of the rheostat; two wires, one black and one blue, run like tentacles from the metal box to the cap on my brother's head; another cord, this one yellow, snakes to the slide projector. I can only think of the display as a torture device, imagined and built by my father. But what was it meant to accomplish? I spin toward the image projected on the wall of the workshop and my breath lodges against the stone in my throat. A young woman stands naked in a field, holding a flower to her nose. Her hair, the color of corn silk, frames her beautiful face. She smiles softly. Sweetly. My gaze traces down her throat to her small round breasts and then over her belly to the mound of golden blonde hair between her legs, and then back up again. The room goes black. The picture of the young woman is replaced by that of a muscled man with a dense pelt of hair covering his chest. Beneath his thick mustache his mouth is twisted into a smirk. He is also naked and his hand grasps the shaft of his penis like the hilt of a knife.

The hum has returned to the workshop. Toby is again arched and rigid. And my confusion is momentarily erased as if I understand this perverse experiment, though I'm certain I do not. It seems that Toby is relaxed when pictures of women cover my mama's bed sheet, but voltage and pain accompanies the images of men. I don't know what this is meant to achieve, but I know it has to stop.

I reach across the workbench. Doing so, I lean over the rheostat and notice the switches and the dial on top. Dashes and numbers run in an arc to accommodate the round black knob. Someone, either Daddy or Toby, has run a strip of black electrical tape like a comic eyebrow, blocking out the lines and numbers on the downside of the arc, and above this, written in red ink, is the word *Danger.* I yank the plug from the wall. Despite the pitch darkness I find my way to the light switch on the other side of the shop and flick it on, and then I turn to my brother, who has managed to get one of his hands loose. He frees his other hand, reaches for the bit in his mouth and pulls it away all the while glaring at me.

"Y-you c-can't be in here, Petey," he says. His voice is dry, and he growls savagely to clear his throat.

Only when I try to answer do I realize that I'm crying, and I can't find my voice. Toby removes the device from his head and I see the red marks at his temples, and I know they're the reason he wears his baseball cap in the house, and the sight of them makes me cry harder.

"It's okay," he says. With a tremendous effort, he sits up on the cot and swings his legs off the side. "*I'm* okay."

"No. No. No." I blubber.

"You're too young to understand," Toby says, wiping at his mouth with the back of his hand. "I wasn't right, Petey. I felt things and did things . . ." His voice trails away. A mask of confusion falls over his face like the darkness between the projector's light. When it passes he says, "Daddy read all about it. He found books in Dallas. He found out what was wrong with me and how to fix it. He had to do something or else he'd have to send me away to an asylum and people would know about me, and they can't know about me. They just can't. Do you want me to go to an asylum, Petey?"

"It's not right," I say between sobs. "It's hurting you."

"It has to," Toby says. His head dips and he observes the floor for a moment. When he looks back at me, the spark I've missed in his eyes has returned, except the light there is hard and cold. A hint of a smile touches the corners of his lips. His expression is hopeful but it's also frightening, because, to me, Toby looks crazy. And when he speaks again, I feel certain his mind has come loose, because he says, "It's working, Petey. I'm getting better. Really I am."

⟶

I pulled into the drive of Toby's house. My car's headlights swept across the front of the shed like a lighthouse beacon. Black paint still covered the windows. A grey light showed beneath the door and then extinguished. Remaining in the parked car, I peered at the shed with trepidation. I'd thought the machine was gone, dismantled, torn apart, and thrown in the trash. That's what Toby had told me; he'd said it was the first thing to go when he moved in after our mother's death. His lie shouldn't have come as a surprise.

Over the years, bits of information came my way. I learned that Toby had made a sexual advance toward his buddy, Duke, which had triggered the fight and the call from Richard Manheim. Of course I'd already figured that out, but Duke himself confirmed it years later. We ran into each other at a bar in Austin, and we got to talking about Toby. He felt bad for my brother. Such a shame, he'd said. Such a waste.

The grey light flashed and I counted to twenty and then it went dark. Leaving the car, I breathed deeply to calm my sparking nerves. The scene inside the shed would be familiar, I knew, but that didn't make it any more palatable.

In the years before leaving home, Toby had used our father's device regularly. Some days he was the golden hero of my early youth, and other days he appeared crazy, eyes wild and mouth shimmering with spittle as he recounted one moral outrage or another. On those days, he went to the shed and wired himself to the apparatus, as if it were a meditative aid. He marched through the broiling gut of hell all the while insisting he was fine in the fire. *I'm getting better. Really I am.* I begged him to stop. My mother never said a word. My father never looked so proud.

It's easy to blame the old man, but he thought he was helping. In college, I did some research of my own, investigating accepted "cures" of the day, and I found a number of references to electro-shock and aversion therapy. I'm sure this was the kind of information he came across during his trip to Dallas. His life was machines, and each part had to work in a particular way to keep the machine running. It would never occur to him that he didn't understand a part or its function. Its value. My father wasn't a villain; he was just a hick who wanted to save his son from a lifetime of sadness and shame—the only future he could imagine for a broken part in the social machine.

At the door to the shed, I lifted my fist and knocked. The gray light poured from beneath the door and then went out. When my second rap went unanswered, I pushed open the door. Toby lay on the cot. He was dead. He'd been gone for a while, maybe since hanging up after leaving me his last message.

The sight of him coiled in my throat along with the odors of urine, burned skin, and singed hair. Deep lines carved in around his mouth and brow; he hadn't even bothered inserting the bit between his teeth. His eyes had poached in the sockets; blood and viscous tears clotted at this temples. He appeared to be smiling, but I had to believe it was the strained rictus of his final shock.

For a moment, I thought I could see the golden boy beneath the layers of weight and folds of skin, but it was only my mind playing tricks, an evanescent denial with no more weight than projected light. I choked on a sob and fought an urge to race to the cot, but a loud voice in the back of my head, reason or dread, warned me away from the coursing voltage. Instead of running to Toby's side, I crossed the shed to disconnect the machine.

As I had done on the first night I'd witnessed my father's therapy, I leaned over the rheostat to reach the wall plug. Toby had turned the rheostat to full power. The white dash on the black dial pointed at a peeling corner of tape and the letter E in the word *Danger,* written in red ink. The ink had faded.

The light went out and then returned with a *shoosh* and a *click*. A deadly hum filled the room. Foolishly, I glanced back at the screen. The image projected there froze me. It was of Toby and our father. The man, younger than I ever remembered him being, stood on a tractor in the parking lot of the John Deere facility. In one hand he held a rag and in the other he held a monstrous wrench. With one foot on the running board and the other on the tractor seat, he looked like a big game hunter, gloating over the carcass of an unfortunate trophy. Toby as a toddler stood on the pavement grinning up at his daddy, clapping his tiny hands together in a display of ecstatic joy.

MAJORLENA

JANE JAKEMAN

She scared the hell out of me.

We never did find out where she came from, before she found us.

After the explosions, three of us scrambled out, away from the road, over the ridge. There was a rocky overhang on the other side. I had the map they'd showed us still in my head. We were bang in the middle of real thick hostiles territory, like jelly in a doughnut.

"Fuck it, man, we stay right here," hissed Leroy.

"You ain't in charge," said Schulz.

"We stay on the ridge," I said.

The explosion had taken out the lead trucks. If we hadn't been straggling, we'd have been gone as well.

There was no movement on the road except for flames. Then came black smoke and a stink. Strange, I knew what it was right away. Like in my mom's kitchen when she made us taffy, stirring away in a boiling-hot saucepan.

"Man comin' up!" shouted Leroy. Then he added, "Jeez, maybe it's a female!"

A helmet outlined above the ridge, then a small figure, hands high, coming up slowly in regulation desert boots, skidding on the sand and shale. People think the Iraqi desert is smooth sand like the beach, but there's places where it's all little stones slipping under your feet. When I think of Major Lena now, and I try not to do that, it's what I remember: the air full of black smouldering stuff and the smell of burning sugar.

We hadn't thought anyone else was alive, but she came from the direction of the road. She was dead cautious, waited, lay on the ground, let Schulz take her rifle and fumble all over her.

"Clean!" he shouted.

She had dog-tags, ID, but it was her voice, more than anything, that was ranking US female military. Though, like I said, we never did find out exactly where she was from. She had a kit-bag and Schulz pushed his hand in it.

"No weapons here," he said.

This was just after dawn and we was stuck there in the desert. Go back down onto the road—no way! A beat-up old wagon came along the road as we were sitting under that ridge; it was full of rag-heads, their rifles all sticking out at odd angles. They didn't spot us. We might have taken them, four of us now, all armed. But something a damned sight more powerful had taken out the trucks—a rocket-launcher, maybe—and whoever fired that might still be around.

This bunch nudged through the smouldering debris with their rifles. It looked like the metal was still too hot to touch—one of them put a hand to a door and drew it back like he'd been scorched. They didn't hang around.

We took a good look at ourselves. Two privates, Leroy and Schulz. Me, the sergeant. And the woman, Major Lena. I guess she had a surname but I don't remember one. Whenever I think of her, which is as little as possible, it's all run together like it was one name—Majorlena. Sounds like a fancy name someone might give a girl. Anyway, that's what we called her. "Yes, Majorlena! Sure, Majorlena! Show us your boobs, Majorlena!"

No, not that. We'd never have dared.

"I'm taking charge here, Sergeant," she said in that voice, slow scraping on steel, flashing her white teeth (that's another reason we was sure she was genuine US of A) but not in any real smile.

She had brown eyes, huge, but not pretty.

"Yes, sir!" I said.

"We'll assess the situation."

We assessed.

Stuck in the middle of a fucking desert surrounded by terrorists, that was our situation.

And no food or water.

Choppers circled above the roadkill like great buzzing flies, and I said, "Sir, we could spread out our shirts or wave something at them."

"Yeah, they're bound to see us," said Leroy. "They're real low."

He ran to the top of the ridge of rock, pulled his shirt off and waved it. There was a burst of machine-gun fire. They had lousy aim. Leroy came running back and we all crowded under the overhang.

"Private Leroy, you take your orders from me," said Majorlena. "Don't move without my say-so. We have to sit it out under the ridge till nightfall. Then we can go down and maybe find some water and ammo." I saw she was eyeing Leroy's bare chest as she talked. He was a good-looking guy, one of them tall, slim blacks.

I forgot about sex. By noon, my eyes felt like they was eggs frying in a pan. I felt like I'd never been in the country before, though I'd been in Iraq for two months. But never really in it, if you see what I mean. Never like this, without iced drinks or showers. I found out you don't rightly sweat when it gets that hot, if you ain't got no water to sweat out of you. Any little trickle off your skin dries instantly. Kind of comfortable after a while, except your head feels like it's in a furnace. Schulz had a shaved head, like a lot of the Pennsylvania boys, unprotected.

We got some shade from the overhang. But my mouth was parching like it was full of sand and when evening was coming I knew we had to get water or we was going to die right there.

Majorlena had been assessing the road situation.

"Sergeant, you and I will go down to the road," she said. "The third truck hasn't been too badly hit. There may be some water, or even a radio."

"That the one you was in, sir?" No one could have survived from the two front trucks. They was nothing but metal frames with charred lumps in the drivers' seats.

"Why, yes, Sergeant," she said. "That's right. I've been travelling with this army."

The melted sugar had poured down the sides of the trucks. There was all kinds of flies and insects there, drawn to the sweetness, I guess. You don't usually get those big fat things in the middle of the desert. It's mostly hard little flies that choke you up when the wind blows a swarm in your face. Majorlena and I were brushing juicy ones off as we got to the third truck. I didn't like the way they flew into my mouth when I opened it.

"Check the tanks and see if you can find some containers," she said.

She climbed up into the cabin. The driver hadn't been burned to cinders. I could see the fire hadn't hit so bad here, though his hair and face was scorched.

Going to unscrew the caps, I went round the side of the truck and looked up. She was there right next to the driver, with her head bent down towards him, when she realised I was watching her. She made a sudden jerking arm movement. Getting down out of the cabin, she showed me something in her hand.

"Got his tags. Give his family closure."

Poor bastard had closure all right. But I still wasn't sure what she'd been doing.

I managed to drain water from the radiator into some big cans, US army property we found in the truck. They was full of coffee. We emptied it into the sand, where it blew away like darker smoke against the dusk.

Before we got back to the top of the ridge, we heard shots.

Schulz was dragging Leroy back up.

"Stupid asshole tried to make a break. They got night-sights."

Majorlena put her hand over Leroy's mouth to stop his screams. They gradually went down to whimpering. He died near dawn. We scrabbled a place for him in the sand and tipped it over him with our hands, then Schulz said some prayers.

⊷

The hunger was like real pain. We had a little water left, tasting of metal and coffee.

"We got to figure a way off here." Schulz was clutching his belly as if he were trying to press it smaller.

"We stay near the vehicles," said Majorlena. She was walking 'round. She didn't look sunk-eyed, not like she had spent the night out in the open with no food or water.

"Yeah," I said, "I know that's official. But there's exceptions."

"There may be some of that melted sugar we could break off," said Majorlena, like she was making a concession.

"I'll go down to the trucks when it gets dark," I said. Just the thought of filling my mouth with that real sweet taste near drove me crazy.

They let me go alone. I figured I would be entitled to extra sugar.

The driver's body was stinking. Stars and moon were bright as electric, so I was afraid I'd be seen by snipers. But nothing. Got to the back of the truck and there was like smooth icicles hanging down. I broke one off and took a suck. Damn me if it wasn't as sweet as candy at a fair. I felt the sugar running through me, its energy coming up in my blood.

When I scrabbled back to the top of the ridge, sending some shale skidding under me, the Major was waiting.

I gave her a piece of sugar.

"Where's Schulz?"

"Getting some sleep down there."

But he was next to Leroy's body and when I shook him he didn't wake up. I called softly for Majorlena to come down.

"What is it?"

She rolled Schulz over towards her and his face was cold and still in the moonlight, his eyes staring up at the stars.

"Jesus! How the hell?—he was okay when I went down." I looked across and saw that Leroy's body was partly uncovered, down to about the waist. Saw what had happened to that smooth skin.

"You reckon Schulz did that?" I said.

"Must have, unless it was wild dogs or something, but I've been keeping watch all the time you were down there. I didn't hear anything."

"Maybe Schulz went a bit crazy, didn't know what he was doing."

"Yeah, sunstroke, heat exhaustion." She sat back. "I'll have to make a report on it when we get picked up."

It was the coldest night I have ever spent. There was no cloud cover. I didn't sleep any, just sat up with my back against the rock. Majorlena was a little ways off, kind of hunched over. I closed my eyes at one point and then opened them a few moments later. She seemed to have shifted a little towards me.

"I ain't going to get no sleep tonight," I said.

Was I warning her or asking her? I still don't know.

But I did go to sleep, and when I woke up, something was moving over Leroy's body. It was a big mass of stuff, like a long beard trailing down from his neck. I stared for a few moments trying to make sense of it, rolling over so I could get a better look. There was a fluttering and crawling going on nonstop over Leroy's chest.

I couldn't see his face. It looked to be moving and heaving, and that was a big swarm of fat blowflies crawling over it and down his body. They glistened, their sticky bodies shifting and pushing, some flying a bit and then settling. In the wounds on his chest, there were flies right in the bloody furrows, twisting round and fluttering like whores in a jacuzzi.

Lying a few feet away, like she and Leroy was in a bed, was Majorlena. And then the flies was coming off Leroy in this black stream, climbing and hopping and flying towards her.

I took a step towards her, thinking she was asleep. I was going to warn her. Then I saw she was awake.

Worse than awake. Her mouth was open and the flies were crawling up over her body and she was saying things. I got closer and heard her whispering.

"Come on my little ones, Mamma's thirsty, Mamma's hungry. You know what she wants. She needs you now."

And the flies were crawling into her dark wet open mouth, scrambling and fluttering over her lips, and she was chawing down on them.

The charred dead in their trucks down on the road was better than that. I sat there all night.

A patrol coming along the road picked me up next day. I told them to look for three more up on the ridge, but they only found two bodies.

I guess she's still travelling with the army.

THE WITHERING

TIM CASSON

It was clear that Miss Appleby trusted nobody associated with my profession. Her attitude was no doubt influenced by her father's disgrace and the tragedy ten years ago in 1881, the details of which, in the form of yellowed newspaper cuttings, I carried in my waistcoat pocket. Still, I persevered, suggesting that an arrangement between us would be to her advantage.

"Or at least advantageous," I added, "to those unfortunate souls that you are blessed to assist."

She wavered, perhaps because of the word *blessed*. A tactical addition on my part: both an appeal to her vanity and a validation of what she doubtless perceived as her selfless and lonely struggle.

"In that case, sir," she said, "if I were to agree, I would insist that you omit the embellishments and half-truths common to the work of your kind."

"Of course . . ."

"Remember your responsibility, Mr. Creswell. Your article could be the final nail in the coffin of an innocent man!"

The outburst coloured her cheeks. When passionate like that, I noticed her eyes were quite lovely.

I insisted that she had the word of a gentleman, and I would write only the truth as I saw it.

◄o►

Her study was gloomy and cluttered; the deep-crimson walls decorated with the masks and tribal carvings that her father had acquired in Africa. I sat there watching her at work, her face paled by the dull morning glow from a window blurred with rain. She sifted through a pile of letters on her desk, tearing each envelope with a paperknife, scanning the handwriting and frowning at something or other.

"Fool!"

She tossed aside the letter, then, as was her habit, began a reply immediately.

I picked it up and read the pleas of a Derbyshire mother whose daughter-in-law's burned remains were discovered in a bread oven. "Hm, agreed. Didn't her son, the baker, confess?"

"Unfortunately much of the correspondence I receive reveals a tacit denial. It's not possible for some folk to accept their loved one's role in any abominable act. My father cautioned in his journals about such time wasters."

"How do you know when they are genuine?"

"Intuition perhaps. And I am familiar with most of the current cases. I follow the reports in the newspapers."

"All those embellishments and half-truths?" I said, winking.

She squirmed. "I am attempting to ease this poor woman's suffering, Mr. Creswell, while at the same time imploring her to accept her son's guilt. Not an easy task."

The next letter caused her lips to tremble oddly. She brushed a stray lock from her forehead, turned and stared through the rainy window. I read the letter, from a Dr. Mortlock in Wales. "What's so different about this one?"

"The brevity perhaps, a sincerity of tone measured in few words." She stood and smoothed her lap, staring at me with a determined look. "Come, Mr. Creswell, we have no time to lose."

She kept a trunk packed ready for such impromptu trips. As always, I travelled light.

◄o►

She stared out of the compartment window at the Welsh countryside, clearly deep in thought. I studied her discreetly, without her or the other travellers noticing, hopefully. The natural light captured an expression of reflective innocence, the delicate symmetry of her face and those lovely eyes. I wondered why such an attractive lady, at thirty now, was not married or at least courted by gentlemen suitors.

Our train arrived late afternoon at a drab little town called Llanilydd, which was enclosed by steep grey hills. The porter loaded Miss Appleby's trunk onto the waiting hansom but she insisted on lugging her strongbox despite its obvious weight. The sky was overcast and there was a chill wind blowing off the hills. She draped a blanket over the strongbox, covering what looked like air holes, hugging it close as we bumped along a muddy valley road—the contents inside tinkling—before arriving at the town's main street. The driver whipped the horses up a sharp hill then halted outside a large dwelling, grand but bleak and uninviting.

A dour servant showed us to our rooms. Miss Appleby asked the whereabouts of the doctor but the fellow had already turned along the landing. My room was adjacent to Miss Appleby's, clad in dark wood panelling, austere though warm thankfully. As I unpacked my travel bag, I noticed the inner door.

I eased out the brass key, knelt, and peered through the ha'penny-sized aperture, trying to convince myself that such behaviour was justifiable, the nature of my work, but in truth hoping to catch a glimpse of her changing, in her undergarments especially. I felt ashamed yet excited also. Across the room directly opposite, the strongbox was positioned on a Turkey rug beside the grate's glowing coals.

Miss Appleby came into view. She used a set of keys to undo an elaborate lock system, opened the lid then unhooked hinge pins that held the side panels in place. The clutter that was revealed—mainly brass components, tubes and glassware—sparkled in the light of the fire. But it was difficult to see the apparatus in any detail.

"There," she said, "a nice fire. That should warm you up."

She uncorked a bottle of greenish mulch—recoiling momentarily from what I imagined was the odour—and fitted a rubber tube to the end. There was a strange sputtering from inside the apparatus; the rubber umbilical coiled like a snake and there was gurgling as the bottle's plankton-like fill reduced an inch.

A knock on the door startled me.

The servant stood there, sniffing with disgust at the sight of me kneeling by the keyhole.

"The doctor asks if you and Miss Appleby would join him in the drawing room for tea."

⟡

I guessed that Dr. Mortlock looked much older than his years; his pallor a bloodless grey, with deep facial lines that seemed to have been shaped by misery, or a hopeless struggle with disease perhaps. His thin frame moved cautiously, wary of the environment, as though some minor collision with the furniture might produce a most painful reaction.

"I imagined you'd be older," he said to Miss Appleby, ushering her to the sofa. "Less appealing to the eye."

She kept her tone formal. "If we could discuss business, Doctor . . ."

"Yes of course. I'm sorry for bringing you here, Miss Appleby. This is indeed a wretched town. But an innocent boy, Tobias Jones, is to stand trial for murder, and that cannot be right."

"Who is he alleged to have murdered?" she asked.

"A girl of seventeen, Charlotte Crane. The daughter of Arthur Crane. He owns the slate quarry here. This town would die without the quarry, and Crane has turned the people against young Tobias."

"What's your relationship with this boy?"

The question seemed to unsettle the doctor. "I have known the family for years, that's all. Should I stand idly by and allow a miscarriage of justice? Tobias is certain to hang."

"How did the girl die?"

"I conducted the post-mortem myself. Marks on the neck indicated a ligature, applied with force enough to fatally deprive the brain of oxygen."

"Was she raped?"

"Her undergarments were undisturbed. There was no physical evidence of molestation."

"What about robbery?"

"Her purse contained two pounds and some odd coins, so no."

"Then why is the boy a suspect?"

"He was discovered with her body at the quarry where he works. Not good, I realise, but . . ."

She stared. "And what did he have to say about that?"

The doctor massaged the deep grooves in his face. "This tragic incident has rendered him mute. A symptom of shock, I believe. He was beaten terribly when found and has not spoken since. You must help poor Tobias. He has a gentle nature, I assure you."

The servant wheeled a trolley in then served tea and fruitcake. Miss Appleby tipped a spoonful of sugar in her cup and stirred it. "Dr. Mortlock, are you familiar with what I do?"

"I have heard you save the innocent from the gallows."

"In some cases that may be true. But what I attempt to do is expose the guilty. I admit though, not always successfully. I must warn you, however, that my work is frowned upon, considered unethical, and certainly not for the faint of heart. Some say it is an abomination. Others, when they see what it is truly about, are quick to turn to superstition and violence. My father was a great man of science, though somewhat trusting, and that cost him his life. I do not wish to make the same mistake."

"Miss Appleby, I nursed my wife through her final moments. Five years ago now. She died in the most dreadful agony. Nothing on earth could be more distressing, believe me. My health has not been the same since. What I mean is, in my time as a physician, I have seen the darkest things this cruel world has to offer."

She shook her head slowly. "Some things you have not seen."

I noticed on the mantelpiece a photograph of the doctor from probably the previous decade, posing stiffly with a lady of similar age, their expressions solemn from the formality of the occasion, yet both healthy looking. Next to this was a picture of a young man, strikingly handsome and smiling without inhibition.

"If I agree to help," she said, "you must do exactly as I say."

He nodded. "Whatever it takes."

"Where is the body of Charlotte Crane right now?"

"In the graveyard, naturally."

"Then we need to exhume."

As she said this, I almost spat a mouthful of tea.

—◦—

An odd sound woke me. It seemed to drift through the door cracks from Miss Appleby's room. I lit the bedside lamp then tiptoed across and peered through the keyhole, surprised, at this hour, to see her sitting on the edge of the bed in a nightgown staring as though in a trance. The sounds were most peculiar and disturbing and appeared to originate from the strongbox apparatus beside the fire. Like the far-off wailing of some nightmarish choir, discordant, spoiled of melody, as though heard through warped pipes perhaps. Miss Appleby stood suddenly and wandered out of sight. I gasped. Something wet and foul-smelling squirted through the keyhole. There was a terrible stinging in my eye.

A voice from behind the door called, "Serves you right, you Peeping Tom!"

"I'm very sorry, Miss Appleby, but I was awoken by strange noises."

"There were no noises when you peeped this afternoon. If the light from a keyhole is obstructed, it does not require Sherlock Holmes to determine what is happening. Fortunately for you the feed is not corrosive."

"Feed?"

"The stinging will subside and your vision will return. Go to the bathroom and wash your face and after that open this door immediately."

"Yes, of course."

Afterwards I perched on the edge of my bed while she sat in a chair opposite. The eerie noises were more pronounced now that the door was open. "I really must apologise, Miss Appleby, but I was curious about that strongbox. In the carriage earlier I saw what looked like air holes."

"I am not ashamed of what I do, Mr. Creswell. That's why I said nothing when you spied this afternoon. But once is enough, wouldn't you say?"

I nodded, smiling weakly.

"The reason I have allowed you to observe my life is simply so that others may know and understand, without prejudice formed through ignorance. However, I must ask you to reserve judgement until you have seen the results, the good that the surrogate can achieve."

"The surrogate?"

"My father acquired him from a shaman in Africa. Every so often, in that village, a mother gives birth to a babe that never grows, as its soul lies between two worlds. If anything, over time, it reduces and shrivels. He is very old now, nearing the end of his existence I fear. His tiny form is not appealing to the eye, quite hideous in fact, so I must ask you not to stare at him. It is he that unwittingly draws the night voices as he sleeps, which are projected through the apparatus's brass vocal horn."

"Night voices?"

"My father's name for them. The native expression does not translate accurately into English. The closest we have is the *withering*."

"I don't understand."

"The dead are speaking, Mr. Creswell. For me, a common enough occurrence at night, yet it never fails to unnerve. Doubtless they are trying to persuade the surrogate to usher them through. Though for what purpose I can only guess. Perhaps it is to do with reliving earthly memories, or the forlorn hope of meeting a loved one again. Usually the sounds are indistinct, soft like the wind, while at other times there's a locution that seems to actually mean something." She tilted her head. "Right now I hear extinct languages, a confusion of tongues, rather like the babble of an audience before curtain up, wouldn't you say? My father, writing in his notes, emphasised the dangers of trying to determine what they are saying, Mr. Creswell, of listening too deeply. To do so can lead to madness. So take heed."

"That isn't very reassuring. In truth, I'd rather not listen to them at all. They frighten me."

"Indeed. They frighten me too."

"Then why . . . ?"

She sighed. "Sometimes I wonder if I have taken the correct path in life, or whether I really had any choice in the matter. Did you hear what the doctor said earlier about seeing his wife suffer?"

"Yes."

"It's clear, with his ill health, that he carries those memories as a burden visible to all. Perhaps, in varying degrees, it is the same for each of us. Just the presence alone of the box is a reminder of my past. As a girl, although I was not directly involved in this work, it shaped my life without me realising."

"In what sense?"

"Back then I did not know the details of my father's occupation, only that he was a scientist and had an assistant he referred to as 'the surrogate.' My mother refused to talk about it, which only added to the mystery and allure. Sometimes I would sneak down to his laboratory in the cellar when he was away, an Aladdin's cave of treasures, which inspired me to also become a scientist.

"I was fortunate to grow up in an age when the laws regarding education were changing. It was over ten years ago now, and women were able to take degrees at the University of London for the first time. I was so happy, studying the sciences in such a learned environment, engaged to be married to Edward whom I loved dearly. I considered myself blessed, believing that bad things happened only to other people. Somewhat conceitedly, I regarded my life almost as a public exhibit, like some beautiful tapestry to be admired by all, with each day weaving a perfect new scene.

"But then the scandal broke. The newspapers vilified my father, branding him a 'necromancer,' whilst his peers dismissed him as a crank dabbling in the black arts. Edward broke off our engagement as a result of such public slurs, fellow students shunned me, and tutors issued poor marks as though I were responsible for my father's theories. The tapestry unravelled, and rewove into something grotesque, depicting images of horror. And, like the doctor, my pain was hung out for all to see."

She stood, wandered over to the door, and looked back with an unbearably sad expression. "I hope the noises are not too disturbing for you. Please try and get some sleep. We have a busy day tomorrow."

After breakfast, she asked the doctor to accompany us to the town gaol. He was reluctant, saying that he felt unwell, but she reminded him of the agreement yesterday.

"Being both a stranger and a woman here," she said, "I need you to gain access to places that might otherwise be barred to me."

She looked beautiful and fresh despite the late night. I imagined she had selected her clothing for comfort and ease of movement: tweed Tartar-style cycling trousers and a matching jacket. A common enough lady's sporting outfit in the London parks, but not, I reasoned, in an industrial backwater such as this. Still, probably better to be fashionably conspicuous than hampered by billowing skirts.

The gaol was within walking distance but the doctor's pace was slow. It was positioned at the highest point in the town and, as I looked back, a view unfolded of bleak terraces, and farther off the grey scar of the quarry against otherwise unspoiled green hills. On arrival, the doctor spoke to the gaoler, a muscular fellow called Pugh.

"Mr. Crane said I'm not supposed to let no one in there, see," said Pugh. His bewildered manner and thick-boned jaw suggested a person of limited intelligence.

"Come on, man!" barked the doctor. "We're here on official medical business."

This seemed to do the trick. Pugh collected his keys and beckoned us to follow. The gaol was a typical provincial establishment; damp stone walls, a single passage leading to just four tiny cells, smelling of mould and faintly of human waste. Pugh showed us the boy's cell then left us to it, slamming the iron door behind.

Tobias Jones lay on a bunk with his knees tucked in his chest. His pale blue eyes were open but did not follow our progress into the cramped space. I saw that he and the striking young man in the photograph on the doctor's mantelpiece were one and the same. With those blond curls, pale clear skin, and melancholic blue eyes, I imagined he had broken the hearts of more than a few local girls. Some faint bruising showed on the side of his face, and there was a partially healed cut above his eyebrow. Miss Appleby began with several straightforward questions. The boy, however, was unresponsive.

"What happened to Charlotte?" she asked. At the mention of the girl, his eyes looked into hers yet still he said nothing. "Do you want to hang?" She thrust a pad and pencil at him. "If you cannot speak then write the answers down." The boy ignored this and buried his head in his arms. From beneath his pillow he had taken a red woollen hat and grasped it close. "We're wasting our time here," she said.

Dr. Mortlock was looking at the boy, on the verge of tears it seemed. "Would you both mind if I spent a moment alone with him?"

I called Pugh. After he let us out, we followed him to the dark recess by the gaol's entrance where he wiled away the hours. He stared rudely at Miss Appleby, as though he had never seen a lady before.

"What's the story there, Pugh?" she asked.

"Uh?"

"With the boy, what happened?"

His dull features grew animated. "Done her with his 'ands like . . . in . . ."

"His hands? Are you sure?"

"Round her neck, aye . . ." He made out he was throttling himself. ". . . *tchsss* . . .like that, see."

I remembered what the doctor had said yesterday about a ligature.

"How do you know it wasn't a belt or a cord?" asked Miss Appleby, clearly thinking along the same lines.

"Mr. Crane said."

"And how would he know?"

"He found 'em up there." Pugh's grin revealed misshapen yellow teeth. "He'll swing for squeezing that sweet kitten. And I'll be on duty, see. Can't wait!"

Looking down now, he seemed to have noticed her shapely legs in fashionable cycling trousers for the first time. He licked his lips and chuckled. "Them's a pair of fancy pants you got on." His hand reached out and squeezed her tweed covered thigh.

Before I was able to intervene, she struck him hard across the face. He cowered, as though expecting another blow.

"Pugh, do you like money?" she said.

"I like to spend it, aye."

"Then how would you feel about earning a good sum?"

◄०►

Afterwards I made notes in my room at the house, thinking about what was at stake here. It was much the same throughout the country. Like Pugh, certain folk delighted at the prospect of another's execution, yet those with an ounce of compassion were naturally repulsed. After an outrage that shocked the public, such as a particularly gruesome murder, society demanded that somebody pay the price. This pressured the police, who were then often too quick to deliver a suspect. It did not matter if the person might be innocent, so long as an example was set. Miss Appleby, I suspected, had a particular aversion to this barbaric toss of a coin, and the noose itself, enhanced by personal experience, which drove her to pursue her work so diligently.

I unfolded the yellowed newspaper cuttings and read them again, except this time from a more personal perspective now that I was acquainted with one of those involved. Miss Appleby had returned home from university one evening to discover a mob hanging her father from the tree overlooking her bedroom window. When she tried intervening, some men held her back, and when she screamed, she was punched in the face. A gang of shrieking women insisted she accompany her father on the tree, and for a wavering moment it almost went that way. She was unable to look, a witness said, so one of the men, with a gleeful expression, gripped her chin and wrenched her face towards her father kicking and squirming. The correspondent, who in a previous article had virtually incited the mob, was this time sympathetic. He called for those responsible to face the noose, which of course they did.

The servant knocked the door and announced that lunch was about to be served.

The meeting with the boy had clearly upset the doctor. We ate watery pigeon soup in the dining room, in silence except for the *tick-tock* of the grandfather clock and a crude slurping as the doctor's spoon met his lips. After a time, Miss Appleby looked him in the eye and said, "Yesterday I mentioned certain terms. On the basis of those terms I agreed to help. And yet you have already broken them, Doctor."

He seemed offended. "That's not true. I feel I must protest here."

"You have not been honest with me."

"In what sense?"

"Why didn't you tell me Tobias is your son?"

He turned his head, looking ashamed. "Is it really that obvious?"

"Your manner with him earlier was paternal, certain physical characteristics are similar, and there is a photograph of him on your mantelpiece."

"Ah, I grow complacent. Sometimes I forget to put it in the drawer. In truth, since my wife died, I'm past caring. Let them think what they like!" He turned defiant for a moment before reverting to the more familiar despondency. "I had a very brief affair with Tobias's mother, just a single occasion where temptation got the better of us. She fell pregnant. Naturally I supported her financially in secret. And we both did a thorough job of hiding it from our respective spouses. Her husband always believed Tobias to be his, and my wife never suspected. She was not able to bear us children. Consequently, over the years, I have felt a growing yet distant affection for the boy. It would break my heart to see him hang. Also, as the presiding physician, I would be expected to examine him afterwards to confirm his passing." He wiped a tear from his cheek with a handkerchief. "I feel that is beyond me."

"What about family? Has he anyone else, any brothers and sisters that may help?"

"His mother died of fever several years ago, his father in a quarry accident. There is an older half-sister. She teaches at the school here. But I fear she is too afraid to speak out and defend him. Crane's donations keep the school running. I suspect he has approached her in private."

She brushed her lips with a napkin. "Then I shall pay her a visit too."

→o→

The high ceiling with exposed beams rendered the schoolroom only marginally less cold than outside. As I closed the door, making a great racket, the children turned and stared. A schoolmistress approached along the aisle, which divided the desks in two sections, her heels echoing over the woodblock floor.

"Get on with your work!"

With her plain, stern features, and hair stretched above her scalp in a stiff bun, there was little resemblance to her handsome half-brother. The doctor spoke almost in a whisper. "I'm sorry for the sudden intrusion. Miss Appleby here wishes to talk to you about Tobias."

"What? Have you lost all sense, Doctor?"

She peered around as if there might be spies among the pupils. Breathing fiercely through her nose, she ordered the doctor to take the class for a moment then led Miss Appleby and me into a windowless storeroom. The smells of boxed chalk, new pencils, water-based paints, and fresh paper reminded me of school as a little boy. Also, the schoolmistress's strict manner prompted a peculiar echo of crimeless guilt, as if we were about to be scolded for our existence alone.

"Who are you?"

Miss Appleby introduced us and said that her business was fighting injustice.

"Injustice?" The schoolmistress spoke as if the word were a profanity. "What can *you* do?"

"I don't know. Perhaps nothing. But anything is worth a try, wouldn't you say?"

"Poking your nose in looking for trouble is bad for everybody."

"I'm not seeking trouble, madam, merely the truth."

"The truth is there is no justice in this life. Tobias is doomed. We just have to accept that and get on with things."

"But if the real murderer is at large still, and we do nothing and he acts again, how could we live with that on our conscience?"

"Don't lecture me about moral duty! You should try spending a lifetime in this town first."

"What if your brother is innocent?"

"Of *course* he is innocent."

"Then who murdered Charlotte Crane?"

"Her father, naturally."

"How can you be certain?"

"Call it instinct, or a good judge of character, whatever you like. Miss Appleby, have you ever been in love?"

She swallowed uncomfortably. "Once, yes."

"Then you understand it would be impossible for Tobias to kill Charlotte. They were sweethearts. It carried on for months in secret but the silly girl read too many novels, *Wuthering Heights* in particular. She was dazzled by romantic notions and grew complacent, visiting him at the quarry for all the men to see. They were planning to marry, to run away together. Crane found out, followed her up there and, after beating Tobias to within an inch of his life, strangled his own daughter. You see, for her to marry a boy of lower class would have brought shame on the Crane family. Such a proud, cruel man, her death was simply about honour over public disgrace."

◦

The bedroom was very dark and cold as I stepped barefoot across the floorboards. I lit the lamp then dressed, my shadow jerking in the half-light. When ready, I knocked on Miss Appleby's door.

She shovelled coal in the grate, ignited twists of newspaper, then dragged the strongbox nearer the warmth. "Each time I prepare, I am reminded of that darkest period of my life, and the moment I first laid eyes on the surrogate. I shall never forget. In that sense, I feel I should warn you."

"Oh?"

"The experience you are about to witness is most distressing."

"Then why do it? What made you want to continue your father's work? I'm interested to know what motivates you."

She seemed annoyed by my questions. "Duty, Mr. Creswell, Papa's final wishes. Can you understand that?"

"To some degree I suppose, but not if—"

"He was lying in his casket in the living room, only hours after he was lynched. The family solicitor paid us a visit. He handed me bundles of papers and a modified oak strongbox. There were detailed instructions for the apparatus, and a recipe for the feed. The final instruction I found most difficult to undertake. But I managed to bring him back for half a minute."

"You brought your father *back*?"

She nodded, tearful now. "He groaned pitifully, but was unable to speak. I wept, tried reassuring him that what had happened wasn't his fault. I didn't know it then, Mr. Creswell, but the newer the corpse means the less work for the surrogate. The surrogate is merely a means to recall rather than a tool for sustaining the process. A returnee to a *fresh* body attempts instinctively to use their own damaged organs and not the surrogate's, their larynx instead of the brass horn. Yet, despite my ignorance at that time, it was obvious Papa's vocal tract had been crushed by the rope. Still, his lips kept puckering until finally I understood what he was trying to communicate and placed a pen in his cold fingers. Naturally it was not the neatest handwriting, but I could make out the words he scrawled."

"Which were?"

"*Save them*, Mr. Creswell. My father implored me to save them. And you ask what motivates me?"

—◦—

Soon after we were outside in the freezing night air. A growing dread was pressing on my heart, and I soon grew fatigued from carrying the strongbox along the dark streets to the chapel. On arrival, I placed it on a patch of grass and leaned against the cold wall, grateful for the rest, yet feeling that I had no control over what I was venturing into. The chapel, a drab building with a single domed window at the front, stood on a sharp gradient like everything else in that town. A hazy sliver of moon cast little light, and my eyes strained to see the silhouetted figure trudging slowly up the hill towards us, past the terraces then the workingmen's club on the corner.

"I fail to see why you employed his services," the doctor said to Miss Appleby, watching the lumbering figure also. "He cannot be trusted."

"I'm not cut out for manual labour and neither are you and Mr. Creswell by the look of it. Sometimes one has to take risks."

Pugh complained about the late hour and the cold, but when the doctor handed over several pound notes, he quieted. We entered through black gates then trod over frosty turf around the headstones until we arrived at the Crane family plot, conspicuous by the pale imposing edifices looming in the darkness. One statue was clean and new, a winged angel sculpted from white marble. Miss Appleby laid the wreaths to one side then Pugh went to work hacking at the icy crust with the spade edge.

We waited in silence; the only sounds Pugh's laboured breathing, the scrape of the spade and the wind rushing through the spindly trees that bordered the perimeter. Fortunately, beneath the hard surface, the soil was softer otherwise it might have taken the gaoler half the night to complete his trench. When his tool struck hollow wood, Miss Appleby jumped down to help lift the casket lid. Pugh crossed himself as the stink wafted up. I stood at the edge of the trench. It was too dark to see anything. Miss Appleby lit an oil lamp and placed it low inside to conceal the glow. Now I was able to see Charlotte's condition. The skin had begun to bloat, ripening to dark coppery tones, a grotesque contrast to the pretty white bonnet and the frock with bows and frills.

"I'm not confident," Miss Appleby muttered to me. "The longer a corpse is laid to rest the harder it is to recall, and the more painful for those brought back if successful. It also means the surrogate will have to work hard, dangerously so, which worries me."

Quickly, she unpacked the box, unravelled wires and tubes and connected them to the cadaver, including a copper disc which she tucked inside the dress's buttons and placed against the heart. She yanked a brass lever. A soft beating sounded, to which Charlotte's body began to gently spasm in rhythm. Pugh, standing in the trench still, muttered a prayer as milky serum sluiced through the catheters and into Charlotte's decayed circulatory system.

"An electrical battery cell powers the false heartbeat," Miss Appleby said. "Anti-coagulants thin the clogged routes."

"Is that what brings her back?" I asked.

"No. It's merely a deception designed to fool her into thinking her body is healthy again. It helps filter unwanted *guests*, shall we say. She will re-enter. Then, after realising her body is useless, she will hopefully answer the surrogate's call and join him in his body."

Pugh cried out. He must have noticed the surrogate nestled amongst the apparatus's rods, wires, and glassware.

"Calm yourself, man," she told him. "If the sight offends, then avert your eyes."

Once again, like last night, I heard the far-off murmuring of voices through the horn. Charlotte's mouth jerked wide open, remaining fixed that way as though an invisible dental clamp were holding it in place. A woeful groan emitted from her, suggesting extreme discomfort. As this cattle-like bellow grew in volume, Pugh cowered, terrified.

"Can't you stop that?" asked the doctor. "Somebody is sure to hear. The entire town will awaken."

"It's too late now," she said. "We must wait for her to pass to the surrogate. At the moment she is confused, struggling inside her own wasted body. Don't worry. This is normal."

"Normal? I disagree most strongly, madam. You have obviously developed immunity to this vile sacrilege. If I had only known . . ."

"If you remember, Doctor, I offered sufficient warning. I must remind you of our agreement."

The horn made a gurgling sound as the groaning from the corpse stopped finally. Charlotte's dark lips remained frozen open, however.

"*Such pain,*" a voice mumbled through the horn.

"Excellent," Miss Appleby said cheerily. "We are successful."

The voice was hoarse and distant, yet also vaguely feminine. "*Why . . . why do this? It hurt so. Let me raast.*"

"I apologise for your distress, Charlotte," Miss Appleby said. "But we need to know what happened to you. Tobias is to hang for your murder."

"*Tob . . . aah? Baah?*"

"Yes, your beloved."

"*Tobah . . . not . . .*"

"What's that?"

"*Wheel . . . wheel, can't fuggus . . . oh the agony . . . not meant to appen . . .*"

"What's not meant to happen, Charlotte?"

"*Stop it, Tobah! Stop it, I beg you . . . No! Release me!*" A piercing shriek, and then Charlotte's stiff arm shot out and her blackened hand locked onto Pugh's wrist.

The gaoler screeched and struggled but the grip would not relax. "Let go of me, devil! Mam . . . Mammy, help me!"

Miss Appleby berated him. "Quiet, Pugh! Have you no feelings? The poor girl merely seeks comfort." She asked Charlotte, "Is Tobias angry, my dear? Is he hurting you?"

An odd whimpering occurred that might have been laughter, before a deeper voice interjected. "*Yes, he throttled me alright, sent me to Hell where all us whores belong! He'll be joining us soon. He deserves it!*"

"Another is present," Miss Appleby said, pushing the lever quickly and yanking the wires free. Serum spurted from the tubes.

"Another?" asked the doctor.

"A malign presence followed her through. It's happened before. Dangerous for the surrogate; therefore, I must shut the procedure down."

Pugh had finally managed to prise away Charlotte's dead fingers. He crawled from the trench and ran into the darkness, blubbering for his mother.

"That's done it," said the doctor, shaking visibly. "I never expected him to keep his mouth shut. What about refilling this grave? I'm afraid I'm not fit enough to shovel dirt."

"I have no desire to either," Miss Appleby said. "Let it be. It's too late now anyway."

"Have you no shame? We cannot abandon it in this condition!"

"Doubtless the gravedigger will put it right. Listen, when we return to the house, I want you to arrange for my things to be taken to the station, including this box here. Pay a guard to ensure nobody touches it. Mr. Creswell and I will need to borrow a horse each. We might require a hasty departure. Come, we haven't much time."

The doctor looked crestfallen. "Time for what? It's clear my son is guilty. You heard what the dead girl said. Justice must be served. Tobias shall hang."

◄•►

As dawn broke, mist covered the icy bridlepath. I followed her up the hill at a measured canter, my face wet and cold from the dew that brushed off the overhanging foliage. We emerged in a clearing, greeted by a hazy view of great unnatural steps carved in the surrounding cliffs.

"Miss Appleby, what exactly are we doing here?"

"Keep up, Mr. Creswell!"

I pursued her up a steep incline until we reached a settlement of stone buildings where blocks were obviously split with hammers and chisels. We tethered the horses to an iron container crammed with slate panels then continued on foot. The area was deserted, though I imagined men would be arriving soon to begin their shift. Below, a steep gravelled slope with rail tracks led far down into the foggy undergrowth. Rusted wagons sat on these tracks, attached to thick cables that coiled around an enormous drum nearby. From a concealed point beyond the drum, I heard the flow of water.

"Over here," she said, striding over the crest.

The embankment was thick with ferns and trees, an odd contrast to the otherwise grey wasteland. I pictured the young lovers meeting here, out of sight of the men, far from the prying eyes of the townsfolk, yet near enough for Tobias to return to work if called. Miss Appleby stepped across the narrow footbridge spanning the stream; the dirty water a shallow trickle, but when released from the pond's dam, I imagined the flow would be substantial. Beside her was the giant waterwheel that powered the drum, a great wooden structure with blades and paddles and riveted iron plates, though motionless now. She pointed at something.

"Do you see that?"

She climbed onto the bridge's handrail, stretched out a leg, and clambered onto one of the paddles.

"Take care, Miss Appleby."

She edged around the paddle, shuffled her feet along a blade, until she neared the hub. Reaching down, she untangled something and stuffed it in her jacket pocket.

A picture began to emerge. As a correspondent, I had developed a skill for recalling conversations verbatim and could replay these in my mind like an actor might a memorised script. This, along with keen instincts, allowed me to view objectively, with empathy or detachment, whatever suited the occasion. Sometimes what appeared perplexing on the surface was really quite a simple affair beneath the complex and emotive behaviour of those closely involved.

The wheel . . . Stop it, Tobias! Stop it, I beg you . . .

Miss Appleby showed me what she had found. It was a sodden blackish colour but when she squeezed the filthy water out its original scarlet showed. The wool had unravelled at one end where it had been cut, probably with a knife.

"Do you see, Mr. Creswell?"

I nodded. "I remember Tobias hugging the shorter end of that scarf in his cell. I thought it was a hat at the time."

"I can visualise them walking here holding hands," she said dreamily, "or perhaps they were warned that Crane had arrived and were making a hurried escape. A gust of wind, the wheel turning, a freak occurrence . . ."

"The constables have been summoned. It's too late for you now."

I turned to see an athletic man with wavy hair and greying sideboards. He stood very straight, slapping a stag horn crop rhythmically in the palm of his hand. "The desecration of hallowed ground and defiling a body are serious offences," he continued. "I imagine you will be imprisoned for a long time."

"That may be so, Mr. Crane," she said. "But it won't bring her back. And neither will the hanging of an innocent boy."

"He had no right to . . . Charlotte was too good for him. Quite simply, if she hadn't been with him, she wouldn't have perished. For him the stakes were high. He knew that. He gambled. There is always a price to pay. It is the nature of the world. Somebody has to pay—blood or coin. I demand to be compensated."

"One cannot be compensated for bad luck, for an act of God. That is an absurd notion."

"Considering what you do, Miss Appleby, you are in no position to judge what is proper. You are a morally repugnant individual, just like your infamous father, who got exactly as he deserved."

"My father cared about people. And not just those close to him, or those of his social class. You, who would permit a grieving boy to die simply to satisfy your rage against God or fate, could never understand that."

"Watch your tongue."

Her tone softened. "They say it is easier to blame, to revert to anger rather than accept the agony of grief. I don't condemn you for that, sir. You lost a daughter. I only ask . . ."

He strode forward. "I am required to contain you before the constables arrive. If you struggle, I'll thrash you."

She ducked under his outstretched arm and ran. I blocked his route, but his fist struck me a thudding blow on the point of my jaw. When I came to, I was lying on the gritty earth, my head aching and my vision blurred. There was no sign of them, but I heard screaming from behind the drum. I stood groggily and staggered up the slope.

He was straddling her, his fingers clamped around her throat, his expression sheer madness now. An image of her father on the tree and the gleefully insane mob came to me. I was not confident of overpowering him, but knew I had no choice but to try. Before I reached them, however, Miss Appleby's hand closed around a slate shard. She swung this at his head. He gasped: a strange sound, like a cough almost. Tumbling off her, he pressed his hand to his forehead, blood seeping through his fingers, which he then attempted to wipe from his eyes with a sleeve.

We left him sitting there muttering to himself then took the doctor's horses and rode fast down the hill. At the house, the servant informed us that the doctor had been incarcerated in the gaol for his role in the graveyard affair. Miss Appleby wrote a brief account of her discoveries and handed this, along with the scarf as evidence, to the servant. We borrowed the horses once again and galloped for the station.

In an office adjoining the waiting room, she was visibly relieved to see the strongbox safe and unmolested.

Still, we did not relax until the luggage was loaded on the train and we were able to stare out of the carriage window at the retreating station.

"Congratulations," I said smiling. "It looks like you have saved a life."

She shook her head. "Crane is a difficult opponent, and there is still much work to be done to free Tobias. Nothing is certain. Those who deserve to stand on the gallows—the Cranes of this world, the industrialists, the slave merchants and warmongers—never do. But sometimes it's possible to thwart their perverse idea of justice. I have contributed all I can. I just hope the doctor is strong enough to see it through. And there is your article, Mr. Creswell. I trust that you will do all in your power."

"Of course. I'll do my best."

Instinctively, I reached across and clasped her hands. For a moment, she seemed to respond to my excitable display of affection. I looked into her eyes and saw a yearning there. But only for a second or two. Quickly, almost as an afterthought, she pulled her hands free and turned to face the window. Her cheeks were flushed, her breathing irregular.

⟶

My editor liked the headline—INNOCENT BOY TO HANG!—but his expression changed the more he read.

"Absurd, Creswell! Do you honestly expect anyone to believe this mumbo-jumbo? Damn it, man, this is a serious newspaper!"

Needless to say, he did not proceed with the story. I did manage to place it, however, except the magazine was somewhat sensational, and my article was sandwiched between two tales of supernatural fiction. Miss Appleby was not pleased, and she refused to talk to me afterwards. I discovered later that Dr. Mortlock had been released without charge after spending only a day in gaol, courtesy of Mr. Crane. The boy Tobias was less fortunate. He was hanged two weeks later.

I sent a telegram to the doctor offering my condolences. I also wrote to Miss Appleby saying that she should be proud of what she had done, and that I would like to see her again because I had grown very fond of her.

She did not reply.

DOWN TO A SUNLESS SEA

NEIL GAIMAN

The Thames is a filthy beast: it winds through London like a snake or a sea serpent. All the rivers flow into it, the Fleet and the Tyburn and the Neckinger, carrying all the filth and scum and waste, the bodies of cats and dogs and the bones of sheep and pigs down into the brown water of the Thames, which carries them east into the estuary and from there into the North Sea and oblivion.

It is raining in London. The rain washes the dirt into the gutters, and it swells streams into rivers, rivers into powerful things. The rain is a noisy thing, splashing and pattering and rattling the rooftops. If it is clean water as it falls from the skies, it only needs to touch London to become dirt, to stir dust and make it mud.

Nobody drinks it, neither the rain water nor the river water. They make jokes about Thames water killing you instantly, and it is not true. There are mudlarks who will dive deep for thrown pennies then come up again, spout the river water, shiver, and hold up their coins. They do not die, of course, or not of that, although there are no mudlarks over fifteen years of age.

The woman does not appear to care about the rain.

She walks the Rotherhithe docks, as she has done for years, for decades: nobody knows how many years, because nobody cares. She walks the docks, or she stares out to sea. She examines the ships, as they bob at anchor. She must do something, to keep body and soul from dissolving their partnership, but none of the folk of the dock have the foggiest idea what this could be.

You take refuge from the deluge beneath a canvas awning put up by a sailmaker. You believe yourself to be alone under there, at first, for she is statue-still and staring out across the water, even though there is nothing to be seen through the curtain of rain. The far side of the Thames has vanished.

And then she sees you. She sees you and she begins to talk, not to you, oh no, but to the grey water that falls from the grey sky into the grey river. She says, "My son wanted to be a sailor," and you do not know what to reply or how to reply. You would have to shout to make yourself heard over the roar of the rain, but she talks, and you listen. You discover yourself craning and straining to catch her words.

"My son wanted to be a sailor.

"I told him not to go to sea. I'm your mother, I said. The sea won't love you like I love you, she's cruel. But he said, Oh Mother, I need to see the world. I need to see the sun rise in the tropics, and watch the Northern Lights dance in the Arctic sky, and most of all I need to make my fortune and then, when it's made, I will come back to you and build you a house, and you will have servants, and we will dance, mother, oh how we will dance . . .

"And what would I do in a fancy house? I told him. You're a fool with your fine talk. I told him of his father, who never came back from the sea—some said he was dead and lost overboard, while some swore blind they'd seen him running a whore-house in Amsterdam.

"It's all the same. The sea took him.

"When he was twelve years old, my boy ran away, down to the docks, and he shipped on the first ship he found, to Flores in the Azores, they told me.

"There's ships of ill-omen. Bad ships. They give them a lick of paint after each disaster, and a new name, to fool the unwary.

"Sailors are superstitious. The word gets around. This ship was run aground by its captain, on orders of the owners, to defraud the insurers; and then, all mended and as good as new, it gets taken by pirates; and then it takes shipment of blankets and becomes a plague ship crewed by the dead, and only three men bring it into port in Harwich . . .

"My son had shipped on a stormcrow ship. It was on the homeward leg of the journey, with him bringing me his wages—for he was too young to have spent them on women and on grog, like his father—that the storm hit.

"He was the smallest one in the lifeboat.

"They said they drew lots fairly, but I do not believe it. He was smaller than them. After eight days adrift in the boat, they were so hungry. And if they did draw lots, they cheated.

"They gnawed his bones clean, one by one, and they gave them to his new mother, the sea. She shed no tears and took them without a word. She's cruel.

"Some nights I wish he had not told me the truth. He could have lied.

"They gave my boy's bones to the sea, but the ship's mate—who had known my husband, and known me too, better than my husband thought he did, if truth were told—he kept a bone, as a keepsake.

"When they got back to land, all of them swearing my boy was lost in the storm that sank the ship, he came in the night, and he told me the truth of it, and he gave me the bone, for the love there had once been between us.

"I said, you've done a bad thing, Jack. That was your son that you've eaten.

"The sea took him too, that night. He walked into her, with his pockets filled with stones, and he kept walking. He'd never learned to swim.

"And I put the bone on a chain to remember them both by, late at night, when the wind crashes the ocean waves and tumbles them on to the sand, when the wind howls around the houses like a baby crying."

The rain is easing, and you think she is done, but now, for the first time, she looks at you, and appears to be about to say something. She has pulled something from around her neck, and now she is reaching it out to you.

"Here," she says. Her eyes, when they meet yours, are as brown as the Thames. "Would you like to touch it?"

You want to pull it from her neck, to toss it into the river for the mudlarks to find or to lose. But instead you stumble out from under the canvas awning, and the water of the rain runs down your face like someone else's tears.

JAWS OF SATURN

LAIRD BARRON

I.

"The other night I dreamt about this lowlife I used to screw," Carol said. She and Franco were sitting in the lounge of the Broadsword Hotel, a monument to the Roaring Twenties situated on the west side of Olympia. Most of its tenants were economically strapped or on the downhill slide toward decrepitude, not unlike the once grand dame herself. Carol lived on the sixth floor in a single bedroom flat with cracks running through the plaster and a rusty radiator that groaned and ticked like it might explode and turn the apartment into a flaming wreck. "I mean, yeah, I hooked up with plenty of losers before I met you. Marvin was scary. And ugly as three kinds of sin. He busted kneecaps for a living. Some living."

Franco flipped open his lighter and set fire to a cigarette. He dropped the lighter into the pocket of his blazer. He took a drag and exhaled. Franco did not live in The Broadsword. Happily, he lived across town in a smaller, modern apartment building where the elevators worked and the central heating didn't rely on a coal-fed furnace. He decided not to remind her that he too damaged people on occasion, albeit only in defense of his employer. Franco didn't look like muscle—short and trim, his hair was professionally styled and his clothes were tailored. His face was soft and unscarred. He didn't have scars because he'd always been better with his guns and knives than his enemies were with theirs. Franco said, "Marvin Cortez? Oh, yeah. My boss was friends with him. If this goon scared you so much, why'd you stick around?"

"I dunno, Frankie. 'Cause it turned me on for a while, I guess. Who the hell knows why I do anything?" She pushed around her glass of slushed ice cubes and vodka so it caught the light coming through the window and multiplied it on the tablecloth. This was late afternoon. The light was heavy and reddish orange.

"Okay. What happened in the dream?"

"Nothing, really."

"Huh."

"Huh, what?"

"Dreams are messages from the subconscious. They're full of symbols."

"You get a shrink degree I don't know about?"

"No, my sister worked as a research assistant in a clinic. Where were you?"

"In bed. The whole bed was on a mountain, or something. Marvin stood at the foot of the bed and there was a drop off. The wind blew his hair around, but it didn't touch me. I was pretty scared of the cliff, though."

"Why?"

"My bed was practically teetering on the edge, dumbbell."

"This Marvin, guy. Did he do anything?"

"He stared at me—and he was too big. Granted, Marvo really was a hulking dude, Ron Perlman big and ugly, but this was extreme, and I got the impression he would've turned into a giant if the dream had lasted longer. His expression weirded me out. I realized it wasn't really him. Looked like him, except not. More like a mask and it changed as I watched. He was turning into someone else entirely and I woke up before it completely happened."

Franco nodded and tapped his cigarette on the edge of the ashtray. "Clearly you've got feelings for this palooka."

"Don't be so jealous. He skipped on me. Haven't heard from the jerk in years. Weirdest part about the dream is when I opened my eyes, the bedroom was pitch black. Except . . . the closet door opened a bit and this creepy red light came through the crack. Damndest thing. I'm still half zonked, so it's all unreal at first. Then I started to freak. I mean, there's nothing in the closet to make a red glow, and the light itself made my hairs prickle. Something was really, really wrong. Then the door clicked shut and the room went dark again. I'd drunk *waaay* too many margaritas earlier, so I fell asleep."

"You never woke up in the first place," he said. "Dream within a dream. The red light was your alarm clock. Nothing mysterious or creepy about that."

Carol gave him a look. She wore oversized sunglasses that hid her eyes, but the point was clear. She snapped her fingers until a waiter came over. She ordered a rum and coke and made him take the vodka away. "Thing is, this got me thinking. I realize I've been having these dreams all week. I just keep forgetting."

"Your boyfriend in all of them?" Franco tried not to sound petulant. His vodka was down to the rocks and he hadn't asked the waiter for another.

"Not only him. Lots of other people. My mom and dad. A girlfriend from high school that got killed in a crash. My grandparents. Everybody guest starring in my dreams is dead. Except for Marvo—and hell, for all I know, he bit the dust. He who lives by the sword and all that."

"This is true," Franco said, thinking of the time a guy swung a machete at his head and missed.

Carol glanced at her watch. She picked up her prim little handbag. "Let's go fuck. Karla's doing my hair later."

II.

He stripped her in a half-dozen expert movements and had her crossways on the low, narrow bed, a pillow under her hips because he wanted to work her over with a vengeance. His blood boiled after their conversation regarding her old goon boyfriend. She was voluptuous as a '50s pin-up and white as milk and her body amazed him. He held her hips and pushed toward climax while she cried out, shoulders and head suspended off the mattress, her fingers twisted in the sheets. He drove, and the bed moved an inch or two with each thrust, adding grooves to the warped and stained floorboards. Then, he came, crashing the bed with enough force to surely jolt the lights in the lower apartment. She swung herself upright and her expression was that of an ecstatic. He met her eyes in the gloom and his brain became jelly; it felt as if it might drain through his nose, suctioned by some force at once ancient and familiar and beyond his comprehension. The iris of her left eye was oblong, out of plumb. It seemed to elongate and slide around like the deformed bubbles in a lava lamp, and for several seconds every piece of furniture, the apartment walls, its doors and fixtures, were distorted, undulating in a way that made him sick in the stomach. Then it passed and he flopped on his back, spent and afraid.

Carol climbed atop him and kissed his mouth. Her breath was hot. Her lips moved wet and swollen against his, "Well, Jesus. Aren't you a voyeuristic sonofabitch." She reached down and her petite fist partially encircled him. She slowly put him back inside her and had her way, mouth against his ear now. He closed his eyes and the vertigo subsided, and he lay in a semi stupor while his body reacted.

When it finally ended, Carol lighted two cigarettes. She gave him one and then dialed her friend the hairdresser and cancelled her appointment. She slurred like she did after the fifth or sixth cocktail.

Franco smoked his cigarette without enjoying it, his mind ticking with the possibilities of what he'd witnessed. She curled against him, her nails digging into the muscles of his chest.

He said, "I think something odd is going on with you."

"Mmm? I feel pretty damned fine."

"Have you been taking drugs? You doing X?"

"Are you trying to piss me off?" She smiled and blew smoke at him.

"I'm trying to decide what I think. You're acting different." He didn't know what to say about her bizarre iris and figured keeping his mouth shut was the best course for the moment.

"Hmm. I've been seeing a hypnotist. Trying to break this smoking habit."

"Uh, did you happen to think that might be the reason you've had lousy dreams lately? Go screwing around in your brain and God knows what'll happen."

"Hypnotism is harmless. All that stuff about them making you cluck like a chicken or do stupid tricks is bullshit. He puts me in a light trance. I'm aware of everything the whole time."

Franco rubbed the vein pulsing in his temple. "Who's this hypnotist?"

"Phil Wary. An old dude. Lives upstairs. He was a magician back in the 1970s."

"This is great."

"It's so-so. I paid him three hundred bucks. I've cut back to half a pack a day, but sheesh, it could be better. That's what I'm saying—sure as shit isn't a cure for cancer."

"Okay," he said. He didn't think anything was okay, and in fact had already made up his mind to pay Phil Wary a visit and set the coot straight. Anybody messing with Franco's girl was in peril of falling from a rooftop.

Franco dreamed of standing in a hallway. He was naked and smelled of sex and bitter perfume. The hallway was dark except at the far end where a pair of brassy elevator doors shone, illuminated by an unseen source. He walked toward the doors and they slid apart. He entered the elevator. It was tight and dim. The doors shut. A panel of glowing buttons floated in the sudden darkness. He pressed the L and waited. The elevator moved, silent and frictionless, and with a sense of tremendous speed and he screamed as his body became weightless and his toes drifted several inches from the floor. He was trapped in a coffin-shaped capsule rocketing into zero g orbit. The control panel flickered and its numerals blackened and popped and died. The overhead strip emitted a hideous red light that caused his skin to smoke and char where it touched. The light dripped like oil, like acid dissolving him.

When the doors opened, he stumbled into the empty lobby of The Broadsword Hotel. Yet the chamber was far too vast, and in the distance one of the walls had collapsed. It was cold, and the gloom thick with a sense of ruin. Furniture lay in broken heaps, and tiles of the vast marble floor were smashed, pieces scattered, and everywhere, curtains and streamers of cobwebs and dust. The tooth of the moon shone through the skylight dome. Carol stood hipshot in its sickly beam. She too was naked except for a silvery necklace, and panties that gleamed white against her delectable buttocks. Her figure was unutterably erotic in its slickness and ripe strength and quivering vulnerability, a Frazetta heroine made flesh. Her head craned toward one of the support columns, arm raised in a defensive gesture. She was a voluptuous conceptualization of Fay Wray transported to some occult dimension, gaping at an off-screen terror.

A shadow moved across the floor and obliterated Carol's paralyzed figure. It stretched unto colossal dimensions until its clawed edge over-lapped Franco's feet and he raced into the elevator that was no longer an elevator, but an endless tunnel, or a throat.

III.

Franco lay in bed alone until noon. This was his first vacation in two years from his millionaire charge, Jacob Wilson. Wilson had jetted off to Paris for the week with his girlfriend of the moment and Leonard and Vernon, the senior bodyguards.

He didn't have any fear of confined spaces, but today the elevator ride was harrowing. He loosened his tie to alleviate a feeling of suffocation. A middle-aged woman in an enveloping dress crowded him and he sweated and squeezed the bridge of his nose and breathed shallowly until the lift thudded to a halt and squealed open a full ten seconds later.

Despite his rather mundane and admittedly coarse occupation, Franco enjoyed a good, thick book and was enamored of classical architecture. The hotel had become a hobby. Almost a century old, and enormous, its caretakers kept alive certain elements and traditions not often present in its modern counterparts. There were at least two sub levels, one of which hosted a barbershop, international newspaper kiosk, cigar shop, and a gentleman's club called The Red Room, this latter held over from speakeasy days. On the ground floor was the lounge, the Oak & Shield restaurant, a largely defunct nightclub called The Owl, and the Arden Grand Ballroom. There were galas every few months and he'd vowed to accompany Carol to one in the near future. Franco was an elegant dancer, comfortable waltzing to a big band.

He went to the lounge and sat at the end of the deserted bar farthest from the double doors and the sun streaming through the windows over-looking the hillside and Capitol Lake far below, and across the way, the Capitol Dome itself, a cracked and grimy edifice that somehow retained its grandeur despite years of neglect. He ordered a Bloody Mary, followed immediately by a double vodka. He lighted a cigarette and pressed his hand to his eyes while he smoked.

Franco had become a regular at the lounge these past months since his dalliance with Carol. The staff knew who he worked for and when he dropped a hint about his interest in resident Phil Wary, the white-suited bartender disappeared, then returned with a hotel business card, Mr. Wary's apartment and phone numbers scrawled on the reverse. Franco glanced at the card, then burned it in the ashtray as a courtesy. He left a fifty on the bar when he finally dragged himself off the stool and went in search of answers. He buzzed Mr. Wary's apartment, then he unfolded his cell and tried the phone number.

Someone picked up and breathed heavily. "What?" The accent was foreign to Franco, although it reminded him of the old Christopher Lee Dracula movies.

"Mr. Wary, hey. Could I have a few minutes of your time? I'm downstairs—"

"I heard you buzzing my intercom. I hate that buzzing. That brash, persistent noise drills straight through my eardrum. No, I think you sound like an oaf, a knuckle dragger. A second generation Italian mongrel, perhaps."

Franco made a fist with his free hand and squeezed until his knuckles cracked. "Very sorry, sir. I just need five minutes. Maybe less. You know a friend of mine. Carol—"

Mr. Wary breathed into the phone. He made an odd noise in his throat. "Then I am convinced I am not interested in your company. My business with her is not for you. Goodbye."

The line went dead. Franco stared at his cell for a several moments. He carefully folded and put it away. He cracked the knuckles of his right hand. It was a long climb to the seventh floor, but there was no chance of his risking the elevator again. He felt homicidal enough without exacerbating his dire mood with an outbreak of latent claustrophobia. By the fourth floor he'd come to regret his decision. His legs were soft from spending too many hours on his ass in limousines and holding down barstools. He'd given up weightlifting and jogging. The endless columns of booze and stacks of unfiltered cigarettes made his sporadic appearances at the gym painful.

He hesitated at Mr. Wary's door to try the knob—locked. He wiped his brow with the silk handkerchief in his breast pocket. Mr. Wary's apartment lay near the stairwell at the far end of the corridor opposite the elevator. The passages in The Broadsword Hotel were slightly wider and taller than typical of such buildings, rounded and ribbed at the peak in a classical manner. Gauzy light filled the window alcove above the stairwell. Shadows stretched long fingers across the carpet and most of the hallway remained in gloom. A fly complained in a darkened overhead light globe.

Franco tucked away the handkerchief and slipped his stiletto from its ankle sheath. He never carried a pistol when off duty. There wasn't much reason to—unlike thugs such as Carol's ex, he didn't need to moonlight as an enforcer. His time off was free and uncomplicated.

Mr. Wary hadn't engaged the deadbolt, so Franco easily jimmied the lock and pushed through the door. The apartment was cramped and hot and smelled of must and moldering paper. Centered in the living area was a leather couch, matching armchairs and a pair of ornate floor lamps, all from a bygone era. Mr. Wary owned numerous paintings of foreign pastorals, vine-choked temples and ziggurats, and men and women in peculiar dress. In a corner was an antique writing desk and above its hutch, poster advertisements of magic shows. Several were illustrations of a man in fanciful robes and bejeweled turban, presumably Mr. Wary himself, presiding over various scenes of prestidigitation that generally featured buxom assistants in low-cut blouses.

A yellow cat hissed at Franco's approach and darted behind the couch.

"So it's like this, is it?" Mr. Wary leaned against the frame of the entrance to the kitchen. Short and brutish, his silver and black hair touched the collar of his expensive white dress shirt. His craggy face was powdered white, his eyes deeply recessed so they glinted like those of a calculating animal. His eyelids were painted blue and his lips carmine. He wore baggy pants and sandals that curved up at the toe. He sneered at Franco, baring a full set of sharp, white teeth. "This wasn't wise of you."

"Hello, Phil," Franco said, bouncing the knife in his hand. He casually reached back and pulled the door closed. "As I was saying, we really need to have a discussion about Carol. You've been trying to help her quit smoking, I hear. Your methods seem unorthodox. She's acting squirrely."

"Her treatment is no concern of yours. You'd do well to depart before matters go too far."

Franco bent and sheathed his blade. He straightened and cracked his knuckles and took a couple of steps further into the room. "Yes, yes, it does in fact concern me. I don't like how she's acted lately. I think you've fucked with her head, got her hooked on dope, I dunno. But I plan to figure it out."

"Fool. Love is a poison in that regard. It robs men of their common sense, inveigles them to pursue their own damnation. If it allays your worry, I promise no drugs are involved. No coercion. A touch of chicanery, yes."

"That doesn't sound very nice."

"You're not a complete barbarian. You comprehend simple words and phrases."

Franco's smile sharpened and he moved slowly toward Mr. Wary, sliding his belt free of his pants loops as he went. "Keep talking, old man. I might enjoy this after all."

"She has a virus of the mind and it's rather transmittable, I'm afraid." Mr. Wary squinted at him. He nodded. "Ah, that's who you are. Such an interesting coincidence. I know your employer. His late, lamented Uncle Theodore as well."

"Jacob?" Franco hesitated. He doubled the tongue of his belt around his wrist and let the buckle dangle. "And, exactly how is that?"

"Olympia is a small town. On occasion we've done business. Your master has, shall we say, esoteric interests. As I am a man of esoteric talents, it's a match made in . . . well, somewhere."

"Carol says you're a washed up magician. Nice posters. You do anyplace famous? Vegas? The Paramount? Nah; you aren't any David Copperfield. You were a two bit showman. A hack." Franco itched to smack him in the mouth; should have done it already. The old man's contempt, his sneer, was disquieting and stayed Franco's hand for the moment as he reevaluated his surroundings, trying to detect the real source of his unease. "Your hands are gone, so now you hustle dumb broads for whatever's in their purses. I get you, Phil."

"Magician? *Magician?* I'm a practitioner of the black arts. Seventh among the Salamanca Seven. You understand what I mean when I speak of the black arts, don't you boy? Since you refuse to leave me in peace, would you care for a drink? Too late now, anyway. I have one every afternoon. The doctor says it's good for my heart." Mr. Wary went to a cabinet and took down a crystal decanter and a pair of copitas. He poured two generous glasses of sherry and handed one to Franco. Mr. Wary sat in an armchair. He clicked his nails on the glass and the cat emerged from hiding and sprang into his lap. "Magician? Feh, I'm a sorcerer, a warlock."

"A warlock, huh?" Franco remained standing. He tasted the sherry, then drained his copita and tossed it against the wall. The small crash and tinkle of broken glass temporarily satisfied his need to inflict pain upon his host. "There's no fucking such thing, my friend."

"That was a valuable glass. I acquired the set in Florence. It survived the Second World War." Mr. Wary's eyelids fluttered and he smiled with the corner of his mouth. "Yes, I practice mesmerism. Yes, I pulled rabbits from hats and pretended to saw nubile women in half. I am conversant in many things, sleight of hand being among these. Camouflage, boy. And amusement. One meets fascinating people in that line. However, my bread and butter, my life's work, lies in peeling back the layers of occult mysteries. I was preparing your delectable girlfriend for myself. Ripening and fattening her on the ineffable wonder of the dark. Upon further reflection, I've decided to let you have her."

"What the fuck are you on, man?" Franco imagined poor Carol blithely acquiescing to Mr. Wary's charms—Franco recognized a predator when he met one. Doubtless the old man with his eccentric garb and quaint accent could pour on the charm. And dear God, what did the creepy bastard do to her when she was incapacitated on that decaying couch? "You sonofabitch. You crazy, fucked up sonofabitch." He whipped the belt buckle across Mr. Wary's face. "You're not going to see her again. She calls you, don't answer. She knocks on your door, you don't answer. She tries to talk to you in the hall, you go the other way." Franco punctuated each directive with a slap of his belt buckle while the man sat there, absorbing the abuse. It wasn't until the fourth or fifth swipe that he realized his victim was grinning.

Mr. Wary caught the belt and jerked Franco to his knees and grabbed him by the hair. "You insect. You creeping, insignificant vermin." He stood, dragging Franco upright so they were nose to nose. "Do you wish to witness my work with your precious, idiotic paramour? Such unhappiness awaits you."

Franco was calm even in his terror. He pretended to struggle against Mr. Wary's iron grip before slamming his knuckles against the man's windpipe. He'd once killed a fellow with that blow on the mean streets of Harlem. His fingers broke with a snap and he grunted in shock. Mr. Wary shook him as a dog shakes a rat in its jaws. Franco's vision went out of focus even as he slashed the edge of his left hand against the bridge of Mr. Wary's nose, and yelped because it was like striking concrete.

"That's quite enough," Mr. Wary said and looped the belt around Franco's neck and drew it snug. Franco went blind. His muscles stiffened and, when Mr. Wary released him, he toppled sideways and his head bounced off the carpet.

IV.

Mr. Wary handcuffed Franco in a closet and strung him up on tiptoes by means of keeping the belt around his neck and the other end secured to a rusty hook dangling from a chain. Mr. Wary left the door partially ajar. He suggested that Franco remain mum or else matters would go poorly for him, and worse for Carol, who was soon to arrive for her weekly appointment.

The closet was narrow and stuffed with coats and mothballed suits, but roofless—the space above rose vertically into blackness like a mineshaft. While Franco struggled to avoid hanging himself, he had ample opportunity to puzzle over how this closet could possess such a dimension. Occasionally, reddish light pulsed from the darkness and Franco relived his recent nightmare.

Afternoon bled into red evening and the stars emerged in the sliver of sky through the window behind the couch. Franco was in a state of partial delirium when Carol knocked on the door. Mr. Wary smoothed his shaggy hair and quickly donned a smoking jacket. Carol came in, severe and rushed as usual. He took her coat and fixed drinks and Franco slowly strangled, his view curtailed by the angle of the closet door.

Franco only heard and saw fragments of the next half hour, preoccupied as he was with basic survival. He fell unconscious for brief moments, revived by the pressure at his throat, the searing in his lungs. He contemplated murder. A few feet away, his lover and the magician finished their drinks. Mr. Wary told her to make herself comfortable while he put on a recording of scratchy woodwind music. He drew the curtain and clicked on a lamp. He cleared his throat and began to speak in a low, sonorous tone. Carol mumbled, obviously responding to his words.

In due course, Mr. Wary shut off the record player and the apartment fell quiet but for Carol's breathing. He said, "Come, my dear. Come with me," and took Carol's hand and led her, as if she were sleepwalking, to a blank span of the wall. Mr. Wary brushed aside a strip of brittle paper and revealed what Franco took to be a dark water stain, until Carol pressed her eye against it and he realized the stain was actually a peephole. A peephole to where, though? That particular wall didn't abut another apartment—it was an outer wall overlooking the rear square and beyond the square, a ravine.

Carol shuddered and her arms hung slack. Mr. Wary stroked her hair. He muttered in her ear and turned slightly to grin at Franco. A few minutes later, he took her shoulders and gently guided her away from the wall. They exchanged inaudible murmurs. Carol wrote him a check and, seeming to secure her faculties, gathered her coat and bade Mr. Wary a brisk farewell on her way out.

"Your turn," he said upon turning his attention to Franco. He unclasped the belt and led him to the wall, its peeling flap of ancient paper. The peephole oozed a red glow. "All this flesh is but a projection. We are the dream of something greater and more dreadful than you could imagine. To gaze into the abyss is to recognize the dreamer and, in recognition, to wake. Not all at once. Soon, however." He inexorably forced Franco's eye against the hole and its awful radiance.

Franco came to, slumped on the coach. Mr. Wary smoked a cigarette and watched him intently. The liquid noises of his own heart, the thump of his pulse, were too loud and he clutched his temples. He recalled a glimpse of Carol's face as dredged from nightmarish limbo. The shape of it, its atavistic lust and ravenous fury terrified him even as a tattered memory. Immense as some forsaken monument, and its teeth—He retched on his shoes.

"It'll pass," Mr. Wary said. The phone, a black rotary, rang. He answered, then listened for several moments. He extended it to Franco. "For you."

Franco accepted the phone and held it awkwardly with his good hand. Across a vast distance, Jacob Wilson said, "Franco? Sorry man, but you're done. I'll have my accountant cut you a check. Kiss-kiss." Across a vast distance, a continent and the Atlantic Ocean, Jacob Wilson hung up.

Mr. Wary took the phone from Franco. "A shame about your job. Nonetheless, I'm sure a man of your ability will land on his feet." He helped Franco rise and propelled him to the door. "Off you go. Sweets to the sweet."

Franco shuffled down the badly lighted hall. A vortex of fire roared in the center of his mind. He stepped into the stairwell. There were no stairs, only a black chasm, and he plummeted, shrieking, tumbling.

"Holy shit! Wake up, dude!" Carol shook his arm. They were in her crummy bed in her crummy apartment. The dark pressed against the window. "You okay? You okay?"

He opened and closed his mouth, biting back more screams. She turned on the bedside lamp and bloody light flooded his vision. He said, "I'm . . . okay." Tears of pain streamed down his cheeks.

"It's three in the fucking morning. I didn't hear you come in. Why the hell are you still dressed?" She unknotted his tie, began to unbutton his shirt. "Wow, you're sweaty. Sure you're okay? Damn—you drunk, or what?"

"I wish. Got anything?" He wiped his eyes. The lamp had now emitted its normal, butter-yellow light.

"Some Stoli in the freezer." She went into the kitchen and fixed him a tall glass of vodka. He guzzled it like water and she laughed and grabbed the mostly empty glass from his good hand. "Whoa, Trigger. You're starting to worry me." She gasped, finally noticing the lumped and swollen wreck of his right hand. "Oh my God. You've been fighting!"

He felt better. His heart settled down. He took off his pants and fell on the bed. "Nothing to worry about. I had a few too many at the bar. Came here and crashed, I guess. Sorry to wake you."

"Actually, I'm glad you did."

"Why is that?" His eyelids were heavy and the warmth of the booze was doing its magic.

"You won't believe the nightmare I was having. I was walking around in a city. Spain or Italy. One of those places where the streets are narrow and the buildings are like something from a medieval film. I could see through people's skin. X-ray vision. There's another thing. If I squinted just right, there were these . . . sort of bloody tendrils hooked to their skulls, their shoulders, and whatnot. The tendrils disappeared into creepy holes in the air hanging above them. The fucking tentacles squirmed, like they were alive."

He'd gone cold. The pleasant alcohol rush congealed in the pit of his stomach. The tendrils, the holes of oozing darkness—he pictured them clearly as if he'd seen them prior to Carol's revelation.

She said, "Right before you woke me with all that racket, there was an eclipse. The moon covered the sun. A perfect black disc with fire around the edges. Fucking awesome. Then, there was this sound. Can't describe it. Sort of a vibration. All the people standing in the square flew up toward the eclipse. The tendrils dragged them away. It was like the Rapture, Frankie. Except, nobody was very happy. They screamed like motherfuckers until they were specks. Wham! Here you were. The screams must've been yours."

"I rolled over onto my fingers. Hurt like hell."

"Wanna go to the clinic? Looks bad."

"In the morning."

"Fine, tough guy."

Franco tucked his broken hand close to his face. He lay still, listening for the telltale vibration of doom to pass through his bones.

V.

Carol was driving the car into Olympia's outlying farmland. The day was blue and shiny. A girlfriend had given Carol a picnic set for her birthday—a wicker basket, insulated pack, checkered cloth, thermos, and parasol. Her sunglasses disguised her expression. She always wore them.

Franco hadn't shaved in four days. He'd worn the same suit for as long. The majority of those days were spent downtown, hunched over an ever mounting collection of shot glasses at The Brotherhood Tavern. His right hand was splinted and wrapped in thick, bulky bandages. His fingers throbbed and he mixed plenty of painkillers with the booze to dull the edge while he plotted a thousand different ways to kill his nemesis, Mr. Wary. Evenings were another matter—those dim, unvarnished hours between 2 a.m. that found him alone in his Spartan bedroom, sweating and hallucinating, assailed by a procession of disjointed images, unified only in their dreadfulness, their atmosphere of alien terror.

He'd dreamed of her again last night, seen her naked and transfixed in the grand lobby of The Broadsword that belonged to another world, witnessed her lift as if upon wires toward the domed ceiling, and into shadow. Blood misted from the heights and spackled Franco until it soaked his hair and ran in rivulets down his arms and chest, until it made a puddle between his toes. He'd awakened, his cock stiff against his belly and masturbated, and after, sank again into nightmare. He was in Mr. Wary's apartment, although everything was different—an ebony clock and shelves of strange tomes, and Wary himself, towered over Franco. The old man was garbed in a flowing black robe. A necklace of human skulls jangled against his chest. Mr. Wary had grown so large he could've swallowed Franco, bones and all. He was a prehistoric beast that had, over eons, assumed the flesh and countenance of Man.

"You worship the Devil," Franco said.

"The Lord of Flies is only one. There are others, greater and more powerful than he. Presences that command his own obedience. You've seen them. I showed you."

"I don't remember. I want to go back." A hole opened in the wall, rapidly grew from pinhole to portal and it spun with black and red fires. At its heart, a humanoid form beckoned. And when he surfaced from this dream into the hot, sticky darkness of Carol's bedroom, he'd discovered her standing before her closet, bathed in the red glow. She cupped her breasts, head thrown back in exultance, sunglasses distorting her features, giving her the eyes of a strange insect. The door had slammed shut even as he cried out, and his voice was lost, a receding echo in a stygian tomb.

Now they were driving. Now they were parked atop a knoll and eating sandwiches and drinking wine in the shade of a large, flowering tree. A wild pasture spread itself around the knoll and cattle gathered in small knots and grazed on the lush tufted grass. The distant edge of the pasture was marked by a sculpture of a bull fashioned from sheets of iron. The highway sounds were faint and overcome by the sigh of the leaves, the dim crooning of some forgotten star on Carol's AM radio.

Franco hadn't told her of his apocalyptic visit to Mr. Wary, nor of his resultant termination from Jacob Wilson's security attachment. The job wasn't a pressing concern; he'd saved enough to live comfortably for a while. Prior to this most recent stint, he'd guarded an A-list actor in Malibu, and before that, a series of corporate executives, all of whom had paid well. However, he *was* afraid to speak of Wary, wouldn't know where to begin in any event.

He lay his head in her lap and as she massaged his temples, he wondered about this radical change in her personality. He'd not known her to savor a tranquil pastoral setting, nor repose for any duration without compulsively checking her cell phone or chain smoking cigarettes. Her calm was eerie. As for himself, one place to get drunk off his ass was the same as another. The wine ran dry, so he uncapped his hip flask of vodka and carried on. Cumulus clouds piled up, edges golden in the midday sun. He noted some were dark at the center, black with cavities, black with the rot of worms at the core. His eyes watered and he slipped on a pair of wraparound shades and instantly felt better.

"Mr. Wary and I are through," she said.

"Oh? Why is that?" Had the crazy bastard mentioned his confrontation with Franco? Surely not. Yet, who could predict the actions of someone as bizarre as Mr. Wary?

She stuck a cigarette in her mouth and lighted up. "I'm cured."

"Wonderful."

"My nightmares are getting worse, though. I've dreamt the same thing every night this week. There's a cavern, or an underground basement, hard to say, and something is chasing me. It's dark and I don't have shoes. I run through the darkness toward a wedge of light, far off at first. It's an arch and red light is coming through it, from another chamber. I think. Nothing's clear. I'm too scared to look over my shoulder, but I know whatever's after me has gained. I can feel its presence, like a gigantic shadow bearing down, and just as I cross the threshold, I'm snatched into the air."

"The tentacles?"

"Nope, bigger. Like a hand. A very, very large hand."

"Maybe you should see a real doctor."

"I've got four pill prescriptions already."

"There's probably a more holistic method to dealing with dreams."

"Ha! Like hypnotherapy?"

"Sarcasm isn't pretty." Franco sipped vodka. He closed his eyes as a cloud darkened the sun and the breeze cooled. He shivered. Time passed, glimpsed through the shadows that pressed against the thin shell of his eyelids.

Branches crackled and the earth shifted. He blinked and beheld a blood red sky and a looming presence, a distorted silhouette of a giant. Branches groaned and leaves and twigs showered him, roots tore free of the earth and grass, and he rolled away and assumed a crouch, bewildered at the sight of this gargantuan being uprooting the tree. He shouted Carol's name, but she was nowhere, and he ran for the car parked on the edge of the country road. Behind him, the figure bellowed and there came a crunching sound, the sound of splintering wood. A dirt clod thumped into his back.

Carol was already in the car, driver seat tilted back. She slept with her mouth slightly open. The doors were locked. Franco smashed the passenger window with his elbow and popped the lock. Carol's arms flapped and she covered her face until Franco shook her and she gradually became rational and focused upon him. Her glasses had fallen off during the excitement and he was shocked at how her pupils had deformed into twin nebulas that reflected the red glow of the sky.

"Drive! We gotta get the hell out of here."

She stared at him, uncomprehending, and when he glanced back, the monstrous figure had vanished. However, the tree lay on its side. She said, "What happened?" Then, spying the ruined tree, "We could've been killed!"

He clutched his elbow and stared wordlessly as the red clouds rolled away to the horizon and the blue sky returned.

"You're bleeding," she said.

He looked at his arm. He was bleeding, all right.

VI.

The doctor was the same guy who'd splinted his fingers. He gave him a few stitches, a prescription for antibiotics, and another for more pain pills. He checked Franco's eyes with a penlight and asked if he'd had any problems with them, and Franco admitted his frequent headaches. The doctor wore a perplexed expression as he said something about Coloboma, then muttering that Coloboma wasn't possible. The doctor insisted on referring him to an eye specialist. Franco cut him off mid-sentence with a curt goodbye. He put on his sunglasses and retreated to the parking lot where Carol waited.

She dropped him at his building and offered to come up and keep him company a while. He smiled weakly and said he wasn't in any shape to entertain. She drove off into the night. He turned the lights off, undressed, and lay on his bed with the air-conditioning going full power. His breath drifted like smoke. He dialed Mr. Wary's number and waited. He let it ring until an automated message from the phone company interrupted and told him to please try again later.

The closet door creaked. The foot of the bed sagged under a considerable weight. Mr. Wary said, "I thought we had an understanding."

"What's happening to me?" Franco stared at the nothingness between him and the ceiling. He dared not look at his visitor. When Mr. Wary didn't answer, Franco said, "Why do you live in a shit hole? Why not a mansion, a yacht? Why aren't you a potentate somewhere?"

"This is what you've done with your dwindling supply of earthly moments? I'm flattered. Not what one expects from the brute castes."

"My dwindling supply . . . ? You're going to kill me. Eat my heart, or something."

Mr. Wary chuckled. "I'd certainly eat your heart because I suspect your brain lacks nutrients. I've no designs on you, boy. Consider me an interested observer; no more, no less. As for my humble abode . . . I've lived in sea shanties and mud huts. I've lived in caves, and might again when the world ends one day soon."

"So much for the simple life of dodging bullets and breaking people's legs."

"You realize these aren't dreams? There is no such thing. These are visions. The membrane parts for you in slumber, absorbs you into the reality of the corona that limns the Dark. Goodbye. Don't call on me again, if you please." Mr. Wary's weight lifted from the bed and the faint rustle of clothes hangers marked his departure from the room.

Franco shook, then slept. In his dreams that were not dreams, he was eaten alive, over and over and over . . .

VII.

Franco collapsed in a stupor for the better part of three days. On the fourth evening, as the sun dripped away, the fugue released him and he finally stirred from his rank sheets. The moon rose yellow as hell and eclipsed a third of the sky.

The sensation was of waking from a dream into a dream.

He loaded his small, nickel-plated automatic and tucked it in his waistband. He drove over to The Broadsword and parked on the street three blocks away. The brief walk in the luminous dark crystallized his thoughts, honed his purpose, if not his plan. No one else moved, no other cars. A light shone here and there, on the street, in a building. Somehow this only served to accentuate the otherworldliness of his surroundings and heightened his sense of isolation and dread.

Carol's apartment was unlocked, the power off. She sat in the window, knees to chin, hair loose. Moonlight seeped around her silhouette. "There you are. Something is happening."

Franco stood near her. He felt overheated and weak.

"Your arm's gone green," she said. "It stinks."

He'd forgotten about the wound, the antibiotics. His jacket stuck to the dressing and tried to separate when he let his arm swing at his side. "Oh, I've got a fever. I wondered why I felt so bad."

"You just noticed?" She sounded distant, distracted. "The moon is different tonight. Closer. I can feel it trying to drag the blood from my skin."

"Yeah."

"I sleep around the clock. Except it's more like I don't really sleep. More like being stoned. I dream about holes. Opening and closing. And caves and dollhouses."

"Dollhouses?"

"Kinda. You know those replica cities architects make? Models? I dream I'm walking through model cities, except these are bigger. The tallest buildings are maybe a foot taller than me. I look in the windows and doll people scream and run off."

"If that's the worst, you're doing all right."

"No, it gets worse. I don't want to talk about that. I've seen things that scared the living shit outta me. I'm losing it. The tendrils; I've seen them for real, while I'm awake." She rested her head against the glass.

Franco gripped the pistol in his pocket. A tremor passed through the walls and floor. Bits of plaster dust trickled from the ceiling. Something happened to the stars, although Carol's shoulder mostly blocked his view. The yellow illumination of the moon dimmed to red.

"We're going into the dark," Carol said. She'd cast aside the sunglasses. Her face was pale and indistinct.

He walked into the kitchenette and drank a glass of tap water. He removed the gun from his pocket and racked the slide. An object thumped in the other room. When he returned, she was gone and the front door hung ajar. The hallway stretched emptily, except for the red glow of the elevator at the far end awaiting him with its open mouth. The stairwell entrance was bricked over. Franco considered the gun. He boarded the elevator and pressed the button and descended.

Everything happened as it had happened in his serial nightmares. She was there in the lobby, gazing toward the vaulted ceiling, and he was too late. A wrinkled hand the size and length of a compact car snatched her up by the fleshy strands as a puppeteer might retrieve a fallen marionette and then blood was everywhere. Franco froze in place, his mind splintering as he registered the tendrils that snaked from his own shoulders and rose into darkness.

An impossibly tall figure lurched from the shadow of the ornate support column. A demonic caricature of an old man, his wizened head nearly scraping the domed ceiling, hunched toward Franco, skinny fingers reaching for him, lips twisting in anticipation. Franco recalled the de Goya painting of the titan Saturn who stuffed a man into his frightful maw and chewed with wide-eyed relish. He fell back, raising his arms in a feeble gesture of defense. The giant took the fistful of Franco's strings, the erstwhile ethereal cords of his soul, and yanked him from his feet; grasped and lifted him and Franco had a long, agonizing moment to recognize his own face mirrored by the primordial aspect of the giant.

Even in pieces, eternally disgorging his innards and fluids, he remained cognizant of his agonies. He tumbled through endless darkness, his shrieks flickering in his wake.

VIII.

He roused from a joyous dream of feasting, of drinking blood and sucking warm marrow from the bone. His sons and daughters swarmed like ants upon the surface of the Earth, ripe in their terror, delectable in their anguish. He swept them into his mouth and their insides ran in black streams between his lips and matted his beard. This sweet dream rapidly slipped away as he stretched and assessed his surroundings. He shambled forth from the great cavern in the mountain that had been his home for so long.

Moonlight illuminated the ruined plaza of the city on the mountainside. He did not recognize the configuration of the stars and this frightened and exhilarated him. During his eons sleep, trees had burst through cracks in paving stones. He squatted to sniff the leaves, to tear them with his old man's snaggle teeth and relish the taste of bitter sap. His lover approached, as naked and ancient as himself, and laid her hand upon his shoulder. They embraced in silent communion as the sun ate through the moon and bathed the city in its hideous blood-red glare.

The couple's shadows stretched long and dark over all the tiny houses and all the tiny works of men.

HALFWAY HOME

LINDA NAGATA

The airliner's safety brochure was like every other I'd seen: laminated and perfect, showing a large jet afloat in calm water, the emergency chutes deployed with inflatable rafts at their ends awaiting the arrival of passengers after a perfect water landing.

"Those diagrams are terribly optimistic," the woman in the seat beside me said, eyeing the brochure as our plane climbed away from Manila. She spoke masterful English, clipped with a Filipino accent. "Let's hope we never have to test that theory."

I turned to her, intrigued. We were seated in the coach section, two women, strangers, traveling alone to Los Angeles. I had the window seat; she was on the aisle. I'd flown a lot, and I knew the social rules for the small talk that goes on between strangers forced to sit side by side for hours on end. A discussion of the false promises illustrated in the safety brochure did not come close to qualifying under those rules.

"Prepare for the worst," I said. "That's my philosophy. At least know where the exits are."

"You're a rare type, then. Most people give no consideration to the worst-case scenario."

She had come onboard late, a slight and lovely woman, maybe forty years old, her brown skin made utterly smooth by a veneer of makeup, her

333

black hair permed into loose curls that framed a balanced face. She dared to wear a salmon-colored business suit that somehow worked for her—a happy color that relieved some of the fatigue visible around her eyes.

After stowing a small bag under the seat with worried haste, she had acknowledged me with a courteous nod and then closed her eyes, seeming to have fallen asleep before we reached the runway.

I was a different sort of woman than my new companion: a tall and rangy California blonde, casually dressed in a cream pullover and cargo pants. I hadn't even bothered with makeup. I was on my way home, a fifteen-hour flight shared with strangers whose opinions and lives had nothing to do with mine.

I refolded the brochure and put it back in the seat pocket. "I've seen the worst case," I told her. "More than once. I've learned to prepare."

She cocked her head, her gaze distracted, a skeptical frown furrowing her brow. "If you *can* prepare," she murmured, more as if she were wondering aloud than speaking to me, "surely it is not the worst case?" Her gaze shifted to meet mine then shot away again, as a self-conscious smile quirked her lips. "Ah, I'm sorry. I've overstepped." She leaned back in her seat, dabbing a tissue against her cheeks, where a sheen of sweat seeped through her makeup. "My occupation leads to an unhealthy fascination with hazard assessments."

"What do you do?" I asked with honest interest.

"Geek work. Engineering appraisals of biohazard containment procedures under laboratory conditions." She settled her small hands one atop the other in her lap. "Modeling the worst-case scenario is just part of the daily grind, but it's always been theory for me. No real-world tests. Not yet. And you? What experience has led you to always map the exits?"

"Call me a professional adventurer."

I was a photographer and a mountain climber. For ten years, I'd scrimped and saved and sought grants, managing to get myself on expeditions around the world. Not all of them had gone well. I told her about a disastrous climb on Denali when an avalanche hit, taking out most of our party and leaving me with a broken arm. And another time on Everest when crowds of amateurs slowed our descent as a storm rolled in.

"I learned not to count on other people, because when disaster strikes, most of them panic. In the worst case? It comes down to everyone for themselves, and if you're not strong enough to accept that, you won't survive. My name's Halley, by the way."

"Anita."

She offered her hand. Its warmth surprised me, almost feverish in its intensity. "Are you all right?"

Anita gave me an indulgent smile. "I have a severe nickel allergy." Touching the far side of her neck, she drew my gaze to a mottled, red rash. "I was given a necklace that turned out to be . . . less than I thought. A slight fever is part of my allergic reaction. It should clear up in a few hours."

"Not a worst-case scenario, then." I kept my voice light, as if it was a joke, but I was uneasy. I didn't want to spend the first week of my homecoming laid out by some exotic Asian fever acquired from a biohazard engineer. Too much irony in that.

Anita laughed again, though this time it sounded forced. "You must be thinking I'm the worst-case scenario for the passenger in the adjacent seat. Gloomy *and* ill."

"No. Worst case would be if something went wrong and I was stuck sitting next to someone too big to push aside or climb over on my way to the exit. Everyone for themselves, remember?" I smiled like it was a macabre joke, but it was the truth, and judging by her somber expression, she knew it.

"Maybe we'll get lucky," she said. "And stay in the air all the way to Los Angeles."

"Best-case scenario," I agreed.

I think it came to us both that we'd said more than we should have, and we retreated into silence.

-o-

I woke with a start. The cabin was dark: just the floor lights and a few reading lamps. The air was too warm, thick with exhaled breaths. A nervous whisper rode atop an ominous silence. Why couldn't I hear any engine noise? I glanced down, to see Anita's white-knuckled hand clutching the armrest between us.

"What the hell is going on?" My ears popped. "Are we descending?" I pulled out my phone to check the time, confirming that it was too soon to be landing, too soon by hours. We were hardly halfway home.

Anita turned to me, her shoulders hunched, reflected light glinting in her dark eyes, her lips parted to admit the quick, shallow breaths that mark the edge of panic. She looked to me like a hunted creature at bay, an impression reinforced by her words. "This can't be happening. It *can't*."

"What is happening?"

"The engines! Listen to them. They've been cutting out, one by one." There was a mad focus to her eyes as she added, "It's a judgment. Against me."

I pulled the buckle on my seatbelt and started to rise. "I'm going to go talk to someone. Where the hell are the flight attendants anyway?"

I jumped as a man's voice, humble with apology, issued from the speakers. "Ladies and gentlemen, we have an emergency."

⊸⊙⊱

The plane was going down.

As the news sank in, passengers wailed, cried, prayed.

I re-buckled my seatbelt and put on my life vest.

Next I looked for the exit sign. It hung above the aisle, four seats ahead. If I survived the impact, I promised myself I would do whatever it took to reach that exit. The pilot had assured us our situation was known. Rescue was already on the way. We wouldn't be in the water long. If I could get out of the plane alive, I'd have a good chance to survive.

Beside me, Anita kept her white-knuckled grip on the armrest, but she wasn't crying, she wasn't praying. She stared ahead at nothing. She'd assessed our odds in her first words to me, when she called the safety brochure *terribly optimistic*. "Anita."

She turned. It was too dark to really see her face, but I saw her hand let go of the armrest. She took my hand; squeezed it, her palm even hotter than it had been before, hot and dry. "You're a survivor, Halley. Do whatever it takes to live through this. Climb over me. Climb over anyone, but live. Someone has to, or it's for nothing."

For nothing?

I wondered what she meant . . . but I didn't really care. It didn't matter. In just a few minutes, all of us on the plane would likely be dead. "Put your vest on," I told her. I helped her with it, buckling it around her waist.

Outside the window, there was only darkness. I pressed my forehead against the plastic pane and peered up, but I couldn't see any stars. I couldn't see the ocean below us. No way to know how much farther we had to fall.

The plane began to shudder.

People screamed—a chaos of animal noises that my fear-filled brain refused to truly hear, blurring and blending the sound with the roar of wind rushing past our powerless wings—all of it abruptly overridden by the pilot's terror-edged voice, "Assume crash position. Assume crash position!"

I grabbed Anita's hand. Then I bent at the waist, my head pressed to my knees and one palm braced against the seat back in front of me—a position that felt to me as useless as a prayer, but I prayed too. I held onto Anita's hand and prayed I would be one of the survivors.

We hit hard. I heard some kind of debris slam against the ceiling. I didn't look up to see what it might be. The plane bounced. We hit again. The fuselage screamed with the voice of aluminum tearing. Luggage exploded out of the overhead rack—and then the fuselage cracked apart.

It broke right in front of me. Darkness swept in, and a howling wind. Fluid sprayed in my face—though whether it was blood or hydraulics or the ocean itself, I couldn't tell because we were tumbling, swirling, cartwheeling on a long chaotic fall into the arms of death.

⟜◦⟞

Or was it life?

We assume it's easy to tell the difference.

⟜◦⟞

Clawing at consciousness, I awoke to a low, rumbling assault of sound, and a raw awareness of pain. Everything hurt. My skull, my face, my back, my hips . . . every muscle along my sides. I blinked, and found myself gazing at black smoke roiling across a starry sky. I was lying on my back, still belted in my seat. The wall of the fuselage was still beside me. The little window framed a fiery light, but the seats that had been in front of me were gone. The fuselage had split right at my feet, and the front of the plane had torn away.

A hysterical little laugh escaped my throat as I remembered my promise to do whatever it took to reach the exit.

The exit was wide open now.

A soft *whump* startled me. A nearby roar of rushing water followed it. My seat shuddered. Rain pelted my face—salty rain, ocean water. The sound I heard was the sound of a breaking wave . . . sweeping around the fuselage? As the wave retreated it left behind a steady, bold roar unlike any ocean sound I'd heard before.

Braced for pain, I turned my head, peering through the window at a lurid light, blurred and refracted by a layer of water droplets clinging to the outside of the window. Something was burning out there, but I couldn't see it clearly enough to know what it might be.

White water surged up and slapped hard against the plastic pane. Instinctively, I jerked back, while the fuselage trembled around me, and more salty water rained down.

A child wailed.

I gasped, realizing this was the first voice I'd heard since waking. The only voice. In the seconds since I'd opened my eyes there had been no screaming, no crying, no pleas for help, no reassurances . . . just the rumble of the ocean, the roar of the fire, and now, one child's despairing wail.

That cry made me move.

"I'm coming," I called out in a rusty croak, groping at my seatbelt until I got it undone. "I'm coming. Don't be afraid."

A stupid thing to say.

I squiggled and shifted and found that my body still worked. I got my feet under me and turned to climb out of my seat—only to discover Anita in my way. Refracted firelight shimmered in her eyes as she lay blinking up at me. Water swirled behind her head. I looked past her, in a direction that was now down, toward what had been the back of the plane. Everything back there belonged to the ocean now. I thought I saw drowned faces beneath the water's unquiet, dark surface but the light was poor. It was hard to be sure.

The child cried again.

Across the aisle, only one other seat remained above the water. The seats that should have completed the row weren't there. I had to assume that, like the front of the plane, they'd been ripped away in the crash.

The child huddled in the sanctuary of that one seat, a boy maybe seven years old. He'd gotten out of his seatbelt; he'd even remembered to inflate his life vest. It looked like a huge yellow pillow strapped to his chest. He clung to the vertical seat cushion, weeping as water rose and fell around his feet, soaking his shoes and his pants.

"I'm coming," I told him.

I told myself, *Go!*

But Anita was in the way. She hadn't moved at all; I needed to know if she could. "Are you hurt?" I asked her, all too aware of currents of hot air moving past my face, missives from the roaring fire just outside.

As Anita opened her mouth to answer, another wave hit. The torn fuselage shuddered, the seat shifted beneath me, and I almost fell on top of her. I caught myself with a hand against her seatback. My fingers came away sticky, smelling of blood.

"Leave me," she said, in a high half-shriek. "Save yourself. *Live.*"

She was right. Injured, helpless, likely with hours to go before rescue came, her prospects were slim. The smart thing to do would be to abandon her and focus on the child.

"*Go,*" she pleaded. "Before you can't get out."

I started to go; I tried to go—what did I care for her life? I hardly knew her. We'd sat together, we'd shared a few words—but then we'd held hands, and our abstract acquaintance had become personal. I couldn't leave her.

I felt for her seatbelt and popped it open, telling myself I was strong enough to help her and the child too. "Come on! We're getting out of here. Put your arm around my shoulder."

She was delirious. She tried to push me away. I grabbed the red tabs dangling from her vest and pulled them. I pulled my own. Both vests inflated and I pushed her into the water that flooded the aisle.

We bobbed at the surface.

I turned her onto her back, gripped the straps at her shoulder, and dragged her with me as I worked my way around the boy's seat. Beyond him, firelight glimmered on open water. That's where I wanted to be. That light was hope glimmering—the desperate hope of not being drowned when the wreckage around us finally pitched over.

I cleared the seat and felt a strong pull of ocean current. Holding one arm out to the boy, I called to him, "Come! Jump!"

He didn't hesitate. He threw himself at me, a skinny little thing strapped into a vest so big he looked like he might levitate. A rumbling growl warned me that a wave was coming. I got an arm around him. He got an arm around me. "Deep breath!" I yelled as a mountain of white water plunged over us.

Like the plane crash, there was nothing I could do except hold on. We tumbled. My head hit against a sandy bottom. I felt the boy thrash. I felt Anita flail, prying at my fingers, trying to get me to let go. Her elbow struck my ribs, but I held on, my fingers locked around the straps of her life vest. I swore to myself we would survive, that we would all three survive together.

The wave let us go.

I rolled onto my back and gasped for air, letting the life vest hold me up. I made sure the boy's face was out of the water, and then Anita. "It's okay," I murmured to them, my voice pitched so high it frightened me. "We're doing okay." The boy had his arm around my neck, so tight it was painful. I was glad. It told me he was strong, not like Anita. She drifted beside us, nearly unconscious.

The wave had carried us maybe fifty feet from the broken fuselage. A fire still shimmered beyond it, though it was less than it had seemed through the window. A yellow fragment of moon floated low above the horizon, illuminating a line of white water that must surely mark a distant reef . . . and I realized then that the fuselage must have been resting on a reef, with waves breaking around it . . . but it made no sense. The north Pacific is vast and nearly empty, and while I could believe our pilot had hoped to come down near some patch of reef or on some spot of an island—Johnston Atoll maybe? Palmyra?—to imagine that he had succeeded was more than I could accept.

With my charges in tow, I swiveled around, where I was presented with more evidence of the impossible.

Visible in the moon's light, not a hundred feet away, was a sand beach, rising steeply to a line of brush and skeletal trees. Water sloshed into my open mouth. I spit it out, sure I was suffering a hallucination, seeing a mirage. Reality had slipped. We had come to a place where the odds did not allow us to be.

Somehow, we had been given a chance—and I took it.

With one hand on Anita's straps and the boy clinging to me with a relentless grip, I kicked my shoes off, kicked at the water, and slowly, slowly, I brought us all to that impossible shore.

The boy stood up as we reached the shallows, but Anita couldn't walk, or maybe she didn't want to. "I'm not going to leave you," I warned her, and I dragged her arm around my shoulder, hauling her up the beach, while the boy ran ahead, scouting beneath the vegetation until he found a hollow that offered shelter from a relentless wind. I got Anita out of her vest, and used it as a pillow for her head. Her skin was hot, but she was shivering so I piled sand around her legs. The boy helped me.

"What's your name?" I asked him as I unbuckled his vest. He gave me a puzzled look, so I tried one of the few Tagalog words I knew. "*Pangalan?*"

"Hilario," he told me in a shy, frightened voice. I tried to remember who he'd been traveling with . . . mama or daddy or both? But they'd been strangers, of no importance to me, and I'd paid no attention. I ruffled his wet hair and gave him a hug.

Out on the reef, the broken fuselage had been pushed over by the waves, submerged just below the surface. Every time a breaker rolled past, spray flew into the air, brilliant white in the moonlight. I watched it and realized: *I survived.*

I was alive, I'd saved two other people, and rescue was surely on its way.

"Come, Hilario." I took his hand and we walked up and down the windswept beach, but nowhere did we find any other survivors, not even a body washed up on the beach, and no debris from the wreck.

This was not reality as I knew it. It was unnatural. All too neat.

As dawn began to lighten the sky, we made our way back to Anita. On the way, I listened for a rescue plane or a helicopter from some passing navy ship, but I heard only the boom and rumble of waves.

"Is there water?" Anita whispered when we returned to her. "*Tubig?*"

"No, there's nothing. But rescue should be coming soon."

I sat cross-legged beside her. Hilario tumbled into my lap, and I held him close. He was mine now. It felt that way. I kissed his salty cheek, and then I put my hand on Anita's forehead. The dry heat of her skin shocked me. Her fever was much worse. "*My God.*"

"Right on time," she whispered.

"What?"

"I meant to die in LA."

"What are you talking about?"

"It doesn't . . . really matter."

Her voice was weak, her words hard to hear. I leaned closer, and my gaze fell on the rash at her neck. Like her fever, it was worse, a collection of tiny pustules, some of them glimmering wet with fluid.

I pulled back. "That's not from an allergy. What's wrong with you, Anita?"

She smiled at me as if we were good friends. "You survived the crash, Halley, just like you said you would." Her whispery voice was almost lost in the wind. "Maybe you'll survive the plague, too. It's possible. One in a hundred should. Maybe two in a hundred, with the best hospital care."

She was delirious. She didn't know what she was saying. Her fever, her head injury, the shock of the crash, had combined to plunge her into the nightmare that must have haunted her career, the worst-case scenario of a biohazard plague escaping one of her labs . . .

That's what I wanted to believe.

But when I looked again at the pustules on her neck, I couldn't hold onto my denial. With Hilario in my arms, I stood up, and backed a step away. Her gaze followed me. "Everyone on the plane," she murmured, "infected by the time we reached LA."

"We didn't make it to LA."

"*You'll* make it. It only takes one. You're that one. The right one, because you'll do what's needed to survive."

◄◦►

It's not true.

That's what I told myself, over and over again as Hilario and I held hands and walked the beach. It couldn't be true.

But what if it was? What if she had made herself the dark angel of the apocalypse, bearing a pestilence that only one in a hundred would survive?

I went back to see her, to plead with her to tell me the truth, but the truth was lost. Her eyes had clouded. She was gone.

◄◦►

I sat on the beach with Hilario, shivering, but not from cold. Wasn't it a miracle the plane had crashed? Euphoria swept over me as I thought about it. Horror rolled in on its heels. Over 330 people had been on that plane. They were gone now, lost. It was a tragedy—and yet if Anita could be believed, so many more, almost all the world, had been made safer because of it.

The drone of a distant helicopter startled me from my musings. I looked up, to see, beyond the reef, the silhouette of a navy ship looming against the yellow glow of the predawn sky. The helicopter was a flyspeck, speeding toward the boiling water that marked the sunken fuselage of the plane.

Hilario leaped up. His eyes went wide as he took in the ship, and a beautiful grin broke out across his face. He whooped, jumping up and down and waving his arms in mad greeting.

I whooped and waved too, but my delirious relief faded as dread descended over me. I sank to the sand, watching Hilario jump up and down, up and down, his high voice crying out in words that I did not understand.

Wasn't it a miracle that our plane had crashed? And wasn't it a miracle that Anita had survived, if only just long enough for me to learn that she'd placed an apocalypse in my hands?

"*Come!*" Hilario screamed, using a rare English word. "*Come!*"

My voice broke as I told him, "No, baby. They can't come here."

He hesitated, turning to me with worried eyes. I got up and ran to the top of the beach where a line of driftwood had collected. I grabbed a large stick. I remembered Anita's last words to me, *You'll do what you need to do to survive.* She'd been so sure of me. I'd been so sure of myself.

I darted back down to where the sand was wet, as close to the wave wash as I dared, and I started scratching deep scars, digging down to the wet, dark sand to form giant letters. Hilario came to watch me with a worried frown on his sweet face. I gave him what I hoped was a reassuring smile but I kept working, because it wasn't the apocalypse that Anita had placed in my hands after all: it was the lives of ninety-nine out of a hundred people—and how personal every one of those lives felt to me, resting in my hands.

Our rescuers read my message and retreated.

Hilario called for them to come back and when they didn't, he ran to me and we cried together as the waves slowly erased my warning and my plea:

TERRORISM–BIOWARFARE

DON'T COME

I wanted to explain to Hilario that the helicopter would be back. That our rescuers would come again, in biohazard suits, bearing miracle drugs, and that against all odds the two of us would survive even in the face of this worst-case scenario.

I wanted to tell him that.

I wanted to believe it.

But an untenable chain of miracles had brought us to this deserted shore. It made no sense to me that the pilot could have guided our plane here with no power in the engines, and it made no sense that only Anita, Hilario, and I should survive the crash and escape the wreckage, the boy and I not even hurt, and no sign of anyone else.

It made no sense.

We should have died on that plane with everyone else, our plague-infected bodies safely lost and unrecoverable beneath the deep waters of the Pacific.

I think maybe we did die.

It could be delirium setting in with the first brush of fever, but the hours since the plane crash do not seem real to me. Looking back, it feels like everything that's happened since I awoke in the wreckage has been a question posed to my soul.

And my answer?

I cradle Hilario as he weeps against my chest.

My answer surprised even me.

THE SAME DEEP WATERS AS YOU

BRIAN HODGE

They were down to the last leg of the trip, miles of iron-gray ocean skimming three hundred feet below the helicopter, and she was regretting ever having said yes. The rocky coastline of northern Washington slid out from beneath them and there they were, suspended over a sea as forbidding as the day itself. If they crashed, the water would claim them for its own long before anyone could find them.

Kerry had never warmed to the sea—now less than ever.

Had saying no even been an option? *The Department of Homeland Security would like to enlist your help as a consultant,* was what the pitch boiled down to, and the pair who'd come to her door yesterday looked genetically incapable of processing the word no. They couldn't tell her what. They couldn't tell her where. They could only tell her to dress warm. Better be ready for rain, too.

The sole scenario Kerry could think of was that someone wanted her insights into a more intuitive way to train dogs, maybe. Or something a little more out there, something to do with birds, dolphins, apes, horses . . . a plan that some questionable genius had devised to exploit some animal ability they wanted to know how to tap. She'd been less compelled by the appeal to patriotism than simply wanting to make whatever they were doing go as well as possible for the animals.

But this? No one could ever have imagined this.

The island began to waver into view through the film of rain that streaked and jittered along the window, a triangular patch of uninviting rocks and evergreens and secrecy. They were down there.

Since before her parents were born, they'd always been down there.

⟨o⟩

It had begun before dawn: an uncomfortably silent car ride from her ranch to the airport in Missoula, a flight across Montana and Washington, touchdown at Sea-Tac, and the helicopter the rest of the way. Just before this final leg of the journey was the point they took her phone from her and searched her bag. Straight off the plane and fresh on the tarmac, bypassing the terminal entirely, Kerry was turned over to a man who introduced himself as Colonel Daniel Escovedo and said he was in charge of the facility they were going to.

"You'll be dealing exclusively with me from now on," he told her. His brown scalp was speckled with rain. If his hair were any shorter, you wouldn't have been able to say he had hair at all. "Are you having fun yet?"

"Not really, no." So far, this had been like agreeing to her own kidnapping.

They were strapped in and back in the air in minutes, just the two of them in the passenger cabin, knee-to-knee in facing seats.

"There's been a lot of haggling about how much to tell you," Escovedo said as she watched the ground fall away again. "Anyone who gets involved with this, in any capacity, they're working on a need-to-know basis. If it's not relevant to the job they're doing, then they just don't know. Or what they think they know isn't necessarily the truth, but it's enough to satisfy them."

Kerry studied him as he spoke. He was older than she first thought, maybe in his mid-fifties, with a decade and a half on her, but he had the lightly lined face of someone who didn't smile much. He would still be a terror in his seventies. You could just tell.

"What ultimately got decided for you is full disclosure. Which is to say, you'll know as much as I do. You're not going to know what you're looking for, or whether or not it's relevant, if you've got no context for it. But here's the first thing you need to wrap your head around: what you're going to see, most of the last fifteen presidents haven't been aware of."

She felt a plunge in her stomach as distinct as if their altitude had plummeted. "How is that possible? If he's the commander-in-chief, doesn't he . . . ?"

Escovedo shook his head. "Need-to-know. There are security levels above the office of president. Politicians come and go. Career military and intelligence, we stick around."

"And I'm none of the above."

It was quickly getting frightening, this inner circle business. If she'd ever thought she would feel privileged, privy to something so hidden, now she knew better. There really were things you didn't want to know, because the privilege came with too much of a cost.

"Sometimes exceptions have to made," he said, then didn't even blink at the next part. "And I really wish there was a nicer way to tell you this, but if you divulge any of what you see, you'll want to think very hard about that first. Do that, and it's going to ruin your life. First, nobody's going to believe you anyway. All it will do is make you a laughingstock. Before long, you'll lose your TV show. You'll lose credibility in what a lot of people see as a fringe field anyway. Beyond that . . . do I even need to go beyond that?"

Tabby—that was her first thought. Only thought, really. They would try to see that Tabitha was taken from her. The custody fight three years ago had been bruising enough, Mason doing his about-face on what he'd once found so beguiling about her, now trying to use it as a weapon, to make her seem unfit, unstable. *She talks to animals, your honor. She thinks they talk back.*

"I'm just the messenger," Colonel Escovedo said. "Okay?"

She wished she were better at conversations like this. Conversations in general. Oh, to not be intimidated by this. Oh, to look him in the eye and leave no doubt that he'd have to do better than that to scare her. To have just the right words to make him feel smaller, like the bully he was.

"I'm assuming you've heard of Guantanamo Bay in Cuba? What it's for?"

"Yes," she said in a hush. Okay, this was the ultimate threat. Say the wrong thing and she'd disappear from Montana, or Los Angeles, and reappear there, in the prison where there was no timetable for getting out. Just her and 160-odd suspected terrorists.

His eyes crinkled, almost a smile. "Try not to look so horrified. The threat part, that ended before I mentioned Gitmo."

Had it been that obvious? How nice she could amuse him this fine, rainy day.

"Where we're going is an older version of Guantanamo Bay," Escovedo went on. "It's the home of the most long-term enemy combatants ever held in US custody."

"How long is long-term?"

"They've been detained since 1928."

She had to let that sink in. And was beyond guessing what she could bring to the table. Animals, that was her thing, it had always been her thing. Not POWs, least of all those whose capture dated back to the decade after the First World War.

"Are you sure you have the right person?" she asked.

"Kerry Larimer. Star of *The Animal Whisperer*, a modest but consistent hit on the Discovery Channel, currently shooting its fourth season. Which you got after gaining a reputation as a behavioral specialist for rich people's exotic pets. You *look* like her."

"Okay, then." Surrender. They knew who they wanted. "How many prisoners?" From that long ago, it was a wonder there were any left at all.

"Sixty-three."

Everything about this kept slithering out of her grasp. "They'd be over a hundred years old by now. What possible danger could they pose? How could anyone justify—"

The colonel raised a hand. "It sounds appalling, I agree. But what you need to understand from this point forward is that, regardless of how or when they were born, it's doubtful that they're still human."

He pulled an iPad from his valise and handed it over, and here, finally, was the tipping point when the world forever changed. One photo, that was all it took. There were more—she must've flipped through a dozen—but really, the first one had been enough. Of course it wasn't human. It was a travesty of human. All the others were just evolutionary insult upon injury.

"What you see there is what you get," he said. "Have you ever heard of a town in Massachusetts called Innsmouth?"

Kerry shook her head. "I don't think so."

"No reason you should've. It's a little pisshole seaport whose best days were already behind it by the time of the Civil War. In the winter of 1927–28, there was a series of raids there, jointly conducted by the FBI and US Army, with naval support. Officially—remember, this was during Prohibition—it was to shut down bootlegging operations bringing whiskey down the coast from Canada. The truth . . . " He took back the iPad from her nerveless fingers. "Nothing explains the truth better than seeing it with your own eyes."

"You can't talk to them. That's what this is about, isn't it?" she said. "You can't communicate with them, and you think I can."

Escovedo smiled, and until now, she didn't think he had it in him. "It must be true about you, then. You're psychic after all."

"Is it that they can't talk, or won't?"

"That's never been satisfactorily determined," he said. "The ones who still looked more or less human when they were taken prisoner, they could, and did. But they didn't stay that way. Human, I mean. That's the way this mutation works." He tapped the iPad. "What you saw there is the result of decades of change. Most of them were brought in like that already. The rest eventually got there. And the changes go more than skin deep. Their throats are different now. On the inside. Maybe this keeps them from speaking in a way that you and I would find intelligible, or maybe it doesn't but they're really consistent about pretending it does, because they're all on the same page. They do communicate with each other, that's a given. They've been recorded extensively doing that, and the sounds have been analyzed to exhaustion, and the consensus is that these sounds have their own syntax. The same way bird songs do. Just not as nice to listen to."

"If they've been under your roof all this time, they've spent almost a century away from whatever culture they had where they came from. All that would be gone now, wouldn't it? The world's changed so much since then they wouldn't even recognize it," she said. "You're not doing science. You're doing national security. What I don't understand is why it's so important to communicate with them after all this time."

"All those changes you're talking about, that stops at the seashore. Drop them in the ocean and they'd feel right at home." He zipped the iPad back into his valise. "Whatever they might've had to say in 1928, that doesn't matter. Or '48, or '88. It's what we need to know *now* that's created a sense of urgency."

◄◦►

Once the helicopter had set down on the island, Kerry hadn't even left the cabin before thinking she'd never been to a more miserable place in her life. Rocky and rain-lashed, miles off the mainland, it was buffeted by winds that snapped from one direction and then another, so that the pines that grew here didn't know which way to go, twisted until they seemed to lean and leer with ill intent.

"It's not always like this," Escovedo assured her. "Sometimes there's sleet, too."

It was the size of a large shopping plaza, a skewed triangular shape, with a helipad and boat dock on one point, and a scattering of outbuildings clustered along another, including what she assumed were offices and barracks for those unfortunate enough to have been assigned to duty here, everything laced together by a network of roads and pathways.

It was dominated, though, by a hulking brick monstrosity that looked exactly like what it was—a vintage relic of a prison—although it could pass for other things, too: an old factory or power plant, or, more likely, a wartime fortress, a leftover outpost from an era when the west coast feared the Japanese fleet. It had been built in 1942, Escovedo told her. No one would have questioned the need for it at the time, and since then, people were simply used to it, if they even knew it was there. Boaters might be curious, but the shoreline was studded at intervals with signs, and she imagined that whatever they said was enough to repel the inquisitive—that, and the triple rows of fencing crowned with loops of razor wire.

Inside her rain slicker, Kerry yanked the hood's drawstring tight and leaned into the needles of rain. October—it was only October. Imagine this place in January. Of course it didn't bother the colonel one bit. They were halfway along the path to the outbuildings when she turned to him and tugged the edge of her hood aside.

"I'm not psychic," she told him. "You called me that in the helicopter. That's not how I look at what I do."

"Noted," he said, noncommittal and unconcerned.

"I'm serious. If you're going to bring me out here, to this place, it's important to me that you understand what I do and aren't snickering about it behind my back."

"You're here, aren't you? Obviously somebody high up the chain of command has faith in you."

That gave her pause to consider. This wouldn't have been a lark on their part. Bringing in a civilian on something most presidents hadn't known about would never have been done on a hunch—see if this works, and if it doesn't, no harm done. She would've been vetted, extensively, and she wondered how they'd done it. Coming up with pretenses to interview past clients, perhaps, or people who'd appeared on *The Animal Whisperer*, to ascertain that they really were the just-folks they were purported to be, and that it wasn't scripted; that she genuinely had done for them what she was supposed to.

"What about you, though? Have you seen the show?"

"I got forwarded the season one DVDs. I watched the first couple episodes." He grew more thoughtful, less official. "The polar bear at the Cleveland Zoo, that was interesting. That's 1500 pounds of apex predator you're dealing with. And you went in there without so much as a stick of wood between you and it. Just because it was having OCD issues? That takes either a big pair of balls or a serious case of stupid. And I don't think you're stupid."

"That's a start, I guess," she said. "Is that particular episode why I'm here? You figured since I did that, I wouldn't spook easily with these prisoners of yours?"

"I imagine it was factored in." The gravel that lined the path crunched underfoot for several paces before he spoke again. "If you don't think of yourself as psychic, what is it, then? How *does* it work?"

"I don't really know." Kerry had always dreaded the question, because she'd never been good at answering it. "It's been there as far back as I can remember, and I've gotten better at it, but I think that's just through the doing. It's a sense as much as anything. But not like sight or smell or taste. I compare it to balance. Can you explain how your sense of balance works?"

He cut her a sideways glance, betraying nothing, but she saw he didn't have a clue. "Mine? You're on a need-to-know basis here, remember."

Very good. Very dry. Escovedo was probably more fun than he let on.

"Right," she said. "Everybody else's, then. Most people have no idea. It's so intrinsic they take it for granted. A few may know it has to do with the inner ear. And a few of them, that it's centered in the vestibular apparatus, those three tiny loops full of fluid. One for up, one for down, one for forward and backward. But you don't need to know any of that to walk like we are now and not fall over. Well . . . that's what the animal thing is like for me. It's there, but I don't know the mechanism behind it."

He mused this over for several paces. "So that's your way of dodging the question?"

Kerry grinned at the ground. "It usually works."

"It's a good smokescreen. Really, though."

"Really? It's . . ." She drew the word out, a soft hiss while gathering her thoughts. "A combination of things. It's like receiving emotions, feelings, sensory impressions, mental imagery, either still or with motion. Any or all. Sometimes it's not even that, it's just . . . pure knowing, is the best way I know to phrase it."

"Pure knowing?" He sounded skeptical.

"Have you been in combat?"

"Yes."

"Then even if you haven't experienced it yourself, I'd be surprised if you haven't seen it or heard about it in people you trust—a strong sense that you should be very careful in that building, or approaching that next rise. They can't point to anything concrete to explain why. They just know. And they're often right."

Escovedo nodded. "Put in that context, it makes sense."

"Plus, for what it's worth, they ran a functional MRI on me, just for fun. That's on the season two DVD bonuses. Apparently the language center of my brain is very highly developed. Ninety-eighth percentile, something like that. So maybe that has something to do with it."

"Interesting," Escovedo said, and nothing more, so she decided to quit while she was ahead.

The path curved and split before them, and though they weren't taking the left-hand branch to the prison, still, the closer they drew to it, darkened by rain and contemptuous of the wind, the greater the edifice seemed to loom over everything else on the island. It was like something grown from the sea, an iceberg of brick, with the worst of it hidden from view. When the wind blew just right, it carried with it a smell of fish, generations of them, as if left to spoil and never cleaned up.

Kerry stared past it, to the sea surging all the way to the horizon. This was an island only if you looked at it from out there. Simple, then: *Don't ever go out there.*

She'd never had a problem with swimming pools. You could see through those. Lakes, oceans, rivers . . . these were something entirely different. These were *dark* waters, full of secrets and unintended tombs. Shipwrecks, sunken airplanes, houses at the bottom of flooded valleys . . . they were sepulchers of dread, trapped in another world where they so plainly did not belong.

Not unlike the way she was feeling this very moment.

—◇—

As she looked around Colonel Escovedo's office in the administrative building, it seemed almost as much a cell as anything they could have over at the prison. It was without windows, so the lighting was all artificial, fluorescent, and unflattering. It aged him, and she didn't want to think what it had to be doing to her own appearance. In one corner, a dehumidifier chugged away, but the air still felt heavy and damp. Day in, day out, it must have been like working in a mine.

"Here's the situation. Why now," he said. "Their behavior over there, it's been pretty much unchanged ever since they were moved to this installation. With one exception. Late summer, 1997, for about a month. I wasn't here then, but according to the records, it was like . . ." He paused, groping for the right words. "A hive mind. Like they were a single organism. They spent most of their time aligned to a precise angle to the southwest. The commanding officer at the time mentioned in his reports that it was like they were waiting for something. Inhumanly patient, just waiting. Then, eventually, they stopped and everything went back to normal."

"Until now?" she said.

"Nine days ago. They're doing it again."

"Did anybody figure out what was special about that month?"

"We think so. It took years, though. Three years before some analyst made the connection, and even then, you know, it's still a lucky accident. Maybe you've heard how it is with these agencies, they don't talk to each other, don't share notes. You've got a key here, and a lock on the other side of the world, and nobody in the middle who knows enough to put the two together. It's better now than it used to be, but it took the 9/11 attacks to get them to even *think* about correlating intel better."

"So what happened that summer?"

"Just listen," he said, and spun in his chair to the hardware behind him.

She'd been wondering about that anyway. Considering how functional his office was, it seemed not merely excessive, but out of character, that Escovedo would have an array of what looked to be high-end audio-video components, all feeding into a pair of three-way speakers and a subwoofer. He dialed in a sound file on the LCD of one of the rack modules, then thumbed the play button.

At first it was soothing, a muted drone both airy and deep, a lonely noise that some movie's sound designer might have used to suggest the desolation of outer space. But no, this wasn't about space. It had to be the sea, this all led back to the sea. It was the sound of deep waters, the black depths where sunlight never reached.

Then came a new sound, deeper than deep, a slow eruption digging its way free of the drone, climbing in pitch, rising, rising, then plummeting back to leave her once more with the sound of the void. After moments of anticipation, it happened again, like a roar from an abyss, and prickled the fine hairs on the back of her neck—a primal response, but then, what was more primal than the ocean and the threats beneath its waves?

This was why she'd never liked the sea. This never knowing what was there, until it was upon you.

"Heard enough?" Escovedo asked, and seemed amused at her mute nod. "*That* happened. Their hive mind behavior coincided with that."

"What *was* it?"

"That's the big question. It was recorded several times during the summer of 1997, then never again. Since 1960, we've had the oceans bugged for sound, basically. We've got them full of microphones that we put there to listen for Soviet submarines, when we thought it was a possibility we'd be going to war with them. They're down hundreds of feet, along an ocean layer called the sound channel. For sound conductivity, it's the Goldilocks zone—it's just right. After the Cold War was over, these mic networks were decommissioned from military use and turned over for scientific research. Whales, seismic events, underwater volcanoes, that sort of thing. Most of it, it's instantly identifiable. The people whose job it is to listen to what the mics pick up, 99.99 percent of the time they know exactly what they've got because the sounds conform to signature patterns, and they're just so familiar.

"But every so often they get one they can't identify. It doesn't fit any known pattern. So they give it a cute name and it stays a mystery. This one, they called it the 'Bloop.' Makes it sound like a kid farting in the bathtub, doesn't it?"

She pointed at the speakers. "An awfully big kid and an awfully big tub."

"Now you're getting ahead of me. The Bloop's point of origin was calculated to be in the south Pacific . . . maybe not coincidentally, not far from Polynesia, which is generally conceded as the place of origin for what eventually came to be known in Massachusetts as 'the Innsmouth look.' Some outside influence was brought home from Polynesia in the 1800s during a series of trading expeditions by a sea captain named Obed Marsh."

"Are you talking about a disease, or a genetic abnormality?"

Escovedo slapped one hand onto a sheaf of bound papers lying on one side of his desk. "You can be the judge of that. I've got a summary here for you to look over, before you get started tomorrow. It'll give you more background on the town and its history. The whole thing's a knotted-up tangle of fact and rumor and local legend and god knows what all, but it's not my job to sort out what's what. I've got enough on my plate sticking with facts, and the fact is, I'm in charge of keeping sixty-three of these proto-human monstrosities hidden from the world, and I know they're cued into something anomalous, but I don't know what. The other fact is, the last time they acted like this was fifteen years ago, while those mics were picking up one of the loudest sounds ever recorded on the planet."

"How loud was it?"

"Every time that sound went off, it wasn't just a local event. It was picked up over a span of five thousand kilometers."

The thought made her head swim. Something with that much power behind it . . . there could be nothing good about it. Something that loud was the sound of death, of cataclysm and extinction events. It was the sound of an asteroid strike, of a volcano not just erupting, but vaporizing a land mass—Krakatoa, the island of Thera. She imagined standing here, past the northwestern edge of the continental United States, and hearing something happen in New York. Okay, sound traveled better in water than in air, but still—*three thousand miles.*

"Despite that," Escovedo said, "the analysts say it most closely matches a profile of something alive."

"A whale?" There couldn't be anything bigger, not for million of years.

The colonel shook his head. "Keep going. Somebody who briefed me on this compared it to a blue whale plugged in and running through the amplifier stacks at every show Metallica has ever played, all at once. She also said that what they captured probably wasn't even the whole sound. That it's likely a lot of frequencies and details got naturally filtered out along the way."

"Whatever it was . . . there have to be theories."

"Sure. Just nothing that fits with all the known pieces."

"Is the sound occurring again?"

"No. We don't know what they're cueing in on this time."

He pointed at the prison. Even though he couldn't see it, because there were no windows, and now she wondered if he didn't prefer it that way. Block it out with walls, and maybe for a few minutes at a time he could pretend he was somewhere else, assigned to some other duty.

"But *they* do," he said. "Those abominations over there know. We just need to find the key to getting them to tell us."

⟨∘⟩

She was billeted in what Colonel Escovedo called the guest barracks, the only visitor in a building that could accommodate eight in privacy, sixteen if they doubled up. Visitors, Kerry figured, would be a rare occurrence here, and the place felt that way, little lived in and not much used. The rain had strengthened closer to evening and beat hard on the low roof, a lonely sound that built from room to vacant room.

When she heard the deep thump of the helicopter rotors pick up, then recede into the sky—having waited, apparently, until it was clear she would be staying—she felt unaccountably abandoned, stranded with no way off this outpost that lay beyond not just the rim of civilization, but beyond the frontiers of even her expanded sense of life, of humans and animals and what passed between them.

Every now and then she heard someone outside, crunching past on foot or on an all-terrain four-wheeler. If she looked, they were reduced to dark, indistinct smears wavering in the water that sluiced down the windows. She had the run of most of the island if she wanted, although that was mainly just a license to get soaked under the sky. The buildings were forbidden, other than her quarters and the admin office, and, of course, the prison, as long as she was being escorted. And, apart for the colonel, she was apparently expected to pretend to be the invisible woman. She and the duty personnel were off-limits to each other. She wasn't to speak to them, and they were under orders not to speak with her.

They didn't know the truth—it was the only explanation that made sense. They didn't know, because they didn't need to. They'd been fed a cover story. Maybe they believed they were guarding the maddened survivors of a disease, a genetic mutation, an industrial accident or something that had fallen from space and that did terrible things to DNA. Maybe they'd all been fed a different lie, so that if they got together to compare notes, they wouldn't know which to believe.

For that matter, she wasn't sure she did either.

First things first, though: she set up a framed photo of Tabitha on a table out in the barracks' common room, shot over the summer when they'd gone horseback riding in the Sawtooth Range. Her daughter's sixth birthday. Rarely was a picture snapped in which Tabby wasn't beaming, giddy with life, but this was one of them, her little face rapt with focus. Still in the saddle, she was leaning forward, hugging the mare's neck, her braided hair a blonde stripe along the chestnut hide, and it looked for all the world as if the two of them were sharing a secret.

The photo would be her beacon, her lighthouse shining from home.

She fixed a mug of hot cocoa in the kitchenette, then settled into one of the chairs with the summary report that Escovedo had sent with her.

Except for its cold, matter-of-fact tone, it read like bizarre fiction. If she hadn't seen the photos, she wouldn't have believed it: a series of raids in an isolated Massachusetts seaport that swept up more than two hundred residents, most of whose appearances exhibited combinations of human, ichthyoid, and amphibian traits. The Innsmouth look had been well-known to the neighboring towns for at least two generations—"an unsavory haven of inbreeding and circus folk," according to a derisive comment culled from an Ipswich newspaper of the era—but even then, Innsmouth had been careful to put forward the best face it possibly could. Which meant, in most cases, residents still on the low side of middle-age . . . at least when it came to the families that had a few decades' worth of roots in the town, rather than its more recent newcomers.

With age came change so drastic that the affected people gradually lost all resemblance to who they'd been as children and young adults, eventually reaching the point that they let themselves be seen only by each other, taking care to hide from public view in a warren of dilapidated homes, warehouses, and limestone caverns that honeycombed the area.

One page of the report displayed a sequence of photos of what was ostensibly the same person, identified as Giles Shapleigh, eighteen years old when detained in 1928. He'd been a handsome kid in the first photo, and if he had nothing to smile about when it was taken, you could at least see the potential for a roguish, cockeyed grin. By his twenty-fifth year, he'd visibly aged, his hair receded and thinning, and after seven years of captivity he had the sullen look of a convict. By thirty, he was bald as a cue ball, and his skull had seemed to narrow. By thirty-five, his jowls had widened enough to render his neck almost nonexistent, giving him a bullet-headed appearance that she found all the more unnerving for his dead-eyed stare.

By the time he was sixty, with astronauts not long on the moon, there was nothing left to connect Giles Shapleigh with who or what he'd been, neither his identity nor his species. Still, though, his transformation wasn't yet complete.

He was merely catching up to his friends, neighbors, and relatives. By the time of those Prohibition-era raids, most of the others had been this way for years—decades, some of them. Although they aged, they didn't seem to weaken and, while they could be killed, if merely left to themselves, they most certainly didn't die.

They could languish, though. As those first years went on, with the Innsmouth prisoners scattered throughout a handful of remote quarantine facilities across New England, it became obvious that they didn't do well in the kind of environment reserved for normal prisoners: barred cells, bright lights, exercise yards . . . *dryness*. Some of them developed a skin condition that resembled powdery mildew, a white, dusty crust that spread across them in patches. There was a genuine fear that, whatever it was, it might jump from captives to captors and prove more virulent in wholly human hosts, although this never happened.

Thus it was decided: they didn't need a standard prison so much as they needed their own zoo. That they got it was something she found strangely heartening. What was missing from the report, presumably because she had no need to know, was *why*.

While she didn't want to admit it, Kerry had no illusions—the expedient thing would've been to kill them off. No one would have known, and undoubtedly there would've been those who found it an easy order to carry out. It was wartime, and if war proved anything, it proved how simple it was to dehumanize people even when they looked just like you. This was 1942, and this was already happening on an industrial scale across Europe. These people from Innsmouth would have had few advocates. To merely look at them was to feel revulsion, to sense a challenge to everything you thought you knew about the world, about what could and couldn't be. Most people would look at them and think they deserved to die. They were an insult to existence, to cherished beliefs.

Yet they lived. They'd outlived the men who'd rounded them up, and their first jailers, and most of their jailers since. They'd outlived everyone who'd opted to keep them a secret down through the generations . . . yet for what?

Perhaps morality *had* factored into the decision to keep them alive, but she doubted morality had weighed heaviest. Maybe, paradoxically, it had been done out of fear. They may have rounded up more than two hundred of Innsmouth's strangest, but many more had escaped—by most accounts, fleeing into the harbor, then the ocean beyond. To exterminate these captives because they were unnatural would be to throw away the greatest resource they might possess in case they ever faced these beings again, under worse circumstances.

Full disclosure, Escovedo had promised. She would know as much as he did. But when she finished the report along with the cocoa, she had no faith whatsoever that she was on par with the colonel or that even he'd been told the half of it himself.

How much did a man need to know, really, to be a glorified prison warden?

Questions nagged, starting with the numbers. She slung on her coat and headed back out into the rain, even colder now, as it needled down from a dusk descending on the island like a dark gray blanket. She found the colonel still in his office and supposed by now he was used to people dripping on his floor.

"What happened to rest of them?" she asked. "Your report says there were more than two hundred to start with. And that this place was built to house up to three hundred. So I guess somebody thought more might turn up. But you're down to sixty-three. And they don't die of natural causes. So what happened to the others?"

"What does it matter? For your purposes, I mean. What you're here to do."

"Did you know that animals understand the idea of extermination? Wolves do. Dogs at the pound do. Cattle do, once they get to the slaughterhouse pens. They may not be able to articulate it, but they pick up on it. From miles away, sometimes, they can pick up on it." She felt a chilly drop of water slither down her forehead. "I don't know about fish or reptiles. But whatever humanity may still exist in these prisoners of yours, I wouldn't be surprised if it's left them just as sensitive to the concept of extermination, or worse."

He looked at her blankly, waiting for more. He didn't get it.

"For all I know, you're sending me in there as the latest interrogator who wants to find out the best way to commit genocide on the rest of their kind. *That's* why it matters. Is that how they're going to see me?"

Escovedo looked at her for a long time, his gaze fixated on her, not moving, just studying her increasing unease as she tried to divine what he was thinking. If he was angry, or disappointed, or considering sending her home before she'd even set foot in the prison. He stared so long she had no idea which it could be, until she realized that the stare *was* the point.

"They've got these eyes," he said. "They don't blink. They've got no white part to them anymore, so you don't know where they're looking, exactly. It's more like looking into a mirror than another eye. A mirror that makes you want to look away. So . . . how they'll *see* you?" he said, with a quick shake of his head and a hopeless snort of a laugh. "I have no idea *what* they see."

She wondered how long he'd been in this command. If he would ever get used to the presence of such an alien enemy. If any of them did, his predecessors, back to the beginning. That much she could see.

"Like I said, I stick with facts," he said. "I can tell you this much: when you've got a discovery like *them*, you have to expect that every so often another one or two of them are going to disappear into the system."

"The system," she said. "What does that mean?"

"You were right, we don't do science here. But they do in other places," he told her. "You can't be naïve enough to think research means spending the day watching them crawl around and writing down what they had for lunch."

Naïve? No. Kerry supposed she had suspected before she'd even slogged over here to ask. Just to make sure. You didn't have to be naïve to hope for better.

She carried the answer into dreams that night, where it became excruciatingly obvious that, while the Innsmouth prisoners may have lost the ability to speak in any known language, when properly motivated, they could still shriek.

⟶

Morning traded the rain for fog, lots of it, a chilly cloud that had settled over the island before dawn. There was no more sky and sea, no more distance, just whatever lay a few feet in front of her, and endless gray beyond. Without the gravel pathways, she was afraid she might've lost her bearings, maybe wander to the edge of the island. Tangle herself in razor wire, and hang there and die before anyone noticed.

She could feel it now, the channels open and her deepest intuition rising: this was the worst place she'd ever been, and she couldn't tell which side bore the greater blame.

With breakfast in her belly and coffee in hand, she met Escovedo at his office, so he could escort her to the corner of the island where the prison stood facing west, looking out over the sea. There would be no more land until Asia. Immense, made of brick so saturated with wet air that its walls looked slimed, the prison emerged from the mist like a sunken ship.

What would it be like, she wondered, to enter a place and not come out for seventy years? What would that do to one's mind? Were they even sane now? Or did they merely view this as a brief interruption in their lives? Unless they were murdered outright—a possibility—their lifespans were indefinite. Maybe they knew that time was their ally. Time would kill their captors, generation by generation, while they went on. Time would bring down every wall. All terrestrial life might go extinct, while they went on.

As long as they could make it those last few dozen yards to the sea.

"Have any of them ever escaped from here?" she asked.

"No."

"Don't you find that odd? I do. Hasn't most every prison had at least one escape over seventy years?"

"Not this one. It doesn't run like a regular prison. The inmates don't work. There's no kitchen, no laundry trucks, no freedom to tunnel. They don't get visitors. We just spend all day looking at each other." He paused in the arched, inset doorway, his finger on the call button that would summon the guards inside to open up. "If you want my unfiltered opinion, those of us who pulled this duty are the real prisoners."

Inside, it was all gates and checkpoints, the drab institutional hallways saturated with a lingering smell of fish. *Them*, she was smelling *them*. Like people who spent their workdays around death and decay, the soldiers here would carry it home in their pores. You had to pity them that. They would be smelling it after a year of showers, whether it was there or not.

Stairs, finally, a series of flights that seemed to follow the curvature of some central core. It deposited them near the top of the building, on an observation deck. Every vantage point around the retaining wall, particularly a trio of guard posts, overlooked an enormous pit, like an abandoned rock quarry. Flat terraces and rounded pillows of stone rose here and there out of a pool of murky seawater. Along the walls, rough stairways led up to three tiers of rooms, cells without bars.

This wasn't a prison where the inmates would need to be protected from each other. They were all on the same side down there, prisoners of an undeclared war.

Above the pit, the roof was louvered, so apparently, although closed now, it could be opened. They could see the sky. They would have air and rain. Sunshine, if that still meant anything to them.

The water, she'd learned from last night's briefing paper, was no stagnant pool. It was continually refreshed, with drains along the bottom and grated pipes midway up the walls that periodically spewed a gusher like a tidal surge. Decades of this had streaked the walls with darker stains, each like a ragged brush stroke straight down from the rusty grate to the foaming surface of their makeshift sea.

Fish even lived in it, and why not? The prisoners had to eat.

Not at the moment, though. They lined the rocks in groups, as many as would fit on any given surface, sitting, squatting, facing the unseen ocean in eerily perfect alignment to one another.

"What do you make of it?" he asked.

Kerry thought of fish she'd watched in commercial aquariums, in nature documentaries, fish swimming in their thousands, singularly directed, and then, in an instantaneous response to some stimulus, changing directions in perfect unison. "I would say they're schooling."

From where they'd entered the observation deck, she could see only their backs, and began to circle the retaining wall for a better view.

Their basic shapes looked human, but the details were all wrong. Their skin ranged from dusky gray to light green, with pale bellies—dappled sometimes, an effect like sunlight through water—and rubbery looking even from here, as though it would be slick as a wetsuit to the touch, at least the areas that hadn't gone hard and scaly. Some wore the remnants of clothing, although she doubted anything would hold up long in the water and rocks, while others chose to go entirely without. They were finned and they were spiny, no two quite the same, and their hands webbed between the fingers, their feet ridiculously outsized. Their smooth heads were uncommonly narrow, all of them, but still more human than not. Their faces, though, were ghastly. These were faces for another world, with thick-lipped mouths made to gulp water, and eyes to peer through the murky gloom of the deep. Their noses were all but gone, just vestigial nubs now, flattened and slitted. The females' breasts had been similarly subsumed, down to little more than hard bumps.

She clutched the top of the wall until her fingernails began to bend. Not even photographs could truly prepare you for seeing them in the flesh.

I wish I'd never known, she thought. *I can never be the same again.*

"You want to just pick one at random, see where it goes?" Escovedo asked.

"How do you see this working? We haven't talked about that," she said. "What, you pull one of them out and put us in a room together, each of us on either side of a table?"

"Do you have any better ideas?"

"It seems so artificial. The environment of an interrogation room, I mean. I need them open, if that makes sense. Their minds, open. A room like that, it's like you're doing everything you can to close them off from the start."

"Well, I'm not sending you down there into the middle of all sixty-three of them, if that's what you're getting at. I have no idea how they'd react, and there's no way I could guarantee your safety."

She glanced at the guard posts, only now registering why they were so perfectly triangulated. Nothing was out of reach of their rifles.

"And you don't want to set up a situation where you'd have to open fire on the group, right?"

"It would be counterproductive."

"Then you pick one," she said. "You know them better than I do."

⟶

If the Innsmouth prisoners still had a sense of patriarchy, then Escovedo must have decided to start her at the top of their pecking order.

The one they brought her was named Barnabas Marsh, if he even had a use anymore for a name that none of his kind could speak. Maybe names only served the convenience of their captors now, although if any name still carried weight, it would be the name of Marsh. Barnabas was the grandson of Obed Marsh, the ship's captain who, as village legend held, had sailed to strange places above the sea and below it, and brought back both the DNA and partnerships that had altered the course of Innsmouth's history.

Barnabas had been old even when taken prisoner, and by human terms he was now beyond ancient. She tried not to think of him as monstrous, but no other word wanted to settle on him, on any of them. Marsh, though, she found all the more monstrous for the fact that she could see in him the puffed-up, barrel-chested bearing of a once-domineering man who'd never forgotten who and what he had been.

Behind the wattles of his expanded neck, gills rippled with indignation. The thick lips, wider than any human mouth she'd ever seen, stretched downward at each corner in a permanent, magisterial sneer.

He waddled when he walked, as if no longer made for the land, and when the two guards in suits of body armor deposited him in the room, he looked her up and down, then shuffled in as if resigned to tolerating her until this interruption was over. He stopped long enough to give the table and chairs in the center of the room a scornful glance, then continued to the corner, where he slid to the floor with a shoulder on each wall, the angle where they met giving room for his sharp-spined back.

She took the floor as well.

"I believe you can understand me. Every word," Kerry said. "You either can't or won't speak the way you did for the first decades of your life, but I can't think of any reason why you shouldn't still understand me. And that puts you way ahead of all the rest of God's creatures I've managed to communicate with."

He looked at her with his bulging dark eyes, and Escovedo had been right. It was a disconcertingly inhuman gaze, not even mammalian. It wasn't anthropomorphizing to say that mammals—dogs, cats, even a plethora of wilder beasts—had often looked at her with a kind of warmth. But *this*, these eyes . . . they were cold, with a remote scrutiny that she sensed regarded her as lesser in every way.

The room's air, cool to begin with, seemed to chill even more as her skin crawled with an urge to put distance between them. Could he sense that she feared him? Maybe he took this as a given. That he could be dangerous was obvious—the closer you looked, the more he seemed covered with sharp points, none more lethal than the tips of his stubby fingers. But she had to trust the prison staff to ensure her safety. While there was no guard in here to make the energy worse than it was already, they were being watched on a closed-circuit camera. If Marsh threatened her, the room would be flooded with a gas that would put them both out in seconds. She'd wake up with a headache, and Marsh would wake up back in the pit.

And nothing would be accomplished.

"I say God's creatures because I don't know how else to think of you," she said. "I know how *they* think of you. They think you're all aberrations. Unnatural. Not that I'm telling you anything you probably haven't already overheard from them every day for more than eighty years."

And did that catch his interest, even a little? If the subtle tilt of his head meant anything, maybe it did.

"But if you exist, entire families of you, colonies of you, then you can't be an aberration. You're within the realm of nature's possibilities."

Until this moment, she'd had no idea what she would say to him. With animals, she was accustomed to speaking without much concern for what exactly she said. It was more how she said it. Like very young children, animals cued in on tone, not language. They nearly always seemed to favor a higher-pitched voice. They responded to touch.

None of which was going to work here.

But Barnabas Marsh was a presence, and a powerful one, radiant with a sense of age. She kept speaking to him, seeking a way through the gulf between them, the same as she always did. No matter what the species, there always seemed to be a way, always something to which she could attune—an image, a sound, a taste, some heightened sense that overwhelmed her and, once she regained her equilibrium, let her use it as the key in the door that would open the way for more.

She spoke to him of the sea, the most obvious thing, because no matter what the differences between them, they had that much in common. It flowed in each of them, water and salt, and they'd both come from it; he was just closer to returning, was all. Soon she felt the pull of tides, the tug of currents, the cold wet draw of gravity luring down, down, down to greater depths, then the equipoise of pressure, and where once it might've crushed, now it comforted, a cold cocoon that was both a blanket and a world, tingling along her skin with news coming from a thousand leagues in every direction—

And with a start she realized that the sea hadn't been her idea at all.

She'd only followed where he led. Whether Marsh meant to or not.

Kerry looked him in his cold, inhuman eyes, not knowing quite what lay behind them, until she began to get a sense that the sea was *all* that lay behind them. The sea was all he thought of, all he wanted, all that mattered, a yearning so focused that she truly doubted she could slip past it to ferret out what was so special about *now*. What they all sensed happening *now*, just as they had fifteen years ago.

It was all one and the same, of course, bound inextricably together, but first they had to reclaim the sea.

◦►

And so it went the rest of the day, with one after another of this sad parade of prisoners, until she'd seen nearly twenty of them. Nothing that she would've dared call progress, just inklings of impressions, snippets of sensations, none of it coalescing into a meaningful whole, and all of it subsumed beneath a churning ache to return to the sea. It was their defense against her, and she doubted they even knew it.

Whatever was different about her, whatever had enabled her to whisper with creatures that she and the rest of the world found more appealing, it wasn't made to penetrate a human-born despair that had hardened over most of a century.

There was little light remaining in the day when she left the prison in defeat, and little enough to begin with. It was now a colorless world of approaching darkness. She walked a straight line, sense of direction lost in the clammy mist that clung to her as surely as the permeating smell of the prisoners. She knew she had to come to the island's edge eventually, and if she saw another human being before tomorrow, it would be too soon.

Escovedo found her anyway, and she had to assume he'd been following all along. Just letting her get some time and distance before, what, her debriefing? Kerry stood facing the water as it slopped against a shoreline of rocks the size of piled skulls, her hand clutching the inner fence. By now it seemed that the island was less a prison than a concentration camp.

"For what it's worth," the colonel said, "I didn't expect it to go well the first day."

"What makes you think a second day is going to go any better?"

"Rapport?" He lifted a Thermos, uncapped it, and it steamed in the air. "But rapport takes time."

"Time." She rattled the fence. "Will I even be leaving here?"

"I hope that's a joke." He poured into the Thermos cup without asking and gave it to her. "Here. The cold can sneak up on you out like this."

She sipped at the cup, coffee, not the best she'd ever had but far from the worst. It warmed her, though, and that was a plus. "Let me ask you something. Have they ever bred? Either here or wherever they were held before? Have *any* of them bred?"

"No. Why do you ask?"

"It's something I was picking up on from a few of them. The urge. You know it when you feel it. Across species, it's a great common denominator."

"I don't know what to tell you, other than that they haven't."

"Don't you find that odd?"

"I find the whole situation odd."

"What I mean is, even pandas in captivity manage to get pregnant once in a while."

"I've just never really thought about it."

"You regard them as prisoners, you *have* to, I get that. And the females don't look all that different from the males. But suppose they looked more like normal men and women. What would you expect if you had a prison with a mixed-gender population that had unrestricted access to each other?"

"I get your point, but . . ." He wasn't stonewalling, she could tell. He genuinely had never considered this. Because he'd never had to. "Wouldn't it be that they're too old?"

"I thought it was already established that once they get like this, age is no longer a factor. But even if it was, Giles Shapleigh wasn't too old when they first grabbed him. He was eighteen. Out of more than two hundred, he can't have been the only young one. You remember what the urge was like when you were eighteen?"

Escovedo grunted a laugh. "Every chance I get."

"Only he's never acted on it. None of them have."

"A fact that I can't say distresses me."

"It's just . . ." she said, then shut up. She had her answer. They'd never bred. Wanted to, maybe felt driven to, but hadn't. Perhaps captivity affected their fertility or short-circuited the urge from becoming action.

Or maybe it was just an incredible act of discipline. They had to realize what would happen to their offspring. They would never be allowed to keep them, raise them. Their children would face a future of tests and vivisection. Even monstrosities would want better for their babies.

"I have an observation to make," Kerry said. "It's not going to go any better tomorrow, or the day after that. Not if you want me to keep doing it like today. It's like they have this shell around them." She tipped the coffee to her lips and eyed him over the rim, and he was impossible to read. "Should I go on?"

"I'm listening."

"You're right, rapport takes time. But it takes more than that. Your prisoners may have something beyond human senses, but they still have human intellects. More or less. It feels overlaid with something else, and it's not anything good, but fundamentally they haven't stopped being human, and they need to be dealt with that way. Not like they're entirely animals."

She stopped a moment to gauge him, and saw that she at least hadn't lost him. Although she'd not proposed anything yet.

"If they *looked* more human to you, don't you think the way you'd be trying to establish rapport would be to treat them more like human beings?" she said. "I read the news. I watch TV. I've heard the arguments about torture. For and against. I know what they are. The main thing I took away is that when you consult the people who've been good at getting reliable information from prisoners, they'll tell you they did it by being humane. Which includes letting the prisoner have something he wants or loves. There was a captured German officer in World War Two who loved chess. He opened up after his interrogator started playing chess with him. That's all it took."

"I don't think these things are going to be interested in board games."

"No. But there's something every one of them wants," she said. "There's something they love more than anything else in the world."

And why does it have to be the same thing I dread?

When she told him how they might be able to use that to their advantage, she expected Escovedo to say no, out of the question. Instead, he thought it over for all of five seconds and said yes.

"I don't like it, but we need to fast-track this," he said. "We don't just eyeball their alignment in the pit, you know. We measure it with a laser. That's how we know how precisely oriented they are. And since last night they've shifted. Whatever they're cued in on has moved north."

◄◦►

The next morning, dawn came as dawn should, the sky clear and the fog blown away and the sun an actual presence over the horizon. After two days of being scarcely able to see fifty feet in front of her, it seemed as if she could see forever. There was something joyously liberating in it. After just two days.

So what was it going to feel like for Barnabas Marsh to experience the ocean for the first time in more than eighty years? The true sea, not the simulation of it siphoned off and pumped into the pit. Restrained by a makeshift leash, yes, three riflemen ready to shoot from the shore, that too, three more ready to shoot from the parapet of the prison . . . but it would still be the sea.

That it would be Marsh they would try this with was inevitable. It might not be safe and they might get only one chance at this. He was cunning, she had to assume, but he was the oldest by far, and a direct descendant of the man who'd brought this destiny to Innsmouth in the first place. He would have the deepest reservoir of knowledge.

And, maybe, the arrogance to want to share it and gloat.

Kerry was waiting by the shallows when they brought him down, at one end of a long chain whose other end was padlocked to the frame of a four-wheel all-terrain cycle that puttered along behind him—he might have been able to throw men off balance in a tug-of-war, but not this.

Although he had plenty of slack, Marsh paused a few yards from the water's edge, stopping to stare out at the shimmering expanse of sea. The rest of them might have seen mistrust in his hesitation, or savoring the moment, but neither of these felt right. *Reacquainting*, she thought. *That's it.*

He trudged forward then, trailing chain, and as he neared the water, he cast a curious look at her, standing there in a slick blue wetsuit they'd outfitted her with, face-mask and snorkel in her hand. It gave him pause again, and in whatever bit of Marsh that was still human, she saw that he understood, realized who was responsible for this.

Gratitude, though, was not part of his nature. Once in the water, he vanished in moments, marked only by the clattering of his chain along the rocks.

She'd thought it wise to allow Marsh several minutes alone, just himself and the sea. They were midway through it when Escovedo joined her at the water's edge.

"You sure you're up for this?" he said. "It's obvious how much you don't like the idea, even if it was yours."

She glanced over at Marsh's chain, now still. "I don't like to see anything captive when it has the capacity to lament its conditions."

"That's not what I mean. If you think you've been keeping it under wraps that you've got a problem with water, you haven't. I could spot it two days ago, soon as we left the mainland behind."

She grinned down at her flippers, sheepish. Busted. "Don't worry. I'll deal."

"But you still know how to snorkel . . . ?"

"How else are you going to get over a phobia?" She laughed, needing to, and it helped. "It went great in the heated indoor pool."

She fitted the mask over her face and popped in the snorkel's mouthpiece, and went in after Marsh. Calves, knees . . . every step forward was an effort, so she thought of Tabby. *The sooner I get results, the quicker I'll get home.* Thighs, waist . . . then she was in Marsh's world, unnerved by the fear that she would find him waiting for her, tooth and claw, ready to rip through her in a final act of defiance.

But he was nowhere near her. She floated facedown, kicking lightly and visually tracking the chain down the slope of the shoreline, until she saw it disappear over a drop-off into a well that was several feet deeper. *There he is.* She hovered in place, staring down at Marsh as he luxuriated in the water. Ecstatic—there was no other word for him. Twisting, turning, undulating, the chain only a minor impediment, he would shoot up near the surface, then turn and plunge back to the bottom, rolling in the murk he stirred up, doing it again, again, again. His joyous abandon was like a child's.

He saw her and stilled, floating midway between surface and sand, a sight from a nightmare, worse than a shark because even in this world he was so utterly alien.

And it was never going to get any less unnerving. She sucked in a deep breath through the snorkel, then plunged downward, keeping a bit of distance between them as she swam to the bottom.

Two minutes and then some—that was how long she could hold her breath.

Kerry homed in on a loose rock that looked heavy enough to counter her buoyancy, then checked the dive compass strapped to her wrist like an oversized watch. She wrestled the wave-smoothed stone into her lap and sat cross-legged on the bottom, matching as precisely as she could the latest of the southwesterly alignments that had so captivated Marsh and the other sixty-two of them. Sitting on the seabed with the Pacific alive around her, muffled in her ears and receding into a blue-green haze, as she half expected something even worse than Marsh to come swimming straight at her out of the void.

Somewhere above and behind her, he was watching.

She stayed down until her lungs began to ache, then pushed free of the stone and rose to the surface, where she purged the snorkel with a gust of spent air, then flipped to return to the seabed. Closer this time, mere feet between her and Marsh as she settled again, no longer needing the compass—she found her bearing naturally, and time began to slow, and so did her heartbeat in spite of the fear, then the fear was gone, washed away in the currents that tugged at her like temptations.

Up again, down again, and it felt as if she were staying below longer each time, her capacity for breath expanding to fill the need, until she was all but on the outside of herself looking in, marveling at this creature she'd become, amphibious, neither of the land nor the water, yet belonging to both. She lived in a bubble of breath in an infinite now, lungs satiated, awareness creeping forward along this trajectory she was aligned with, as if it were a cable that spanned the seas, and if she could only follow it, she would learn the secrets it withheld from all but the initiated—

And he was there, Barnabas Marsh, a looming presence drifting alongside her. If there was anything to read in his cold face, his unplumbed eyes, it was curiosity. She had become something he'd never seen before, something between his enemies and his people, and changing by the moment.

She peered at him, nothing between them now but the thin plastic window of her mask and a few nourishing inches of water.

What is it that's out there? she asked. *Tell me. I want to know. I want to understand.*

It was true—she did. She would wonder even if she hadn't been asked to. She would wonder every day for the rest of her life. Her existence would be marred by not knowing.

Tell me what it is that lies beyond . . .

She saw it then, a thought like a whisper become an echo, as it began to build on itself, the occlusions between worlds parting in swirls of ink and oceans. And there was so *much* of it, this was something that couldn't be—who could build such a thing, and who would dream of finding it *here*, at depths that might crush a submarine—then she realized that all she was seeing was one wall, one mighty wall, built of blocks the size of boxcars, a feat that couldn't be equaled even on land. She knew without seeing the whole that it spanned miles, that if this tiny prison island could sink into it, it would be lost forever, an insignificant patch of pebbles and mud to what lived there—

And she was wholly herself again, with a desperate need to breathe.

Kerry wrestled the rock off her lap for the last time, kicking for a surface as far away as the sun. As she shot past Barnabas Marsh, she was gripped by a terror that he would seize her ankle to pull her back down.

But she knew she could fight that, so what he did was worse somehow, nothing she knew that he *could* do, and maybe none of these unsuspecting men on the island did either. It was what sound could be if sound were needles, a piercing skirl that ripped through her like an electric shock and clapped her ears as sharply as a pressure wave. She spun in the water, not knowing up from down, and when she stabilized and saw Marsh nearby, she realized he wasn't even directing this at her. She was just a bystander who got in the way. Instead, he was facing out to sea, the greater sea, unleashing this sound into the abyss.

She floundered to the surface and broke through, graceless and gasping, and heard Colonel Escovedo shout a command, and in the next instant heard the roar of an engine as the four-wheeler went racing up the rock-strewn slope of the island's western edge. The chain snapped taut, and moments later Marsh burst from the shallows in a spray of surf and foam, dragged twisting up onto the beach. Someone fired a shot, and someone else another, and of course no one heard her calling from nearly a hundred feet out, treading water now, and they were all shooting, so none of them heard her cry out that they had the wrong idea. But bullets first, questions later, she supposed.

His blood was still red. She had to admit, she'd wondered.

⟶

It took the rest of the morning before she was ready to be debriefed, and Escovedo let her have it, didn't press for too much, too soon. She needed to be warm again, needed to get past the shock of seeing Barnabas Marsh shot to pieces on the beach. Repellent though he was, she'd still linked with him in her way, whispered back and forth, and he'd been alive one minute, among the oldest living beings on the earth, then dead the next.

She ached from the sound he'd made, as if every muscle and organ inside her had been snapped like a rubber band. Her head throbbed with the assault on her ears.

In the colonel's office, finally, behind closed doors, Kerry told him of the colossal ruins somewhere far beneath the sea.

"Does any of that even make sense?" she asked. "It doesn't to me. It felt real enough at the time, but now . . . it has to have been a dream of his. Or maybe Marsh was insane. How could anyone have even known if he was?"

Behind his desk, Escovedo didn't move for the longest time, leaning on his elbows and frowning at his interlaced hands. Had he heard her at all? Finally he unlocked one of the drawers and withdrew a folder; shook out some photos, then put one back and slid the rest across to her. Eight in all.

"What you saw," he said. "Did it look anything like this?"

She put them in rows, four over four, like puzzle pieces, seeing how they might fit together. And she needed them all at once, to bludgeon herself into accepting the reality of it: stretches of walls, suggestions of towers, some standing, some collapsed, all fitted together from blocks of greenish stone that could have been shaped by both hammers and razors. Everything was restricted to what spotlights could reach, limned by a cobalt haze that faded into inky blackness. Here, too, were windows and gateways and wide, irregular terraces that might have been stairs, only for nothing that walked on human feet. There was no sense of scale, nothing to measure it by, but she'd sensed it once today already, and it had the feeling of enormity and measureless age.

It was the stuff of nightmares, out of place and out of time, waiting in the cold, wet dark.

"They've been enhanced because of the low-light conditions and the distance," Escovedo said. "It's like the shots of the Titanic. The only light down that far is what you can send on a submersible. Except the Navy's lost every single one they've sent down there. They just go offline. These pictures . . . they're from the one that lasted the longest."

She looked up again. The folder they'd come from was gone. "You held one back. I can't see it?"

He shook his head. "Need to know."

"It shows something that different from the others?"

Nothing. He was as much a block of stone as the walls.

"Something living?" She remembered his description of the sound heard across three thousand miles of ocean: *The analysts say it most closely matches a profile of something alive.* "Is that it?"

"I won't tell you you're right." He appeared to be choosing his words with care. "But if that's what you'd picked up on out there with Marsh, then maybe we'd have a chance to talk about photo number nine."

She wanted to know. Needed to know as badly as she'd needed to breathe this morning, waking up to herself too far under the surface of the sea.

"What about the rest of them? We can keep trying."

He shook his head no. "We've come to the end of this experiment. I've already arranged for your transportation back home tomorrow."

Just like that. It felt as if she were being fired. She hadn't even delivered. She'd not told them anything they didn't already know about. She'd only confirmed it. What had made that unearthly noise, what the Innsmouth prisoners were waiting for—that's what they were really after.

"We're only just getting started. You can't rush something like this. There are sixty-two more of them over there, one of them is sure to—"

He cut her off with a slash of his hand. "Sixty-two of them who are in an uproar now. They didn't see what happened to Marsh, but they've got the general idea."

"Then maybe you shouldn't have been so quick to order his execution."

"That was for you. I thought we were protecting you." He held up his hands then, appeasement, time-out. "I appreciate your willingness to continue. I do. But even if they were still in what passes for a good mood with them, we've still reached an impasse here. You can't get through to them on our turf, and I can't risk sending you back out with another of them onto theirs. It doesn't matter that Marsh didn't actually attack you. I can't risk another of them doing what he did to make me think he had."

"I don't follow you." It had been uncomfortable, yes, and she had no desire to experience it again, but it was hardly fatal.

"I've been doing a lot of thinking about what that sound he made meant," Escovedo said. "What I keep coming back to is that he was sending a distress call."

⟨⟩

She wished she could've left the island sooner. That the moment the colonel told her they were finished, he'd already had the helicopter waiting. However late they got her home again, surely by now she would be in her own bed, holding her daughter close because she needed her even more than Tabby needed her.

Awake part of the time and a toss-up the rest, asleep but dreaming, she was still trying to get there. Caught between midnight and dawn, the weather turning for the worse again, the crack and boom of thunder like artillery, with bullets of rain strafing the roof.

She had to be sleeping some of the time, though, and dreaming of something other than insomnia. She knew perfectly well she was in a bed, but there were times in the night when it felt as if she were still below, deeper than she'd gone this morning, in the cold of the depths far beyond the reach of the sun, drifting beside leviathan walls lit by a phosphorescence whose source she couldn't pin down. The walls themselves were tricky to navigate, like being on the outside of a maze, yet still lost within it, finding herself turning strange corners that seemed to jut outward, only to find that they turned in. She was going to drown down here, swamped by a sudden thrashing panic over her air tank going empty, only to realize . . .

She'd never strapped one on to begin with.

She belonged here, in this place that was everything that made her recoil.

Marsh, she thought, once she could tell ceiling from sea. Although he was dead, Marsh was still with her, in an overlapping echo of whispers. Dead, but still dreaming.

When she woke for good, though, it was as abruptly as could be, jolted by the sound of a siren so loud it promised nothing less than a cataclysm. It rose and fell like the howling of a feral god. She supposed soldiers knew how to react, but she wasn't one of them. Every instinct told her to hug the mattress and melt beneath the covers and hope it all went away.

But that was a strategy for people prone to dying in their beds.

She was dressed and out the door in two minutes, and though she had to squint against the cold sting of the rain, she looked immediately to the prison. Everything on the island, alive or motorized, seemed to be moving in that direction, and for a moment she wondered if she should too—safety in numbers, and what if something was *driving* them that way, from the east end?

But the searchlights along the parapet told a different story, three beams stabbing out over the open water, shafts of brilliant white shimmering with rain and sweeping to and fro against the black of night. *A distress call*, Escovedo had said—had it been answered? Was the island under attack, an invasion by Innsmouth's cousins who'd come swarming onto the beach? No, that didn't seem right either. The spotlights were not aimed down, but out. Straight out.

She stood rooted to the spot, pelted by rain, lashed by wind, frozen with dread that something terrible was on its way. The island had never felt so small. Even the prison looked tiny now, a vulnerable citadel standing alone against the three co-conspirators of ocean, night, and sky.

Ahead of the roving spotlights, the rain was a curtain separating the island from the sea, then it parted, silently at first, the prow of a ship spearing into view, emerging from the blackness as though born from it. No lights, no one visible on board, not even any engine noise that she could hear—just a dead ship propelled by the night or something in it. The sound came next, a tortured grinding of steel across rock so loud it made the siren seem weak and thin. The ship's prow heaved higher as it was driven up onto the island, the rest of it coming into view, the body of the shark behind the cone of its snout.

And she'd thought the thunder was loud. When the freighter plowed into the prison, the ground shuddered beneath her, the building cracking apart as though riven by an axe, one of the spotlights tumbling down along with an avalanche of bricks and masonry before winking out for good. She watched men struggle, watched men fall, and at last the ship's momentum was spent. For a breathless moment it was perfectly still. Then, with another grinding protest of metal on stone, the ship began to list, like twisting a knife after sticking it in. The entire right side of the prison buckled and collapsed outward, and with it went the siren and another of the searchlights. The last of the lights reeled upward, aimed back at the building's own roofline.

Only now could she hear men shouting, only now could she hear the gunfire.

Only now could she hear men scream.

And still the ground seemed to shudder beneath her feet.

It seemed as if that should've been the end of it, accident and aftermath, but soon more of the prison began to fall, as if deliberately wrenched apart. She saw another cascade of bricks tumble to the left, light now flickering and spilling from within the prison on both sides.

Something rose into view from the other side, thick as the trunk of the tallest oak that had ever grown, but flexible, glistening in the searing light. It wrapped around another section of wall and pulled it down as easily as peeling wood from rotten wood. She thought it some kind of serpent at first, until, through the wreckage of the building, she saw the suggestion of more, coiling and uncoiling, and a body—or head—behind those.

And still the ground seemed to shudder beneath her feet.

It was nothing seismic—she understood that now. She recalled being in the majestic company of elephants once, and how the ground sometimes quivered in their vicinity as they called to one another from miles away, booming out frequencies so deep they were below the threshold of human hearing, a rumble that only their own kind could decipher.

This was the beast's voice.

And if they heard it in New York, in Barrow, Alaska, and in the Sea of Cortez, she would not have been surprised.

It filled her, reverberating through rock and earth, up past her shoes, juddering the soles of her feet, radiating through her bones and every fiber of muscle, every cell of fat, until her vision scrambled and she feared every organ would liquefy. At last it rose into the range of her feeble ears, a groan that a glacier might make. As the sound climbed higher, she clapped both hands over her ears, and if she could have turtled her head into her body, she would've done that too, as its voice became a roar became a bellow became a blaring onslaught like the trumpets of Judgment Day, a fanfare to split the sky for the coming of God.

Instead, *this* was what had arrived, this vast and monstrous entity, some inhuman travesty's idea of a deity. She saw it now for what it was to these loathsome creatures from Innsmouth—the god they prayed to, the Mecca that they faced—but then something whispered inside, and she wondered if she was wrong. As immense and terrifying as this thing was, what if it presaged more, and was only preparing the way, the John the Baptist for something even worse.

Shaking, she sunk to her knees, hoping only that she might pass beneath its notice as the last sixty-two prisoners from Innsmouth climbed up and over the top of the prison's ruins, and reclaimed their place in the sea.

-‹o›-

To be honest, she had to admit to herself that the very idea of Innsmouth, and what had happened here in generations past, fascinated her as much as it appalled her.

Grow up and grow older in a world of interstate highways, cable TV, satellite surveillance, the Internet, and cameras in your pocket, and it was easy to forget how remote a place could once be, even on the continental United States, and not all that long ago, all things considered. It was easy to forget how you might live a lifetime having no idea what was going on in a community just ten miles away, because you never had any need to go there, or much desire, either, since you'd always heard they were an unfriendly lot who didn't welcome strangers and preferred to keep to themselves.

Innsmouth was no longer as isolated as it once was, but it still had the feeling of remoteness, of being adrift in time, a place where businesses struggled to take root, then quietly died back into vacant storefronts. It seemed to dwell under a shadow that would forever keep outsiders from finding a reason to go there, or stay long if they had.

Unlike herself. She'd been here close to a month, since two days after Christmas, and still didn't know when she would leave.

She got the sense that, for many of the town's residents, making strangers feel unwelcome was a tradition they felt honor-bound to uphold. Their greetings were taciturn, if extended at all, and they watched as if she were a shoplifter, even when crossing the street, or strolling the riverwalk along the Manuxet in the middle of the day. But her money was good, and there was no shortage of houses to rent—although her criteria were stricter than most—and a divorced mother with a six-year-old daughter could surely pose no threat.

None of them seemed to recognize her from television, although would they let on if they did? She recognized none of them, either, nothing in anyone's face or feet that hinted at the old, reviled Innsmouth look. They no longer seemed to have anything to hide here, but maybe the instinct that they did went so far back that they knew no other way.

Although what to make of that one storefront on Eliot Street, in what passed for the heart of the town? The stenciled lettering—charmingly antiquated and quaint—on the plate glass window identified the place as THE INNSMOUTH SOCIETY FOR PRESERVATION AND RESTORATION.

It seemed never to be open.

Yet it never seemed neglected.

Invariably, whenever she peered through the window, Kerry would see that someone had been there since the last time she'd looked, but it always felt as if she'd missed them by five minutes or so. She would strain for a better look at the framed photos on the walls, tintypes and sepia tones, glimpses of bygone days that seemed to be someone's idea of something worth bringing back.

Or perhaps their idea of a homecoming.

It was January in New England, and most days so cold it redefined the word *bitter*, but she didn't miss a single one, climbing seven flights of stairs to take up her vigil for as long as she could endure it. The house was an old Victorian on Lafayette Street, four proud stories tall, peaked and gabled to within an inch of its moldering life. The only thing she cared about was that its roof had an iron-railed widow's walk with an unobstructed view of the decrepit harbor and the breakwater and, another mile out to sea, the humpbacked spine of rock called Devil Reef.

As was the custom during the height of the Age of Sail, the widow's walk had been built around the house's main chimney. Build a roaring fire down below, and the radiant bricks would keep her warm enough for a couple of hours at a time, even when the sky spit snow at her, while she brought the binoculars to her eyes every so often to check if there was anything new to see out there.

"I'm bored." This from Tabitha, nearly every day. *Booorrrrred*, the way she said it. "There's nothing to do here."

"I know, sweetie," Kerry would answer. "Just a little longer."

"When are they coming?" Tabby would ask.

"Soon," she would answer. "Pretty soon."

But in truth, she couldn't say. Their journey was a long one. Would they risk traversing the locks and dams of the Panama Canal? Or would they take the safer route, around Argentina's Cape Horn, where they would exchange Pacific for Atlantic, south for north, then head home, at long last home.

She knew only that they were on their way, more certain of this than any sane person had a right to be. The assurance was there whenever the world grew still and silent, more than a thought . . . a whisper that had never left, as if not all of Barnabas Marsh had died, the greater part of him subsumed into the hive mind of the rest of his kind. To taunt? To punish? To gloat? In the weeks after their island prison fell, there was no place she could go where its taint couldn't follow. Not Montana, not Los Angeles, not New Orleans, for the episode of *The Animal Whisperer* they'd tried to film before putting it on hiatus.

She swam with them in sleep. She awoke retching with the taste of coldest blood in her mouth. Her belly skimmed through mud and silt in quiet moments; her shoulders and flanks brushed through shivery forests of weeds; her fingers tricked her into thinking that her daughter's precious cheek felt cool and slimy. The dark of night could bring on the sense of a dizzying plunge to the blackest depths of ocean trenches.

Where else was left for her to go but here, to Innsmouth, the place that time seemed to be trying hard to forget.

And the more days she kept watch from the widow's walk, the longer at a time she could do it, even while the fire below dwindled to embers, and so the more it seemed that her blood must've been going cold in her veins.

"I don't like it here," Tabby would say. "You never used to yell in your sleep until we came here."

How could she even answer that? No one could live like this for long.

"Why can't I go stay with Daddy?" Tabby would ask. *Daddeeeee*, the way she said it.

It really would've been complete then, wouldn't it? The humiliation, the surrender. The admission: *I can't handle it anymore, I just want it to stop, I want them to make it stop.* It still mattered, that her daughter's father had once fallen in love with her when he thought he'd been charmed by some half-wild creature who talked to animals, and then once he had her, tried to drive them from her life because he realized he hated to share. He would never possess all of her.

You got as much as I could give, she would tell him, as if he too could hear her whisper. *And now they won't let go of the rest.*

"Tell me another story about them," Tabby would beg, and so she would, a new chapter of the saga growing between them about kingdoms under the sea where people lived forever, and rode fish and giant seahorses, and how they had defenders as tall as the sky who came boiling up from the waters to send their enemies running.

Tabby seemed to like it.

When she asked if there were pictures, Kerry knew better, and didn't show her the ones she had, didn't even acknowledge their existence. The ones taken from Colonel Escovedo's office while the rains drenched the wreckage, after she'd helped the few survivors that she could, the others dead or past noticing what she might take from the office of their commanding officer, whom nobody could locate anyway.

The first eight photos Tabby would've found boring. As for the ninth, Kerry wasn't sure she could explain to a six-year-old what exactly it showed, or even to herself. Wasn't sure she could make a solid case for what was the mouth and what was the eye, much less explain why such a thing was allowed to exist.

One of them, at least, should sleep well while they were here.

Came the day, at last, in early February, when her binoculars revealed more than the tranquil pool of the harbor, the snow and ice crusted atop the breakwater, the sullen chop of the winter-blown sea. Against the slate-colored water, they were small, moving splotches the color of algae. They flipped like seals, rolled like otters. They crawled onto the ragged dark stone of Devil Reef, where they seemed to survey the kingdom they'd once known, all that had changed about it and all that hadn't.

And then they did worse.

Even if something was natural, she realized, you could still call it a perversity.

Was it preference? Was it celebration? Or was it blind obedience to an instinct they didn't even have to capacity to question? Not that it mattered. Here they were, finally, little different from salmon now, come back to their headwaters to breed, indulging an urge eighty-some years strong.

It was only a six-block walk to the harbor, and she had the two of them there in fifteen minutes. This side of Water Street, the wharves and warehouses were deserted, desolate, frosted with frozen spray and groaning with every gust of wind that came snapping in over the water.

She wrenched open the wide wooden door to one of the smaller buildings, the same as she'd been doing every other day or so, the entire time they'd been here, first to find an abandoned rowboat, and then to make sure it was still there. She dragged it down to the water's edge, plowing a furrow in a crust of old snow, and once it was in the shallows, swung

Tabby into it, then hopped in after. She slipped the oars into the rusty oarlocks, and they were off.

"Mama . . . ?" Tabitha said after they'd pushed past the breakwater and cleared the mouth of the harbor for open sea. "Are you crying?"

In rougher waters now, the boat heaved beneath them. Snow swirled in from the depths overhead and clung to her cheeks, eyelashes, hair, and refused to melt. She was that cold. She was *always* that cold.

"Maybe a little," Kerry said.

"How come?"

"It's just the wind. It stings my eyes."

She pulled at the oars, aiming for the black line of the reef. Even if no one else might've, even if she could no longer see them, as they hid within the waves, she heard them sing a song of jubilation, a song of wrath and hunger. Their voices were the sound of a thousand waking nightmares.

To pass the time, she told Tabby a story, grafting it to all the other tales she'd told about kingdoms under the sea where people lived forever, and rode whales and danced with dolphins, and how they may not have been very pleasant to look at, but that's what made them love the beautiful little girl from above the waves, and welcome her as their princess.

Tabby seemed to like it.

Ahead, at the reef, they began to rise from the water and clamber up the rock again, spiny and scaled, finned and fearless. Others began to swim out to meet the boat. Of course they recognized her, and she them. She'd sat with nearly a third of them, trying trying trying to break through from the wrong side of the shore.

While they must have schemed like fiends to drag her deep into theirs.

I bring you this gift, she would tell them, if only she could make herself heard over their jeering in her head. *Now could you please just set me free?*

HONORABLE MENTIONS

Abbott, Megan "My Heart Is Either Broken," *Dangerous Women*.

Allan, Nina, *Vivian Guppy and the Brighton Belle* (novella), *Rustblind and Silverbright*.

Antosca, Nick, "Burial Grounds," *Exotic Gothic 5 Volume I*.

Atkins, Peter, "Postcards From Abroad," *The Imposter's Monocle*.

Barron, Laird, "Ardor," *Suffered From the Night*.

Barron, Laird, *Termination Dust* (novella), *Tales of Jack the Ripper*.

Cadigan, Pat, *Chalk,* This is Horror, chapbook.

Chinn, Mike, "Cheechee's Out," *Second City Scares*.

Cluley, Ray, "The Festering," *Black Static #36*.

Crow, Jennifer, "Anna They Have Killed" (poem), *Mythic Delirium issue 0.2*.

Ford, Jeffrey, "A Terror," Tor.com July.

Frost, Gregory, "No Others Are Genuine," *Asimov's* SF. Oct/November.

Gardner, Cate, *This Foolish & Harmful* (novella), *The Transfiguration of Mister Punch*.

Gavin, Richard, "A Cavern of Redbrick," *Shadows & Tall Trees, #5*.

Gerrold, David, "Night Train to Paris," *F&SF* January.

Grant, John, "Memoryville Blues," *Memoryville Blues*.

Graves, Rain, "Hades and its Five: The Ferryman" (poem), *Four Elements*.

Harman, Christopher, "Dark Tracks," *Supernatural Tales 25*.

Hobson, M.K., "Baba Makosh," *F&SF* November/December.

Hodge, Brian, "We, The Fortunate Bereaved," *Halloween*.

Hook, Andrew, "Rain from a Clear Blue Sky," *Black Static #33*.

Janes, Andrea, "The Last Wagon in the Train," *The Tenth Black Book of Horror*.

Johnstone, Carole, "21 Brooklands: Next to Old Western . . . "*For the Night is Dark.*

Jones, Stephen Graham, "Interstate Love Affair," *Three Miles Past.*

Kiernan, Caitlín R., *Black Helicopters* (novella), chapbook.

Langan, John, *Mother of Stone* (novella), *The Wide, Carnivorous Sky.*

Llewellyn, Livia, "Furnace," *The Grimscribe's Puppets.*

Maberry, Jonathan, "Mister Pockets," *Dark Visions 1.*

Marolla, Samuel, "Black Tea," *Black Tea and Other Tales.*

McHugh, Ian, "Vandiemensland," *Next.*

Miéville, China, "The Design," *McSweeney's* 45.

Nevill, Adam, "Always in Our Hearts," *End of the Road.*

Nickle, David, "Black Hen a La Ford," In Words, Alas, Drown I.

Oliver, Reggie, "Come into My Parlour," *Dark World: Ghost Stories.*

Oliver, Reggie, "The Silken Drum," *Fearie Tales.*

Partridge, Norman, *The Mummy's Heart* (novella), *Halloween.*

Reed, Kit, "The Legend of Troop 13," *Asimov's Science Fiction* January.

Schanoes, Veronica, *Burning Girls* (novella), Tor.com June.

Schanoes, Veronica, "Phosphorus," *Queen Victoria's Book of Spells.*

Schow, David.J., "A Home in the Dark," *Nightmare #15* December.

Snyder, Maria V., "The Halloween Men," *Halloween.*

Swirsky, Rachel, "Abomination Rises on Filthy Wings," *Apex #50.*

Tem, Steve Rasnic, "Bedtime Story," *Black Static #32.*

Volk, Stephen, "The Peter Lorre Fan Club," *The Burning Circus.*

Warren, Kaaron, "The Unwanted Women of Surrey," *Queen Victoria's Book of Spells.*

Warrick, Douglas R., "Rattenkőnig," *Vampires Don't Sparkle/Plow the Bones.*

Watt, D. P., "Laudate Dominium (for many voices)," *Shadows & Tall Trees, #5.*

Watt, D. P., "With Gravity, Grace," *The Transfiguration of Mister Punch.*

Williams, Conrad, "Raptors," *Subterranean Winter.*

ABOUT THE AUTHORS

Nina Allan was born in Whitechapel, London, grew up in the Midlands and West Sussex, and wrote her first short story at the age of six. Her fiction has appeared in numerous magazines and anthologies, including *The Best Horror of the Year Volume Two*, *The Mammoth Book of Ghost Stories by Women*, and *The Year's Best Fantasy and Science Fiction 2012* and *2013*. Nina's most recent books include the novella *Spin* and *Stardust: The Ruby Castle Stories*. Her first novel, *The Race*, set in an alternate near-future version of southeast England, will be published in summer 2014. She lives and works in Hastings, East Sussex.

"The Tiger" was originally published in *Terror Tales of London*, edited by Paul Finch.

◄○►

Stephen Bacon's fiction has appeared or is forthcoming in *Black Static*, *Cemetery Dance*, *Shadows & Tall Trees*, *Crimewave*, and many other anthologies, and has been reprinted in *Best Horror of the Year Volume Five*. His debut collection, *Peel Back the Sky*, was published by Gray Friar Press in 2012. He lives in Rotherham, South Yorkshire, United Kingdom, with his wife and two sons.

"Apports" was originally published in *Black Static*, edited by Andy Cox.

◄○►

Dale Bailey lives in North Carolina with his family, and he has published three novels, *The Fallen*, *House of Bones*, and *Sleeping Policemen* (with Jack

Slay Jr.). His short fiction, collected in *The Resurrection Man's Legacy and Other Stories,* has won the International Horror Guild Award and has been twice nominated for the Nebula Award.

His website is: www.dalebailey.com.

"Mr. Splitfoot" was originally published in *Queen Victoria's Book of Spells*, edited by Ellen Datlow and Terri Windling.

—◊—

Nathan Ballingrud is the award-winning author of the short story collection *North American Lake Monsters*, from Small Beer Press. He lives with his daughter in Asheville, North Carolina, where he is at work on his first novel.

"The Good Husband" was originally published in *North American Lake Monsters*.

—◊—

Laird Barron is the author of several books, including *The Croning, Occultation,* and *The Beautiful Thing That Awaits Us All*. His work has also appeared in many magazines and anthologies including *The Magazine of Fantasy & Science Fiction, Lovecraft Unbound*, and *Haunted Legends*. An expatriate Alaskan, Barron currently resides in Upstate New York.

"Jaws of Saturn" was originally published in *The Beautiful Thing That Awaits Us All*.

—◊—

Tim Casson's short fiction has been published in various anthologies and magazines including regular appearances in *Black Static*. He has just completed the dystopian YA novel *Underclass* and is working on putting together his first collection. He lives by the sea in south Wales.

"The Withering" was originally published in *Black Static*, edited by Andy Cox

—◊—

Simon Clark lives in Doncaster, England, with his family. When his first novel, *Nailed by the Heart*, made it through the slush pile in 1994, he banked the advance and embarked upon his dream of becoming a full-time writer. Since then, he's written the cult zombie classic *Blood Crazy*. Other titles include *Darkness Demands*, *Vampyrrhic*, *On Deadly Ground*, and *The Night of the Triffids*, which continues the story of John Wyndham's classic *The Day of the Triffids*.

Simon's next novel is *Inspector Abberline & the Gods of Rome*, a crime thriller featuring the real-life detective who led the hunt for Jack the Ripper.

"The Tin House" was originally published in *Shadow Masters*, edited by Jeani Rector.

—◦—

Ray Cluley's stories have been published in the magazines *Black Static, Interzone, Crimewave*, and *Shadows & Tall Trees*, and a variety of anthologies, including *Wilde Stories 2013: The Year's Best Gay Speculative Fiction* and in French translation for *Ténèbres 2011*.

His story "Shark! Shark!" recently won the British Fantasy Award for Best Short Story. *Within the Wind, Beneath the Snow*, a limited edition novelette, will appear later this year as a chapbook from Spectral Press, while his debut collection, *Probably Monsters*, is due from ChiZine Press in 2015. This is Ray Cluley's second appearance in *Best Horror of the Year*.

You can find out more at probablymonsters.wordpress.com

"Bones of Crow" was originally published in *Black Static*, edited by Andy Cox.

—◦—

Jeannine Hall Gailey recently served as the Poet Laureate of Redmond, Washington, and is the author of three books of poetry: *Becoming the Villainess, She Returns to the Floating World*, and *Unexplained Fevers*. Her work has been featured on NPR's *Writer's Almanac, Verse Daily*, and in *The Year's Best Fantasy and Horror*. Her poems have appeared in *The American Poetry Review, The Iowa Review*, and *Prairie Schooner*. Her web site is www.webbish6.com.

"Introduction to the Body in Fairy Tales" was originally published in *Phantom Drift*, edited by David Memmott, Martha Bayliss, Leslie What, and Matt Schumacher.

—◦—

Neil Gaiman is the Newbery Medal–winning author of *The Graveyard Book* and a *New York Times* bestselling author. Several of his books, including *Coraline*, have been made into major motion pictures. He is also famous for writing the *Sandman* graphic novel series and numerous other books and comics for adult, young adult, and younger readers. He has won the Hugo, Nebula, Mythopoeic, and World Fantasy awards, among others. He is also the author of powerful short stories and poems.

For more information: www.neilgaiman.com/

"Down to a Sunless Sea" was originally published at *www.guardian.com*

◄◦►

Brian Hodge is the award-winning author of eleven novels spanning horror, crime, and historical. He's also written around 110 short stories, novelettes, and novellas, and five full-length collections. His first collection, *The Convulsion Factory*, was ranked by critic Stanley Wiater among the 113 best books of modern horror. Recent or forthcoming books include *Whom the Gods Would Destroy* and *The Weight of the Dead*, both standalone novellas; *No Law Left Unbroken*, a collection of crime fiction; a newly revised hardcover edition of *Dark Advent*, his early post-apocalyptic epic; *Worlds of Hurt*, an omnibus edition of the first four works of his Misbegotten mythos; and *Leaves of Sherwood*.

Hodge lives in Colorado, where more of everything is in the works. He also dabbles in music, sound design, and photography; loves everything about organic gardening except the thieving squirrels; and trains in Krav Maga, grappling, and kickboxing, which are of no use at all against the squirrels.

Connect through his web site (www.brianhodge.net) or on Facebook (www.facebook.com/brianhodgewriter).

"The Same Deep Waters as You" was originally published in *Weirder Shadows over Innsmouth*, edited by Stephen Jones.

◄◦►

Jane Jakeman is a British author who has published crime and ghost stories in *Supernatural Tales*, *Ghosts and Scholars*, and *All Hallows*, some of which were reprinted in the collection *A Bracelet of Bright Hair*. She has travelled widely in the Middle East and lives in Oxford, United Kingdom, with her Egyptologist husband and two small black cats.

"Majorlena" was originally published in *Supernatural Tales*, edited by David Longhorn.

⚬

KJ Kabza's short stories have appeared in *Nature*, *The Magazine of Fantasy & Science Fiction*, *Beneath Ceaseless Skies*, *Daily Science Fiction*, AE: The Canadian Science Fiction Review, *Buzzy Mag*, *Flash Fiction Online*, *New Myths*, and many others.

He currently lives in sunny Tucson, but he sort of misses the Gothic atmosphere of late autumn in New England, if he's being honest. For updates on forthcoming releases and links to free fiction, you can follow him on Twitter @KJKabza and peruse www.kjkabza.com.

"The Soul in the Bell Jar" was originally published in *The Magazine of Fantasy & Science Fiction*, edited by Gordon Van Gelder.

⚬

Derek Künsken has built genetically-engineered viruses; worked with street children in Latin America; served five years as a Canadian diplomat; and, most importantly, teaches his nine-year-old son about superheroes, skiing, and science. He writes science fiction, fantasy, and sometimes horror in Ottawa, and can be found at www.derekkunsken.com.

His fiction has appeared in a number of magazines and anthologies, and he recently received the 2012 *Asimov's* Readers' Award for his novelette *The Way of the Needle*. "The Dog's Paw" had been kicking around in his head for a while, but came out of his pen in Port-au-Prince in the weeks after the earthquake of 2010.

"The Dog's Paw" was originally published in *Chilling Tales: In Words, Alas, Drown I*, edited by Michael Kelly.

⚬

Linda Nagata is the author of multiple novels and short stories including *The Bohr Maker*, winner of the Locus Award for best first novel, and the novella *Goddesses*, the first online publication to receive a Nebula award. Her story "Nahiku West" was a finalist for the 2013 Theodore Sturgeon Memorial Award. Her newest novel is the near-future military thriller *The Red: First Light*. Linda has spent most of her life in Hawaii, where she's been a writer, a mom, a programmer of database-driven websites, and lately an independent publisher. She lives with her husband in their long-time home on the island of Maui. Find her online at: *MythicIsland.com*

"Halfway Home" was originally published in *Nightmare Magazine,* edited by John Joseph Adams.

◄○►

Kim Newman was born in Brixton (London), grew up in the West Country, went to University near Brighton, and now lives in Islington (London).

His most recent fiction books include *Professor Moriarty: The Hound of the d'Urbervilles, Anno Dracula: Johnny Alucard,* and *An English Ghost Stories.* His nonfiction books include *Ghastly Beyond Belief* (with Neil Gaiman), *Horror: 100 Best Books* and *Horror: Another 100 Best Books* (both with Stephen Jones), and a host of books on film. He is a contributing editor to *Sight & Sound* and *Empire* magazines and has written and broadcast widely on a range of topics, scripting radio documentaries and TV programs. He has won the Bram Stoker Award, the International Horror Critics Award, the British Science Fiction Award, and the British Fantasy Award. His official website, "Dr Shade's Laboratory," can be found at www.johnnyalucard.com.

"The Only Ending We Have" was originally published in *Psycho-Mania,* edited by Stephen Jones.

◄○►

Lynda E. Rucker is an American writer currently living in Dublin, Ireland. Her fiction has appeared in such places as *The Magazine of Fantasy & Science Fiction, Black Static, The Mammoth Book of Best New Horror, The Year's Best Dark Fantasy and Horror, Postscripts, Shadows & Tall Trees,* and *Supernatural Tales.* She is a regular columnist for *Black Static,* and her first collection, *The Moon Will Look Strange,* was published in 2013.

She blogs very occasionally at lyndaerucker.wordpress.com and tweets more frequently as @lyndaerucker.

"The House on Cobb Street" was originally published in *Nightmare Magazine,* edited by John Joseph Adams.

◄○►

Priya Sharma went to medical school when anatomy was taught by dissection of cadavers and inappropriate mnemonics. "The Anatomist's

Mnemonic" started life as a love story but Priya soon got a grip of herself and made it into something darker. However, long before she learned where the scaphoid bone is located, she was taught about heart, head, and life lines.

Her work has appeared in *Interzone*, *Black Static*, *Albedo One*, and *Alt Hist*, as well as on Tor.com and has been reprinted in previous editions of *The Best Horror of Year*, edited by Ellen Datlow, and *The Year's Best Dark Fantasy and Horror*, edited by Paula Guran.

More information can be found at www.priyasharmafiction.wordpress.com

"The Anatomist's Mnemonic" was originally published in *Black Static*, edited by Andy Cox.

—◇—

Robert Shearman has published four short story collections, and between them they have won the World Fantasy Award, the Shirley Jackson Award, the Edge Hill Readers Prize, and three British Fantasy Awards. The most recent, *Remember Why You Fear Me*, was published in 2012. He writes regularly in the United Kingdom for theatre and BBC Radio, winning the *Sunday Times* Playwriting Award and the Guinness Award in association with the Royal National Theatre. He's probably best known for reintroducing the Daleks to the twenty-first century revival of *Doctor Who* in an episode that was a finalist for the Hugo Award.

"That Tiny Flutter of the Heart I Used to Call Love" was originally published in *Psycho-Mania*, edited by Stephen Jones.

—◇—

Simon Strantzas is the author of four short story collections, including most recently *Burnt Black Suns*. His fiction has appeared in *The Mammoth Book of Best New Horror* and *The Year's Best Dark Fantasy & Horror* and has been nominated for the British Fantasy Award.

He resides in Toronto, Canada.

"Stemming the Tide" was originally published in *Dead North: Canadian Zombie Fiction*, edited by Silvia Moreno-Garcia.

—◇—

Steve Rasnic Tem's latest novel is *Blood Kin* from Solaris, his second novel for them after 2012's *Deadfall Hotel*. His two most recent collections are

Celestial Inventories and *Here with the Shadows*. Upcoming are a novella, *In the Lovecraft Museum*, and a massive 225K collection of uncollected horror—*Out of the Dark, A Storybook of Horrors*.

"The Monster Makers" was originally published in *Black Static,* edited by Andy Cox.

◄○►

Lee Thomas is the Lambda Literary Award and Bram Stoker Award–winning author of *The Dust of Wonderland, The German, Torn, Like Light for Flies*, and *Butcher's Road*. You can find him online at *www.leethomasauthor.com*.

"Fine in the Fire" was originally published in *Like Light for Flies*.

◄○►

Steve Toase lives in North Yorkshire, England, and occasionally Munich, Germany.

His work has been published in *Scheherezade's Bequest, Liquid Imagination, Jabberwocky Magazine, Sein und Werden, Cafe Irreal, streetcake magazine, Weaponizer* and *nthPosition* amongst others. He is currently working on his first novel. His website can be found online at: www.stevetoase.co.uk

"Call Out" was first published in *Innsmouth Magazine #12,* edited by Silvia Moreno-Garcia and Paula R. Stiles.

◄○►

Conrad Williams is the author of seven novels, four novellas and more than one hundred short stories, some of which are collected in *Use Once, then Destroy* and *Born with Teeth*. In addition to his International Horror Guild Award for his novel *The Unblemished,* he is a three-time recipient of the British Fantasy Award, including Best Novel for *One*. He's also editor of the acclaimed anthology *Gutshot*.

He is currently teaching creative writing at Edge Hill University and working on a new anthology for Titan Books as well as a sequel to his 2010 novel *Blonde on a Stick*.

"The Fox" was originally published as a chapbook by This is Horror.

ACKNOWLEDGMENT IS MADE FOR REPRINTING THE FOLLOWING MATERIAL

"Apports" © 2013 by Stephen Bacon. First published in *Black Static 36*, September/October. Reprinted by permission of the author.

"Mr. Splitfoot" © 2013 by Dale Bailey. First published in *Queen Victoria's Book of Spells*, edited by Ellen Datlow and Terri Windling, Tor Books. Reprinted by permission of the author.

"The Good Husband" © 2013 by Nathan Ballingrud. First published in *North American Lake Monsters*, Small Beer Press. Reprinted by permission of the author.

"The Tiger" © 2013 by Nina Allan. First published in *Terror Tales of London*, edited by Paul Finch, Gray Friar Press. Reprinted by permission of the author.

"The House on Cobb Street" © 2013 by Lynda E. Rucker. First published in *Nightmare Magazine #9*. Reprinted by permission of the author.

"The Soul in the Bell Jar," © 2013 by KJ Kabza. First publishing in *The Magazine of Fantasy and Science Fiction*, November/December. Reprinted by permission of the author.

"The Dog's Paw" © 2013 by Derek Künsken. First published in *Chilling Tales: In Words, Alas, Drown I*, edited by Michael Kelly, Edge Science Fiction and Fantasy Publishing. Reprinted by permission of the author.

"Fine in the Fire" © 2013 by Lee Thomas. First published in *Like Light for Flies*, Lethe Press. Reprinted by permission of the author.

"Majorlena," © 2013 by Jane Jakeman. First published in *Supernatural Tales 24*, edited by David Longhorn. Reprinted by permission of the author.

"The Withering" © 2013 by Tim Casson. First published in *Black Static 32*, edited by Andy Cox. Reprinted by permission of the author.

"Down to a Sunless Sea" © 2013 by Neil Gaiman. First published online on www.guardian.com on March 22, 2013. Reprinted by permission of the author.

"Jaws of Saturn," © 2013 by Laird Barron. First published in The *Beautiful Thing That Awaits Us All*, Night Shade Books. Reprinted by permission of the author.

"Halfway Home" © 2013 by Linda Nagata. First published in *Nightmare Magazine #12*. Reprinted by permission of the author.

"The Same Deep Waters as You" © 2013 by Brian Hodge. First published in *Weirder Shadows Over Innsmouth*, edited by Stephen Jones, Fedogan & Bremer. Reprinted by permission of the author.

ABOUT THE EDITOR

Ellen Datlow has been editing science fiction, fantasy, and horror short fiction for more than thirty years as fiction editor of OMNI Magazine and editor of *Event Horizon* and SCIFICTION. She currently acquires short fiction for Tor.com. In addition, she has edited more than fifty science fiction, fantasy, and horror anthologies, including the annual *The Best Horror of the Year, Lovecraft's Monsters, Fearful Symmetries*, the six volume series of retold fairy tales starting with *Snow White, Blood Red*, and *Queen Victoria's Book of Spells: An Anthology of Gaslamp Fantasy* (the latter anthologies with Terri Windling).

Forthcoming are *Nightmare Carnival, The Cutting Room,* and *The Doll Collection.*

She's won nine World Fantasy Awards and has also won multiple Locus Awards, Hugo Awards, Stoker Awards, International Horror Guild Awards, Shirley Jackson Awards, and the 2012 Il Posto Nero Black Spot Award for Excellence as Best Foreign Editor. Datlow was named recipient of the 2007 Karl Edward Wagner Award, given at the British Fantasy Convention for "outstanding contribution to the genre" and was honored with the Life Achievement Award given by the Horror Writers Association, in acknowledgment of superior achievement over an entire career.

She lives in New York and co-hosts the monthly Fantastic Fiction Reading Series at KGB Bar. More information can be found at www.datlow.com, on Facebook, and on twitter as @EllenDatlow.